the
tramp

www.tigerdreaming.com.au

Publisher: Tiger Dreaming www.tiger dreaming.com.au
First published in 2016

Title: The Tramp

Author: Michael Cannon

ISBN-13: 978-0-9953997-0-9

Conceptualised, written, edited and typeset in Australia.

Printed by CreateSpace.

Cover design, illustration and page layout: Design Eye Creative
www.designeyecreative.com.au

To Kathy
for your endless support

A special thank you to Kathy Hill, Janice Bird, Roger Jaensch,
James Talbot, Brenda Slavoff, Mary Reilly, Susan Scott,
Sonia Guizzo and Teri Mammini.

... and an even bigger thank you to dreams.

SUPPORTED BY

Tasmanian
Government

This project was assisted through
Arts Tasmania by the Minister for the Arts

the tramp

MICHAEL CANNON

Self-imposed exile sentenced him

to twenty years of hell

Also in this series:
The Tramp. Music of Robert Aitken by Michael Cannon
Available from 2017 on CD or digital download
from www.tigerdreaming.com.au
www.amazon.com & www.bandcamp.com

THE TRAMP
by Michael Cannon

PART ONE

RECOGNITION

CHAPTER ONE

'Cheers.'

Samantha Pearson raised her glass before taking a deep swallow of dark ale. She wiped her mouth with an exaggerated gesture and smacked her lips.

'I needed that. Well, go on mate, what are you waiting for?'

Matthew stared at his wife's glass, now half empty or half full, depending on one's outlook. His own still had its unblemished wheat-coloured head and was frosted with condensation.

'You know what I think,' he began, 'sometimes the expectation is better than the actual drink.'

'Rubbish.' Samantha laughed. 'Get outside of it before I finish mine and drink yours, too,' she stabbed a finger at him, 'and you'll miss out.'

'Keep yer bleedin' 'ands orf.' Matthew thickened his London brogue to sound more like a Cockney. As he took his first drink he noticed how the light from the window brought out chestnut hues in his wife's hair.

'It's my pint an' not yours, even if you do look like a gawjus red'ead.'

Samantha smiled at the compliment as she picked a hot potato wedge and dunked it first in a bowl of sour cream, then the chilli sauce. She cooled the wedge and bit the flavoured end.

'Not that bad a place after all', she said, being more than a little forgiving.

'Apart from the ogre at the bar', Matthew chuckled.

'Don't be a pig.'

Matthew had had little opportunity to be a tourist since their whirlwind romance and subsequent wedding three years earlier. Despite their burgeoning public relations business in Hobart being all-consuming,

Samantha kept promising to show her husband some parts of Tasmania she had not visited since her childhood. They had finally managed to take a week off and Matthew was getting to appreciate places he had previously seen only in tourist brochures or ads.

They had followed the Lyell Highway northwest from their home in New Norfolk to the sulphur-scarred landscape of Queenstown, and on to the tourist magnet, Strahan, where they had stayed overnight. The next morning, they drove through the isolated west coast mining towns of Zeehan, Rosebery and Tullah, negotiated the winding Hellyer Gorge and continued on to the coastal town of Wynyard. In answer to an imminent call of nature, they found themselves in a pub off the highway, just outside town. As they had used the facilities, they considered it only fair to have something to eat while they were there.

'If it looked more appealing from the outside, they might get more backsides on seats in here,' Matthew observed in a whisper. He looked about and counted: only nine, apart from them and the staff.

Three heavy-set men wearing uniforms sporting forestry logos sat at the bar, looking very much at home, almost as if the seats had assumed the shape of their rears. A fourth man sat alone at the end of the bar; his unkempt beard and scraggy hair framed a scowling face. The few other customers seemed to be enjoying a Sunday lunchtime beer, and one couple sat in an intimate coffee conversation. It appeared as though Matthew and Samantha were the only patrons actually having something solid to eat.

'Maybe you're right,' Matthew added with a hint of sarcasm, 'not too feral after all.'

'Not now we've turned up.' She smiled and tucked into another wedge.

The scruffy man picked up his drink and walked over to a stage, a simple triangular plinth of worn timber boards on a pine frame, with old screws and bent rusty nails sticking out of the edge. The stage had been wedged tightly into a corner of the room to afford space for a modest herringbone parquetry dance floor. It was also the only area without natural light.

Two chairs sat on the platform and on each rested an acoustic guitar. A weathered mauve fedora hung over the headstock of the instrument on the right. The man picked up the other guitar, lifted the strap over his head and made himself comfortable on the chair behind the microphone. He switched on a small flexible desk lamp that was gaffer-taped to the side of a music stand, illuminating an open folder. He thumbed through the pages and settled on one before flicking the switch on a small amplifier to his right. He mumbled into the microphone and strummed a chord, made an adjustment and cleared his throat. Incidental light reflected upward into his face and dishevelled hair, casting strange shadows on the wall behind.

'Doesn't look like an entertainer,' Samantha whispered.

'Beard too shaggy?' Matthew asked mischievously.

'Drink your beer.'

The opening notes of 'Fire and Rain' pervaded their senses, and they both visibly relaxed another notch.

'Do it justice,' Matthew whispered, and he was not disappointed. The musician sang as if he had written the song himself; the rendition was faultless and, while the vocals did not try to replicate the original, they were nevertheless beautifully performed. The audience applauded as the final chord sounded, as did one appreciative staff member, an attractive dark-haired woman who looked out of place in the ramshackle pub.

The singer began another classic, Elton John's 'Goodbye Yellow Brick Road', until one of the foresters called, 'Hey, Pom, how's about "Cows With Guns"?' His heckle was met with laughter and applause from his mates. The singer stopped, and without displaying any affinity with his small audience, performed the strangely humorous tale of bovines who have learned to fight back. Familiar with the song, the regulars joined in by blowing trumpet sounds to replicate the recorded song's horn section.

'I wanted to hear "Goodbye Yellow Brick Road",' whispered Samantha as the Dana Lyons song ended.

'Hard to sing,' Matthew added. 'He might have crucified it.'

He started another tune with a cascading finger-style pattern in the key of D. Each corresponding melody line and bass note sounded clear and true, despite being played on strings that were obviously, to Matthew's musical ear, very old. A fan of good music and lyrics, Matthew became absorbed in the song.

Samantha refocused on making the most of this rare time away from the demands of their business, and started making suggestions about their schedule for the rest of the afternoon. She paused, wondering if she had her husband's attention.

'Matt, are you listening? Matthew?'

'Sorry love, what?'

'Have I been talking to myself these past two minutes?'

'I was distracted. Those lyrics – have you taken notice of them?'

'No, I've been talking to you.'

'Listen,' he whispered.

'Something about loss; something about music.' She sighed. 'What time do you want to leave?'

'No, this is powerful stuff. I wonder whose song it is. The lyrics could be Taupin but the music's more like, what was his name, the "Streets of London" bloke?'

Samantha sighed again. 'McTell.'

'Nah, not him.'

'Yes it was,' she insisted, 'Ralph McTell.'

He remembered. 'Shit, I hate it when you're right. Shhh, listen.'

There was just one verse and chorus remaining but Samantha appreciated what she understood of the story. 'The song sounds quite bouncy, but sad all the same, don't you think?'

'Shall we stay a while longer?' he nodded. 'Does it matter if we're running late?'

She shrugged. 'I guess not. I'll get another round, but you're driving, so only light beer for you.'

Matthew smiled. 'Fair enough, boss.'

They sat for another hour listening to the strange man with the two guitars and the enigmatic hat. He played a range of classics, from the Beatles to Dire Straits and, eventually, 'Goodbye Yellow Brick Road', but between the past hits he performed numbers they had not heard before, despite their collective musical knowledge. These unknowns were well played, and seemed connected to something deep inside this rough man.

The singer took another break.

'Best go then,' Matthew said.

They finished their drinks, gathered their gear and made to leave, but not before giving the guitarist an appreciative wave, although he chose not to respond.

'We see you again?' the young woman behind the bar asked in a strong Italian accent.

'Might well do that.' Matthew said as he returned her smile, before heading for the door.

· · · · ·

Samantha's navigation skills kept Matthew on track, with a little help from a Jamie Cullum CD thumping through the speakers. They followed Bass Highway east along the coast past Burnie, then took a left turn at a roundabout near the tiny hamlet of Howth, inspiring Matthew to feign a lisp. They drove through the scenic but strangely named Sulphur Creek and on to their bed and breakfast in the quaint seaside town of Penguin. Penguin's claims to fame included a picture-postcard church and an ocean vista that rivalled better known tourist destinations throughout Australia, not to mention the much photographed Big Penguin statue on the town's foreshore.

They checked into the B&B – a historic Federation weatherboard house – and unpacked before going for a walk along the beach. They passed close to the giant cement penguin that was covered in gull droppings, then wandered down to the shore and took off their shoes to paddle in the shallows. In no time at all the chilly spring Bass Strait waters had changed their minds about a long, romantic walk along the water's edge.

CHAPTER TWO

'Peter Gabriel!' Matthew said, as if he'd just discovered there really was life on Mars.

'What?' Samantha almost spilled her coffee.

'That's who he sounded like.'

'Who?' she said, 'I'm not following you.'

'Peter Gabriel, you know, "Sledgehammer"; "Solsbury Hill"? The bloke in the pub yesterday sounded like him. Listen.' He rose from the breakfast table and walked over to the radio and tweaked the volume up. Peter Gabriel's 'In Your Eyes' was now playing quite loudly. Other B&B guests looked over from their tables, wearing expressions ranging from distraction to displeasure.

'I know who Peter Gabriel is, you nong. Just go and turn the music down, for Pete's sake.'

He lowered the volume and returned to his seat. 'Sounded like him, I'm right, aren't I?'

Samantha mouthed 'sorry' to anyone still looking their way.

'Maybe the guy did, and maybe he didn't. Now finish up, we're off to Cradle Mountain.'

'No rush though,' he stretched his arms above his head. 'Time for anuvva cuppa, yeah?' he added in his mock Cockney.

They eventually made their way back to the room, packed up, settled their account and headed for their next destination, but not before the customary pose in front of the Big Penguin, silver gull crap and all.

Matthew's memory of the pub performer was compelling, and it was reflected in his choice of music on the ninety-minute meandering drive, with songs by artists from a similar time and place in his memories. They continued east along Bass Highway, took a right through Forth and up into the highlands, their car pounding like a mobile jukebox.

'You know there's something I'll never get used to,' Matthew turned the volume down, 'the road kill everywhere you go. Like a bloody battlefield with the critters losing the war.'

'Come a time when there'll be nothing left to run over,' Samantha agreed. 'It wouldn't surprise me if some even do it deliberately.'

'Don't know what you've got till it's gone,' Matthew added before he turned the music back up. He recalled hitchhiking through South Australia and Victoria before he'd found his way to Tasmania, where the mainland's native fauna seemed to have been reduced to large kangaroos and emus; probably drivers showed those creatures more respect – unless you were driving a truck. A collision with a large animal could cause serious, expensive damage to a small car and its occupants. *Damn the critters if they weren't big enough to make a dent,* he mused.

The drive was relaxing and scenic, apart from the distraction of shattered marsupial bone, blood and guts. Matthew and Samantha checked into the lodge and quickly changed into hiking gear to spend the afternoon walking some of the kilometres of well-trodden boardwalks and marked trails. Those so inclined could walk all the way down to Lake St Clair, sixty-odd kilometres south, via the renowned Overland Track, but not on this trip, they had agreed.

· · · · ·

In Tasmania's climate, one could become burned by the sun on a chilly day. The mid-afternoon air was only six degrees but, due to their fast walking pace, they had already peeled down to their T-shirts.

'All roads lead to Rome,' Matthew said, after they had completed the short walk between the ranger station and the lodge. Having a pub at the end of a long walk is a canny piece of marketing, he decided.

'All roads lead to beer.' Samantha pursed her lips. 'Thank you, my good man,' she added as Matthew held the door open for her.

'Chivalry ain't dead yet, ma'am,' he responded with a wink, but Samantha was already on her way towards the bar.

They checked the menu and decided to order something light, then took their beers outside to a table on the raised, timber decked dining area. 'Ah,' Matthew swallowed and sat back, 'that's hitting the spot!'

'Back to nature,' Samantha agreed.

'I could sit here all night and watch those,' he said, looking down to the grounds beneath them, at the grazing wallabies and wombats, and a solitary echidna snuffling out an insect meal.

A pair of black currawongs flew close and silently perched on the balustrade next to their table.

'Friends of yours?' Samantha grinned as Matthew reached for his camera.

DO NOT FEED THE WILDLIFE signs were strategically placed around the alfresco dining area but, as one of the sleek raven-like birds hopped onto their table within arms' reach and stared at them hopefully, its bright yellow sclera accentuating its bold glare, Matthew guessed that not all patrons heeded the request. The bird eventually lost interest and took to the air, with its mate following suit.

'It's cooling down all of a sudden.' Samantha shivered as she rubbed goose bumps from her neck. 'Should have taken an inside seat by the fire after all.'

'Na, it's because we've cooled down. Besides, it was too stuffy in there,' Matthew said. 'This would have been a welcome breeze an hour ago.'

'Well, it's not welcome now.' She zipped her quilted sleeveless jacket up to her neck and pulled her possum-wool scarf around her ears.

A further ten minutes passed without words while they dipped into the bowl of hot chips that had arrived conveniently after the currawongs had left. She noticed Matthew had also zipped up his jacket. 'Welcome breeze a little less comfortable?' she asked.

He shrugged and raised his collar.

'Getting cold now,' he said, as he rummaged through his daypack. 'Where's that bloody beanie?'

The light began to fade but, considering they were only a two-minute walk from their accommodation, they decided to have another beer before heading back to freshen up for dinner.

'Bugger it. We're on holiday,' Samantha said with a slight slur, as if she needed to justify another pint.

The temperature plummeted as the sky turned from glorious golden to deep twilight, prompting their return to the cabin, for showers and a change of clothing. With an overnight forecast of two degrees Celsius, Samantha switched the gas log fire heater to its highest setting before they left for the restaurant.

· · · · ·

'Matt and Sam Pearson, cabin Forty-One,' Samantha said as they stood obediently beside the WAIT HERE TO BE SEATED sign.

The uniformed waitress wore a broad, welcoming smile straight out of the training handbook, greeting them as if they were bosom buddies.

'Hi, I'm Jacinta, and I'll be attending your table tonight.'

She drew a line through their names in an open book on the counter, took two menus from the stack and hugged them to her chest as she turned, beckoning Matthew and Samantha to follow.

Jacinta gestured for them to take their seats at a table overlooking the lake. As they made themselves comfortable she asked, 'Been a great day for it, where did you walk?'

She appeared interested in how they had spent their day and responded appropriately to their answers with nods and, 'Yes lovely walk,' or 'I must do that one.' Matthew could not help but wonder if her interest, too, was straight out of the training handbook.

If they had not been so weary they might have enjoyed their meals or Jacinta's occasional banter more.

'So, what's planned for the morning?' Samantha asked Matthew, making conversation during another lull.

'Early start, more walks,' he yawned, tapping a spot on the Parks Tasmania map. 'What say we take the car to here at dawn, then walk up to Marions Lookout, and maybe on to Kitchen Hut if we have time?'

'Back by ten for checkout. Sounds good to me.' Samantha's yawn matched his.

'Time for bed,' Matthew suggested as he drank the last of his water.

Samantha raised her eyebrows. 'Promises, old man, promises.'

· · · · ·

Despite the heater's fan droning away throughout the night, a distinct chill remained in the cabin, and Matthew was not surprised when he opened the curtains to find an emerging morning scene of crisp white frost blanketing the ground. A snow-capped Cradle Mountain, edged with brilliant sunlight against a clear blue sky, formed an inspiring backdrop – so sharp it seemed unnatural.

'Where are we off to this afternoon?' Matthew asked.

'You know we're off to Longford,' Samantha said, shaking her head. 'What's going through your mind?'

'I've been wondering if that bloke might be playing today. It might be a week day but one never knows.'

Samantha's husband never failed to surprise her. Ordinarily it was one of his most endearing traits, but not on this occasion. 'You want to go *back*?'

'Um.'

'What's up with you, Matt? We only have a week off to see a bit of

Tasmania and you want to backtrack to a joint we dropped into a couple of days ago to watch some shaggy guy play the guitar. What is it with him, or is it really the cute barmaid I couldn't help but notice you noticing?' she suggested, mischief in her tone.

'Well, I did think it would be nice. He's a good player and the pub could use the custom. Besides—'

'Besides,' she stopped him, 'I'd sooner go to Longford. Remember the small detail that my sister and your best friend will be expecting us.'

'Okay, no sweat. I just thought of being spontaneous.'

'Look, we've not seen Nicky and Dennis since they bought their new place. We can drive back to the pub any time, come up for the weekend, and we could head to Stanley while we're there.'

'You know I don't like Dennis.' His pouting sincerity proved unconvincing.

'You're an idiot, Matthew.' Samantha watched him take four small bread rolls and assorted pre-packed butters and jams from the mini-bar, and put them into his backpack. She raised her eyebrows as he stood to go outside to pack the car.

'What?' he said in answer to her stare as he turned away, 'I liberated them last night at dinner. I knew we'd not have time to have the breakfast we've paid for.'

They locked their cabin and took the meandering drive to Ronny Creek car park, where they grabbed their walking gear and cameras, and set off on the icy boardwalk across exposed buttongrass plains. The raised pathway, with galvanised netting applied, offered safety and traction underfoot in such conditions, and allowed them to keep a brisk pace. In no time their early morning shivers waned as they climbed towards the beautiful vista at Marions Lookout.

· · · · ·

Three hours later they returned to the lodge to check out, and by nine-thirty were heading towards Longford, singing along to *Hotel California*. After the music had faded, Samantha switched the player off and idly counted the roadside guide posts for a while. She could not help wondering whether something was bothering Matthew, prompting his desire to turn away from their plan to visit her sister and brother-in-law.

'Okay,' she spoke through the silence, 'spill the beans.'

'Spill what beans?'

'You know.'

He hesitated. 'Something is niggling me; something about Ilford ... Something about Ilford and that bloke.' He had been searching his memories, back to his late teens and early twenties, doing the clubs and pubs of London, the nightlife, the people, the bands. 'Mostly through blurred vision,' he mumbled.

'Sorry?'

'Oh, nothing. That muso at the pub brought back some memories I just can't put my finger on.'

'Good memories?'

'Good, bad, nothing specific. You know when you smell something and it takes you back to a point in your life? You eat something you haven't had for years and, whammo, you're transported back to nowhere in particular – but more than likely where you last ate that whatever-it-was ... just an essence of your past.'

Samantha nodded.

'And he reminds me of Peter Gabriel.'

'You've already told me that.'

'And more to the point, Peter Gabriel and Kate Bush.'

' "Don't Give Up"?'

'Yes, yes!' She had hit the proverbial nail on the head. 'But I won't be giving up until I work out what the bloody hell this bloke's voice is bringing back to me.'

'You should give the pub a call and ask his name,' Samantha suggested. 'Find the link and it may help get this out of your system.'

'Good idea.' Matthew said. 'Maybe I can call when we get to Longford.' Samantha rolled her eyes, but she was nonetheless relieved.

Matthew flicked through his iPod, found Bob Marley & The Wailers, turned the volume to high and together they let out loud 'Woooo's' in time with Marley's introduction to 'Lively Up Yourself'. The car filled with poor renditions of Jamaican accents and laughter.

CHAPTER THREE

As soon as Samantha and Matthew arrived, Nicky and Dennis Hooper took them on a quick tour of their Georgian home. While the nineteenth-century property would once have been the homestead of a wealthy family, it had not fared well in more recent times, and had drifted into disrepair, until the Hoopers stumbled on an auction for its sale. Nicky explained how their modest bid proved attractive enough that day, and in no time they had become the proud owners of a substantial renovation project.

'Your dog's found a new companion!' Samantha sat at the dining table in the large kitchen, as Matthew ruffled the jowls of the Hooper's pet miniature schnauzer. 'What's his name again?'

Nicky smiled. 'Harry. He doesn't usually warm to males at first meeting, in fact he can be a bit wary. We think a consequence of his pre-rescue life, sad but true.'

'Well, there's no wariness in him at the moment,' Matthew laughed as Harry slid to the white tiles for a chest rub.

'Matt doesn't like you, Dennis. Did you know?' Samantha said with attempted sincerity.

Dennis looked at Samantha then to Matthew. Nicky raised her brows.

'He can get stuffed then, because Matthew's a fekkin' pompous git.' Dennis grinned, his deep London timbre accentuating the taunt.

Matthew left Harry where he was, slid his chair back and stood, puffing out his chest. The taller of the two with an imposing physique, Dennis rose and stepped away to the area between the table and island workspace. He popped his knuckles and snapped his head up, silently suggesting show us what you've got. Matthew followed him, balled his hands into fists and did his best to stand eye to eye, to reflect his opponent's challenge. Matthew made his move, lunged at Dennis, grabbed him by the shirt and wrenched him off balance. Both clattered to the floor, grunting and taunting each other: 'Is that all you got, tosspot?' and 'You ain't arf pafetic!'

Dennis gained the upper hand, grappling with Matthew as they rose to their knees and finally back to their feet.

'You Chelsea-supporting bell-end,' Dennis groaned as he picked Matthew up, twisted him upside down and bounced him, as if the smaller man had been wrapped in a tangled bungee cord. An excited Harry leaped, barked, and licked Matthew's exposed face.

'I got you now, Den, you Tottenham bloody Hotspurs prat,' Matthew's taunt squeezed out through Dennis' unrelenting grip and Harry's wet lapping tongue.

'It's Hot ... spur ... you ... ignorant ... git,' Dennis said as Matthew's head repeatedly stopped a fringe length above the tiles.

'Put him down, you brute, or you won't get a biscuit,' Nicky giggled. Not for the first time, she righted teetering cups as grappling limbs rattled chairs and jolted the table.

Dennis lowered Matthew until his shoulders rested on the floor, and then let him go.

'Okay Mum, but can I have a Tim Tam, not these rubbish crème ones?'

Matthew stood and, while he rearranged his dishevelled clothing, held Dennis' aggressive stare for a moment more, and then enveloped his friend in a manly, backslapping hug.

They resumed their seats at the table, their wheezing and coughing suggested neither was as fit as he might have been in times past.

'I still can't believe you guys are going to run an art gallery,' Samantha said. 'It's so exciting!'

'I still can't believe Dennis friggin' Hooper knows what a bloody art gallery is,' Matthew grinned. 'Art gallery? His Spurs mates would piss themselves laughing!'

Dennis responded with a poor attempt at a refined accent. 'I have always had an artistic side, don't forget, Matty old chap; light and dark, positive and negative and all that.'

'The only art you know is giving some poor travelling supporter a bloody good kicking.'

'I never did, Ref!' Wearing an angelic expression, Dennis held his arms wide, but his theatrics vanished when he noticed Nicky's scowl. 'Hey, come on love, I wasn't one of those blokes.'

Nicky's glare passed from Matthew to her husband, and back again.

'I'm pulling his leg, Nic,' Matthew said, 'I never went to his games unless Chelsea were playing. Of course, we'd be on opposite sides of the stadium, but supporters' clubs knew the troublemakers to watch out for, and the name Dennis Hooper never got a mention, as far as I'm aware. Come on Nic, we all know Dennis has never shirked finishing something someone else has started, but he was never known to be a serial instigator.'

Nicky searched their faces and, choosing to accept Matthew's back-pedalling, finally nodded.

Dennis punched Matthew on the arm. 'You troublemaking shit. Now fermé yer bloody bouche or I might give you a proper kickin', like every good 'ooligan would.'

Londoners Dennis and Matthew first met at their local school in Fulham as nine-year-olds. Almost inseparable as children, they maintained their close friendship long after school life became history. They played for the same amateur football club, formed a band focused on impairing the eardrums of the Hooper's neighbours, and had similar tastes in mainstream music. As they came of age they learned about the local pub scene as well as developing a burgeoning interest in the fairer sex, with all the joys and challenges that invited.

Where the teenagers differed was on which football team should merit their hard-earned pocket money or, later, wages. Despite living in Fulham,

Matthew was an avid Chelsea fan. Dennis' entire family had traditionally followed another of London's high-profile clubs, Tottenham Hotspur, whose ground was even further from their home. The great rivalry between these teams promised, and delivered, animated banter between the friends.

At twenty-seven, Matthew felt depressed after being retrenched from his first job at a small public relations business, and was considering what his future might hold when, over a consolatory pint or two at their local one evening, Dennis suggested they invest in a spot of globetrotting and be nomads for a while. Their ale-inspired stratagem of that session gathered momentum, and over the coming weeks they formulated a plan of action. They informed their families and friends, Dennis left his job at a master joinery, and they boarded a plane bound for Australia as soon as their documents were in order.

They spent a number of months working their way around mainland Australia until, on a whim, they took advantage of cheap flights from Melbourne to Hobart. While in a pub in Salamanca Place one Sunday afternoon, pints in hand and watching Premier League football, Dennis was distracted by the pub's attractive manager, Nicky Brookes. From that moment the football held little appeal as he and Nicky exchanged anecdotes and dreams. Later that evening Dennis told Matthew he was thinking of hanging around Hobart for a while, and Matthew was happy to support his smitten companion and stay on. A few weeks later, Nicky invited her sister Samantha on a blind date to 'meet my boyfriend's closest mate', and from that moment the couples became almost inseparable.

It was not long before a double wedding transpired, with radiant sister brides, and Dennis and Matthew being each other's best man, to the amusement of those attending.

· · · · ·

'Hey, Den,' Matthew began as he rattled his empty cup on its coaster.

'Don't call me 'Den', Matty.' Both grinned like children at the phrase they had used since childhood.

'Cast your mind back to the late eighties.'

'Oh feck, you don't want much do you?'

'Ilford,' Matthew continued.

'Here we go,' Samantha turned to Nicky with a pained expression. 'Come on, let's have a proper girls' look at the place my sister now calls home.' Samantha picked up her cup and peered theatrically at what remained of her coffee, before glancing up at the large and impressive French-style country-kitchen clock. Still, she turned to her husband and asked, 'Darling, what's the time?'

He looked up at the same clock. 'Twelve-thirty,' he said. 'Aren't the numbers big enough for you?'

Dennis snorted.

'Haven't got anything more appropriate for a Sunday morning special occasion strollette around my very favourite sister in the entire world's beeeeautiful home?'

'Of course there's a Charday in the fridge,' Nicky put on her Kath & Kim drawl. 'Faaancy a glass, do woiy?'

'Is the Pope a Catholic?' Samantha posed the metaphorical question as she went to the refrigerator to select a bottle. Before she returned to the table, Nicky had two glasses ready, her fingers marking 'the spot' on each. 'Only a half, mind, because it's still early.'

'It's mid-afternoon in New Zealand, Sam,' Dennis suggested.

Samantha nodded. 'A half glass will still do for now, thanks all the same for your advice!'

The girls headed off down the hallway with wine glasses in hand. 'So your first exhibition has to be your photography?' Samantha asked as they walked away.

'Sure is, I already have ten printed and framed; perhaps five or six more will fill the first gallery space. I'll show you after we've seen the bedrooms.'

'No,' Dennis called to the retreating women. 'Don't you girls worry about us for a second.'

'You know where the fridge is,' Nicky said, as their voices echoed from the hallway.

'Right couple of pisspots we've got there,' Matthew said.

'Fancy a home brew?' Dennis asked.

'Cracking idea!'

'I got this state-of-the-art keg system and it is bloody brilliant. You'd never know the beer wasn't the real deal.'

'I've read about those, so if it's as good as you say, then just to the top if you would, my good man – got to be better than your old shite.'

Dennis grabbed two pint handles from the kitchen dresser and in a camp American drawl urged, 'Not a moment to lose, Bobin, let's make for the Ratcave.'

'To the Ratcave.' Matthew laughed at the memory of more childhood banter as he followed Dennis down a flight of timber stairs, directly from the open-plan kitchen-dining room.

'Hey,' Matthew began as he slid his hand along the curved banister rail, 'excellent craftsmanship! I'd bet it's your work?'

'Yup.'

'Figures.'

The stairs took them to a spacious cellar, where the walls, ceiling and floors had been insulated appropriately, not only to maintain the perfect environment for wine and, apparently, the brewing of beer, but also to serve as a getaway for Dennis. A competition-size snooker table was the first thing Matthew noted as the full extent of the cellar came into view, and then in the corner, around one of the four brick ceiling supports, a bass guitar and compact amplifier.

On a nearby desk sat a computer, an electric piano, relevant audio and midi interfaces for music recording, plus the usual black, white and orange studio spaghetti: the tangled mess of cables required to connect a computer with sound modules, pedals and instruments.

'Holy shit, Ratman, is that your old Music Man, the StingRay fretless bass? I thought you'd left that behind.'

'Sure is: the Pino Palladino special. Dad had it shipped over for me a month ago. Remember him?'

'Of course I remember your dad. It was all his fault you were sired.'

'Palladino, not my dad, you dickhead.'

Matthew smiled. 'Oh! How could one forget? Palladino's playing on "Wherever I Lay My Hat" was quality – gave us musos a reason to listen.'

'The opening notes were borrowed from Stravinsky; didn't you know?'

'Get out,' Matthew said. 'You were always full of useless crap.'

'Yes, well, my compendium of useless crap helped us win a few pub trivia nights, remember? All you ever contributed was football statistics and bugger all else.'

'Piss off,' Matthew laughed. 'Palladino's still going strong.'

'That doesn't surprise me.' Dennis filled the glasses with his version of Guinness and handed one to Matthew. 'So, whaddya reckon?'

A nod accompanied the first sip, and then a longer draught followed.

'Good,' Matthew said, 'really, good.' He wandered over to the guitar, ran his fingers down the fretless neck. 'Do you mind?'

'Go for it. Finding any time to play lately?'

Matthew shrugged, put the glass to one side of the amplifier and sat on the other, but didn't switch the power on. He strummed a few three-note chords, and then did his best jazz run.

'Yep, you're still shite,' Dennis grinned.

'Your turn.' Matthew handed him the bass, picked up his glass and creaked himself into a director's chair.

'Should have brought your acoustic, then we could have played a couple.'

'Didn't want to leave it in the car while we were being tourists.'

'Sensible, my son,' Dennis said. He flicked the amplifier on, waited for a couple of seconds then began to play. Dennis demonstrated he was still a good bassist with command of some challenging techniques. Despite his rugged demeanour, he was a sensitive and skilled musician, with the touch of a strings player.

Dennis clicked the phaser unit on and played the opening bars from 'Wherever I Lay My Hat' while Matthew tapped out a tempo on his thighs and sang the opening lines.

'Still got it, amigo,' Matthew said when Dennis had finished.

'Now,' Dennis began as he picked up his pint and took a swallow, 'what's all this waffle about Ilford?'

'Do you have any memories?'

'Of course I do. I mean, it wasn't that long ago. Mind you, there was loads happening in those days, between football, band and the pubs. If it's football I don't want Mr Smugness rubbin' in just how good your boys-in-blue are doing.'

'No mate, I'm talking music here.' Matthew stood, took his beer over to the snooker table and rolled the white ball across the baize covered slate surface. 'Where did you get this beauty?'

'Came with the place. They couldn't get it out without pulling it to bits. I offered them a couple of hundred for it, and Bob's yer relation. Rack 'em up and tell me about Ilford,' Dennis said as he followed and flicked the overhead lights on.

'I'm not sure, but whatever it might be is driving me nuts ... something to do with Peter Gabriel.'

Dennis struck the cue ball into the triangle of reds, they scattered in all directions, with one creeping slowly up to the far right pocket, before rolling over the edge into the knitted bag. 'A brilliant gig in ninety-two, wasn't it?'

'What, mine or Gabriel's?'

'Gabriel's, of course. We all recognise you were and still are rubbish,' Dennis winked and leaned over to prepare for his second shot.

'Shut your face, you pillock. I'm talking about someone who sounded like Peter Gabriel.'

The blue ball dropped into the far right pocket. 'What, you mean like a karaoke night?'

'Don't be a knob, you know what I mean.'

Dennis stood, his forehead creasing in thought for a moment, before he walked around to the other side of the table to address another red.

'You know,' he said after a pause, 'I do have this vague recollection of a band ... no, a duo, doing a cover of "Don't Give Up".' He dropped the red, but the white spun back and into the pocket by his hand.

'Oh, hard luck old boy,' Matthew sniggered. 'but yes, you are on the money. I want you to say that to my missus, because she thinks I'm going well and truly bonkers.'

'Who's bonkers?' Nicky asked from the top of the stairs. 'No, never mind. We're going out for a light lunch. Sam has some ideas for the gallery reopening. Coming along?'

'Yup, I'm famished,' Dennis shouted.

'But I've only just started my pint,' Matthew said.

'Better knock it back then,' Samantha called, 'or we'll leave you to it.'

Dennis looked to Matthew and together they grinned.

'For old times' sake then,' Matthew said.

They chinked glasses and downed their home-brew Guinness. Both wiped their froth-moustaches as if part of an old ritual, and perhaps it was. They looked at each other, spread their fingers over their bellies and let go two loud belches that had the sisters' laughter echoing from above.

'That's our boys,' Nicky called. 'Now tuck your shirts in and get up here or we'll leave without you.'

CHAPTER FOUR

'So, this Peter Gabriel sound-alike,' Dennis began as he tucked into his bruschetta, 'have you stumbled onto something on the internet?'

'Nothing as clear cut as that,' Matthew said, 'or all my questions would have been answered. Samantha and I pulled into this grotty pub a few days ago. Not inviting in the least but, you know, Sam's legs were twisted together and she moaned every time the wheels hit the smallest bump. It was either pull in there or squat by the roadside and expose her lilywhite arse,' he chuckled and Dennis raised his glass.

Despite chatting to her sister, Samantha overheard their conversation.

'I was sure I was going to pee myself! I don't mind watering a plant in the woods, but never so close to a road and constant traffic.' With that detail clarified, the girls returned to their own discussion.

Matthew continued: 'There were only a few people in the bar. Then this bloke began to play. He looked like a feral but really knew his stuff. Played songs from the seventies and eighties and did them well. Not, you understand, word and note for word and note, but in his own style. The pub was rough, he looked rough, but his performance was excellent. You know, something about him took me back, back to somewhere I just can't put my finger on.'

'It was strange,' Matthew continued, 'this bloke performed alone but there was an extra seat with a guitar and a mauve hat, you know the kind with a wide, floppy brim.'

'Like a woman's fedora,' Samantha added, 'hanging over the head of the second guitar.'

'But no sign of the wearer,' Matthew said.

'Maybe she was in the loo?' Nicky joined in.

'For forty-five minutes?' Matthew questioned. 'There was only one music stand, one microphone.'

'No shit, Sherlock,' Dennis said.

'Maybe she didn't need a microphone. You know, like an opera singer,' Nicky continued.

Samantha rolled her eyes and sighed. 'Don't get too involved sis.'

'You have to admit, Sam, it does sound intriguing,' Nicky whispered.

'I know,' Samantha smiled. 'Just don't get him going!'

Matthew pointed his last asparagus spear at Nicky. 'That's the word, it was intriguing.'

'More than intriguing,' Samantha said. 'You've been obsessed ever since and it's driving me nuts.'

'Look,' Matthew sat back and wiped his mouth on a napkin. 'This has gripped me, sort of like a TV whodunit.'

'Oh, now there's been a suspicious murder, has there?' Dennis asked sarcastically, 'somebody killed Lord Reginald Smythe wiv' a dibbler in the pottin' shed.' He laughed.

'Oh fuck off, chum,' Matthew snapped, his frustration emerging in an angry retort. 'If you're gunna take the piss then ... never mind.' He scraped his chair back and stood. 'I'm off for a real one.'

Nicky released the breath she had taken in, certain that there were few men who could speak to Dennis in that tone, without at least having their lapels creased.

'That came from the blue,' Dennis said as he watched the door to the toilet close behind Matthew. He absently noted the creative, gender-specific illustrated characters on the adjacent doors, and wondered if he should do something inventive on the gallery's restroom door. He let the idea go just as quickly, because his wife was the creative one, and she would never agree.

'I've not seen him like this before,' Samantha said.

'I have,' Dennis said. 'Something's messing with his head. What *was* with this bloke, Sam? Anything you can offer? Because Matt sure as hell can't put his finger on it.'

'He's right,' Samantha said. 'The guy was talented, despite looking like he'd just walked in from a homeless shelter.'

'Maybe he had,' Nicky noted.

Moments later Matthew reappeared and walked towards the bar. 'He's got this thing about that voice,' Samantha said, 'and it's like, what do you call it, a brain worm?'

'That's the term; bored its way in and refuses to leave,' Dennis said.

Samantha began to speak, until Matthew returned with four drinks and placed each on a coaster. He dragged his chair in a little less noisily than before and sat.

'Sorry mate,' Matthew said.

Dennis shrugged, raising his pint. 'No matter, old mate, bottom's up.'

Samantha rested her hand on Matthew's thigh. 'I was just talking about that guy's voice.'

She had given him leave to continue, and Matthew spoke as if his dummy-spit had never happened:

'You know like a TV talent show where some seemingly hopeless case shuffles out in front of the judges and ends up performing like a pro? Well, this bloke did it to me. I reckon he lives on his own, you know, with no woman to make sure he washes behind his ears. He had this thick greying beard and his hair looked like it was on its way to becoming dreadlocks. His clothes were really shabby and I noticed his shoes were only half laced. Then he sat behind his guitar and something changed – it was uncanny.'

'His eyes were sad though, you know, sort of void of life.' Samantha interrupted but Matthew didn't mind; she was taking an interest and that was all that mattered.

'Yes, but his voice was strong, his playing just oozed confidence and the way he ripped through the songs it was like, in his mind, it was another place, another time.'

'Like the London bleedin' Palladium?' Dennis laughed.

'Yes, just like the London bleedin' Palladium,' Matthew said as he tapped on the tabletop.

'You know, I remember watching this show a few years ago,' Dennis recalled. 'Some musician had been disguised behind a beard and long hair, then was stuck on a thoroughfare somewhere to play guitar, as if he was a homeless guy busking for a few coins.'

'I remember that,' Matthew said. 'I reckon it was Jonnie Brice, at Southbank in Melbourne.'

'That's the fella!'

'We saw him in Hobart,' Samantha said. 'He's very clever, and quite gorgeous with it.'

'I think he kinda looks strange,' Nicky said.

'What?' the others spoke in unison.

'You know, the way his head rolls around when he sings.'

'Drink your wine, you twit,' Samantha giggled.

Dennis looked at the sisters with a smile. 'Finished? I think the point of the sketch was to see if people would recognise and appreciate talent where it's least expected; and, let's face it, while Jonnie is a good singer, he's a freak on the guitar. He's changed perceptions of how the instrument can be played – and now there's a bunch of budding heroes worldwide who're taking the guitar to another level, thanks to him and others like him.'

'Woohoo,' Nicky said, 'listen to Mr Preacher!'

Dennis slapped her forearm playfully. 'Anyway, he received some attention, but mostly people just ignored him, and some looked like they wanted to tell him to get a real job.'

'Got it in one,' Matthew said. 'I bet this bloke has an amazing history and probably no-one else at the pub would have a clue.'

'Or care?' added Samantha.

'You think you've seen him before, back in London,' Dennis said.

It was not a question.

'Yes, in another life, as it were.'

'What was the name of the pub?' Nicky asked.

'What, in Ilford?'

'No, Wynyard, you twit,' Dennis said.

Matthew shrugged, 'I don't remember seeing a sign.'

'Wheatsheaf,' Samantha recalled. 'I saw a rusty old sign lying on the ground in the car park, when I got out the car.'

'Sterling way to market your business,' Nicky said.

'How did you know it was a pub if it didn't have an obvious sign?' Dennis asked.

'I didn't care. It was a big Federation building with a car park at the side and a sandwich board out the front saying 'OPEN' – and don't forget I was about to pee my smalls. I was going in, regardless.'

'You were walking as if you were about to give birth,' Matthew chuckled.

'Are we boring you?' Samantha asked her sister, who had taken an iPad from her bag and seemed no longer part of the conversation.

'Love, it wasn't you I was calling a twit,' Dennis tugged his wife's sleeve.

Nicky looked up. 'What? Sorry, no, I'm trying to find this Wheatsheaf pub online. They don't seem to have a website.'

'That wouldn't surprise me,' Matthew said. 'Yellow Pages?'

'I'm trying, but the connection is soooo slow.'

'Let's get out of here and head back home,' Nicky said. 'We can continue the search there.'

Harry's excited bark echoed through the hallway as Nicky unlocked the front door. 'Hello Harry,' she sang, almost face to face as the schnauzer leaped repeatedly.

'Get your rope,' Dennis urged, and Harry spun, galloping off down the hall, his claws scrabbling on the hardwood floor, to disappear around the corner and into the kitchen.

'You'll have to chase after him, love,' Nicky laughed. 'You know he'll be on his bed waiting for you to come and play.'

'C'mon Matt, let's take him outside for a run.'

Ten minutes later Harry bound in from the back garden and flopped on his bed in the kitchen, only to jump up and trot back to the laundry for a noisy drink. He reacquainted himself with his bed, after leaving a trail of watery drool across the kitchen floor. Dennis slid in, with an old towel jammed beneath his foot, to clean up the mess. Matthew followed, commentating on Dennis' skating form.

The schnauzer was much loved in the Hooper household. Of course, Harry could not help making a mess, any more than he could control his snoring, which began almost the moment he closed his eyes.

Four steaming coffee mugs had been set on their coasters around the table, with two already claimed by the chatting sisters. One spare place had a pad, pen and cordless phone sitting beside it. Samantha looked to Matthew and pointed. 'That's for you.'

Matthew dragged his chair in and picked up the pad, on which was written 'Wheatsheaf' and a telephone number.

'Not easy to find,' Nicky stated with satisfaction.

Matthew laughed to himself at his apprehension as he picked up the phone, ran a finger across the pad and dialled the number. The ring tone seemed to sound for an eternity. Matthew cleared his throat.

'Hello?' The heavily accented voice sounded uneasy.

'Hi,' *finally*, thought Matthew, 'is this the Wheatsheaf?'

'*Sì*,' the voice said.

'Er, can I speak with the manager please?' He held his palm over the mouthpiece, 'No wonder they don't have any custom—'

'Rusty,' a voice growled.

'Hello, my name's Matt Pearson. My wife and I dropped in for a drink the other day.'

There was a pause. 'Hmm, nice pins, I recall. Don't get many new, er, faces 'ere.'

I'm not surprised, you prat, Matthew thought. 'Ah, that's no good,' he said. 'I was wondering who the musician was?'

''E don't do gigs.' Rusty's voice hovered between apathy and aggression.

'Fine, I just wondered what his name is and hoped you might be able to tell me.'

'Rob the Pom, and 'e don't do gigs.'

'Rob the Pom?'

'Rob the Pom. He's not for 'ire.'

'I thought I knew him,' Matthew tried to keep melody in his voice while really wanting to say something to the manager about his abrupt, offensive telephone manner.

'No-one knows Rob the Pom,' the manager said with a snort. 'That's the way 'e likes it.'

Matthew thought for a moment until the manager added, 'Anyfin' else?'

'Er, yes. Sorry. I wonder when he's next playing?'

'Oo knows?' the manager said offhandedly. 'Comes an' goes as 'e pleases.'

'Isn't he on your books?'

'None o' yer business, mate,' the manager snapped, and then hung up.

'That went well,' Matthew stared at the handset. 'Arrogant prat.'

'Pass me the phone, Matthew,' Samantha said. Although they both worked in public relations, she thought she might have better luck. Matthew slid the phone and pad over to her and she dialled the number. Again it took a while to be connected.

'Hello, is that the Wheatsheaf?

Ah, *Salve*!' Samantha began conversing in what, to their untrained ears, sounded like authentic Italian.

Dennis looked at Matthew and mouthed, 'Anything yer missus can't bloody well do?'

'Sam usually only speaks like that when we're in the cot,' he whispered with a glint in his eye.

'Oh puleeeese,' Nicky cringed.

Samantha spoke with the person for a few minutes then ended with, '*Grazie mille. Ciao!*'

They looked at Samantha expectantly. 'Her manager is *un cazzo,* so she tells me.'

'What's that?' Dennis asked.

'Not really sure,' Samantha said, 'but I think it's something to do with a penis.'

'Well, at least he's not a chauvinist,' Matthew snorted. 'I gather he treats everyone with the same contempt. So what did she have to say, other than her boss is a *muchos* schlongo?'

'That's Mexican,' Dennis remarked, with satisfaction that he understood the difference.

'What is, schlongo?' Matthew laughed at his own retort.

'Her name's Adelina. She doesn't like answering the phone as she's not confident with her English, but nobody else there seems to want to.'

'Either she's really well paid, or she just needs the dosh,' Dennis decided.

'So,' Matthew sounded impatient, 'did she give you any clues about the muso guy?'

'Not really. She's only been working there for about seven months, and he's only been in a handful of times. She says he comes in to play every now and again, probably just because he's bored. Seems he is a bit of a loner, and it also seems she likes him, despite his appearance.'

'I guess she didn't have an address for him?' Matthew searched.

'She thinks he lives somewhere out Waratah way, says one of the patrons who dropped a load of firewood off once told her the place was *Baracca,* which I think means hovel.'

'Here yer missus goes again', Dennis said. 'Cor!'

'A bit like the pub,' Matthew was smiling.

'Was it that bad?' Nicky wrinkled her nose.

Samantha nodded. 'The building had that I-need-a-good-wash feel, everywhere you looked.'

Matthew slumped back in his seat. 'So, we're none the wiser then?'

'Sounds like our best bet's just to take pot luck and turn up in the hope that he's playing, I guess,' Dennis sympathised.

The phantom musician had teased all four companions' sense of wonder and they sat in contemplation for a while, except for the occasional slurp, idle chink of spoon on cup, or Matthew's knee, that bounced restlessly.

'Keep your jimmy leg still mate,' Dennis said, 'or I'll kick the bastard.' Matthew relaxed immediately.

Samantha sat back and clapped, 'At last, thanks Dennis, I will know how to cure it next time!'

'Well, that's that then,' Nicky sighed as she finished the last of her drink, 'best we start dinner.'

'Isn't it a bit early?' Matthew asked, checking his watch without actually looking at the time.

'We grew up in a household where the Sunday roast would chug away all afternoon in a cooker much like that,' Samantha said, pointing to the antique wood-burning range, 'isn't she a beauty?'

'Sure is,' Nicky grinned, 'C'mon Sam, the beef's been marinating in the fridge since last night.'

'I've gone off beef,' Dennis pouted.

'Bullshite, caveman,' Matthew laughed, 'you'll eat anyfink wiv legs, wings or fins.'

Dennis pursed his lips and nodded. 'Need a hand, girls?' he asked.

'We've got four hands and girl talk aplenty,' Nicky replied, as if to give them leave to get out of their hair.

'Thank God for that,' Dennis sighed. 'Come on Matt, back to the Ratcave; we've a game to finish. Shame you didn't bring your guitar,' he said as they headed down the stairs.

'Did I mention this was a groovy hand rail?' Matthew said.

· · · · ·

'We've decided to go back to Wynyard on the off-chance,' Dennis said at dinner.

Matthew groaned. 'Christ! Not now, you fekkin' oaf.'

'What? We decided, so now I'm telling 'em.' Dennis was never known for subtle diplomacy.

Matthew looked at Samantha; Samantha was looking at him. Around the dining table, everyone was still. She sighed, 'I guess *we* are.'

'Er, *we*?'

'That's what you said,' Nicky smirked.

'Oh, of course,' Matthew said. 'I thought you'd tell us to leave well enough alone.'

Nicky finished the last of her modest portion and pushed her plate away. 'While the boys were making that racket downstairs, the girls were upstairs planning a nice weekend in the northwest, get away for a bit, and revisit the Wheatsheaf, too.'

Matthew sat up straighter. 'When do we go?'

'You two can go any time you please,' Nicky said, 'but we're in the middle of some heavy renovations and can't afford to take days off, so if you want us to join you, you'll have to wait, probably until March.'

'And we're taking our first time out for a while,' Samantha agreed, 'and I don't want to put the staff under undue pressure just yet, especially with two of them still cutting their teeth.'

Matthew appeared to fret. 'But, what if Rob the Pom moves on?'

'There's no indication he's itinerant,' Samantha said, 'but from what Adelina told me it's pointless going too soon, and our friendly landlord will tell us nothing in advance. We can make it four days over Easter or three on the Queen's Birthday long weekend. There are plenty of things to see and do around there, so we can just be flexible and play it by ear, maybe ring the pub every afternoon and, if he's there, then we can drop in for a drink and a listen.'

Matthew shrugged. 'Easter? That's over six months away. I hope it won't be too late by then.'

'Or ...' Dennis paused, and the others turned expectantly, 'if previous years are anything to go by, we'll be staying over at your parents' for Christmas, right? Tradies won't work over the holidays so there won't be anything going on here – are you with me?'

'Go on,' Nicky said. *Tread carefully*, her tone suggested.

'I can make sure I am up with everything they will need for when they're back on site in January.'

'You bet you will,' Nicky said.

'Sam, are you and Matt closing the doors over the silly season?'

'Er, I guess so ... I haven't even thought about it, to be honest.'

'Then, why not pack up our camping gear and take it with us to the Brookes' place on Christmas day, don't go nuts on the alcohol front and we can take off early the next morning for a few day's camping somewhere around Wynyard?'

'There'll be bugger-all traffic so hopefully we should have a good run,' Matthew said.

Samantha and Nicky looked to the other. 'Ned's?' Samantha whispered.

Nicky nodded. 'Think you can make it work?'

'I'll give it my best shot.'

Dennis overheard their whispers. 'What are you girls cookin'?'

'Doesn't matter,' Nicky said, 'We'll let you know soon enough.'

'I assume you'll be bringing Harry anyway,' Samantha said, 'so he can just stay on with Mum and Dad.'

'We will, and they love Harry.'

'This sounds more the ticket,' Matthew grinned, 'and not so long to wait for the mystery to unfold!'

Dennis looked at Nicky, his brows raised. 'Payback's going to be a bitch, I just know it.'

'Be afraid,' she joked.

'Now,' Samantha began, 'do you think we can have a nice evening and talk about other things apart from Matthew's rock-star doppelgänger? What about these renovations, this fabulous gallery and how you intend to open her?'

Matthew laughed, 'Dennis fekkin' Hooper running an art gallery!'

'You really are a prat, Matty,' Dennis said as he disappeared down the hallway and into the office. He returned a few moments later with a yellow manila folder, bulging with stapled sheets of plans, costings and a design sample board.

'I'll be lackey to the stonemasons and roofers, and build stud walls, door and window frames myself. In fact, I've already completed four of the seven window frames, and have ordered the sash windows, which will arrive the second or third week of January, so we have been assured. Hopefully we can sign off on time, as planned.'

'And on budget,' Nicky added.

Dennis nodded, and pointed to an outbuilding on the plan. 'This one will be the gallery, connected to the house via a corridor to the boot room, right here. We're putting the small kitchen in the corner here, and turning this bit into a climate-controlled storeroom here,' he tapped the place on the drawing.'

'And this bit's where your stud walls will be?' Matthew asked.

'Yup, just in the corridor, which will have the same exterior stonework as the rest of the place – oh, and a loo over here, of course. The rest will remain stonework outside and re-rendered walls inside.

'And the gatehouse?' Matthew asked.

'We've worked on that ourselves, me and Nic. As you saw, it's not far from being finished.'

Samantha referred back to the gallery plan and said 'This will be a fantastic expanse of hanging space.'

'Sure will Sam. Once the windows are in I can start to render the walls.'

Nicky scowled. 'Dennis, I thought we'd decided to get professionals in for the rendering?'

'I know love, but remember the astronomical quotes?' Dennis flicked through the document and tapped a relevant spot on a page. 'You'd have thought they were frigging cosmetic surgeons or something.'

'Well, look at it this way,' Nicky shrugged. 'If we, and I mean you, do the rendering, we might save some dollars initially, but it will likely cost us in the end. And how can you expect to work such large walls with no experience, and do it better than the professionals? You're a brilliant timber craftsman Dennis, not a tradie. Want the best job? Be prepared to pay for it.'

'Just like you'd tell your prospective customers,' Matthew agreed.

'I know, I know, but it's such a lot of money,' Dennis shrugged. 'Remember when the Camerons next door got those guys in to render their lounge-room walls and they botched it up? The surface started flaking within a few weeks and Chris went ballistic.'

Nicky nodded. 'And didn't they go for the cheapest quote? Lesson to be learned: don't employ jacks-of-all-trades; get the specialists, no matter the cost. Keep your raptor gaze on them, they'll work quicker and better than even you will, and we'll get a good night's sleep.'

'Fair point,' Dennis sighed. 'I'll make some calls tomorrow.'

'Finished?' Samantha asked.

'Sorry about that, sis.' Despite the apology, she knew their private conversation would not offend these particular guests.

'So,' Dennis began, 'all raise a hand if you are up for a Boxing Day sortie to the northwest.'

Matthew sat back, slapped his imaginary gavel into his palm and said 'SOLD to the man wearin' the funny 'at.

CHAPTER FIVE

Returning to their home in New Norfolk, a thirty-minute drive north of Hobart, spelled the end of the Pearsons' September sojourn from normality. With the excitement, relaxation and mystery of those past few days behind them, they refocused on their business, seven staff and an ever expanding portfolio at Pearson PR, Hobart.

Samantha and Matthew made an agreement to take a break from all things Rob the Pom for the time being, although Matthew could not completely rid himself of the nagging feeling that the enigmatic musician was somehow familiar and, with the nickname 'the Pom', must obviously be English. That was one possible part of the jigsaw in place, but what about the rest of the unknown pieces?

Samantha, on the other hand, hardly gave Rob the Pom a second thought. She arranged to borrow her parent's state-of-the-art camper trailer, and spent a day with Matthew, in her parents' shed, getting familiar with the spacious fold-out unit. With its separate sleeping quarters, one over the trailer wheels and the second off to the side at ground level, plus a separate annex and an amazing slide out kitchen unit, roughing it was not likely to be on the cards, although they could still pretend.

. . . . .

In early October, Samantha and Matthew were enjoying a lazy Sunday-morning breakfast in bed.

'Honey?' Samantha cooed, as she circled a finger through the hairs on his forearm.

'Okay, just how much is '*honey*' going to cost?' Matthew said as he brushed toast crumbs from his bare chest onto the floor. He raised a single eyebrow and waggled it in mock suspicion.

His comical expression seldom failed to bring a smile to Samantha's face, even if she might not feel like smiling at the time. 'It won't cost much, not much at all,' she said, but then her smile faded. 'I hope you are going to clean that up?'

'Of course, as soon as our lie-in is over. So, what won't cost much, not much at all?'

'Just a little petrol money,' she said, 'that's all – oh, apart from giving up your Saturday.'

'Go on.'

'There's an arts festival in Burnie next week. Jess Poulton is performing on Saturday.'

A Brookes' family friend, Jess Poulton was a talented young comedic actor, with enough energy and charisma to give her a chance of opening a couple of those opportunity doors. Matthew had said in the past he thought Jess was brilliant: great ironic humour, delivered by an irreverent Aussie larrikin. Neither were too surprised when they learned Jess had announced she was relocating to the mainland, in search of a larger pond to dip into.

'She's coming back to Tassie, then,' he said, stating the obvious. 'That girl's funny as shite!'

'Evidently she's decided to launch her first Australian tour, right here in her home state.'

'Good on her. When and where?'

'Saturday evening, an outdoor gig on the Burnie waterfront lawns.'

Samantha watched Matthew's allegorical brain cogs whir, knowing it wouldn't take long for him to piece a scenario together. 'You are soooo transparent, Matt.' She poked him in the ribs. 'I know, *exactly*, what you are concocting.'

'Not far from the Wheatsheaf then?'

She pretended a long-suffering sigh. 'I guess not, dear.'

He cupped a hand on his chin and tapped his top lip. 'Drop in to the pub, if Rob the Pom is there, we find out something about him, back to Burnie for a quick bite then off to see Jess.'

'Management accepts your proposal.' Samantha said.

'I assume I'll get that in triplicate?' he jokingly suggested. 'Have you asked Den and Nic?'

'It was Nic who told me about Jess being at the festival, and no, they can't make it.'

'Shame. Are they okay with that? Dennis is pretty interested.'

'If they've got other things to do, that's their decision I guess,' Samantha said. 'Doesn't mean we can't still go.'

'I suppose you're right, I'll give him a call later anyway.'

· · · · ·

It was mid-afternoon, October 15, when Samantha drove their car into the Wheatsheaf grounds. Only four other vehicles occupied the weed-infested car spaces, one being a battered white utility, sporting a familiar, flaking forestry logo on the driver's door. Matthew peered beneath the tattered tonneau that failed to cover the ute's tub, and spied a weathered chainsaw, a sawdust-encrusted chain-oil container, and a stained white plastic container with a label hanging from its side, stating: *Warning 1080 Poison. Sodium flouroacetate. DEADLY TO DOGS.*

Just as deadly to a shitload more creatures than just the beloved man's best friend, Matthew thought. He tried to resist the same thought he had already had a dozen times on the journey. But he thought it just the same: *I hope Rob the Pom is playing today.*

He pushed through the entrance door and peered into the pub. His excitement built, as the sound of an acoustic guitar rang clearly in his ears.

His eyes took a moment to adjust from bright outside sunshine to dull pub lighting, then he recognised the three heavy-set men, on the same stools as the last time, but this time not wearing their forestry uniforms. They sat, beers in hand with their backs pressed against the bar. Matthew felt the blood pulse through his neck as he followed their line of vision towards the stage, only to find it was empty; no guitars, no microphones, no singer. The music was not live at all. The men had simply assumed their normal positions, entertainer or not.

'What is it, love?' Samantha asked as he made no move to go further.

'He's not here.'

'Well who's ...' She stopped herself as a female voice joined the guitar. 'Oh, it's a recording ... well, are you going in?'

'What's the point?'

'What if he's starting late and hasn't set up yet?'

Matthew pursed his mouth and moved inside just the same, but only as far as the first table. He stood and looked around at the empty, dark corner, the three workers who paid him no attention, and the bar. Despite the three men, it appeared as if the pub was not open.

Samantha felt a moment's irritation towards her husband. She sighed, and walked around him and on to the bar. She pressed her elbows into the bar top and looked for somebody who might serve them. She even peered over the bar, almost as if she expected someone crouching there, just out of her line of sight, to jump up, glass and towel in hand and say, 'Can I get you something, madam?'

She tapped her fingernails on the timber surface, and waited.

'Betts.' A voice called from behind, and Samantha turned to see one of the workers looking at her. 'Rusty ain't here, nor is Loren,' he explained, 'so Betts's holding the fort. BETTS!' he called again.

'Who's Loren?' Samantha asked.

'The Italian chick, y'know, Sophia.'

Samantha responded with a patient smile, and then said, 'I thought her name was Adelina ...'

'Too bloody hard to pronounce, so me mates and me call her Loren, don't we?' His companions nodded without turning. 'The gaffer calls her Italiano, but Betts calls ...'

'I'm coming, Johnno,' Samantha cocked her head towards a distant voice, 'there in a tick.' The cook emerged from down the hallway, carrying a carton of plastic-wrapped soft-drink cans. 'Oh, hello dear,' she puffed, 'I didn't hear anyone come in. What can I get you?'

'I, er, we were wondering if the musician was due to play today?'

'No dear, he is down the road with my husband, busking at the festival.'

'Oh.'

'Can I get you anything?'

Samantha turned to Matthew, and beckoned for him to come over.

'The musician's not here today, Matt. Do you want a coffee or something else while we're here?'

Matthew frowned dejectedly.

Betty looked from Samantha to Matthew. 'No need to feel obliged to have something for something's sake, dears.'

'Is that okay, really?' Samantha felt a pang of guilt.

'It is fine, dearie.'

'We won't tell Rusty you let a couple of punters go without fleecing their pockets,' Johnno, who had been eavesdropping, chuckled.

'Don't be naughty, Johnno,' Betty said without taking offence. 'You're not trying to weasel a free beer out of me again, are you?'

'That's blackmail, Betts, dontcha know?' one of his friends said, still without turning.

'There is a free beer for you and your layabout brothers,' Betty said, 'but only if you restock the fridge for me.'

'Right y'are, Betts.' Johnno emptied his glass and pushed it towards her. 'Consider it done!' He walked around the bar and down the darkened hallway, clearly not for the first time. 'Come on lads, give us a hand,' he called, 'the landlord's shouting the bar.'

'Righty ho, I'm in,' one of his friends slapped the counter top, as both stood and followed.

. . . . .

As Samantha turned right onto the highway and headed east, Matthew opened one of the packets of potato chips they acquired at the Wheatsheaf; an obligatory purchase. He puffed the bag open and wedged it, within easy reach, between Samantha's knees.

'There you go love,' he said, as he opened a packet of his own and began, mid-crunch. 'So, any ideas where he might be playing?'

'Being he's not officially a part of the festival, we can only guess. You know,' she interrupted herself, 'Rusty has some nerve, taking advantage of this Rob the Pom to go busking at a festival, and then probably holding on to most of the proceeds.'

'Sounds like most managers,' Matthew mused.

Samantha found a vacant parking space near the Burnie town centre, and they took a pleasant stroll to the foreshore, following a growing number of people carrying fold-up chairs, blankets and hampers, towards the surf club.

They neared a stage, protected by a three-sided marquee, with banks of coloured lights, and stacks of speaker cabinets flanking the stage. Technicians and road crew were busily making ready. A man who did not appear to be a performer, kept repeating 'One two, one chew, two, chew, one two, wunnuh, chewuh,' into a microphone. There was no sign of Rob the Pom.

'Let's try that way,' Matthew suggested, and they kept walking, picking their way against the gathering crowd. They continued halfway along a boardwalk that skirted the shoreline but, after realising they were leaving the action, retraced their steps. After they crossed a railway line, heading south towards town, they found Rob the Pom, sitting on a small stool outside the entrance to a hotel playing his guitar. The enigmatic mauve fedora was perched on a microphone stand that had not been extended to its usual height. The open guitar case by his feet contained an assortment of coins, and several notes.

Matthew and Samantha stood away from the constant line of foot traffic, and watched Rob the Pom play. He seemed to be mostly ignored by the people passing through, although an occasional hand might extend to drop a token of a listeners' appreciation into the case. He played renditions of popular classics, but none of his own songs. He played, and the Pearsons applauded, but Rob the Pom ignored his audience of two, as if he sang, singularly, for his own enjoyment.

'Great playing,' Matthew said when he took a break.

Rob the Pom made eye contact with him for the briefest of moments, before turning back to his guitar to adjust the tuning keys.

'You know,' Matthew said, 'you seem really familiar, and I've been wondering if we've met before?'

Again, the briefest moment's attention. 'Unlikely,' Rob the Pom said.

'You sound as if you come from London.'

The musician paused, as if he barely tethered his rage.

'Like what you hear?' he grated, 'Well, how about throwing me a few coins to keep Rusty happy? Then you can be on your way, to wherever you are going.'

Matthew decided to press him. 'I don't want to be a pest, but I'm sure we've met before, and it's driving me nuts trying to work out where.'

Rob the Pom looked up again, biting back the urge to tell Matthew to fuck off, when he noticed Samantha. His mouth clamped shut, for reasons he failed to comprehend.

'We love your work,' Samantha said with a smile as she leaned forward to drop five dollars into the guitar case. 'We just wanted to say hello, and tell you so.'

Speak with them, my love. The beautiful voice, that only he would hear, said to him.

'... don't want to.'

'I beg your pardon?' Samantha said.

He looked at Samantha, studied her as if Matthew no longer existed. He felt his throat tighten, as if she was the most emotional force he had encountered since ... since. *You must trust them*, the voice urged. *Trust them.*

'Will you move on, please?' he said, his tone ragged.

They are your chance, my love.

Rob the Pom continued to stare at Samantha, as if his vision had developed some super power that permitted him to see into her soul. His face softened, barely noticeable but still there. *Would it really hurt that much?* he wondered.

No, it would not.

Maybe it's time.

Yes, it is time.

No, it's not. You only need me.

There, that other voice.

I'm tired ... so tired. Tired of running.

You can – and must – trust them, my love.

'Hey, Pom,' Rusty Faulkner's grating call shattered his internal dialogue. Rusty approached from the pub next door and growled, 'Why the 'ell aren't you playing, while all these people are bloody well just walkin' on by? Shit, Pom, you've not even 'anded out any of me flyers.' He looked down at the guitar case, and sighed. 'S'pose it's time we found another spot anyway.'

Rusty pushed between Samantha and the case. ''Scuse us lady, we're off.' He turned to Samantha, and she smelled beer on his breath. 'Unless you wanna show your appreciation of the great Rob the Pom by chucking a couple o' tenners in the case before 'e puts 'is guitar away?'

'Thank you, but I have already donated to the musician.'

'Well if it's all the same, missus, be on your way so we can be on ours.' Rusty turned away and began thrusting his homemade Wheatsheaf flyers at passers-by close enough to reach.

Cheeky bastard. Matthew chose to keep that to himself.

'Well, I have not yet donated.' Matthew held his own note, folded between finger and thumb, in the space between them. 'We were chatting to him, and would like to continue to do so.'

Rusty Faulkner turned to him and frowned.

'Do I know you?' he asked. Again, beer breath. Matthew shook his head. 'Well then, conversation over.' Rusty snatched the five dollars with the barest nod of thanks.

He shoved the note and flyers into his pocket, turned and crouched by the guitar case to scoop the takings of an hour's busking into a plastic zip-lock bag.

'Time's getting on, Matthew,' Samantha said, 'we'd best leave them to their work and find somewhere to eat.'

Rob the Pom watched them walk away, watched them both take an occasional look over their shoulder. He felt empty, as if he had missed out on an opportunity, but didn't know what that might have been.

He heard a soft, guttural laugh, somewhere over his shoulder, but didn't turn, because he knew who that was.

Samantha and Matthew retraced their steps to the marquee and, deciding against a restaurant meal, made themselves comfortable on the lawn to eat their paper cones of fish and chips. The audience was being entertained by a young woman with a fresh voice, who accompanied herself on the ukulele, and a group of taiko drummers who lathered themselves into a sweating, hollering frenzy, until Jess Poulton took the stage at eight o'clock.

Jess Poulton did not disappoint, and it was great to catch up with her after the show. However, the mood was sombre as Samantha and Matthew settled into their hotel room for the night.

CHAPTER SIX

Christmas morning arrived, and the four companions reconvened at the boisterous family gathering at Samantha and Nicky's parents' home in New Norfolk. Despite the reverie it was not long before Matthew and Dennis found a quiet place to talk, revisiting the apparition that continued to flitter, tantalisingly, outside the boundary of their recollections.

Matthew had told Dennis about their close encounter with Rob the Pom at the Burnie festival, but it offered no more insight into the enigma.

Despite his initial derision, Dennis admitted he had spent some time researching the music scene of the nineteen eighties, trying to help his brother-in-law solve the riddle, although his attempts, up to that point, had been fruitless.

He was prepared for the entire mystery to prove to be no more real than one of Matthew's confused dreams.

The lifelong friends had been in touch more regularly since the acquisition of the Longford property, and Matthew's fleeting brushes with Rob the Pom. However, Christmas was about celebrating with the Brookes family rather than being on their own, as Samantha insisted when she found them out in the workshop, sitting beside the camper trailer with Harry at Matthew's feet.

'What on earth are you two doing out here anyway?'

Matthew shrugged. 'We came out to check the trailer ... and just got talking about stuff.'

Samantha sighed 'We're heading off tomorrow so surely it can wait? Come and join the fun – it's starting to get noisy in there!'

Dennis watched her as she left through the shed doorway. 'Did you notice that? I reckon that was a cab-sav walk if ever I've seen one!'

Matthew looked around too late. 'Quite likely Den, but Boxing Day hangovers will not be part of the plan for us chauffeurs this year. Come on mate, let's be sad old bastards and grab another light beer.'

'At least we're allowed to eat as much as we like!'

The sisters had proposed that they head to the family's old camping place near Waratah. With the Wheatsheaf only an hour away, if nothing came of the mysterious Peter Gabriel sound-alike, then at least they could find solace in beautiful northwest scenery. Neither husband had heard of the Brookes' hidden gem before, but Samantha and Nicky knew they would appreciate the isolated paradise.

The Brookes family had named it Ned's Camp.

They left at eight; first Dennis and Nicky's Nissan Patrol, followed by the Pearsons' Mitsubishi Outlander towing the camper trailer. It was a five-hour journey to the well-hidden camping spot, on a river near Waratah.

The sisters' dearly departed old Uncle Ned Brandscombe was a real bushman and, despite being somewhat domesticated through marriage, occasionally preferred his own company and would pack up his beaten up off-roader without notice and vanish, for days or sometimes even weeks of hunting, fishing and solitude. He almost always returned with some produce, either fresh or, as he had the means, smoked fish or wallaby.

Ned would stand at his own front door and knock as if he were a visitor, holding a bunch of ragged flowers behind his back in the hope that his long-suffering wife would forgive him, yet again. Aunt Enid (the young girls were instructed to dispense with the Great) usually did, after a suitable period of silence. 'Your uncle has gone to Coventry for a while,' Aunt Enid would tell the children, even if they had not asked. Flowers would be transferred to the compost bin and any fish placed in the freezer, to be likewise ignored, for the time being.

When Aunt Enid had deemed Ned had suffered enough, she would make a ceremonial pot of tea, using her best china, and invite Ned to join her, to mark an end to the punishment. Of course, Ned would relish the silent treatment, but go along with the ritual in good humour. They had been together so long, they accepted each other's ways with flexibility and unspoken love.

Samantha and Nicky adored their old uncle, with his gnarled hands and weathered face, a memory seemingly etched into every crease. As kids they would sit for hours listening to his tales and songs, usually in front of the fire with the lounge-room lights out, as if they were away camping with him. The old man would play his mandolin and sing songs he had made up while he was away. The beaten-up instrument had only five rusty strings, because Ned had never bothered to replace the three broken ones, but that never mattered to the girls. They would sit, absorbed, as Uncle Ned's deep, craggy voice conjured images to them of rich brown earth.

Ned often told them the story of when, as a child back in the early nineteen-thirties, he would visit the last captive Tasmanian tiger in Hobart Zoo; a sad narrative with a sadder ending. But most of all they loved it when Uncle Ned swore he knew where a family of wild tigers lived, but would never tell anyone, even his dear nieces.

'If I told', Uncle Ned would say, 'some mindless idiot would come and kill them, as a sport to brag to their mates.'

Not once did the girls ever doubt his word.

Young Samantha and Nicky accepted that the old man could sometimes be a handful for Aunt Enid but they considered him a hero, the kind seldom found anywhere these days, people who knew him would say.

One weekend, when Uncle Ned was closing in on his eighty-fourth birthday, he took Nicky, Samantha and their parents to one of his getaway places. He was becoming quite frail and forgetful, and they later assumed that he had finally wanted to share, or show off, the gem he had held secret, before he was no longer able to. Timely it was, as old Uncle Ned curled up his toes (as he would have said) within the month. Lovely, generous old

Aunt Enid, with her world torn from her, followed Uncle Ned only a week later. All those memories, all those experiences, all that kindness, gone in one final sigh.

· · · · ·

The access track to Ned's Camp was virtually hidden from the road, but, after forty minutes bouncing along plantation tracks, farmland and old forest owned by Uncle Ned's old mate, Bushy Lavender, Matthew's patience with Samantha's directions was justified. Back and forth through a pristine Gondwanan wilderness of majestic celery-top pine, myrtle, sassafras and a dense understory of tree ferns, they finally found the landmark: an overgrown flat table of basalt. While at first it appeared to be a barrier, it provided the narrow and only access to the magnificent secluded campsite.

'Ned's Camp,' Nicky announced to Dennis as they crested the rock to see a beautiful amphitheatre, almost totally encapsulated by a circular ridge of basalt, scree and dolerite above a verdant tree line. At first glance it appeared as a miniature volcano crater, not much more than a kilometre across. Narrow vertical rifts running northwest and southeast allowed the Hellyer River to cut through on the far edge, on its way to meet with the Arthur. A small rivulet had funnelled away from the main watercourse, and opened out into a wider, slower-moving reservoir in the clearing before them, before gathering momentum to cascade into a gulley outside the crater's southern edge.

Mindful of Tasmania's changeable weather, Matthew parked on a bank of sand-like silt, above indications of the lake's high-water line. Dennis and Nicky pulled alongside and they all got out of the vehicles and stood for a moment listening to birdsong, the buzz of flying insect and gentle gurgle of the water.

'Doesn't get much better than that,' Matthew said.

Dennis took a deep breath of air while he gazed in wonder at a vista that reminded him of scenes in *Jurassic Park*. 'Who owns this place again?'

'Belongs to Uncle Ned's best mate, Bushy Lavender.' Nicky spoke almost at a whisper. 'He's a cantankerous old sod who doesn't abide trespassers.'

'And we're not trespassing?' Matthew asked in a similar tone.

'Watch out for shotgun pellets peppering yer arse,' Dennis joked.

'The Brookes are exempt from Bushy's shotgun,' Nicky said with a shiver, as memories of Bushy filtered through.

'What's his take on two ornery Londoners?' Matthew posed.

'I phoned last week,' Samantha said. 'None of us should get shot at.'

'Should? That's comforting to know we might *not* get shot,' Matthew said, 'So, why are we all whispering?'

'She started it,' Dennis directed a nod towards his wife.

'Bushy not only doesn't like trespassers, he doesn't like company of any kind,' Samantha remembered, 'apart from old Ned, Aunt Enid and, it seems, us Brookes girls.'

On the rare occasions they met, Bushy did not intentionally go out to scare the young girls, but his appearance was like Uncle Ned's without the charm, and his voice 'sounded like a telling off', as Samantha recalled once saying to her parents.

'Bushy's a very old man now but probably still gets about. His grandson, William, has taken over the property. That's who I spoke to when I rang. We're okay here.'

'One doesn't get this kind of quiet back in London.' Matthew was still whispering.

'Very true, old chap,' Dennis agreed, 'good old Uncle Ned.'

'Good old Uncle Ned's mate, too, let's not forget,' added Matthew.

Samantha wrapped her arms around herself. 'I can feel him,' she sighed, 'Uncle Ned is still here.'

'Why wouldn't he be?' Matthew agreed.

'Hey Ned,' Dennis' call echoed around the distant rock walls, 'how're they hangin'? We're about to crack a coldie. Fancy one?'

Nicky shook her head; trust Dennis to break the spell. 'No beer until we're all set up, you oaf,' she said in her normal tone.

'Hear that, Ned?' Dennis continued, 'Henpecked, that's wot we are, not real men like you old geezers, nicking orf on yer tod.'

'Give it a rest and unpack the Patrol,' Nicky laughed.

'So ...' Dennis hesitated while he watched Matthew flick through his own hand written camper trailer assembly instructions. 'You reckon this is where Uncle Ned found the family of Tassie tigers?'

'Who knows?' Samantha thought aloud. 'Just imagine if only ...' The words hung in the air as they paused again, breathing in the sights, sounds and smells.

'Right,' Dennis said after a minute, 'let's get back to it.'

Nicky grabbed her camera bag. 'Back in a mo,' she said.

'Go on, leave us to it,' Dennis called as she walked away. 'Would you like me to bring you a fekkin' cushion to sit on?'

· · · · ·

Dennis stretched on his camp chair, belly full after a hearty meal. 'What's our plan of action tomorrow?'

'I phoned the Wheatsheaf on Wednesday,' Samantha said, 'and the Italian girl, Adelina, has a feeling he might appear in the next couple of days. She wasn't certain but said Rusty mentioned something about Rob the Pom.'

'Lucky you keep getting her,' Nicky said.

'She did say nobody else bothers to answer the phone.'

'What does she think about our interest in this bloke?' Dennis asked.

'She hasn't commented on that, but said she doesn't know much about him; thinks he's polite, likes his voice but doesn't recognise many of the songs he plays.'

Dennis shook his head. 'She's probably twenty and not aware of much before nineteen ninety.'

'She'd be mid-twenties at least,' Samantha suggested, 'but another culture, perhaps a different radio hit list.'

Matthew was sitting on the sand, poking at the fire and following the embers as they danced high into the deep sunset. 'So, what's the plan?'

'A few more bevvies, a good night's sleep,' Dennis said as he stood and stretched. 'Come on mate, let's wash these dishes before it gets too dark and the Waratah Wisp snatches us at the water's edge.'

Nicky looked out at the still water that reflected the low crimson sky. 'Thanks for that, Dennis, you idiot,' she sighed.

They remained by the light of the fire and a small gas lamp, and it wasn't long before the expected campsite tales of ghosts, ghouls and strange creatures were shared, mostly by the men.

'It was nineteen forty-nine,' Dennis began another tale, but Nicky raised her hand in submission.

'Dennis, no more, please!'

'Last one,' he urged. 'As I was saying; nineteen forty-nine, when Mountain River was terrorised by a strange being that left both town and bush people alike pretty well shittin' themselves. Some said the creature sort of looked like a dog but was the size of a bear, and a call like that of a … bansheeeeeee.'

He paused for effect, looking into the eyes of each of his companions in turn. 'The phantom sent shivers through not only man, woman and child, but dogs went bleedin' bonkers when it was around … stock even crashed through fences.'

'The wonders of the human subconscious.' Samantha felt a spiritual chill on her neck.

'Whatever, it spooked the township for months,' added Dennis. 'Even the authorities got themselves involved.'

'Probably just a thylacine.' Nicky used the Tasmanian tiger's formal name. 'Just another persecuted creature trying to survive. Anyway, where do you find this stuff?'

'Good old Google!'

'Well, that was so long ago,' Matthew said with an air of one-upmanship. 'I have it on very good authority,' he said with theatrical smugness, 'Two friends who climbed da, daaaa – da da da daaaa ... Black Bluff.'

'It wasn't just two friends,' Samantha said.

Matthew recalled the mockery he endured when he related the story – not the first time, to his new bride, but later to a group of friends. He found it easier to tell the tale if he distanced himself by telling it in the third person, but apart from that he described events just as he remembered.

He leaned forward in his chair, so close to the glow of the fading fire that he looked positively weird. 'So, my mates are keen trekkers, and one weekend they decided to bag Black Bluff, you know, starting near Loongana.'

'Bag?' Nicky asked.

'Bag. You know, get to the top, strike it off your bucket list.'

'Really?' Samantha queried. 'So, Sir Edmund Hillary bagged Everest?'

'I suppose so,' Matthew said with a shrug. 'Just back old boy. Put the kettle on and cook me a kipper, there's a good chap; we bagged the blighter, what ho!'

'Not quite in the same league though, is it?' Dennis added, ignoring Matthew's poor rendition of a neo-romantic British accent, and overlooking the fact Hillary was a New Zealander.

'Well, okay, maybe you conquer a monumental mountain but bag a, um, smaller one?'

Preferring general conversation on a dark, still night in the bush to monster stories, Nicky asked, 'What, like you sail a boat but drive a ship?'

After thinking about it, Matthew mimicked teenage disdain, 'Wotevva.'

The sisters decided they would rather not hear any more. They collected their things and made to retire.

'Best to have yer last waz before the fire dims, girls,' Dennis said. 'We won't look.'

'Yes, you will,' Nicky said, 'come on Sam, let's go this way.' They grabbed head torches and a roll of toilet paper from inside the annex, and headed off into the bushes.

'Watch out for vampire leeches on yer arses,' Dennis called as he and Matthew watched the torchlights flitting this way and that.

'Girls are spooked,' Dennis chuckled, despite hearing distant giggles.

'And you're not?' Matthew asked and Dennis agreed with a nod of his head. They stared into the fire for a while, until bobbing lights announced Samantha and Nicky's return.

'So, my mates ...' Matthew made to resume his tale.

'I thought these bloody stories had finished,' Nicky said with a sigh.

'No, but I bet this is a good'n. Go on Matt, me ol' China,' Dennis said.

Nicky resumed her seat. 'It better not be scary.'

'Oh it is, little sister.' Samantha patted Nicky's hand.

Matthew looked at Dennis and shook his head. 'So these blokes met at the campsite at Loongana and started their uphill climb. It was a brilliant clear day ... by all accounts. The walk is pretty constant up the Brookes Track, with little relief for legs and lungs.'

'Brookes Track?' Dennis asked.

'No family connection,' Samantha said, 'at least I don't think so.'

'Anyway,' Matthew continued, 'we, er they climbed for a good hour or so, before the wind started to pick up, clouds gathered and the temperature dropped. Before long they were trudging through a blizzard, wondering how the weather could change so quickly. They kept heading upward but, by the time they reached Paddys Tarn, had decided it wasn't safe to head for the summit, nor was it a good idea to head back down.'

'Paddys Tarn?' Dennis asked.

'A lake, towards the summit of the bluff. Anyway daylight was fading with the heavy cloud, despite it being only mid-afternoon, and then a heavy fog began streaming over the white caps on the lake. They found a reasonably flat, clear space between clumps of tussock grass and pitched their tents, using rocks to help secure the pegs. One guy had a four-season, two-man tent and the other a swag, but the swag would have felt more secure in the storm. They hunkered down for what they expected to be an uncomfortable night, both relieved they had provision for nasty weather.

'Talking was more like shouting but they persevered for a bit while they ate their packet meals in the larger tent, a few squares of chocolate and a slurp of scotch. Eventually they bedded down after braving the elements to have night-time pees that could have carried all the way back to Loongana, then Jack slid into his swag.

'The storm broke throughout the night, and then it became so quiet one could hear every breath. Bloody eerie it ... I heard it was.'

Dennis began to inhale, slow and raspy as he placed more wood on the fire, turned and dragged his leg exaggeratedly.

'Shut up, you dick,' Nicky whispered and, to Dennis' amusement, she pulled her jacket tighter around her neck.

'Some time during the night, Jack got up for another pee. He crawled out and was standing there with his head light on. The next thing you know he ripped the zip open and jumped into the other bloke's tent ...'

'Does the other bloke have a name?' Dennis asked with a hint of mischief in his tone.

'Piss off, Dennis you prat; okay, it was me. This is scary shit, just speaking this out loud.'

'Sorry mate, go on.' Dennis saw the angst in Matthew's flame-lit face, making the story far more potent. 'Go on, this is bloody brilliant!'

Matthew cleared his throat. 'I looked at Jack and his eyes were wide. I asked him what was wrong and I remember exactly what he said. "Fuck, fuck, fuck, there's something out there." He pulled his knees up under his chin and was shaking. I couldn't get him to make sense so I put my head light on and peered through the flysheet ...'

He looked at Samantha: despite knowing the tale, her eyes were as wide as saucers. He looked at Nicky: her hood was up and her hands were wringing the jacket tightly.

'Don't stop now,' Dennis said with a breathy voice, not looking quite as smug as before.

'There, outside ...' Matthew hesitated again.

'Spit it out, you bastard.' Dennis demanded.

'You'll think I'm stupid,' Matthew said.

Samantha rested her hand on Matthew's. 'No, they won't.'

Matthew looked into their faces in turn. 'There was this strange creature; about a metre tall, thin, hairless. Narrow green eyes on the sides of its head. It stood close to the front of the tent. Long, feathery upright ears that constantly flicked. Apart from that it didn't move. It had short, thin arms that hung loose by its side. The creature's skin, pale and wet like a fish, glistened in my head light.'

'Nooo,' Nicky sighed.

'The strangest thing is it didn't look solid, as if you could almost see through it.'

The campsite was so silent, the crackle of the embers seemed to increase their volume, until Dennis began to roar, laughing so hard his entire body shook. The others just stared at him while he gripped his knees, pulled himself together and, finally, cleared his throat.

'D'yer know what it was?' he squeaked at their silence, 'it was fekkin' Gollum, Frodo friggin' Pearson. You saw Gollum ... how bleedin' precious!' Again he howled and fell, chair and all, backwards onto the sand.

Matthew lowered his face to hide his eyes, stood and looked down at Dennis for a moment before he turned away from the fire.

'Dennis,' Samantha said. 'Didn't you look at him? I guess not, because if you did, you'd have thought twice about ridiculing him.'

'What?' Dennis looked over his shoulder towards Matthew as he disappeared into the annex. 'It was a piss-take, surely.' He sat up and shook the sand from his short hair.

'It was nothing of the sort,' Samantha said. 'To my knowledge, he's only told that story three times since it happened: to me right after he got back from the bluff, to some people who acted just like you and took the piss, and then tonight.'

Dennis' mouth hung open for a moment while he tried to think of something to say. 'I ... I thought he was telling porkies.'

'No, Dennis, he's not telling lies. Strange as it seems, he believes what he saw.'

'Shite,' Dennis said. He stood, brushed himself down and followed Matthew to the annex.

'What just happened?' Nicky asked, suddenly wishing she was back home in Longford.

Samantha thought for a moment then said, 'Something happened that night on the top of Black Bluff. Real or not, he believes he saw what he just said he did.'

The sisters could hear them talking, before the men returned and resumed their places by the fire.

'For the record,' Dennis began after righting his chair, 'I am really sorry and I know now to take me old mate seriously. Finish your story. It's as scary as shite and I guess that's just how I dealt with it. Go on. Won'tcha?'

Matthew sat staring at the embers for a while. When he began to speak his voice sounded tired:

'There's not much more to tell. We looked at the creature looking at us ... we were both frozen with fear. It did nothing threatening, just stood, gazing at us or past us, we couldn't really tell. Then it started to walk, right on past, and for all we knew at the time, it was still there, out of sight, watching us.'

'I am crapping myself,' Nicky laughed nervously. 'Come on guys, tell me this is a joke, because I'm not a happy camper just at the minute.'

Matthew shook his head. 'I know the story sounds ridiculous. I probably had a nightmare but if I did, Jack had one exactly the same.'

'Have you checked out other trekker's experiences? Maybe it's just a trick of the elements,' Dennis suggested.

'I've since discovered others have stories of strange occurrences up there,' Matthew shrugged.

'And they're just as reluctant to talk about it,' Samantha added.

Nicky shivered. 'Won't be getting much sleep tonight.'

Matthew sat back and put his hands behind his head.

'Well, come in spinners!' Samantha grinned.

'No,' Dennis gasped. 'You bastards, I don't believe it.'

Nicky laughed, more from relief than mirth.

'Time to bed down,' Samantha said. 'Goodnight.' She kissed her sister's cheek and Dennis' hair then disappeared inside the annex. Nicky followed shortly after, without saying anything.

Matthew refuelled the fire, for no other reason but to retain an ambient glow around the campsite.

'Best get our heads down. See you in the morning.'

Dennis grabbed Matthew's wrist. 'You weren't lying, were you?'

Matthew looked at him, and Dennis thought he perceived the slightest shake of Matthew's head.

'See you in the morning,' Matthew repeated. He eased away from Dennis' grasp and left him alone by the fire.

It did not take long before weird tarn creatures started to manifest in Dennis' periphery: the delicate foraging of an unseen wallaby turned sinister and threatening, or a fish breaking the water's surface transformed into some unmentionable creature, about to drag itself slowly from the lapping of water of the lakeside, each one another conjured figment of his heightened mind games.

'Sheer bloody genius,' Dennis chuckled as he placed another log on the fire for good measure. He took one last look around, to see what else his imagination might offer up, pulled his collar over his tingling neck, and headed for the annex.

The night was still and quiet save for an occasional breeze sighing through the treetops, the call of a nightjar or brushtail possum foraging in the campsite for leftovers. Nicky lay awake, listening to the guttural growl and snuffle from, she hoped, just a Tasmanian devil. Her mind wandered; Dennis' stupid Waratah Wisp and Matthew's creature sent another shiver through her; beings of fantasy dragging themselves from the river. *Idiots!*

She reached out, found Dennis' arm and gave it a hard pinch.

He snorted and turned over. 'Ow! What ... what's up?'

'Nothing, dear,' she said, satisfied she wasn't the only one awake. 'Go back to sleep.'

She heard a movement from the other side of the partition where Samantha and Matthew were sleeping, on a bed above the trailer itself. She rolled over and pulled her covers about her neck. *Damn Matt and his stupid story*, she thought, and tried her best to exorcise the illusion from her mind.

· · · · ·

Light filtered through the PVC annex window, heralding a mild and beautiful morning. Meandering slow and glassy, the lake's surface held reflections of the far tree line, as surreal as a computer animation. One bleached, skeletal stringybark stood, twisted but powerful, as if it had died, mid-bow, while acknowledging an unseen audience.

The ghouls of darkness, woven by those graphic campfire stories, were long gone, as Dennis sat on a chair by the remnants of the previous night's fire. Alone in a perfect dawn with his fingers linked around a mug of hot coffee, he remained in silent contemplation until Matthew emerged from the annex, gave him a grin and walked around the back of the Patrol and into the bush with trowel and toilet roll in hand. Dennis nodded and smiled, feeling sheepish that he had been completely fooled the previous night. *Or had he*? The thought still reverberated.

A while later, Samantha emerged wearing a loose-fitting tank top and brief PJ shorts. Dennis noticed that, despite her cheeks being smeared with makeup and dramatic bed hair, she was an elegant-looking woman.

Samantha is family, Dennis thought, *one does not perv on family*.

'Morning love,' he said. 'No, don't go that way, your hubby is conjuring another of last night's bog monsters.'

Samantha grimaced and turned theatrically, stepping away as if she were walking on hot coals. 'Thanks for the heads-up,' she said and decided on another direction.

Several minutes later Nicky stood by the annex wrapped in a towel, toiletries bag and her environmental liquid soap bottle in hand.

'I'm glad that night is over,' she said. 'A curse on you and your numbskull friend. I'm off for a strip wash, and no dear, I don't want you to scrub my back.' She turned, wandered down to the water's edge and followed it until she was out of sight of the camp.

Matthew returned a few moments later, collected his camera from the annex and wandered off towards the lake. 'Whatever you do,' Dennis said just loud enough for his friend to hear, 'don't point that thing to your left.'

Matthew naturally turned, but quickly looked away. 'Hey, nice tits, Nic,' he called as he angled away, back to the camp.

'Piss off, Matthew!' Nicky yelled, and Dennis chuckled as he rose from his chair, went to the annex and set water to boil. Matthew joined him and they began to prepare a not altogether healthy breakfast.

As he transferred sliced mushrooms from cutting board to bowl, Dennis thought back yet again to Matthew's tale. If the story was true it was simply amazing. If it was a fabrication it was no less amazing, and even more powerful, considering Samantha had been part of the ruse. He shook his head and opened a bag of tomatoes.

· · · · ·

'So,' Matthew said as he finished eating, 'I wonder if we'll have any luck at the Wheatsheaf today.' Nicky pumped her fist and he saw they all grinned at him. 'Why are you all looking at me like that?'

'We had bets on how soon you'd ask.' Samantha looked at her husband and saw last night's memory had been locked back in its cage, perhaps indefinitely this time.

'And I'm guessing Nic won?'

Nicky returned a broad smile and bowed as formally as she could from her fold-up chair.

Matthew slapped his thigh. 'Well, glad that's out of the way, so, what's the plan?'

Samantha and Nicky had already put their heads together. 'We think if we head off by ten, back to the road in thirty minutes or so, we should be in Wynyard by noon.'

'Sounds the goods,' Matthew smiled, bubbling with anticipation. 'Now Dennis, shall we chuck in a line for half an hour and see if we can catch us some good old Tassie tucker?'

The sisters remained in their chairs and chatted while the boys fished. Everyone appeared to have decided to avoid discussing Matthew's tale, which had at first been akin to a horror story, then seemed to be nothing more than an elaborate hoax, or ... Dennis and Nicky were not convinced either way.

'What was last night about?' Nicky could not hold back any longer.

'What do you mean?'

'You well know what I mean, Sam. Matthew wasn't just telling a scary story, that's for sure. Something spooked him by that tarn and you helped him make light of it, didn't you!' It was not a question.

'Look sis, you are right about him being spooked. He came home almost out of his wits, so did Jack. Either they were the butt of some practical joke by other trekkers, or something weird happened, real or imaginary.'

'I gather he has researched it since?'

'We've both read reports that say others have been spooked by something around that place, but then plenty of people have been there without anything strange happening.'

'Perhaps it was subconscious, something they read about the bluff?'

'Both swear not to have known anything. I mean, it's not like they're avid trekkers who belong to a club or anything.'

'Does he still go trekking, after that?'

'Sure, mainly local walks because work takes up so much of his time. He's gone on his own, as well as with others, and he's fine; but, I tell you something, he will never go anywhere near Black Bluff again. His memory of whatever they saw that night hasn't faded with time.'

Nicky thought for a moment. 'It's odd he hasn't confided in Dennis before now.'

'Well, he's never really confided in anyone but me, until last night. As I said before, he told some mates soon after it happened but they laughed at him, so since then he's kept it to himself so he wouldn't be ridiculed again.'

'Quite right,' Dennis' voice made both girls jump.

'Shit, Dennis. Don't do that!' Nicky growled.

Dennis had gone to the Patrol to plug in their cold box, but returned to his seat to dismantle and pack away the rods. Matthew was still down at the water's edge, gutting and cleaning the catch. While there was not enough for dinner, it would offer them a taster.

'He said it was a joke,' Dennis said quietly. 'I don't believe the sod.'

'I suppose, throughout the ages, people have always had strange experiences that die with them, unexplained,' Nicky said.

'Look,' Samantha said, gazing over at Matthew as he worked, 'he was spooked by something, and haven't we all been? I mean, I thought I saw a ghost once. She was clear as, well, a ghost could be, and it scared the crap out of me at the time. No other explanation, and I don't even believe in ghosts. Matthew's incident was no different, and not life-altering by any stretch of anyone's imagination.'

'Apart from your hubby won't go up Black Bluff again,' Nicky suggested.

'Okay so we beefed it up a bit for effect,' Samantha sighed. 'We were sitting around a campfire telling spooky stories don't forget, and no, he won't go again and he doesn't really want it to be that big a deal.'

Matthew brought the cleaned catch to the kitchen area, wrapped each in cling wrap and took them to the Nissan to put them into the cold box.

'You should get a bloody Oscar for last night's performance,' Dennis said as he reached down and flicked a leech off his friend's leg.

Matthew smiled and said with a flourish 'One has to ... become.'

'Make sure you're all cleaned up properly before we go,' Nicky called. 'Don't want you lot to make the Hoopermobile smell as if it belongs to a fishmonger.'

'Not that there's anything wrong with that,' Dennis and Matthew said in unison.

'Always the comedians,' Nicky mumbled to nobody in particular.

It was unlikely someone would stumble on their camping spot but they chose not to chance it: while most trekkers and anglers were respectful, they still locked the Outlander, secured the padlock on the trailer's tow-ball, and packed up their valuables to take with them. With the camper's annex all zipped up to keep wildlife out they bundled themselves into the Nissan and headed over the rock, and back down the rugged track. Finding their way was still slow and bumpy but the track was clear and easier than coming in, and they didn't pass anyone on their way. Soon they were on bitumen on their way to Wynyard.

CHAPTER SEVEN

Dennis turned onto Murchison Highway to follow the scenic drive through Hellyer Gorge: magnificent forests of myrtle beech, towering tree ferns and orchids fringing the serpentine bitumen proved a picturesque distraction from the previous evening's stories.

They meandered around sharp and tricky bends to the bridge, bringing them back, briefly, to the Hellyer River.

'Any chance we can stop for a minute so I can take some piccies?' Nicky asked, directing the question hopefully at Matthew, who shrugged and nodded resignedly.

Dennis pulled over to let a faster vehicle pass. 'Idiot boy racer. Here is as good a place as any, I s'pose.'

'I think I can see a car park a bit further on through the trees,' Matthew pointed. 'That might be better: less chance another brainless twerp will take the bend too shallow and push us over the edge into the gorge?'

'Fair enough, Matty.' Dennis checked behind and edged the vehicle back onto the bitumen.

'No problems, Den.'

They pulled into the car park where two camper vans and a small red sedan were parked.

'One of those boy racers?' Nicky suggested, pointing at damage on the sedan's front quarter.

Dennis pretended to spit. 'No self-respecting lout would drive summ'ink like that. Reckon it belongs to a woman, or it's a rental.'

'Well, probably she was hit by some lunatic male driver,' Nicky smiled as she grabbed her camera bag and tripod, opened the door and moved towards the trees with the silent purpose of an expert. She clicked a wide-angle lens onto the camera body as she walked, and looked up into the bright morning canopy with its subtle hues glowing beneath the labyrinth of limbs, branches, twigs and foliage.

Nicky relished the chance to shoot the scene before her as long exposures, capturing a second, or seconds of time in one frame; the brilliant reflections cutting shafts of hazy gold through verdant olive, glorious carpets of soft russet, and bright, almost unreal yellow-greens, the edges of gossamer leaves softened by the sighing breeze. She envisaged the river, tethered in a moment of time as if a silk scarf, floating above a surreal forest floor. She could already imagine her images framed and hanging in the gallery.

She had walked only a short distance along the riverbank when her neck prickled with excitement; a platypus was feeding in the shallows, no more than twenty paces ahead. She edged as close as the terrain would allow and sat quietly in the dappled shade of a myrtle overhang by one of a number of small pools, etched into the bank. She held her breath while she slowly and deliberately set the camera onto its tripod.

Nicky could have stayed for hours, just the river and click of the shutter in her awareness. Again she held her breath as the creature turned, swam towards her, dived under twisted tree roots, and resurfaced in the pool beside her.

She could not believe her fortune. So many hours, hours amounting to days throughout her life, spent in hope of capturing the elusive platypus. And here, one of the world's animal wonders had come so close she could have reached down and touched it. Nicky's movements were liquid as she unclicked the camera from the tripod and refocused on the pool. She took shot after shot after shot, reminding herself to keep breathing; reminding herself that this opportunity might never again come her way.

She paused to watch the platypus slide out of her sight beneath the tangled roots, to resurface in the river and continue on its journey. The distance between them now as close as most people would ever get, and they'd still be enthralled.

She heard a whisper from over her shoulder, no louder than the sigh of the breeze through the trees: 'Nic.'

'Nicky.' Again, no louder, but her sister's voice broke the spell.

'Did you see that?' Nicky whispered.

'My word I did,' Samantha returned. They watched the elusive monotreme create V-ripples as it ventured further upriver, and finally out of sight.

Nicky turned with tears in her eyes. 'What's up, sis?' she said.

'Time's ticking on and the boys are keen to make a move.'

Nicky brought the camera back to rest on her shoulder and sighed. 'That was amazing. Am I likely to get that kind of opportunity again?'

'Glad I was here to catch a glimpse,' Samantha said, and really meant it. 'I guess you now have the rest of your exhibition.'

'The weekend is young, Sam,' Nicky said. 'Who knows, maybe something else will present itself.'

The companions continued their journey northward. In her mind, Nicky relived her close encounter with a platypus, while Matthew pondered on something just as elusive.

The constant drone of the engine lulled Nicky to sleep: in her bathroom, she sat on an antique oak bath stool in a white towelling robe, watching a platypus in the teal waters of her bath. As she aimed her coffee cup to snap a photograph, the platypus dived and the waters began to churn, darken and fill with thick algae streamers that waved and twisted in some preternatural undercurrent. The bathroom light faded as a pale, gangly creature burst upwards from the water, eagerly grasping at the platypus, which wriggled in evasion before sliding back under the surface. The creature stood panting, knee-deep in the bath, picking strings of slime from his face while he searched the spot where the platypus had vanished. He looked up, noticed Nicky, and his eyes narrowed in indignation.

'Nicky,' the creature said throatily as he reached forward and grabbed her by the knee.

'Nicky!' Dennis' voice this time. 'We're here.'

The bathroom, the creature and the dream evaporated.

'This is a pub?' Dennis asked as he unbuckled his seat belt. 'You guys must've had some balls to walk in here in the first place.'

'No,' Samantha reminded him. 'A bursting bladder, if you recall.'

'Well, it could have been a biker den for all you knew.'

'What's more, and I hate to say it, but my second coffee's come through,' Samantha added as she opened the door and stepped onto the car park gravel. 'This is becoming a habit at this place.'

'What a positively horrible dump,' Nicky said. 'Are we really going in there? Surely there are nicer pubs if we go into Wynyard?'

'We're here for this one, don't forget,' Matthew said over his shoulder as his purposeful stride took him towards the entrance.

Nicky shrugged and grabbed her camera bag and purse. Dennis ensured the windows were all up, pressed the remote lock, then jogged to catch up with his wife.

'Make mine the beer I had last time,' Samantha said as she ducked under Matthew's arm, tickling it as she passed. 'C'mon Nic, this way.' Her sister did the same, including the tickle.

Dennis walked up to the bar while Matthew stared into the dark corner, hardly believing what he saw: on the rough dais sat two chairs, two guitars, one microphone and a mauve fedora.

Dennis checked the logos on three beer taps in front of him. 'What's Sam's poison?' he asked when Matthew had joined him at the bar.

'Pint of Eddings Dark Ale,' Matthew said as if in a trance, 'same for me.'

Dennis opened his wallet and waited expectantly until a tall, heavyset man approached.

'What'll it be?' the man asked flatly.

Dennis assumed this was the guy with the poor telephone manner. He appeared to be in his late sixties, but a second look suggested life, genetics or both might not have been kind to him and he could have been younger. Six foot one and, despite the evident stoop and wide girth, Dennis guessed that at one time he might have been a handful. His rolled sleeves revealed faded tattoos over wrinkled forearms. There was no evidence etched on the man's face that smiling had been a common pastime, and at that particular time the man obviously saw no reason to break with tradition.

'Four pints of, er...' Dennis glanced at Matthew, '... what?'

'Eddings Dark Ale, please,' Matthew said.

'Keg's down,' the man said with little interest. 'Got bottles of Eddings Dark, or there's draught and light on tap.'

'Four of the dark ale bottles then, ta. Dennis is my name.'

'That's nice.' The barman looked over to Matthew and, as if it was an unusual occurrence said, 'You been 'ere before.'

'September last year,' Matthew answered, as Samantha walked from the toilets and sat at the table Nicky had chosen.

'Oh yeah, I remember,' the bar man said absently, while flicking his gaze between the sisters. 'Menu?'

'Sure. My name is Dennis.' The introduction was a little less friendly than the first time.

The barman turned to Dennis and looked down at his extended hand. Perhaps he was having second thoughts about being a tough man.

'Rusty, because o' this.' He pointed to the thinning, long red hair, tied back from his face. He took Dennis' hand firmly. 'Rusty Faulkner.'

'My good buddy, Matthew,' Dennis said.

As if all he wanted was for someone to stand up to him, Rusty's demeanour changed, although his face remained devoid of friendliness.

'Pleasure I'm sure. Feeds for all then,' he assumed and handed over four folders. 'Menu ain't large but me missus is quite the cook.' He turned his head and called, 'Italiano. Hey, ITALIANO! I'm sure that bloody woman is deaf.'

A woman rushed from the kitchen, through the battered nineteen-seventies–style saloon doors that squeaked with every swing.

She wiped her hands on her apron and said, 'Yes, Mister Rusty?'

'Make sure Bets has got the oven up,' he turned to Dennis and Matthew expectantly.

'Sì, Mister Rusty.'

'Not sì, woman. Bloody yes. Yes!' He turned back to Dennis. 'Damn foreigners,' he sighed and shook his head as if they would agree, although both decided no response would be best.

'So,' Rusty reminded himself, 'four dark ales comin' up. She'll bring 'em to the table. Pay before ya leave – and don't forget.' He walked off without another word.

A rough-looking man, leaning on the bar next to Dennis had overheard.

'Not many people get anything more than agro out of Rusty.'

'Looks like he hates his job,' Dennis suggested.

'Rusty hates everything,' the man said, before turning back to idly pick at the dried remnant of someone's meal.

'You the muso?' Dennis asked, studying his bearded face for any hints of recognition, but the stranger ignored him.

'No, that's him at the end of the bar,' Matthew whispered.

Dennis leaned forward and raised his voice slightly to address the man Matthew had pointed out.

'Hey mate, buy you a drink?'

'No,' Rob the Pom said.

Dennis shrugged and made his way over to the table.

'I reckon that big bloke would be the rude porker your Italian friend spoke about,' he said.

'Adelina is her name,' Samantha gestured towards the attractive dark-haired woman as she flitted quickly from bar to table under Rusty's watchful gaze. 'And that's her.'

'She's gorgeous, isn't she?' Nicky said.

'Didn't notice, Sam,' Dennis lied. 'Did you, mate?'

'Notice what?' Matthew followed with his own innocent look of guilt.

'I'd like to say hi,' Samantha said and made to get up.

Matthew looked at Adelina. 'I'd wait until Mr Bossman leaves the room or she'll cop a bollocking. Besides, she'll be over in a minute with the beers. Hey Dennis, did you find anything familiar in the face of the muso?'

'Nah, the light's no good in here. Might have looked a bit obvious if I'd walked over and started studying his features.'

'Well, can you see him better from here?'

'Hardly.'

'I think he looks like a hairy homeless person,' Nicky decided.

Eventually Adelina came over with the beers then produced a pad and pen from her apron pocket.

'Sorry I take long time. You ready to order?' she asked in an accent they all found delightful.

'Hello, I am Samantha,' she said, before beginning a hurried conversation with Adelina in whispered Italian. Adelina held her pen poised as if discussing menu options.

'They dunnarf saand sexy,' Dennis said, adopting his Cockney persona for effect.

'Cor notarf,' Matthew said, equally as broad.

Adelina indicated that she needed to get back to work, memorised their orders and scampered back around the bar to the kitchen.

'Now, I'm reading between the lines a bit,' Samantha began, 'but I'm gathering she's kind of trapped here. No money to move on, and says what she earns here hardly covers her board.'

'And she said that to an almost stranger?' Dennis questioned.

'Perhaps I'm the only one she's been able to have a personal conversation with in a while.'

'Can we find her work in or around Longford or Evandale?' Dennis said.

'Love,' Nicky began, 'I'm sure we might, if we knew anything more about her than having a sexy voice and looking cute.'

'Damn cute.' His mumbled comment earned him a slap on the hand.

'She studied at the Accademia d'Arte in Florence some years ago she told me, so how's that for a coincidence?' Samantha said, as if evidence of an art background made her employable.

'Impressive indeed but we don't need anyone for the foreseeable future,' Nicky said.

'I know; I was just saying. Perhaps some bar work with a decent boss?'

Nicky shrugged. 'We can ask around, can't expect any more than that.'

'So how old is she then?' Dennis asked.

'That's not the kind of thing one asks, Dennis! But, around mid-twenties, at a guess?'

'Looks younger. I'll order another round; these little bottles hold bugger all for a bloke with a decent thirst.'

Dennis walked to the far end of the bar, stood next to the musician and had what seemed to be a one-sided conversation, until he received his change and grasped the four drinks. He said something over his shoulder and walked back to the table.

Matthew concentrated on Rob the Pom and watched as the musician finished what looked like a soft drink and made his way over to the guitars. He slipped a strap over his head, sat and adjusted the microphone. Without any introduction or ceremony, he moved into a version of a song Dennis and Matthew recognised as being by Elvis Costello.

While the sisters listened with muted interest, Dennis and Matthew focused intently, not only on how skilfully he worked the fretboard but how smoothly his voice eased through Costello's melody.

'He's good,' Dennis whispered; Matthew nodded. Both wondered how many of the other twelve patrons would have heard the original, or much cared how Rob the Pom delivered it. When he strummed the final chord, barely a ripple of appreciation could be heard other than from the Pearson-Hooper table.

The guitarist clipped a capo over the first fret and began a new song, and it wasn't long before it became clear the guitar was barely an adjunct to a poem of loss. Matthew and Dennis focused on the lyrics as the musician's story unfolded:

Here comes another day and it's hauntingly familiar
She left without a word, there's not much one can say
But I remember too well, that awkward shadow at the door
Anguish and compassion – I can't listen any more.

Dancing circles 'round our used-to-be's
But now, what's done is done
Wishes count for none.

Someone's scream broke the silence. White knuckles on the table
Now clasped to her uniform. Don't let me go or I'll fall
I said 'there'll be no more times where we laughed at silly things
No more harsh words fighting over stupid things'.

I am lost for words and there's not much one can say
Words of comfort melt like snow on a summer's day
That awkward shadow at the door.

Here comes another day, another torn from this world
The image keeps returning, to haunt me like a nightmare
So when will I forget? There were no time for goodbyes
That is where it all started, that awkward shadow at the door.

No more will sunshine light her hair, nor will winter make her shiver
Words of comfort melt like snow on a summer's day.

No more will strange things make her smile, or sad songs make her quiver
Words of comfort melt like snow on a summer's day
That awkward shadow at the door.

Here comes another day and it's hauntingly familiar
She left without a word ... not much one can say.

The final line was left hanging, as if the story did not have an end; the chord diminished and was swallowed by the general murmur of conversation, grating of chairs and chinking of glasses. Few had even paid attention but Matthew and Dennis were mesmerised. Even the sisters had stopped talking and listened intently. Samantha thought she saw Rob the Pom wipe something from his eye.

In general, the patrons seemed unresponsive due to lack of interest in anything other than a song to tap their toes or sing along to. The four companions, on the other hand, reflected on the sombre tale Rob the Pom had delivered.

'What a sad, sad story,' whispered Nicky, 'I wonder if there's something behind the tale.'

'I can see your point, Matt,' Dennis said. 'There is something more to this singer than meets the eye.'

Rob the Pom didn't dwell, and broke into something with a lighter mood; James Taylor's 'Carolina in my Mind', which appeared to be a favourite at the Wheatsheaf, as the song earned applause from the locals before he'd finished the first line.

Accolades or none, Rob the Pom's reaction was the same: indifference. Adelina took him a soft drink and he had a swallow before starting a slow acoustic rendition of 'Message in a Bottle'.

'Love this one,' Samantha said.

'They obviously like it too,' Matthew said, indicating to a group on the other side of the dining room, who were singing along.

Rob the Pom moved immediately into another song, which had the expat Londoners sitting up attentively.

'Bugger me if he's not doing "Solsbury Hill", Matthew said through a broad smile.

It was a lively rendition of an already upbeat song, and members of the audience stamped their feet on the timber floor, which gave Rusty cause for further irritation.

The singer changed the tempo and moved immediately into another Peter Gabriel song, the sultry 'Mercy Street'. A beautiful introduction invited the listener to pay attention, and Dennis found he agreed with Matthew: the man's voice indeed had similarities to Gabriel's smoky tones.

The acoustic treatment was so sensitive, Dennis was sure he could imagine the familiar bass and drum line, as well as a lower octave reflection of Rob the Pom's voice, as if the musician was playing over a backing track. Dennis realised it was in fact Matthew's voice he could hear, producing the octave harmony.

Dennis leaned towards his friend and whispered, 'This guy is brilliant – what the hell is he doing in this dump?'

The song's ending brought loud applause from Dennis and Matthew while Nicky took a snapshot of the musician.

'Did you notice he sang the wrong words in the last verse?' Matthew said. 'The woman in Gabriel's original was Mary, but he used another name? Apart from that it was bloody perfect.'

Samantha also noticed: 'I think he sang Hayley.'

A chill ran through Dennis. 'Who?'

'He sang "kissing Hayley's lips".'

Dennis sat back and ran his nails down the stubble on his cheek, waiting for the neurotransmitters in his brain to make the connection.

'Well, bugger me!' Dennis whispered.

Matthew looked at him. 'Den, what is it?'

'You ain't gunna believe it; I know who this geezer is.'

Matthew rested his bottle on the coaster, fearing it might slip from his grasp. 'You're shittin' me, Dennis bloody Hooper.'

'No, I'm not Matt.' Hardly believing it himself he said 'that bloke is the Tramp. I'd stake my life, and your life, on it.'

CHAPTER EIGHT

Dennis sat staring at the musician, paying no attention to his next song. 'Remember late-eighties London, and yes, Ilford, to be precise?' he asked.

Matthew had been leaning back in his chair, searching distant or vague memories. He sat forward, close to Dennis' shoulder.

'Of course I remember; Ilford has been nagging at me for months; but the late eighties? Have to peer through too many pints.'

'Just look at you two,' Samantha laughed, 'like you've both seen a ghost!'

'We would've been eighteen? I reckon it was at the Cauliflower,' Dennis said, 'you know the 'aunted pub?'

Nicky sighed. 'Here we go again. This is your fault, sis.'

Dennis turned to his wife. 'So the story goes, a bunch of teenagers snuck into the cellars at the Cauliflower and met with a nasty end – don't know what, but of course they shouldn't've been down there. One of the kids, a girl, supposedly keeps returning in ghostly form, calling out for help, so the spook followers tell us. Anyway I reckon we would have seen Hayley and the Tramp half a dozen times at the Cauliflower. Hayley was gorgeous and had a voice like, er ...'

'Sam Brown!' Matthew recalled.

'Pretty blonde girl,' Samantha remembered. 'Had some hits in Australia as well.'

'Well, bugger me, Den, you're a fekkin' genius,' Matthew shook his head and chuckled, 'Hayley and the Tramp eh?'

'Never heard of them,' Nicky shrugged.

'You've never lived in London,' Dennis smiled. 'Long way to travel from

Tasmania to London to support England's best and worst about-to-be or wannabes.'

Nicky glanced from Dennis to Matthew, then at her sister. 'What on earth is he doing here then, in this dump?'

'That's the million quid question,' Dennis said, 'but then we were there and now we're here too.'

· · · · ·

Matthew watched Rob the Pom stand, set the guitar on his chair and then walk, ponderously, towards the bar. He hoped Dennis had solved the puzzle, and Rob the Pom was indeed the Tramp.

'Now's as good a time as any,' Matthew nudged Dennis. 'Let's see how right you are, me ol' china. Hey, Tramp,' he called, 'buy you a beer?'

Rob the Pom stopped mid-step, and jerked his head towards them, wearing an expression that flickered from indifference to something else – surprise, even dismay. He turned away from the bar and took a set of keys from his pocket as he walked towards the exit, taking the briefest of glances at them from the corner of his eye. The closing of the door behind him snuffed out his haloed silhouette.

Rusty had heard the call, saw Rob the Pom's reaction and marched over to their table. He spoke to them in a restrained growl:

'What the friggin' 'ell do you think you're doin', offendin' my friggin' drawcard?' His pitch, rising higher and louder with every syllable made Dennis stand and prepare for trouble. Rusty was now yelling: 'How dare you idiotic blow–ins insult him just cos he's a bit down an' out?'

Rusty threw his towel back towards the bar, not caring that it fell short of the mark. He rolled his sleeves and barked, 'You, you, you and you,' his finger stabbed at them in turn, 'finish your drinks and piss orf.'

'Mate,' Matthew began, but Rusty was not open to discussion.

Rusty's trembling finger confirmed his rage. 'You're no mate o' mine, pal.

I said drink up and get out.'

Everyone present looked at the manager, back to Dennis, and now at Matthew, who had risen to stand beside his friend: a shield between the threat and their wives.

The locals may have relished the idea of someone standing up to big, moody old Rusty, who often, it was said, could do with being taught a few manners. What's more, a brawl might just have made their Christmas. Adelina looked at Samantha and Nicky, but of course speaking up would be more than her job was worth.

While Dennis stood his ground, furious they had been spoken to in such a tone, he was aware the manager probably had every right to throw them out. Matthew felt downhearted that they were losing a possible link to their past, and the sisters were eager to leave, wanting no further trouble.

Nicky looked at Rusty and mouthed, 'Sorry,' then turned and walked out without waiting for a response she didn't expect to receive.

As they left the door to close by itself, Dennis growled 'Let's go before I decide to teach old Rusty how you don't treat customers.'

'You'll do nothing of the sort,' Nicky demanded as she climbed into the Patrol and buckled her seat belt. Samantha was standing by the rear passenger door, looking away.

'Come on Sis,' Nicky said over her shoulder, 'I don't want to stay here a moment longer.'

'Wait, I'll be back in a minute.' Samantha pushed the truck door to and walked across the gravel to an old station wagon, with dark blue cracked paint and dented bodywork. She slowed as she approached the door, noticing the driver's mirror was no longer in its place, just a few wires and rusty screw holes betraying its past existence. Inside, Rob the Pom sat with his head back against the headrest while his fingers tapped erratically on the cracked rubber seal on the side window. Her shoes crunched on the gravel and he turned for a second, saw who it was and frowned, anxiety etched across his forehead.

'I, er, I'm sorry if my husband said something to offend you.' He did not respond. 'Only he wasn't calling you a tramp, he just thought you were somebody he used to know, many years ago.'

'Go away.'

'A singer from the UK,' she added.

'Please,' he whispered. He didn't move, didn't put his seat belt on or turn the ignition key, he just closed his eyes and continued tapping. Samantha watched him, wondered what it was he was hiding, or running from. She looked over her shoulder at the Patrol and saw three faces staring at her, like expectant children waiting to go on an outing.

'Anyway, I'm sorry but we never intended to offend you.' She turned, took a step, and then froze at the sound of his voice.

'I've not been called that in years.' His voice was soft, sad and not at all indignant.

'Called what?' Samantha said without turning.

'The Tramp.'

Samantha held her breath while he slowly released his. She noticed the drone of traffic and the caw of a nearby raven.

'I went by that name ... long ago in ... another life.'

Samantha felt the pulse quicken in her temples. *Oh my God*, she thought, *they were right*.

She turned and said, 'Matthew, my husband, really would like to buy you a beer.'

'I don't drink ... not while I'm working.'

'I sure could use one.' Samantha smiled when he looked up at her. 'Please, come with us somewhere, just for a coffee. Matthew would like the opportunity to apologise.'

'He has no need,' Rob the Pom said, 'and I have to go back and finish my set or Rusty will keep my dollars in his pocket. Perhaps I'll see you back in there, and when I'm done your husband can say sorry if it will make him feel better.'

'I don't think we can go back inside,' she said looking around at the Wheatsheaf. 'I don't think we are the manager's favourite customers, just at the moment.'

'What happened?' For the first time Rob the Pom, or the Tramp, was interested, to his own surprise.

'Well, Mr Rusty was pretty upset we had offended his musician, and then chucked us out, on our ears as it were.' She noticed his fingers had relaxed.

'Rusty is a prick,' he said without expression. 'Appears as tough as nails but isn't the man he might once have been.' He took the keys from the ignition, got out of the car and closed the door. 'Come in with me, I can handle him.'

'I'm Sam, Samantha Pearson. By the way, you've left your window open.'

'Take a look,' he said without turning, 'nobody would pinch that.' He knew he should not really complain, as the car did not even belong to him.

He stopped mid-stride, and stared at his feet. 'My name ... is ... Robert. Robert Aitken.' His words appeared strained, as if conversation was alien to him. 'I really don't care for Rob the Pom,' he said, and walked on.

Samantha looked towards the Nissan and beckoned to her friends to come quickly, although Nicky decided to remain where she was, should the manager decide to throw them out again.

Rob the Pom waited for them at the door. His head was down, eyes focused on his weathered shoes but, as Dennis and Matthew neared, he looked up at them briefly. They both said apologetic hellos, but he chose not to respond. Rob the Pom turned, opened the door and walked back inside, across the parquetry dance floor and picked up his guitar. He sat and started to play 'Cavatina'.

Matthew hesitated at the door. 'Well?' he demanded of his wife.

'When we're inside,' Samantha said, as she walked in and took her place at the same table.

· · · · ·

'Well?' Dennis and Matthew were leaning forward, and spoke in near perfect unison.

Samantha looked over her shoulder, and saw Adelina watching them. She held the Italian's nervous glance for a moment, but smiled, as if to say everything was fine. But then Rusty emerged through the squeaky kitchen doors, and began to weave his way past the empty tables towards them. In his haste, he knocked a chair with his thigh and it clattered to the floorboards. Before he was able to demand they leave, the guitar paused and the musician's voice spoke through the PA.

'Rusty, it's fine.'

The manager paused, looked at Rob the Pom, and then the visitors, as if he was disappointed. He glared threateningly at them for a second then turned, righted the chair and strode back towards the kitchen. The saloon doors crashed back against the door jambs as he barged through.

Matthew reached for his wife's arm.

'What happened?' he whispered through clenched teeth, then he turned to see Adelina pick up the towel Rusty had earlier thrown to the floor, and fold it into one of her pockets as she walked over.

'Miss Betty shout and he now reeeally mad, is Mister Rusty,' Adelina whispered.

Samantha nodded. 'We are sorry. We'd like to order some coffees, if we can? Thanks,' she said as Adelina handed her a menu, held open at the drinks page.

'What does Rob, er, the musician, drink?' Matthew asked, looking to his wife for clarification.

'He drink tonic water with honey when he sing. He nice man, but he sad,' Adelina sighed. 'He called Roberto, not like Robeh the Pomeh.'

'Yes, I've heard,' Samantha agreed, and gave her their order.

'Can you take a drink to him and add it to our bill?' Samantha asked. 'I'd best tell my sister the creature is in his cage.'

She whispered something to Adelina, who snorted a brief laugh before regaining her composure. Adelina turned back towards the bar before Rusty saw, and chastised her for actually enjoying her work – albeit at his expense.

'What did you say to Adelina?' Dennis asked.

'*Cinghiale.*' Samantha stood and turned for the exit.

'What's that mean?'

'Wild boar.'

'About right, I reckon,' Matthew agreed, 'and when you come back you'll have something to tell us?'

Samantha waved without turning.

After she and Nicky had returned, Samantha shared all she had learned in that brief conversation by the car. While they spoke, Rob the Pom worked through the rest of his set, from songbook or memory, and Samantha saw he would occasionally glance in their direction, and once even returned the subtlest of smiles.

While Robert performed, he felt strangely at ease, considering the day's unexpected events. He had not warmed to anyone in years, apart from Adelina with her lovely manner, beautifully broken English and funny laugh, and Betty's motherly attention. Yet he still held them at arm's length. There was something about Samantha, however, who he remembered from that day at the festival, when he treated her in his usual brusque manner. She seemed different – it was almost as if *he* wanted to learn about *her*.

Is it time? Robert wondered.

Yes, it is, my love.

But I don't know how ... it's been too long.

Robert waited for the other voice, but it remained absent. *Sometimes, silence is worse.* He looked over at the group and felt he had actually returned Samantha's smile. He realised there were no flutters of dread or even the nausea he usually felt when acknowledging someone. When he made eye contact with Samantha and her friends, it seemed to be okay. He had recognised Matthew and Dennis' London nuances from the few words they had spoken to him, and Samantha's soft Australian tones. Robert accepted the emptiness in his world; a longing for ... companionship.

That longing had been missing for many years. An unexpected interest in other people, a craving to be accepted. The normal Robert Aitken would not care, not even register their existence. It was easier to shun society, only surfacing to earn a few hand-to-pocket dollars in exchange for a few hours of performing or, perhaps if he felt inclined, a little manual labour. People knew little about him, and that's how he preferred it.

But now?

Robert Aitken was perplexed; feeling uncomfortable about feeling comfortable about these four people, knowing as much as they did. But that discomfort was surely less than the alternative he had grown used to these past decades. He imagined a set of balance scales and began to weigh up options that sat inside the two metaphorical pans. He felt the fulcrum tip, tantalisingly away from the world that had become his norm.

He played an old favourite, 'Streets of London', for the locals, while he mused on how the day was turning out to be stranger than a self-imposed loner could have imagined. His regular final number was the nineties hit 'Don't You Forget About Me,' which was an odd choice considering his preferred existence. The song usually brought warm applause, and he didn't mind singing it, especially that day, because the words he sung seemed to float back into him.

Without fanfare or goodbyes, he stood, placed his guitar on the seat, picked up his drink and walked to the bar. As he passed the jar labelled ROB THE POM'S TIPS he upended it and pocketed the contents, aware the ten-dollar note was the one he'd put in there earlier; an incentive that seldom achieved its aim.

He went to take his usual seat at the far end of the bar, but then remembered. He looked over at the four at the window table; they held his gaze. He didn't know why the change, but then he didn't care; he weaved his way over to them.

'Mind if I join you?' he asked as he dragged up a chair and sat.

Rusty watched, his dislike of the strangers growing by the minute, but Adelina could not restrain her smile.

In the months she had worked at the Wheatsheaf, Adelina had grown to like this strange man who looked like a *vagabondo* but acted politely, in a detached way, and – just as important to her – 'Roberto' always smelled nice: not perfumed, just clean.

For a while Robert sat staring at his glass, regretting his decision to join the four. Conversation was sparse at the table. Despite the four having a plethora of questions for him, they were loath to broach any.

Samantha's achievements included a psychology degree, and she relished any opportunity to study people. She watched Robert's mannerisms, appreciated the effort he was making, but feared that at any moment he could revert and slide back into his shell. Someone had to break the awkward silence.

'Robert,' she began, 'I can't quite pick your accent, but I gather you're from London?'

He turned the glass in his hands, sat back in the chair and raised his eyes to the ceiling. *This being normal is hard*, he decided. He looked towards his usual stool at the bar and a shudder ran through him, as if he sensed tendrils of grimy fog reach out towards him. He thought he heard a voice that said, *Robert, what are you doing over there? Come back and sit with me.*

'Push it away, Robert,' Samantha surprised herself, guessing his fears. He turned to her, and stopped himself from asking if she could actually see his unwanted, invisible companion, because that would have been absurd.

'Born off Fulham Road,' he answered with a sigh, after another prolonged hesitation.

Dennis laughed. 'Bugger me if I'm not from the same neck of the woods. Landridge Road actually.'

'Oxberry,' Robert said. He began to remember other things he had chosen to forget many years ago, as if his memory contained countless tiny, dark rooms, and someone had just started to switch a few lights back on.

A brief but genuine smile appeared on Robert Aitken's face. He brushed his shoulder as if pushing the darkness aside, met Samantha's gaze and they exchanged nods.

'I went to school at All Saints Church of England,' Dennis said without invitation. 'As did Matthew.'

Robert glazed over for a moment. 'Hurlingham and Chelsea.' Yes, he remembered his childhood, but that wasn't the part of his life he had forced himself to dismiss. 'Whereabouts, er ... Matthew?'

'Cloncurry Street, near the vicarage.'

Robert shrugged. 'Don't recall the vicarage: never had much time for religion. Parents shunned it. Said it caused more oppression and violence in the world than it does good, and who can argue with that?'

Robert was stunned but tried not to show it: that simple sentence flowed from him more easily than any words he had spoken to anyone in years. *Conversation for conversation's sake.* Again he noticed Samantha looking at him; *no, she is studying me.* Despite the feeling that she was reaching into his head, or his soul, which had every chance of pushing him away, he instead decided he liked her – as much as one could after so little time. He returned a smile, brief but there, and he didn't feel threatened at all.

'You sound more like Matthew than Dennis.' Nicky observed.

Robert knew why: one facet of distancing himself from his past was to change the way he naturally spoke; rid himself of his London voice. The first way to *no longer be* Robert Aitken from Fulham was no longer to sound like he was from Fulham.

'Er, did you enjoy school?' Nicky asked.

'Music was my passion. That's where I met ...' he became silent and Samantha saw him emotionally withdraw.

Samantha had to work fast. 'Hey Robert, what are you up to later today?'

Robert sat with hunched shoulders and steepled fingers.

'Robert, it's okay,' Samantha's voice pushed through the wall he had begun to rebuild.

'I, er, I'll head home for a while and then go fishing. Thanks everyone,' he said as lightly as possible, 'it's been um … a breath of fresh air. Well, I'll be off.'

He picked up his glass and stood, searching the room for Adelina. He walked over to her and, after a brief conversation, headed around the bar, through the squeaky doors and into the kitchen.

'Well,' Matthew said after a moment of silence. 'At least it was nothing we said this time.'

'You're not going to leave it there, are you?' Dennis asked.

'I suppose so. I mean we know now he really is who we thought. To be honest I'm knackered.'

Samantha held Matthew's hand while speaking to the other three. 'He seems like a very complex and sad character.'

She watched Robert as he re-emerged from the kitchen and walked towards the stage, folding a couple of notes into his top pocket. She noticed how he kept his head down, and imagined the wall coming up again.

'Nic,' Samantha began, 'would you mind if we shared our family secret?'

'For him,' she gestured towards Robert. 'Why would you do that? And, more to the point, what would Bushy say if we brought a stray back to his hidden gem?'

'Bushy won't mind what Bushy doesn't know, sis. I feel Robert desperately needs someone to talk to but won't ask, and everyone is too afraid of his angst, or fragility, to reach out to him. I'm guessing he's come further today than he has for a long time – and he is this elusive Tramp that has driven the boys nuts for ages, after all.'

'Well, if you're so sure, I can't really stop you, can I?'

Matthew had been thinking of the Fulham hotel where he would have last seen the Tramp all those years ago, and heard only half of this conversation.

'What the hell are you girls talking about?'

'Just sit back. I'm going to have a word with Robert.'

'Might be one last chance.' Dennis had understood.

Samantha walked across the dance area; a relic from the Wheatsheaf's grander times, and crouched next to Robert as he put one of the guitars into its case.

'Robert, I don't mean to pry but I think you really would like to talk with someone. I see you have pain, and assume you hide it by retreating – and I must say you've done a sterling job of it, but how long do you want this to continue?'

Robert clipped the final fastener on the case. As he stood to pack the second guitar she heard his knees crack.

He stared at his feet and mumbled, 'It's been too long.'

He picked up the fedora, put it in a battered cardboard box, and slipped that inside a hessian shopping bag. He could not bring himself to talk to her, but feared she would leave.

He held the bag out to her. 'Carry this for me?'

Samantha hesitated. *This is more than a stage prop.* She took the bag from him, its lightness a contradiction to the weight of the significance she imagined it had in Robert's world.

'Mind how you go with it.' He still did not look at her.

'It's safe with me,' Samantha assured him, and herself.

Robert packed the second guitar, picked up both cases and walked out through the side doorway, turned right and down the hall with Samantha following. He stopped by a heavy steel door, put the guitars down and said, 'Wait there.' He opened the door and disappeared into the gloom of the strongroom with one of the cases.

Samantha imagined there was something secret in that dark, secure place. The memory of Rusty's craggy, uncompromising face conjured images of stolen goods or drugs hidden in the dark recesses of the strongroom. *What if there was a hidden cellar beneath the strongroom?* She amused herself at her own creative thoughts at work.

'Something funny?' Robert said without challenge, as he emerged for the second case.

'Just having fun inside my head,' Samantha said, inspiring Robert to consider the last time he had had fun in his head.

'Robert,' Samantha's voice invaded his musing. He looked at her and nodded for her to go on.

'If I ask you something, will you promise not to walk away?'

He studied her face, did not warm to her inoffensive request, but tried not to stiffen. 'Can't make any promises.'

Samantha took a breath. 'How can you give yourself permission to sing her name, but not speak of her?'

Robert felt himself swoon, and he gripped the edge of the open door beside him.

'Please, Robert.' She noticed him look down the hall past her, as if marking his line of retreat.

Robert squinted at her through the sudden feeling of grit in his eyes, the caring in her face; not love, not lust, just empathy. He thought back to that day at the Burnie festival. The crowds, the disgruntled, choleric acceptance of his alienation. He remembered being the animal, with an opportunity to escape but, still caged in its mind, somehow not knowing how to make that first move. He hated Rusty for taking him there, as if on a leash, but he hated himself even more for allowing himself to be used that day; the performing monkey for somebody else's gain.

What an idiot I've been.

But then, these caring souls who had reached out to him, and him even daring to consider their collective gesture of fellowship, until Rusty returned to rend that gossamer opportunity to shreds.

Robert Aitken was weary of beating himself up, but as he had finally accepted he would just have to get over it, get back to his self-imposed life of anguish and alienation, here she was again ... *must not let it go this time.*

No, you must not, my love.

As he looked down at his shoes, Robert felt in his heart that this may be his last chance, knew he could not spurn another opportunity. He looked up at her, holding back the urge to wrap his arms around her, but discovered he had no need, as Samantha placed the box near the skirting board, stepped forward and pulled him to her.

Overwhelmed, he pressed his face into her neck, held her shoulders, felt the softness of her breasts against his chest, and the floodgates opened: years of pent up, silent guilt gushed from him like a torrent.

Robert Aitken sobbed and heaved, as he had never done before; every rasp, weep and groan a release of hour upon day upon month upon year of torment. She whispered soothingly into his hair and held him tightly. He uttered no words; his throat would not allow. He stayed there, grasping tightly to this woman who might rescue him from his emotional prison.

Eventually Samantha felt his grip weaken and she relaxed her own, to allow him his space. Robert slid to the floor, his elbows on his knees and his face in his hands.

'Oh God, let this end,' he groaned through his fingers.

She hoped that did not mean his life.

From the next room, Samantha heard Sting singing about an Englishman in New York, and wondered if the music had just started, or their situation had blocked peripheral sounds from her awareness. She turned to see Betty Faulkner standing further down the hallway, wide eyed, by the open door. She bunched a stained tea towel in her clenched fingers.

'He's okay,' Samantha mouthed. *I hope.* Betty nodded, turned and closed the door quietly behind her. Samantha kneeled in front of Robert and touched his forearm. 'I am so sorry to bring this out in you,' she said, meaning every word.

Robert felt exhausted, foolish, pathetic. He shook his head and sniffed. *Should have kept the wall in place.*

She helped him to his feet. 'Robert, would you happen to have a tent?'

He looked at her: such an odd question to ask at that time. He pulled a handkerchief from his pocket and honked into it.

'I've got a swag in the car,' he snuffled, 'but it's not a tent. Do you need to borrow one?'

Samantha laughed brightly, and a light flickered in another room of Robert's hidden memories.

'No, we're set up at our special place for the weekend but thanks for offering. Only … you said you liked to go fishing.'

He nodded.

'The boys enjoy fishing, our campsite is not too far from here, and I wondered if a couple of days away would do you good. So, if you've nothing better to do, why not come and join us?'

Robert flinched at the violence of his inner voice: *They don't know what I am, so don't be so fucking ridiculous to even consider it.*

And then: *Do not allow this opportunity to escape, my love.*

He looked at Samantha. *That would not be possible*, he thought. *I don't do these things*, he rationalised. *That is not me*, he reasoned.

A wave of nausea fluttered in his gut and he felt the usual need to flee, but as he fought through blurring vision, the ease of what he said surprised him to the core:

'Okay.'

One simple word.

One step through the prison door.

He looked over Samantha's shoulder as Adelina walked hesitantly down the hallway.

'Roberto, Samanta?'

'Roberto okay,' Robert said as he tried to make himself look presentable. He hooked one ragged shoe behind the other calf and rubbed it, as if that might polish away the scruffiness of his appearance.

Adelina walked up to him and smiled. She then caressed his cheek with the back of her fingers.

'It is good, my friend.'

She turned to Samantha and said 'Miss Betty; I do not say their other name because it sound like I say bad word,' she laughed, despite the tense setting. 'Miss Betty say Roberto sad so I come to see my friend.'

Robert reached out his hand and she held his in hers for a moment.

'I go now before Mr Rusty shout me again.' Adelina turned, kissed Samantha's cheek in the Italian fashion, and then hurried back the way she had come.

'We need to get her away from here,' Robert said as he heard the door close with a creak and a click.

We, thought Samantha. *Another good sign.*

'Nicky and Dennis live in Longford; when they get home they're going to make some enquiries, try to find her some kind of job there. I must get her phone number before we head back. Now, I hope you won't change your mind about coming away with us for a day, or so.'

Robert's first reaction was to renege, but his raw emotions, the simple act of releasing his fears, anger and self-hatred had chipped a few bricks from the wall he had maintained around himself. A few rays of hope crept into his mind, forcing the depression he referred to as *the beast* marginally further from him.

'No,' he said with relief, 'I've not changed my mind.'

As he picked up the other guitar, Samantha said, 'Can I ask one other small request of you?'

He felt less trepidation than at her first suggestion. 'Go on.'

She pointed at the guitar case. 'Do you think you might bring your guitar with you?'

Robert looked down at the case, and knowing his guitar was his lifeline said, 'No reason why I shouldn't.' *I'll feel better having it with me.*

Samantha left Robert after he'd promised to meet her outside fifteen minutes later – with his guitar, she had insisted in the nicest way. She guessed he could not walk back through the pub looking and feeling as he did, and would make his exit another way. She closed the hallway door behind her and walked across the parquetry dance floor while Brian Johnson sang (or screamed, depending on one's musical taste), 'You Shook Me', careful not to move in time with the song's thumping beat.

The few remaining patrons paid her little attention, apart from those who might notice an attractive woman walking to a raunchy rock song, but she felt self-conscious all the same.

CHAPTER NINE

Samantha wore a bashful smile when she resumed her seat next to Nicky and Matthew, relieved that the few seconds of strutting limelight had distracted her for a moment. The closing bars of the song rattled through the tired speaker system as she looked over her shoulder, following Nicky's gaze: Dennis stood at the bar, talking with the Faulkners. Betty appeared amiable while Rusty wore his usual cantankerous expression.

'What's happening, sis?'

'Not sure,' Nicky said. 'When you disappeared with Robert, Rusty began to take an interest so Dennis went up to keep him distracted. I think it's general conversation now but one can never tell with Dennis. He never really shows if he is, you know, displeased.'

Matthew noticed Samantha's smile was strained, and she appeared drawn and tired; he saw her hands tremble slightly as she poured a glass of water. 'Okay, love? What happened out there?'

Samantha shrugged. 'Hard work, that's what happened.'

'That's it?' Nicky asked, 'We saw the cook wander out then rush back all a fluster and speak with your Italian friend, who did likewise.'

'So, where's the Tramp, how is he?' Matthew pressed.

'You can ask him yourself in a while, if he keeps his promise.'

Nicky cocked her head. 'He said yes to your invitation?'

Samantha looked around at Dennis, Rusty and Betty. 'Yes, he promised to come back with us to Ned's Camp.'

'Nooo!' Matthew and Nicky said in almost perfect unison.

'He's bringing his guitar,' she said, as if that made everything okay, then added before they entered into a discussion, 'Listen, I should wait until Dennis comes back but he's obviously in the middle of something. I won't go into any details just now but Robert had a bit of a meltdown. Seems I reopened old wounds. I don't know about our boys' past connection with him, and I'm not at all sure why, but I for one want to help this man. I want to know his story and he sure as hell can't, or won't, tell it here. I'm positive he has desperately needed to tell it – probably for years, but maybe the opportunity never presented itself.'

Matthew sat back. 'Holy shite, that's some public relations coup!'

Samantha questioned her motives for the moment, in the privacy of her own mind. Was it because of her ingrained, genetic penchant for wanting to help others, because he had shared a fleeting past with the man she loved, or was it no more than a psychological challenge? She checked her watch.

'He's going to meet us by his car in about ten minutes and I must be there when he comes out, or he might just take off and keep driving.'

Adelina was doing the rounds, pressing to get the few hangers-on to buy just one more drink before they settled their account and departed. Adelina approached and spoke to Samantha in Italian.

'No, thank you.' Samantha said after a while, 'We're about to leave.'

Adelina touched Samantha's wrist in the only show of affection she dared within view of her boss. 'Please do not go away without say goodbye,' she said in English. '*Grazie Samanta.*'

'*Prego*, we will see you again,' Samantha said, her smile warm and genuine.

The waitress returned the gesture, nodded to Matthew and Nicky then continued with her duties.

'It's a wonder you didn't invite her as well,' Nicky said, not intending it as demeaning. She turned to Dennis and said, 'My sister was always the one to bring home the strays.'

'Thanks for that, Nicky.' Matthew laughed; he always maintained it was one of his wife's most endearing characteristics, and he loved her for it.

'Matthew, you'd best go and drag your mate away from Rusty and Co.,'

Nicky said, preferring not to be anywhere near the temperamental owner.

Matthew pushed his chair back and walked over to the bar.

''Scuse me.' He nodded to Rusty and Betty. 'Dennis, we have to make a move soon.'

· · · · ·

'He's not that bad a bloke,' Dennis gestured behind them as they walked away, 'once you get talking with him, and Betty is the lovely and, I reckon, long suffering missus.'

'Yes, perhaps we might ask the Italian lass what she thinks, Den. Don't overlook the possibility the grumpy old git's only nice to you because he's wary of you.'

'If he was twenty years younger the bloke'd be a handful,' Dennis agreed. 'So, what's happenin' then? I see Sam's back.'

'You'll never guess what,' Matthew said, but carried on without giving Dennis the opportunity, 'Samantha has had a long chat with Robert and it appears he's coming to crash our secret hideout.'

'What the ...?'

'That's what I thought,' Matthew agreed with a smile.

'Well, who's been praying to the god of getting things to go yer way, then?' Dennis nudged his friend's elbow.

'I know Den, simply amazing. But word of warning, careful what you say because if he's that fragile about his past we might send him packing before he's actually unpacked.'

They met the girls at the door and left as a group. True to his word, Robert was leaning against his car, guitar at his feet. Samantha walked over and said, 'I assume you'll need to go home for some clothes?'

'No,' Robert indicated with a twist of his head. 'I always carry a change of clothes, and my swag is in the back. I don't have any provisions, so I'll head into Wynyard and pick up a few things.'

Robert had a powerful urge to get in his car and flee to the dilapidated house he called home, return to that garden surrounded by scrub; the familiar birdlife, reptiles and various marsupials he spent most of his days, and sometimes his nights with. He could so easily slide back into the isolated world he had fashioned for himself and had become used to, among those living, breathing and growing things that did not judge him. He failed to hear Samantha say, 'Don't worry Robert, we have plenty of everything.'

Robert glanced into the shadows of the alcove around the pub's entrance and thought he could make out the dark mist of his doom calling him back. He shivered and, more determined to rid himself of *the beast*, took his car keys from his pocket and said, 'Follow me.'

They tailed Robert to Wynyard, where Samantha took the liberty of accompanying him around the supermarket; while he felt unnerved that something altogether different was walking in his shadow, he preferred not to refuse her.

They wandered the aisles in silence while Robert chose vegetables, potatoes, a loaf of grain bread in a brown wrapper, cheese and what seemed to be a small extravagance, a bar of dark chocolate. *So, at least he cares for his health*, Samantha decided as he dropped each item into the basket she carried for him.

Robert loaded the bags behind the drivers' seat of his car and gestured for them to follow him. He pulled into the traffic, passed through an intersection and turned off into a bottle-shop car park.

Although Robert appeared almost to have become the tramp that once was his performing name, he certainly enjoyed expensive tastes in alcohol. Emerging from the shop with a boxed bottle of Drambuie, he looked over to the Patrol and gave them a nod to indicate he was finished.

'Doesn't drink like he's about to top himself,' Dennis said irreverently as they followed Robert's car.

Samantha nodded, more to herself. 'Some things he said made me think he desperately clings on to his life, despite being overburdened by something from his past, and I think I've guessed what it might be about.'

Robert slowed and allowed them to pass. They drove east towards Burnie, took a right turn and found Ridgley Highway. When a male Scottish voice announced through the Patrol's speaker system 'You have reached your destination', Dennis switched the sound off.

'See you leturrr, Bullie, we'll no' be needen' you for a wee while.' Dennis' attempt at the Glasgow accent brought groans from his friends.

'We've got to get one of these,' Samantha laughed as they drove through a spectacular rolling patchwork of open farmland, a stark contrast to the morning's ancient rainforest vista.

'Love him,' Matthew agreed. Billy Connolly's lilting voice seldom failed to make them smile, even through the simple art of giving directions.

Eventually they turned into the hidden entrance, down the road's shoulder away from the usual line of a driver's vision and to the innocuous rusted steel farm gate. Behind them, Robert's wagon had also slowed and was indicating. Matthew's belly bubbled with anticipation.

The vehicles weaved their way along the difficult track and, despite the manufacturer boasting all-wheel-drive capabilities, Robert's vehicle struggled with clearance on some of the terrain. When the party reached the raised basalt rock entrance, Dennis hitched a towrope from the Patrol to help keep Robert with them.

Robert sat behind the wheel watching as Matthew unhooked the towrope, while a pulse thumped perfect bass rhythm in his neck and temples. *The beast* sat, somewhere unseen over his shoulder, constantly goading him to leave, as this was no place for Robert Aitken – he who should keep his silence.

Rob the Pom. Rob the Guilty. Rob the Nobody.

Robert Aitken, at home with his animals and grief and self-loathing, *and me, the beast* would tell him. *You are mine Robert, mine.*

Then, the other voice; soft, gentle, beautiful. His eyes prickled. *Stay, my love,* the voice sang, *it is time you did.*

She had come to him occasionally, this voice, usually only when *the beast's* hold was tenuous. Her words of comfort could also heighten his torment, opening the door to that other entity that had commanded his mind for decades.

'I wish you would both leave me alone,' he groaned.

Robert, thankfully, did not hear other voices, save for *the beast* and *her*. Two voices in his head other than his own were more than enough.

'Are you with us?' Matthew tapped on the driver's window. Robert had driven the last fifty metres in a daze, consumed by the entities that had controlled his moods for years. It was then that he noticed the camper trailer in front of him and the Hoopers' Patrol parked to its left. He realised he had been sitting, grasping the steering wheel, as if it would tether him to that reality.

Robert's newfound companions were milling about, resetting the fire and lining up mugs on the foldaway camping table. He watched them, still unable to fully comprehend what he had actually done.

'Hey Robert,' Dennis called, 'cuppa?'

Robert did his best to shake *the beast* away. *I refuse to listen to you any more.* He cleared his throat and answered as brightly as he could; 'Great, tea thanks.'

Dennis and Nicky watched Robert as he finally turned his ignition off and got out of the car.

'Was this a good idea?' Nicky whispered.

'That remains to be seen,' Dennis responded with a hint of hope.

PART TWO
CONFESSION

CHAPTER TEN

Robert stood at the water's edge, gazing at the lake's gentle meandering, such a contrast to his churning internal chaos. He had wanted to make a change to his life, but had no impetus, but now, these strangers had turned up, perhaps for a reason beyond his ken? Could it be that *she* sent them to help him?

No, that would be ridiculous.

She is dead, Robert.

But she speaks to me.

No, Robert, she is dead.

'Is it here?' Samantha's voice was soft, reassuring.

Robert hugged his mug of tea and turned, seeing her do likewise. He hesitated for a moment, then said, 'You are amazing. Can you see right into my mind?'

'No,' Samantha shrugged. 'I read your body, that's all.'

Robert smoothed a space in the dirt with his foot and sat, beckoning her to do the same. This woman, this stranger, made him feel safe, although fleetingly. But it proved to him the gloom could be forced away.

'Can I call you Sam or ...?'

'Sam, or Samantha, I'm happy with either.'

'Well, Sam, I can't lie, but this, being here ... terrifies me.'

Samantha nodded, 'I can't pretend to understand, but there's no pressure and you can leave any time you want. You don't even have to,' she thought for the right word, but it evaded her, 'hang out with us. Head over there and set up if you need your space.'

Robert shrugged. 'God knows, I almost turned back a dozen times since Wynyard, but I didn't.'

The challenge of accepting Samantha's request was nothing short of terrifying, but he was determined to see it through, no matter what the outcome. His smile wore the pain of years of tormented silence.

'Well, at least, all I can do is give it a go … can't I?'

She nodded and took a breath. 'So, do I assume *it* has come along for the ride?'

He liked her humour. 'The bastard isn't happy – chewed my ear off all the way from the pub.'

Samantha snorted loudly. 'I'm so sorry, I never imagined it could be quite that bad.'

Her laughter was an icebreaker, and she watched the bunched muscles in Robert's face relax, just a little.

She glanced around to see Matthew and her sister, on their chairs around the fire. They were watching her and returned her nod, seeming to understand what she was trying to do, knowing that, for a while, the two of them should not be disturbed. Dennis joined Matthew and Nicky with three freshly brewed drinks and they sat around the unlit fire, their murmur a low comforting addition to nature's soundscape.

'Have you given it a name?' Samantha asked.

'Oh yes but I'll not speak of it in front of a woman.'

She took a swallow of her coffee and absently picked grit, or coffee grounds, from her tongue.

'Here's a challenge for you,' she began. 'See that clearing on the far side of the lagoon, over there?'

Robert followed her finger. 'Where the dead tree is?'

'Yes. Do you think you could banish your unwanted companion there for a while?'

'Ha! If it was only that easy. I mean, it's not like I've ever invited it anywhere, not like I've ever *wanted* it gnawing into my brain.' He took a swallow of tea and turned back to watch the water.

She searched memories of her university days. 'Have you ever been given means to deal with it?'

'What, like fucking napalm?' His words rang with bitterness.

She assumed he'd never spoken to a professional about his life. 'Techniques, or mind tools, for the want of a better description.'

He turned to her and shook his head. 'I've not spoken to anyone about it; really, well, until you showed up, that is. Oh, sorry about the language, by the way.'

Samantha waved it away. 'You want to hear those two jokers when they get going,' she thumbed over her shoulder to Matthew and Dennis, 'and I've been known to drop the F-bomb when necessity dictates, and not always out of anger. Nicky is no angel either, so don't you go worrying that we might be a pious bunch; it really is the word for all seasons.'

'So,' he looked over to the dead tree, with its bleached white trunk and branches devoid of bark, colour and life. While it reached upwards like a spectre frozen in time, it still wore an air of serenity. 'Got any of those mind tools I can borrow?'

'Are you serious about this? I'm not a certified practising psychologist or anything.'

'I couldn't give a rat's arse about that. This is friend to friend ... if you like.' Again, Robert shocked himself with the words that left his mouth, words that seemed to hang in the space between them.

'Okay,' she spoke through a nervous smile, 'but don't worry if some of the things I ask you to do seem uncomfortable, even stupid.'

'Listen,' Robert said, 'I used to be in the music industry and loved it while I was there, and that all turned out to be bullshit. But for a time I still revelled in it.'

'Okay,' she paused, 'nothing is going to harm you.'

'Just don't make me cluck like a chicken.'

While Robert's expression had not changed, Samantha knew he was making light of the situation. She sat quietly for a while as she formulated a strategy.

'You know,' Robert started, 'this thing, whatever I might call it, of course is not a creature.'

Samantha nodded.

'Only I found I was able to deal with it better if there was something to challenge, and nothing better than a dark, threatening ... *beast*.'

Samantha understood how he had dealt with his depression over the years: a constant showdown.

'Well, shall we try a different tack?'

Robert shrugged, as if to say 'go ahead'.

'Okey dokey Robert, let's see how we fare: close your eyes, or perhaps focus on the surface of the water.' She watched him, saw his eyelids lower; heard him breathe out slowly. 'Try and relax and go with the flow.'

When she was a psychology student (before she grasped the offer of a job in public relations), Samantha had learned about hypnotherapy and other relaxation techniques, using triggers to calm a person's anxiety. But this was different: a real subject who was, in her opinion, trapped in an ever circling, dispirited existence. Her own anxiety was gathering like deep, sinister clouds on a horizon.

How wrong could this go? she wondered. *No wrapping his anxiety in a pink bubble, or other metaphysicals, for this man.*

She decided she needed to present something to Robert that he could find tangible, something he might relate to.

She began with some basic relaxation techniques: 'Okay Robert, sit calmly and hold your hand out in front of you. Close your eyes. Feel your hand getting lighter. Keep your concentration. Try not to move. It's important to hold your hand in the same position, despite it not weighing much, not much at all.' She saw the creases on his face lessen as he became more relaxed. His arm rose slightly.

'Make sure you hold your arm steady, despite its lightness.'

Samantha led Robert through a technique she envisaged would help relax his entire body, and therefore his mind. She saw in him a willingness to participate that belied his rough exterior. He was an artist, after all, she assumed, with a predisposition towards the incorporeality of the mind, whether consciously or not.

'Now, I want you to ball your hand into a fist, clench as tightly as you can and hold the fist while I count; twenty, nineteen, eighteen ...' Samantha counted down. 'Three, two, one, relax your fingers. Concentrate on the sensations in your hand, the blood that now returns to the veins. Tell me what you feel.'

'... Tingling ... cool in my palms ... heat in my fingertips ... pulsing.'

'Look with your inward eye, down into the tiny spaces inside your veins, Robert, as if you are blood searching its way back into your fingers. Discover the parts of you that are largely ignored by your conscious mind. Let the subconscious take over for a while.'

Samantha guided Robert's mind through his body, the dark but no less vital parts of Robert Aitken that he would usually ignore, rarely consider or have no awareness of at all.

'Is your *beast* here?' Samantha's voice seemed strangely distant to him, as if in a dream.

His speech was slow. 'Yes.'

'Where is it?'

'Don't know,' he shrugged imperceptibly. 'Don't think it likes you.'

Glad about that, she thought. 'Robert, will you trust me on this?'

'Too late to go back now,' he answered slowly, his humour lingered.

'Call it to you.'

Robert shook his head.

'You have to control it, Robert. Demand it comes to you.'

'Shit,' he said through gritted teeth. While his eyes remained closed, he turned his head towards the bank, to his left.

'Imagine it there,' she said. 'Can you do that?'

'I don't want to ...'

Robert was quiet, concentrating deeply. Then he growled, 'Bastard.'

'Describe it to me.'

Again: 'I don't want to.'

'Robert?' Samantha's tone was soft. Reassuring. Safe.

His head turned towards the reeds at the water's edge.

'Grimy smoke,' he began, 'swirling. A million cartwheels. Faceless. No eyes, sometimes ... no.' With the emerging apparition there came an edge of anguish in his tone. 'Fuck ... and then this happens,' he groaned.

'What happens?'

'Grey cartwheels in my belly ... in my head ... like they feed on anything ... good in my mind. They eat the fireworks.'

She hesitated. 'Fireworks?'

'In my mind ... when I close my eyes. The cartwheels eat hope. Light. Contentment.'

'Control them.' Samantha held her breath, feeling out of her depth.

'How the hell do I do that?' he said with dreamy bitterness.

'Shush,' she whispered. 'Relax, Robert. I'm right here, here to help you.'

Robert continued to surprise Samantha with his willingness to go on her journey, even here, in the privacy of his mind. They focused on his *fireworks*; closed-eye visualisations, myriad pulsations of colours and flashes, as if they revealed the manifestations of mind-created thoughts and memories. Not, as Robert had grown to accept, the ever present growth of his spinning cartwheels of despair.

'You have just brought your fears to the fore,' she continued. 'Now I want you to conjure a net using the power of your mind, a substance so strong and fine nothing in heaven or earth can break, or find a way through.'

Robert struggled to comprehend the sense of what her distant voice was asking him to do, despite desperately wanting to.

'Remember, a mesh that is unbreakable and inescapable.'

She watched his struggle, the setting of his jaw, the minute flexing of the muscles around his eyes; a rapid eye movement, as if he slept restlessly. Whether it was with the entity he had brought to the surface, or the concept of her psychology, she could not tell, nor did she want to break the concentration he fought to maintain.

'Nothing can pass through this mesh,' she insisted with all the confidence she could garner. 'Remember, nothing can break through.'

Robert nodded. His jaw knotted again, and the lines in his forehead deepened further.

'The mesh is a magnet; the cartwheels are dark steel. Remember the magnet. Wrap the cartwheels from your belly up in the mesh,' she said, 'and they cannot escape because of the magnet. Bring the mesh into your head and allow the cartwheels to be drawn into the net. They cannot resist the pull of the magnet.'

Samantha paused while Robert dealt with her mind-play.

'Have you managed this, Robert?'

He frowned, and then nodded.

'Now send your net over to the rest of your *beast* and find it is attracted to it, see the mesh wrap around those cartwheels, again and again, until all you can see is the net you have created. Now there are no edges, no ends: the net has become totally sealed like an impregnable orb. Send the ball to the dead tree, your *beast's* prison.'

Samantha studied Robert, looked behind the rough unkempt dark beard and long peppered hair, behind the lines gouged by years of wear, tear and torment. Despite all that, she thought he had a pleasant face. She would even call it handsome.

'Robert, how are you doing?'

'Hnn,' he grunted, slowly opened his eyes and rubbed them. They seemed to have escaped the weathering of time and tide; she thought them kind, even beautiful.

'So, how did you go?' she asked. 'Well, how did *I* go, actually?' She smiled, not really seeking his approval.

'Went well, on both counts,' Robert said as he scratched his beard. 'Got the bastards in the net, made my own football and kicked them over the water. Pele would have been proud of that. The ball is now hooked in one of those dead branches.' He pointed to the tree. 'Of course only I can see it, unless you're smarter than even I give you credit for.'

Samantha appreciated his banter. She rested her hand on his and said, 'Small steps, Robert; I hope the first of many.'

'Forget small bloody steps, Sam. I want genocide. I want every fucking nanoparticle of *the beast* to burn in hell, or Gehenna, or anywhere but my brain and belly.'

'So,' she was wary that his reaction was too good to be true, 'how are you feeling after all that?'

'Absolute shit,' he smiled, 'but I've never let that stop me.'

He rose and walked to the waters' edge to fill his mug.

'Hey, best not to drink that, Robert. In the annex there's a twenty-litre container of drinking water. Feel free to help yourself. There's also a bucket of water and a towel for hand-washing.'

Robert took a drink. 'Figure if I swallow some of that botulism stuff I might just pass it on to *the beast* and that would really piss him off.'

Samantha read the humour in his cynicism. 'All the while he's over there he won't catch anything though, will he?'

Robert looked towards the tree and mumbled 'Fair point!'

CHAPTER ELEVEN

While the mood around the unlit campfire appeared subdued, no-one felt impelled to keep idle chatter coming, for as they sat bathed in late afternoon sunshine and gentle breeze, all felt at ease in nature's restorative vitality.

Robert was there because Samantha made him feel safe, alive and understood. Because of his comfort there was no longer the urge to flee – well, not at that moment anyway – and *the beast* had been banished to his periphery, at least for a while.

'Sorry to burst everyone's lazy afternoon bubble,' Dennis broke the spell, his voice almost a grating disparity to the sigh, buzz and babble of Ned's Camp. 'But we'll need an extra fish or two for later. Robert, fancy a bit o' bloke time?'

Robert's impulse was to say no thanks, so he could remain close to Samantha. There was nothing sexual in his desire, he did not covet her or resent Matthew, only she had become his safety, his lifeline; a respite in a harrowing existence. Regardless, he liked them all, especially Dennis, who was brash and loud, but Robert deemed them all to be good people. Nicky was as yet unreadable; while polite and friendly, she had not shown enough of herself for Robert to form an opinion.

He blinked slowly and looked at Samantha.

'Sure,' he said, 'I'll get my gear.'

Matthew and Dennis soon learned Robert was a skilled fisherman, a natural without need of fancy and expensive equipment. His rod and reel were old in comparison to their expensive, flashy gear; still, he cast fluidly as if the line was a projection of his arm, effortless and habitual.

They worked silently from their own spaces on the lake bank, as fishing seldom proved successful when the angler combined his art with idle chatter. After a while Robert had landed two brown trout in quick succession, without the others getting a nibble. When he had secured the second fish, Robert turned and said, 'Enough?'

'Good work, Robert,' said Matthew. 'Your success has made me thirsty. Let's head back.'

A light wisp of smoke lifting into the sky told them the fire had been lit; the sight was welcoming as they approached the campsite. As Robert drew level with the dead tree on the far bank, he looked over the water and stared intently.

'See something?' Matthew asked.

'Just keeping things in order,' Robert frowned.

As he turned and walked on, Matthew and Dennis looked at the tree, then each other, shrugged and followed.

Robert found he was better able to bite back his misgivings, and relax in the surroundings he had forced himself to endure. Matthew and Dennis, being from his old patch in London, had a common past link, including his largely forgotten love of football. Nicky's initial reservations towards Robert began to fade and she engaged more with him, but Samantha was simply a breath of real air to his soul, and Robert had to keep himself in check when he felt he asked too much of her attention.

A couple of hours had passed, the fire was pushing out a decent heat and the last round of hot drinks had come from water boiled on a billy, more for mood than convenience. The men prepared the fish while the sisters set salad onto the plates and kept an eye on the foil-wrapped potatoes, cut and plied with butter and garlic, nestled around the stone edges of the fire.

Robert placed each fish on its own square of foil, and stuffed each with butter and seasoning, courtesy of the sisters' stores. He then folded the foil into triangular parcels and rolled the edges together, placed them on a grill rack suspended over the flames and returned to his seat.

While Robert engaged in idle talk of fishing, the Wheatsheaf, even the attractive Italian barmaid Adelina, there was no mention of his past life in London. Mindful of Samantha's warning, Dennis and Matthew suppressed their curiosity.

'How long will they take?' Nicky asked Robert, again more to keep a conversation alive.

'Just about now,' Robert said.

Nicky picked up the plastic camping plates and laid them out on the ground. Dennis unearthed the potatoes and sat one on each plate, cursing and blowing his fingers as he opened each hot foil wrapper. 'Woohoo! Smell that garlic,' he said as steam erupted from the first. 'That'll keep the wampires at bay!' Dennis mimed pulling an imaginary cape across his face.

'Don't start,' Nicky moaned, and when Robert looked at her she added, 'Spooky stories last night, just about scared me to death.'

Robert prodded one of the bags, and Samantha watched, feeling that his small smile was a genuine, relaxed expression. She made a silent wish that their session had indeed proved beneficial.

'Ready,' Robert announced, and placed each foil parcel on its own plate.

'My beer's dead,' Matthew said. 'Who fancies a fresh one?'

'Does Raggedy Ann have cotton-wool knockers?' Dennis joked.

'We're on Chateau Cardboard,' Samantha said, waving her plastic glass in Nicky's direction.

Robert shook his head. 'No thanks, perhaps a bit later.'

Matthew wanted desperately to know about Robert's past, but he remembered Samantha's warning, *bide your time, he will speak only if and when he wants.*

Robert had been looking around while he ate. He turned to Samantha and asked, 'You say your uncle kept this place secret almost his entire life?'

'Yes,' said Samantha, 'Uncle Ned loved to be on his own, just him, his fishing rods and the wild.'

Nicky agreed. 'He was getting on a bit when he took Sam and me for a weekend of fishing, camping and stories.'

Dennis joined in: 'Never met the bloke but it sounds as if he was the salt of the earth.'

'Ordinarily not a great one for conversation,' Nicky added, 'but occasionally he would come out of his shell. Those were the times Sam and I would think him the most interesting man in the world.'

'Aunt Enid worshipped him,' Samantha added.

'On your mother's or father's side?' Robert asked.

'Mum's uncle,' Nicky said.

'Dad's an accountant,' Samantha said. 'Chalk and cheese were Dad and Uncle Ned, despite them getting on quite well.'

The conversation lulled, and they finished their meal in comparative silence.

Robert sucked garlic butter from his finger, leaned forward and stacked his plastic plate on top of the rest. 'How did your aunt cope when your uncle died?'

Samantha wondered if Robert's question had an ulterior purpose.

'Poor love only lasted a couple of weeks.' Samantha studied Robert's reaction closely. 'I guess she had nothing else to live for, once her life partner had gone.'

There, an invitation, an opportunity for Robert to finally tell the tale of his own life; tell of the forces that ripped him from a world of normality to one on the very fringes of society. While he had worn the facade of a bitter man, where the real Robert would rarely make an appearance, it was only when he took his guitar to an audience he would engage, and then only by the emotion of his talent as an entertainer.

Still, the sadness, the longing would be all-consuming, but at least he had come to this place, to be with a group who really seemed to care, to finally speak of his life. All had been confirmed by that sad tale of one person's love for another.

Above all, Aunt Enid's tale would prove to be the catalyst.

'Terrible business.' Robert cleared his throat and stood. 'I need a Dram and my guitar. I've a story to tell you all, if you're willing to hear?'

Matthew's belly fluttered with excitement. He looked at Dennis and mouthed a silent 'Wow'.

Robert took their expressions as an invitation, and he left the light of the campfire and walked to collect his guitar, songbook and bottle. On the way he became light-headed, staggered and reached for the bonnet of his car. He knew the feeling well; the giddiness, usually preceding a visit by *the beast*.

'All right, mate?' Dennis called.

Robert waved without turning; his mouth dry and his skin clammy, as the dreaded sensations took hold. *I can't. I just can't.*

Samantha and Matthew exchanged glances. She rose and walked to where Robert stood.

'Do you need anything?' she whispered.

As he reached for his brow she noticed his hand tremble. 'How's that net holding out?'

'Some of the bastards have escaped,' he strained through clenched teeth.

'Well, catch them and put them right back where they were.' Samantha reached for him but Robert evaded her touch.

'I'm sorry. I didn't mean that, just a natural reaction.' *Unnatural*, he challenged himself.

Samantha leaned back against the driver's door and crossed her arms; Robert kept his hands on the bonnet, feet placed wide as if he were about to be arrested.

'Happens that quickly then?' Samantha observed, and he nodded.

'Robert, you have come a long way today. You don't need to do more, why not come back, sit and just ... be?'

Robert's head hung low; he did not move or respond to her, as if he had fallen asleep where he stood. Samantha resisted the urge to touch his shoulder, to bring him from his trance.

'Robert?' she whispered.

Another voice; the soft dream of the woman spoke to him. *You have the chance to face this, my love.*

'I know. I want to.'

'Sorry?'

He realised he had spoken aloud. 'Got the bastards back.' His smile, and voice, sounded strained.

'Come and sit with us,' she said.

'Give me a moment,' Robert said, and she made to walk away. 'No. Stay, just a minute please?'

She looked over to her family, across to the water to the dead tree, and Robert's invisible but no less dreadful *beast*. 'Take as long as you need.'

· · · · ·

'I always feel better when I play,' Robert sighed after a ten-minute battle re-tethering *the beast*.

He stood, straightened his shirt and said, 'Now, that music therapy.'

He walked to the back of the wagon, opened the hatch and slid the guitar case out, and then grabbed his music folder and the box containing his Drambuie.

Robert looked at her. 'If I don't do it now, I might just as well pull the shutters closed again for another twenty years.' He turned to the other faces around the fire.

'Fancy a song?' he called, as brightly as he was able.

CHAPTER TWELVE

Robert sat on the edge of the camp chair and tuned his weathered six-string. He strummed a few chords and tried to feel at ease, both physically and emotionally.

'I have a Takamine too, at home.' Matthew referred to a guitar that was similar to the one settled on Robert's thigh.

Robert looked down at the beloved companion that had been through everything with him. 'W— I bought it, or I should say them, in eighty-nine after playing at a demo workshop in London.'

It was a start, he thought, and to his surprise it came out easier than he had expected. He idly picked chords introspectively, until the chord pattern segued into the opening to the Kinks' 'Sunny Afternoon'.

Robert recalled how his plumber father would sing the song, then ramble on about the idle youth of the day. 'Useless bloody layabout musos getting rich plunking a few notes on a guitar,' he would say, with Yorkshire-esque inflections, then end with, 'Hope you do that when you grow up, son.'

He smiled at the memory of his dad, a mountain of a character who gave his young son endless encouragement to chase his dreams. *I wonder where he is now?* A metaphorical door opened and a light switched on, as he recalled snapshots of his childhood in Oxberry Avenue, Fulham.

Fellow Londoners, the Kinks had been an inspiration to budding schoolboy musicians Matthew Pearson and Dennis Hooper, so much so that they called their own teenage band 'The Brothers Davies' after the Kinks' founding members Ray and Dave Davies. They loved the music of the sixties and seventies, and often performed cover versions of charting nineteen-sixties' songs.

Matthew and Dennis sang along with Robert enthusiastically, even throwing in improvised harmonies during the chorus. When the final chord rang out, the campsite filled with applause and whistles.

Robert's face beamed and he laughed genuinely. 'Thanks for your help with that one.'

Samantha noticed how he glanced quickly over the water to where the white tree stood, and his expression changed: *You can't touch me now.* Robert turned to Samantha and she thought how much a real smile changed his face.

'Did you come from a musical family?' Nicky asked.

'My father played the guitar and sang. He was into the Everly Brothers, Simon and Garfunkel ... anything with harmonies. He had tradesman's hands, and only seemed to be able to get his fingers around three chords, but could fudge just about any song. Mum? She was a good singer but didn't play any instruments well. Dad used to say even if she played the spoons she'd do it badly.'

Samantha laughed. 'Sounds like my musical abilities.'

'What were your influences, apart from the Kinks?' Dennis asked.

'Good songwriting, meaningful lyrics, strong melodies,' Robert said. 'George Harrison's work always seemed to come right from the core of his being.' He began to play 'Something' by the 'quiet Beatle'.

As the song progressed he was aware that everyone was listening, almost as if in a trance, and when he finished he said, 'See what I mean?'

'What about one of *your* songs?' Matthew dared.

Robert looked at him, then at Samantha before casting another glance over to the tree, which appeared moody under the darkening sky. *Still locked safely away*, he decided.

He adjusted the guitar's tuning, focused on the fret board and flexed his fingers. Samantha noticed that he swallowed deliberately, almost painfully, before playing a soft, lilting tune with simple lyrics:

We're always dreaming, Hayley, you and me
Where we will everlasting be
We'll get away, we really will some day
Dreams of our cottage by the sea.

Sit yourself down, cup your hands and keep the cold at bay
We will sing and laugh about our melancholy ways
Wrapped in our blankets in the dark of our cottage by the sea
Hayley, you and me.

As Robert sang her name, shivers coursed through Matthew, as if he sensed the power in those two syllables. For a moment Matthew's thoughts were centred on a still frame of the Cauliflower's smoky room, with a blurred image of Hayley and the Tramp. This tramp, this core of the old Robert Aitken, who sat playing to them.

The strings' resonance faded and Robert hung his head. Samantha watched him; she was aware her eyes were wet.

'Robert.' It was not a call, not a question or a statement, just a reminder that they were with him.

The guitar picked up where it had left off; Robert continued with a tale, she guessed, of a dream that could never be. Hayley was the reason Robert had turned into who he was, and such a powerful presence she remained.

Windswept hills, angled reaching cypress
Roaring fire, mist on shuttered panes
Wet jackets dripping, puddles on the floor
Dreams of our cottage by the sea.

Two recluses flee the bustle of London town
We will never wish to change our melancholy ways

Playing riddles, guesses in the dark of our cottage by the sea
Hayley, you and me
It's where we want to be.

Dog curled up, snuggled by the hearth
Cat gazing at the world outside
Together times, Hayley you and me
Immersed in our tranquillity.

We write our names, scratched in frost patterns on a winter pane
We will write songs about our melancholy ways
Two lovers huddled in the warm of our cottage by the sea
Hayley, you and me. It's our tranquility
The world's simplicity, Hayley, you and me.

While his playing remained confident, he sang the final lines of the song through a throat so tight that words almost failed in their bid to escape. But escape they did and everyone around the fire knew they had shared, in some small way, a hint of Robert's pain. Dennis wanted to speak but knew anything he said would have sounded trite, so he remained quiet.

Samantha wiped her eyes: 'Robert, that was beautiful.'

The sweet voice in his head urged, *Tell your story, my love.*

'Confession time,' Robert sighed. 'Hayley was my wife, and I killed her.'

They were stunned into silence. Samantha conjured images of her inviting an emotionally scarred psychopath to their campsite in the middle of nowhere. The beauty of Ned's Camp proved nothing more than a place of isolation, far from the safety net of society and its rules. *What have I done?*

She overcame the urge to put distance between herself and Robert; instead she said, 'Robert, you didn't kill anybody.'

Robert did not respond.

You did not kill me, the voice in Robert's mind said, but of course the others could not possibly hear.

'Robert, please,' Samantha whispered, 'you're scaring me.'

As Robert finally looked at her she recognised the window to his soul wore the unmistakable cloak of hopelessness. She knew she need not turn to the tree; *the beast* was again within him, although the term now wore something more sinister. She held his gaze and prayed that he had spoken metaphorically.

'Robert,' she said, 'cast your net again.'

He rose to his feet, groaning, 'Too late, too late.'

'No!' Samantha demanded, and the power of her command shocked Robert back down into his seat.

'You've come too far to give in now,' she added in a softer tone.

'What net?' Dennis mouthed, but Matthew held a finger to his lips; he didn't think Robert was a murderer, and believed, or hoped, the confession was allegorical. In reality he knew he could only hope, for the moment.

Samantha moved to Robert's chair, knelt before him and saw how his left hand gripped the guitar's neck as if it were a weapon to protect himself. The strings twanged discordantly as she prised his fingers away and held the instrument out for her husband to take. She then reached for the other hand that cupped his open mouth, held his two hands together, and rested them on his knee.

Matthew looked at the guitar, studied the neglected strings, the stained and finger-worn fret board, where the lacquer had rubbed away from between the tarnished frets, the numerous scuffs and nail scrapes on the soundboard. There was so much history with that instrument, and while those scrapes and scratches should have been a declaration of his love and joy of music, every mark on Robert's guitar now seemed, to Matthew, to express only sorrow and pain. Matthew did not dare strum it.

Samantha looked up at Robert. 'Ply your net. You did it before and can do it now.'

Samantha was right. Robert clawed through the fog of his misery. He nodded, closed his eyes and forced himself to concentrate.

'You have to trust in your net, Robert.' Samantha gave his hands a squeeze. 'Close the space they found to free themselves.'

Gather them, seal the hole perfectly. You can do this. Robert realised the voice, soothingly rhythmic and angelic as Samantha's, was not hers but the other voice – the Hayley in his head.

He dug his fingernails into his clenched palms to help him focus, wondering in his confusion if the encapsulating warmth around his hands was that of Samantha or Hayley. *It doesn't matter.* He focused and worked, collected and herded until the tiny, spinning, agonising cartwheels were again bound securely and sent, as a shimmering black orb, across the water and back to the prison tree. His belly felt free and he breathed deeply.

He opened his eyes to see the people watching him, an altogether different kind of audience. Nicky was standing, her arms clinging to Dennis beside her. Matthew was leaning forward in his chair, focusing on his wife. Ready to react, if needed.

Robert concentrated on the face closest to him, the face of Samantha Pearson, and he knew there was no-one living in this world that he trusted more than her.

'I am no danger to any of you,' he sighed. 'I'm not a danger to anyone but myself.' The words seemed to hang in space. 'It all happened so long ago and I am no threat. Thank you, Sam.'

Robert eased away from Samantha's grip, sat back and swallowed as if his throat bled.

'I've never wanted or needed anyone's strength since, yes, since Hayley left. Dennis, Nicky, please sit. I must tell you a story now ... and there's no going back. A true story ... I haven't talked about any of this since ... since the inquest.'

Inquest. The small word summoned all manner of scenarios and outcomes and seemed to suspend itself above the fire, hanging there for all to see, and fear.

'Please,' he gestured to the empty seats. Robert reached forward and squeezed Samantha's hand and nodded, as if to say, *I know, you are right here, because I cannot do this without you.*

He waited patiently while Samantha, Dennis and Nicky took their seats. He poured a small amount of Drambuie into his mug, took a sip then pressed the mug into the sand at his feet. Matthew held the guitar out for him, for as long as it took.

'I don't know where to start.' Robert shook his head, and finally accepted the guitar.

'How's about wherever you need to?' Dennis said.

Robert saw that, while Dennis sat in his chair, he appeared coiled, ready to defend, ready to attack. *Okay* he accepted; *I'll endure their distrust until my story has ended and then they can decide for themselves. Guilty as charged, Your Honour. No matter, I deserve everything I get, but I've gone too far to stop now.*

He played idle notes on the guitar, considering where and how to resume the story.

'I was a gawky teenager,' he began, 'all bone and sinew, hair that stuck out all over the place. School life in London pretty much focused on football, music and not much else. I was about fifteen ... or sixteen ... looking to get out of school as quickly as I could. A musician ... footballer? Anything but endless, boring lessons. Didn't care much for my appearance. I mean, what was the point?

'One day a new face turned up at school. From out of town, this girl seemed a bit of a square peg, round hole kind of person. Tall, quiet, shy. She didn't mix with anyone for a while. Probably found herself torn from a nice school in another county and dumped in the rabble of our madhouse in Fulham; she must have felt completely out of place. She spoke so ... not posh like the Royals, but posh all the same. There we all were, not an aitch or an ell in the place, including most of the teachers.'

Dennis agreed with a chuckle. 'Where we *wuz brung* up, an aitch was as rare as a bloody triffid.'

'The new girl spoke with a slight West Country accent,' Robert continued, 'all rounded vowels with this delightful, musical lilt. She pronounced her aitches, like, "home", "hospital".'

Matthew likened Robert's description of the girl's accent to colourful Somerset and Dorset tones. 'I know what you mean, Robert.'

Dennis leaned forward in his chair. 'So, you were looking to get out of school and play music?'

'Well, that was the plan. Coincidentally around that time I started to like school ... even had my hair cut.'

Samantha smiled, 'A teenager smitten?'

'Wasn't just me. Half the boys seemed to take pride in their appearance all of a sudden.'

'Now, I'm only guessing here,' Dennis began, 'but I reckon she was drop dead *gawjus*.'

Robert nodded, 'A few of us were distracted from the routine of mischief, music and football, and yes, I thought she was gorgeous.'

Nicky was intrigued, as if she was reading one of those real-life stories in a women's magazine.

'So, this girl became the centre of attention in a new school and revelled in it. Good move, Mum and Dad!'

'Not really. See, she was a strange one, because what she saw in herself and what others saw were two different things. I don't think she had high self-esteem. As I said, she was shy and, I think, uncomfortable in her own skin. Equally uncomfortable with the attention she received from the males. You know, what she thought was gangly, everyone else saw as elegance.'

Samantha studied him closely, trying to ascertain just how at ease Robert was. He appeared comfortable, with no sign of his recent meltdown. While he spoke of this girl in a detached kind of way, she knew this being became the most important person in his life.

'Let me think,' Samantha said, 'she offended the boys by turning down their attentions, and offended her fellow girls because of the attention she received at their expense?'

Robert nodded. 'She did find friends, girls who focused on studying, rather than playing around in class.'

'Robert,' Samantha dared, 'want to tell us her name?'

Robert turned to Samantha. *My trusted friend.* He closed his eyes.

'The girl's name was Hayley Louise Sutton.'

There, it had been said. Robert was silent for a while and the others respected his need to be. Suddenly he broke into Cockney Rebel's 'Make Me Smile'. If there were any tensions, they dissipated in seconds as everyone joined along with harmonies and the catchy, 'ohhh, la la la's' of the song's chorus line.

By the time Robert had finished everyone was indeed smiling, and applauding.

CHAPTER THIRTEEN

Nicky filled the kettle from the water storage container, and lit the stove while Dennis prepared five mugs in readiness. They watched Robert through the annex windows. As he strummed his guitar, Samantha sat close and Matthew stoked the fire. Dennis noticed that, although Matthew had said there was no need to fear Robert, he kept a watchful eye on the singer, being so close to his wife.

'What do you make of it, love?' Nicky whispered.

Dennis shrugged. 'Something happened, some disaster. I really don't think he killed his missus, just assumed the blame for whatever transpired.'

'You said you remembered him and his music; surely if something happened it would have been in the papers, and on the news?'

Dennis scratched his chin.

'It's all a bit sketchy, Nic, but it's not like they were famous or anything. We used to see loads of bands and drink loads of beer back in those days. They used to play at the Cauliflower now and then. It wasn't like we'd say, "oi, why aren't those geezers 'ere this week?" It was more like "This band is great" or "These losers are shit, make mine a pint".'

'He is one troubled man.' Nicky reflected, her reservations hanging in the balance. 'If not for my sister he'd have self destructed, or packed up and gone by now.'

'If not for Sam he wouldn't be here at all, but I reckon Robert's tough and if he was going to end it all he would have done it long ago. But I agree, without Sam he'd never be opening up.'

The rattle of the stove announced the water had come to the boil. Dennis filled the mugs, added milk and sugar as required and they headed back to the chairs by the fire.

Samantha resumed her seat next to Matthew, her eyes on Robert as he accepted the mug from Nicky. Robert had a sip of his tea, pushed the mug down into the indent in the sand, and resumed his idle playing.

'Me and my friends would have bets on who would pluck up enough guts to ask Hayley out. Even Charlie Roddick received the cold shoulder from her, and he was the school hunk. Great football player was Charlie, good looking and made the most of it. If he couldn't score, then us ordinaries hadn't a snowball's chance in hell.

'Problem with Charlie was, if a girl didn't come across, then he'd badmouth her at every opportunity. Of course he'd had the proverbial door slammed in his face, and he gave poor Hayley grief at every opportunity.'

'Someone should have given him a smack in the moosh,' Dennis growled.

'No-one gave Charlie a smack,' Robert said. 'He was one tough cookie, with a gang of mates around him and a tougher family to boot. Nobody messed with the Roddicks.'

'Dennis may just have, in that situation,' Matthew smiled.

Robert looked at Dennis. 'I have little doubt.'

'Tim Tam, Robert?' Nicky asked, feeling better about him.

'I don't think I've tried them,' Robert said as he took one from the packet. He looked at each in turn and then said, 'I hope you all realise what you're doing for me. I don't do this,' he opened his hands, biscuit pinched between thumb and forefinger, not referring to the wide open outdoors, but the sociability. 'I can't remember the last time I sat anywhere with other people and chatted about anything, let alone ...' he paused again, 'this.'

He had a bite of the biscuit and perched the remainder on his knee. He picked up his tea and took a sip.

'I was quite smitten with Hayley Louise Sutton, and being a fan of Dire Straits, especially "Romeo and Juliet"; it kind of became my song to her in those early days.'

'Overlooking the meaning behind the lyrics,' Dennis said, 'because they're not really befitting for one with a boyhood crush.'

'True, but the teenage me didn't pick up on that.'

'A request, Robert,' Samantha asked, 'would you play it for us?'

Robert nodded, adjusted the guitar's tuning and closed his eyes to conjure the chord progressions from memory, then began the trademark arpeggio signature that hinted at Mark Knopfler's style. He performed the song admirably, and when he reached the parts the sisters loved the most, they sang along under their breath.

Samantha and Nicky whispered the words and felt the joy of the pain expressed in the lyrics. Robert kept the beat perfectly and delivered a fine acoustic rendition of the work.

When the final chord rang out Nicky said, 'So many people have found so much in that wonderful song.'

Robert took another sip of his tea, which had cooled in the evening air. He assessed his feelings, assessed *the beast* and decided, to his astonishment, he felt calmer that he could have hoped. Another glance in the direction of the tree; all well and secure.

'I know it might sound corny, but Hayley was like a shaft of sunlight on a dismal day,' he continued, 'to me and plenty of others.'

'Was she in your class?' Matthew asked.

'No, she was only five months younger than me but she was put in the year below. I didn't play so much football during the breaks for a while. Instead I'd find myself watching her eat her lunch, or sitting on her own reading a book, or chatting with her friends.'

'You were a fekkin' stalker,' Dennis said irreverently, although Robert took it as the joke that had been intended.

'I'd try to act cool, walk past humming a tune, see if she'd look my way, but she never seemed to notice that skinny layabout.'

'Maybe she did,' Samantha said. 'Girls have always been good at not noticing someone's advances. You know the saying, a boy chases a girl until she catches him?'

'Well, she seemed extremely good at not noticing me then. I discovered she played badminton ...'

'A toff's game!' Matthew said, tongue in cheek.

'I thought so at the time too, but I just had to go along to find out. Turns out, the school was putting on a demonstration tournament for the next athletics day.'

'Of course, you were there,' Matthew said.

'See, I told you; a stalker,' Dennis whispered loudly.

'I was. But then I didn't need to go and join the badminton team, because my parents had twisted my arm to audition for a part in a school musical production, and Hayley happened to be there, too. I quickly discovered how well she could sing.'

'And that's when she started to notice you?' Nicky's engagement in his story increased as her misgivings subsided.

'Not really,' Robert said. 'Hayley scored the lead role, but – despite getting my hair cut and copping the ridicule of my football mates for my troubles – I was ushered into the dark of the so-called orchestra pit, to plunk on a bass guitar.'

'I guess business as usual, then,' Dennis laughed. 'Still perving on that girl unseen!'

Robert glazed as light filtered through the dusky rooms in his mind that held memories of those early times.

'You know,' he said, 'The musical was quite a success. Hayley became darling of the school dramatics just about overnight, which I suppose was an incentive for Charlie to try his luck again.

'Well, her reaction caused a stir. Evidently he walked up and asked her out one morning, in front of all his gang mates, and she said no. He got stroppy and groped her because, well, Charlie was Charlie, and he assumed every girl was his for the taking. But not this one, because Hayley slapped his face and stood her ground.

'He stormed off into the street and took his anger out on a car windscreen. His mates followed suit and they all went nuts – maybe it was just an excuse for a spot of wilful destruction. Police were called and Hayley's parents nearly took her from the school. After that, rumours began to circulate about her being his girl, and she'd struck him because she'd discovered Charlie had been cheating on her. I don't think many believed it but, well, you know, youth will be youth.

'I slipped a note into her book one day at lunch. It said something like, "We don't believe Roddick. You are not alone".'

'At least she knew you were on her side,' Nicky sighed.

'I didn't sign it.'

'You pillock!' Dennis smirked.

'Why not?' Samantha asked.

Robert scratched at his beard. 'I thought it would be more powerful if it didn't come from the scrawny kid she never noticed anyway.'

Nicky was impressed. 'So you gave up an opportunity to be the hero.'

'No,' Matthew said, 'he was the hero, only an unsung one.'

'Come on, Robert,' Nicky said, 'the suspense is killing me. Cut to the chase, won't you?'

'Shush, Nic, let him tell his story the way he wants to.' Samantha urged her sister to be patient.

Robert still felt at ease, and the unfamiliar feeling energised as much as it confused him. He looked at Nicky and nodded.

'I have to tell this in my own way. It's been a long time since I've even thought about this … I'm remembering as I go.'

'In your own time,' Matthew said, 'the night is young. Fancy another Dram, by the way?'

Robert drained his mug and offered it to Matthew, who had held the bottle out expectantly.

'Help yourself,' Robert said.

'I'm good thanks, got a red on the go.'

Robert took a sip and set the mug down.

'Roddick was expelled and, with their leader gone, the gang crumbled. Some were never seen again at school and the rest seemed to change their attitude, whether this was because the boss had gone, or their parents, the police or the school had given them an ultimatum: one more strike and you're out. One of the gang members, Derry Derrick, turned his attention to music and ended up a more than handy lead guitarist. In fact, we did gigs together for some time.'

Nicky snorted, 'Derry Derrick, really?'

'Hey, he could have been the Derry that worked at Music Man for a while,' Dennis wondered, 'the shop on High Street?'

'Yes, Derry worked there,' Robert thought back. 'Handy, as he wangled discounts for us on new strings, music sheets and other bits and pieces.'

'I heard him perform a few times,' Dennis remembered, 'he was a good guitarist and singer, and played in the shop to anyone willing to listen. Well, Derry eh? Small world!'

'Real name was Roderick Derrick,' Robert continued, 'but, as Derry told me later, Charlie thought it sounded too much like Roddick, and "ordered" him to change it or he'd not be allowed in the gang. He couldn't abbreviate his first name to Rod, because Rod Derrick sounded like Roderick and they would be back at square one, so he was only ever known as Derry, and it just stuck.'

'My brain's exploding,' Dennis chuckled.

'Some parents should be accountable,' Matthew said with a wink. 'Calling your kid by that name is just condemning him to a life of pretend speech impediments – you know, Wodewick Dewwick!'

'Names aside,' Nicky grumbled, 'how did you allow this person to be a part of your musical life when he'd been so awful to the girl of your dreams?'

'I don't believe he did directly, and he was full of remorse. He admitted he'd been too easily led, and if he'd apologised one more time I might have clocked him myself. But, as Dennis said, he was a fine guitarist and actually a great bloke, once he'd left his gang life behind him.'

'So,' Matthew mused, 'with Roddick and the gang gone, things settled down at school?'

Robert nodded. 'All those scared of the Roddick gang started to re-emerge, me included I suppose, but Hayley was polite in saying no to anyone game enough to ask. After that happened a few times, some kids started to suggest she just had no interest in males, then rumours started that, you know, she was batting for the other team.

'One night, Mum asked why I was acting so morose so I told her, and she said I had to let the girl know I was sweet on her. Dad agreed. He said I shouldn't die wondering, should show her where I carved her initials in a tree or something, just let her know.'

Robert shook his head. 'It got so bad that I would break into sweats just thinking about talking to her. One morning at school I decided, there and then, to ask her out. I started to walk towards her, but the next thing you knew I'd carried on right past. If I turned and tried again I'd have looked like an idiot.'

'Poor boy,' Samantha pouted, 'you really were hopelessly smitten.'

'Then one wet winter's afternoon, walking with a couple of friends on our way home from a game, I saw her, sitting at a window seat in a café with two of her school friends.'

Robert stared into the fire as another room of memories presented itself. The dull, rainy Saturday afternoon, bright café lights illuminating everybody inside; shimmering reflections on the wet pavement outside, like a Parisienne rainy-day oil painting.

'A Gene Kelly movie set?' Samantha's question brought him back to her and the campfire.

'A Gene Kelly movie set,' Robert agreed. 'My belly squirmed with fear, or anticipation, and I knew that had to be the time, I simply had to pluck up the courage. I told my friends what I was about to do, and they should carry on home.'

He hesitated, again finding himself across the road from the café. His friends laughing at him, asking – no, telling him not to waste his time, because he'd only back out. They said she would tell him to get on his bike. Robert recalled their expressions, giving him all the more determination to go through with it.

'I jogged across the road, got myself soaked by spray from passing traffic, but not even drenched trousers would deter me this time.'

Robert was there again, standing beneath the brightly coloured café awning, brushing down his wet trousers, taking a deep breath, opening the door and stepping inside. He could hear the door close with a jingle behind him, aware that people turned to the movement and sound, but with nothing particular to hold their interest longer than a moment, turning away again, back to their own lives. Hayley was engrossed in a discussion about something or other with her friends and he just stood there, feeling timid and out of place. Looking at his feet, he watched small puddles forming on the grey-and-white chequered linoleum floor.

His recollection was suddenly so vivid he could feel the warmth of the room burn into his cold face, hear the chink of cutlery, smell the pastries, the perfumes around the room. He was back there, after all those years – a memory so amazing and clear he could hardly believe it.

Robert thought of *the beast*, and knew it could not reach him here, in the safety of his past.

He had felt ridiculous standing at that door, shivering from the cold, wet and terrified in a warm room where everyone else seemed to be happy and relaxed. He peered back through the window at his friends, remembering how they mimed hilarity, holding their bellies in mock laughter, pointing at him. His resolve grew as he walked over to her table. The young, scared, determined youth cleared his throat and the three girls turned to see the skinny, bedraggled and terrified Robert Aitken.

He recalled how his voice cracked when he tried to speak.

'I said hello, and while the other girls laughed, Hayley didn't. She said hello right back, before telling me that I looked drenched.'

Hayley had smiled genuinely, and Robert remained tongue-tied. All he could say was that the bus had splashed a puddle over him. He remembered that the other girls mocked him, and Hayley asked them not to. She said he looked cold, and he lied that he wasn't.

'My teeth were chattering,' Robert spoke through his recollection.

Despite the cold and wet, he remembered feeling the heat on his cheeks.

'I said I just wanted to say hi.'

The other two girls snorted and continued with their derisive whispering, but Hayley's smile remained welcoming.

'She said she had seen me around at school, and remembered I'd played bass guitar in the musical.'

'So she remembered you after all,' Nicky said with a sigh.

Robert nodded. 'Yes, she did, Nicky. She did at that.'

He began to sing:

I remember seeing you here
And then I'd see you there
Then I'd find you in my dreams
I saw I lacked the courage to introduce myself.

You, the reluctant beauty
I stood shoulder to shoulder
with all the other guys who thought you unapproachable
Fearing to make their move.

I thought you'd not consider second best
I thought I'd be a ghost to you
I thought you'd not take heed of the likes of me
That is when I first saw you.

Robert continued his account of perseverance and belief; told the story of what he saw in the young woman who had become the focus of his emotional world – and later, even more.

Thinking you'd be amused
Expecting ridicule
Firming my courage, I approached the table where you gathered
With some of your school friends.

So how was I to know when
we were both seventeen, that
you'd assume that you'd no female charms, an awkward homely schoolgirl
Just how wrong were you?

I thought you'd not consider second best
I thought I'd be a ghost to you
I thought you'd not take heed of who is me, but I found
I did not know you.

I had just the slightest notion
of your poetry in motion
You returned my hello with a smile; believe me, my heart faltered
When you noticed me.

And now you're standing here
Behind that microphone
With your voice open for all to witness every talent you have
Now I know you more.

And now I know you don't think me second best
I can't believe I'm so close to you
And now we both pay heed of who are we
But I still recall when I first saw you.

CHAPTER FOURTEEN

Robert sighed, sad to have returned from that powerful, wonderful, sensory experience. He closed his eyes, took a breath and shivered once in the cooling air.

'We started to see each other. I just wanted to be in her company and Hayley seemed so comfortable in mine. There was no pressure to be or do anything, we'd just go for walks, or we might just sit and talk.

'Word soon spread at the school that the tall, quiet Hayley Sutton had been seen out walking with the tramp, because that's what some of the kids used to call me. I didn't care about the nickname and I don't think Hayley did either. I could don a brand new set of clothes and still look scruffy, even after my haircut, which was still by no means short. Hayley, on the other hand, could wear rags and look elegant.'

Robert's rattling laugh took them by surprise. He coughed.

'Sort of like a posh girl dating a homeless kid! After a month or so, I finally plucked up the courage to introduce Hayley to my parents. She looked out of place in our daggy home, like an alien. Mum and Dad took to her, and of course Mum had to tell Hayley to her face how beautiful she was, which was embarrassing. I remember, that first night, as I was about to walk Hayley home, Dad pulled at my sleeve and told me I was a dark horse, or an old trouper, or something like that. You know, followed by a wink. I remember he laughed later, saying I was punching above my weight.'

'Didn't you find that demeaning?' Nicky asked.

'No, I never took it that way because he meant well. Just my dad and his sense of humour.'

Dennis stood. 'Sorry Robert, a call of nature. I'll stick the kettle on while I'm up. Back in a mo.' As he walked off he asked over his shoulder, 'Sounded all too perfect, but surely she must have had some skeletons in her handsome closet?'

'None, apart from avoiding the dating game, as Charlie Roddick, among others, discovered.' Robert recalled how Hayley would prefer a ramble up a hillside to partying, or seeing a movie over a noisy, smoke filled pub. 'I was happy to, you know, just to be with her.'

'Well, give us the dirt, Robert. What about romance?' Nicky asked.

'There wasn't any early on, well nothing physical. She never gave me any signals and I wasn't going to force the issue. I didn't want to lose what we had and really was in heaven just being around Hayley Louise Sutton.' He was enjoying the freedom of just speaking her name.

'Come on now Robert,' Nicky pressed him, 'surely there was at least some snogging?'

Dennis returned and sat. The chair creaked as he leaned forward, with his elbows on his knees.

Samantha searched Robert's face for his reactions, not only to the memories that were resurfacing and he was finally sharing, but also to the questions posed by his audience. She had become aware of how he was formulating his sentences – more detailed and colourful accounts, in contrast to his truncated statements at the beginning of the tale. But she cringed twice in as many minutes at the nature of her sister's questions. Robert had hesitated, and it was clear he was uncomfortable sharing this intimacy. The kettle's whistling came to his rescue.

'Oh,' Dennis remembered, '... the kettle. Drinks anyone? Robert?'

'I'm fine, thanks.'

'We'll get them. Come on, sis,' Samantha knew what the others would want and didn't bother asking. They gathered the mugs and headed for the annex. When they were inside Samantha whispered 'Nic, I don't think it's wise to ask about intimate things.'

'What?' Nicky whispered back, 'Robert's enjoying himself and wants to talk, dontcha think?'

'Just be careful, that's all I'm saying.'

While Nicky was filling the mugs she called, 'Robert, tell us about Hayley's parents.' She raised a questioning eyebrow at her sister, who nodded her approval.

Robert answered loud enough for all to hear, 'Very polite people they were. He was some kind of engineer and she was, er, a librarian, or assistant. She scored a part time job at the library.'

'The old Georgian building on Fulham Road.' Matthew said.

Robert nodded, although he could not remember.

'Hayley's love of books probably came from her mum, and singing from Mr Sutton: he was into amateur dramatics. I went to see a couple of productions when Hayley and her dad both had singing roles. He was more outgoing than Hayley's mum, but still not the life of a party, if you know what I mean. I suppose Hayley had traits from both parents. And though she wasn't that keen on general socialising, I discovered she was more comfortable performing on stage.'

Dennis smiled as he took the mug from Nicky, before sharing a slice of personal observation.

'It's a strange thing how people assume all artists and musicians are gregarious, but some are really quite shy. It's almost like being up on a stage gives some performers permission to be loud and out there. All a part of the act.'

Nicky watched her husband share another of the many facets that made up his personality. Big and loud, soft and sensitive, she loved them all.

Robert agreed. 'We started playing guitar and singing together, mostly at our place because Hayley's mum liked her peace and quiet. That was okay because Mum and Dad loved all kinds of music, especially when played by their son, who they thought was talented.'

Robert closed his eyes in retrospection, reflecting on how his father liked some blues music, which, he assumed, was the reason he had caught a little of the bug. Hayley wasn't a big fan although she didn't mind it occasionally, and would do it well, but they mostly played styles they both enjoyed.

'We both liked acoustic – you know, people like Simon and Garfunkel – and did a fair rendition of "The Sound of Silence"; and yes, of course, I did the Paul Simon bits.'

'Will you play that for us now?' Samantha asked. 'Matthew can do the Garfunkel line if you like.'

Robert quickly ran through the chord progression that suited his voice best. He began the slow introduction and they synchronised their voices faithfully to the original. As the final notes rang, their audience of three applauded the impromptu collaboration.

Robert finessed the guitar's tuning and strummed a few chords as he began to speak.

'Hayley was a good guitarist. I always thought she was better than me. We'd often perform songs with one of us playing open chords and the other embellishing higher up the fretboard.

'At first we only played for our parents but then we started to sing at a few of our friends' places. When she donned the guise of a performer, Hayley enjoyed venturing out more.

'Once, we were asked to play at the Cauliflower to fill in for a band that had pulled out. It was a quiet Wednesday night and there was only a handful of punters. I didn't care, and though she was nervous playing in a pub, Hayley enjoyed herself. When we were packing up, the manager asked us if we'd be Wednesday regulars, for twenty quid in our pockets. And that's really where it all started.'

'Hey Den,' Matthew started to wonder, 'we went to a couple of those Wednesday sessions, didn't we? I remember there being bugger-all people there and, pardon my French, Robert, but this gorgeous woman was up there singing the empty place down.'

'That's right,' Dennis agreed, 'we'd drop by after training and have a pint or three. May not have been the first night, but we saw you play. My memory tells me you sounded polished.'

Robert smiled. 'We only did half a dozen Wednesdays before we were asked to do the Friday gig: more patrons and more in our pocket, although then it had to be official and we needed to register with the musicians' union. We did the Friday slot with other acts, and found a few more venues that didn't mind slipping some cash in our pockets on other nights.'

'What kind of music did you play?' Nicky asked.

'We developed a repertoire the punters wanted to hear, like Fleetwood Mac, UB40, Simply Red … you know, acoustic versions of the usual charting bands. Simple renditions at the start but we practiced one or two new songs every day and after a few weeks had quite a list behind us. Hayley could even lend her voice to Joan Armatrading numbers, so we were quite diverse.

'We decided we needed to be more than just us two, so we auditioned and scored a good young drummer called Pete Hardcastle, who was happy to be there for the experience and a few quid, and Derry Derrick on lead and acoustic guitar. I played bass and acoustic, with Hayley alternating between guitar and electric piano. Hayley, Derry and I all did vocals and we became, for all intents and purposes, a proper band.'

'Were you always Hayley and the Tramp?' Nicky asked.

Robert thought. 'We didn't really have a proper name in those early days, and I think we just performed as Hayley and Robert, but that wasn't so appropriate when the others joined. We threw some options into the mix and decided on Hayley and the Tramp. Some thought it had the same ring as Katrina and the Waves, although that had never entered our minds at the time. We simply used Hayley's name and my nickname. Derry and Pete agreed it sounded enigmatic.'

'You play other venues?' asked Dennis.

'The Cauliflower was sort of our home base, but we did play other spots around London like, um,' he opened another metaphorical locked door, 'the George Robin?'

'Sir George Robey?' Matthew suggested.

'That's it! They had been hosting some big name acts, bands and performers who already had an international following.' Robert shook his head, astounded at how deep some of these memories had been buried.

'We had a spot at a local folk festival somewhere, and even played a wedding, but that was a horrible experience. The mother-in-law requested some, to us, lame stuff like "Tie a Yellow Ribbon" and one old duck insisted we play "Agadoo". Hayley thought it was fun but Derry and Pete nearly walked out on us. We had to promise never to take on another wedding or they'd leave.'

'Shite, I'm not surprised,' Dennis said, then started to sing the chorus of the proclaimed cheesiest party dance of the nineteen-eighties, and they all joined in *a cappella*.

'Enough, enough,' Matthew was laughing so much his eyes streamed, 'before Uncle Ned comes back and demands we stick a sock in it!'

Robert sighed. Rediscovering these lost memories proved sound therapy, as much as the pleasure his music was giving to his new friends. Robert Aitken was connecting with his audience, and that had not happened for years. He started to play a recognisable seventh-fret twelve-bar introduction, and they all started to applaud.

'We used to do "It Ain't Proper" regularly at the Cauliflower,' he spoke over the chords, 'I'd sing the verses and Hayley would harmonise in the chorus. We used to camp it right up and the pub would love it.'

A surprise even to himself, Robert stood to strike a guitar hero pose, and the others stood to join with him, playing air guitars and singing heartily. By the time the song's final crashing chords rang out they were all laughing.

'Time for another Dram, I think,' Robert cleared his throat and sat down. 'I met Lenny Kerslake once.'

'Jeez,' Dennis began as he opened a bottle of Barossa Shiraz, 'Kerslake was a bloody character! He kept the hits happening even after Fagin Schmagin broke up! Did you do something together?'

'He was back in England for a TV appearance, and dropped into the Cauliflower one night, came up-stage, borrowed my acoustic while I was playing bass, and we did 'It Ain't Proper". He came back the next night and did a few more songs. Lenny Kerslake and Hayley and the Tramp gigging together was the talk of the Cauliflower for a while after that, and there were rumours that we had joined forces.'

'Shit,' Dennis laughed, 'how long did that last?'

'Only two days, then Lenny went back to America – that's where he was living at the time.'

'Bugger,' Dennis looked to Matthew, 'we must've been on another fekkin' planet, Matt. How the hell did we not know Lenny was in town?'

'I remember none of it, Den. Maybe we weren't as regular at the Cauliflower as we thought we were. Robert, you're telling me he used that guitar, right there?'

Robert held the instrument out as far as the strap over his shoulder would allow, as if it was to be revered to others as much as it was to him.

'This very guitar,' Robert winked.

'A polite and friendly man was Lenny, not quite what you'd expect from his on stage persona.'

Constantly assessing, Samantha wondered if Robert was telling a white lie, just having a little fun with his newfound companions. *Having fun is good*, Samantha decided.

'Did your experiences with performing and rubbing shoulders with the famous inspire you to start writing your own material?'

'I'd never written a serious song before I met Hayley ... never felt the need. There was so much good stuff out there already. Hayley, on the other hand, had been writing songs since her early teens and recorded some on cassettes. She'd record a guitar or piano and vocals, then play it back and overdub, if you like, harmonies and another instrument on a second recorder. On some songs, her dad helped out with extra harmonies. The sound quality was pretty ordinary, but it was great that she had an archive of her really early work.'

'Do you still have any?' Samantha dared.

'What, the cassettes? Yes, in my rucksack back at my place. I don't have a player and have no idea what condition they're in – and I wouldn't want to try, in case something were to happen to them.'

Dennis was not certain he wanted the responsibility, but decided to offer anyway:

'Mate, if I can get the right equipment, I should be able to transpose them to digital for you, put them on a CD.'

Robert acknowledged the offer with barely a nod.

'Shame we can't hear Hayley now,' Nicky said.

Samantha wondered if Robert would be relieved that they couldn't. Hearing Hayley's voice may well have been too much too soon.

'That's that, then,' Dennis began, 'I'll see what I can do.'

'That would be good,' Robert said, indeed uncertain he would be ready to actually hear Hayley's songs again. The real Hayley that is, not the ghost in his head. He stared into the fire.

'Are you okay?' Samantha asked, after a while.

'Yes, I'm fine, Sam.'

Needing to keep the music going, Robert strummed a few chords.

'Here's one that just about sums up the mess I've made of my life,' he said, and began to run through the chords to 'Nowhere Man'.

Recognising the sound, Dennis asked, 'Want some help? Matthew and I used to do this one, we know the harmonies.'

Robert glanced at the tree to keep *the beast* at bay, and nodded. He counted them in for the idiosyncratic three part *a cappella* of Lennon, McCartney and Harrison, and Robert introduced the guitar after the second line. When the song finished they sat in quiet reflection.

'You could record that and it would be a seller,' Samantha said after a while. 'Wonderful, you guys are so clever.'

'There's a new band about to take the North West by storm!' Dennis said with a hand cupping his ear, mimicking a radio announcer.

'Matt, Hooperman and the Tramp,' Matthew laughed.

'Back to your songwriting?' Samantha asked.

'The first song I ever wrote was just after we started playing together,' Robert remembered. 'We were doing covers, and slipping a few of Hayley's originals into our sets. I wrote the song over a week and played it to Hayley the next weekend. She said she really liked it, but then, it was about *her*.

'See, Hayley had this ability to write about anything. Her music wasn't just "I love you and you don't love me and I'm going to step off a cliff" kind of mush. She could see a caterpillar on a leaf and write a great song about it. But as for me, I struggled making any concept believable. Everything sounded corny when I did it and most of my stuff ended in the bin before, as Hayley would say, I'd given it a fighting chance. Anyway, I'll play that first song if you like.'

Without waiting for a response, he introduced a lively chord sequence, and began to sing:

Suddenly it hit me – a bolt in from the blue
Suddenly my life took a left turn
Or was it a right one? I really couldn't see
But I knew too much to go back and pretend.

Suddenly it hit me when I walked into the room
I knew then my life was soon to change
I felt my senses tingle and my fears evaporate
'Cause I knew too much to go back and pretend
I knew my old life was at an end.

You are so wonderful
You know I won't change how I feel

Suddenly it hit me when I looked into your eyes
Suddenly I knew you felt the same
You made your decision it was me you were looking for
And you knew too much to go back and pretend
You knew your old life was at an end.

You are so wonderful
You know I won't change how I feel - 'cause this is real.

'Love the beat,' Nicky said, 'although I had expected you'd play the one about the cottage by the sea again.'

'No,' Robert said, 'that was something we often spoke about – the cottage by the sea, not the song. You see, I didn't actually write that one until ...' he hesitated, 'until after ...'

Samantha saw the change in his face, heard an edge return to his voice, read his reluctance to continue to where that was leading. She asked, more for distraction than conversation:

'Robert, did yours and Hayley's works harmonise with each other?'

Robert turned to her. *Still reading me like a book.*

'Well, they kind of had to. Most of our band numbers were Hayley's, although I'd play some part in their construction, but mostly they were her babies with real eighties beats and energy.

'My work was usually built around the acoustic guitar, with Hayley adding touches here and there, improvising vocally and coming up with some great embellishments.'

Robert recalled how she loved the mandolin, and would sneak it into his songs occasionally. It never bothered him, because he loved her playing – and the joy that instrument offered.

'Between the two of us we had a fair bit of diversity in our compositions.'

'A real partnership,' Nicky understood.

'Collaborative songwriting,' Dennis agreed.

Robert shrugged. 'I knew all too well Hayley was the magic behind our music, and I was just happy to be a part of it all.'

'Will you play us one of Hayley's songs?' Nicky glanced to her sister, and immediately regretted asking.

'No,' Robert said a little more harshly than he intended. Seeing Samantha glare at her sister, he continued in a more amiable tone, 'I can't do her work, Nicky, to be honest.'

'Although ...' He ran through a chord sequence to refresh his memory. 'Perhaps this one. We scored this New Year gig in eighty ... something, last minute, because the main act had pulled out. I recall the guitarist had sliced a chunk out of his hand and couldn't play. Probably stoned, knowing the Little Creechas.'

'The who?' Nicky asked.

'No, different band,' Dennis joked.

'We supported the Creechas a couple of times. They had been touted as the next big thing to come out of London. They definitely showed real flair and promise, but we heard they indulged in the alternative substances, crap that would addle anyone's brains. Ashley Drewes, their guitarist, was in the year above me at school – I'd played football and music with him and he came across as a nice bloke. Unfortunately, his and the others' brains appeared to have been well and truly messed up by that time.'

'Why do bands do that?' Nicky sighed.

'Easy,' Dennis shrugged, 'all of a sudden they have money and the promise of fame, and dealers swarm like wasps, trying to snare them. Give them free drugs on a plate knowing if they try it they'll come back asking for more, and next time they'll have to pay, and again, and again.'

'Well, aren't you the know-it-all,' Nicky said.

'There was this one song ...' Samantha prompted Robert, hoping he would retain focus.

'We found out about the New Year gig late morning on the day. We spent some time working on a suitable repertoire, you know, plenty of dance stuff, but we didn't actually know any New Year songs. Anyway, Haley had this idea and a chord progression. She went through the song with me in the afternoon, we jotted down some lyrics, and then a few hours later we were on stage.

'At five minutes to midnight we played the song in its entirety, no band rehearsal, no real written music, just words and chords on paper.' Robert slipped the capo onto the seventh fret and began the lively chords that gave the guitar a mandolin-esque tone.

'Derry and Pete had not even heard a note before their copies were shoved under their noses, but we all still managed to start and stop at the same time, which is always a good thing. I'm guessing no-one actually listening would have realised the song was only a few hours old. Of course it wouldn't have won any awards, but it worked okay. People were dancing and singing, so it did its job admirably. A class act, was Hayley!'

He began to sing:

Everyone, won't you join us as we sing the night away?
Every single one of you, won't you join us as we sing the night away?

It's that special time of year, releasing old, inviting new
Time to change perspective. Everyone; me and you
We will join in celebration. Thought this time would never come
Da da da, da da da, da da da da.

Everyone, won't you join us as we sing the night away?
Every single one of you out there, won't you join us as we sing the night away?

All those memories that we'll cherish. Remember times, remember names
Remember those no longer with us, amid the fireworks and the games
Old acquaintance not forgotten as the clock starts ticking down
Da da da, da da da, da da da da.

Think of what it is you've wanted, now's the time to turn around
A year of searching; let us see what you have found
Deciding what's important. Perhaps no need to look that far
Now by the firelight, just remember who you are.

Everyone, won't you join us as we sing the night away?
Every single one of you out there, won't you join us as we sing the night away?

Robert spoke over the song's continued chord progression, 'As I said, it wouldn't have won a competition, but it achieved its purpose, and it was a great party song, as enjoyable to sing as to hear I always felt.' He sang as if still part of the song, 'I'm not sure they were all the lyrics, so that will have to do for now.'

Dennis laughed. 'I reckon that would hold its head up against other New Year songs!'

Robert rested a hand over the strings to smother the chord, took a drink and cleared his throat.

'One evening, a little into the New Year, Hayley did something that completely changed my life. *Not for the last time.* We'd been out walking on a freezing night, and as we crossed over Putney Bridge, I slid on the icy pavement, went down like a ton of bricks and cracked my scone on the kerb, and there was blood everywhere.'

'Scone?' Nicky asked.

'Head,' Matthew translated.

Robert began a progression of slow arpeggios, which made his narrative seem more like a documentary.

'I remember hearing this voice, soft like an angel. *The same soft voice in my head.* I gather I'd blacked out because when I opened my eyes, Hayley was kneeling and my head rested on her lap. She said, "What am I to do with you?" She wiped blood from the cut on my forehead and laughed, said I was going to take some looking after, and added we would need to get married so she could do it properly.'

'Oh my God,' Nicky cried, 'how beautiful, how romantic!'

'What, the proposal or the crack on the noggin?' Matthew snickered.

'Shut up, Matthew, you ninny. But of course you said yes?'

'I didn't feel in a very romantic mood, so didn't say too much at the time.'

He remembered they had walked to his home, where his mother brought cups of hot chocolate and a pack of frozen peas to hold against the lump. He thought it a strange remedy for an ice injury, and said as much at the time. Once she was satisfied Robert was going to recover, his mother had left them alone.

'After we had a laugh at my expense, I asked Hayley if she meant what she'd said on the bridge. She said yes, then added that she wouldn't mention it again because it was a man's job to propose.'

'So you did?' Samantha smile was wide.

'I wasted no time blurting it out. Even got down on one knee to do it, you know, properly.'

'Did Hayley cry?'

'I think we both did. I was over the moon because, frankly I'd been wondering how long her interest in me was going to last.'

'That is so lovely,' Nicky crooned, then, 'No, I mean not that you were worried, I ...' She giggled. 'I ... you know what I mean, Robert. It is such a lovely story.'

Samantha looked at her sister and shook her head.

'Tell us about the wedding,' she dared.

Robert silenced the guitar and glanced around at the people with him. It had still only amounted to a handful of hours since they had come into his life, but they made him feel safe and, for that, gave him the drive to keep on going.

'April, three months later,' he said after opening another metaphorical locked door and flicking on the light. 'A small gathering, just our immediate families and a few friends. Yes, including Derry, before you ask.'

'Don't tell us he was your best man?' Dennis said.

'Yes he was. He also performed a song he had written about us, just for the occasion.'

'Was it a church wedding?' Nicky wanted details, although didn't expect to get them.

'It was at All Saints, near Putney Bridge. Seeing the bridge was close to home and a catalyst for the proposal, it seemed the right place. Hayley's mum was adamant we should be married in a church, in the proper fashion, and they generously paid for the lot.'

Samantha was confused. 'But wasn't All Saints your school?'

'All Saints Anglican, it's a very old and picturesque church, not far from the Thames.'

'Did you have a honeymoon?' Nicky asked.

'Couldn't afford one because the church cost our parents a packet, and we didn't want to miss our regular Fridays at the Cauliflower. If we dropped out for a week or two, there were always other acts waiting to step in, and we were worried the punters might lose interest in us.'

'Like a hot spud?'

'What are you talking about Dennis?' Nicky asked.

'Dropped,' he said, as if that answered her question.

'Idiot,' Nicky said, glaring at her husband for making light of a serious matter. Robert enjoyed their banter, and his smile was genuine.

'Hayley's folks got us a room at another pub for the night, and we ended up playing a number of acoustic shows there after that. I think it was called the Mayflower.'

'Why not the Cauliflower?' Nicky asked.

'Hayley's dad was a regular at the other pub, his local – and, who knows, he might have struck a deal. It was their gift, after all. Nice room too.'

'Your bookings were steady, then?' Samantha asked.

'At the Cauliflower, yes. We started to get gigs at other places too – all Derry's doing. He was building some amazing contacts around the place.

Hayley and the Tramp started to attract the interest of a few of the bigger London clubs and it was all down to Derry. He evolved into our player-manager, which was okay, as it allowed Hayley and me the luxury of focusing on the music.'

'And your young marriage,' Nicky suggested.

Robert searched deep into himself and discovered, not *the beast*, but a surge of melancholy.

'Those were amazing times,' he blurted all too quickly, 'one in particular. We were performing at the Robey and, the manager told us later that George Martin had been there and heard a few of our songs.'

'Holy shite!' Dennis and Matthew said in almost perfect unison.

'Did you meet him?' Matthew asked.

Robert peered around the metaphorical door and looked inside.

'While Hayley and I were doing an acoustic set, Derry saw him and went over to introduce himself as our manager. George Martin said he was impressed, especially Hayley's songwriting, so Derry told us later.'

Matthew's eyes were wide like a child's. 'Did he say anything else?'

'That was about it. Derry told us he left shortly after.'

'Who is he?' Nicky's question was met with incredulous stares from all three men.

'George Sir bleedin' Martin? And you ask who he is?' Dennis spoke to his wife as if she must have been living in a bubble.

'The guy of Star Wars fame?' she clutched.

'That was George Lucas, sis,' Samantha sighed.

'George Martin was a genius. He helped the Beatles mature from rock-and-roll to seasoned musical pioneers,' Dennis made it sound like a lecture.

'What did he do, then?' she asked.

'The list is impressive,' Robert said. 'Arranger, producer, director, composer and innovator all rolled into one.'

'So,' Nicky repeated, 'what did he *do,* then?'

Matthew could see Robert was struggling, so he said, 'It's complicated,

Nic. Even the most gifted musicians can benefit from other points of view, a bit of guidance. The Beatles had been writing some amazing music, probably the best of their time, but George Martin helped hone and inspire them beyond that. He arranged and produced a kind of music that had hardly been considered before. Think of the impact that *Sgt. Pepper's Lonely Hearts Club Band* had.

'George Martin was responsible for some of the classical elements of the Beatles' music. He blurred the lines between pop, highbrow, even experimental music.'

'That's right,' Dennis said, 'he composed a string arrangement for "Yesterday", and we all know how iconic that song became. His influence is there, in many of the Beatles' later recordings.'

'Hmmm, I think I get it.' Nicky said.

'So,' Dennis began, 'you both started to attract interest. Did you audition for Sir George?'

Robert hesitated. 'Sir George?'

'Knighted in nineteen ninety-five, or was it ninety-six?' Matthew turned to his friend.

'Six I reckon,' Dennis said. 'Our Robert 'ere brushed shoulders with the soon-to-be titled.'

'So, I was more of a hermit than I thought,' Robert said with a shake of his head. 'I never knew, but shouldn't really be that surprised.'

'I suppose you don't know McCartney was also knighted in ninety-seven, then?' Matthew added.

'Didn't know that either.'

'You must have heard of Lennon's murder and Harrison's passing?' Dennis said.

Robert nodded. 'Yes, those found their way into my world of indifference. Terrible business.'

Robert sipped on his Drambuie and stared into the fire. He took a deep breath, put the mug down and continued:

'Derry said he spoke to Martin and perhaps he mentioned us to someone else. Anyway, one day Derry got a letter from Donnington Records offering us an audition, at Abbey Road Studios no less. I was so ecstatic I hardly slept for days. We had a few weeks to get ourselves together and work on three originals to perform in the studio to a Donnington rep.'

'Wow, what a buzz!' Matthew said, 'but, why didn't the rep simply come to one of your gigs?'

Robert thought ahead in his story's timeline.

'I'll get to that,' he grunted.

'Ah, okay. Was it difficult deciding which songs you'd play?'

Robert saw that Matthew and Dennis were leaning forward in their chairs, as if afraid to miss a word.

'Was at first, but we settled on two of Hayley's and one of mine. We were asked to bring our instruments but no amps or drums, so Pete Hardcastle got to play on a studio kit other famous drummers had used, and he was pretty chuffed about that. We swore our parents to secrecy, but didn't tell anyone else about the audition.

'Hayley's parents had bought her a small car for her birthday and decided to give it to her early, you know, to celebrate. They said a pop star couldn't go through life without wheels. Nothing fancy mind, just an eighty-three Austin Maestro hatchback, which proved handy for transporting the guitars and keyboard.'

Robert leaned back and sighed as he returned to *the now*.

'That began three weeks of emotional mayhem.'

CHAPTER FIFTEEN

Robert strummed a few slow jazz chords.

'Hayley wasn't an experienced enough driver to go traipsing across London and I didn't drive at all, so we decided to take the tube, meet with Derry and Pete at Maida Vale Underground. It was only a fifteen-minute walk to the studio from there.

'By the time we'd reached Paddington we realised we'd be far too early and, as Hayley was feeling anxious, we got off and went for a walk, guitars and all. She said she was having second thoughts but I assumed she was nervous of meeting with the "Donnington scary suits", as she called them.'

Robert recalled Hayley suddenly deciding she was underdressed. They walked around looking for a clothing shop as he tried to help put her mind at ease.

'We stumbled upon this hand-me-down clothing place.' Robert paused while he searched for a name. 'Too Good to Chuck, it was called, and we had a laugh as we peered through the window. The sign on the door said "closed" but we could see someone inside, behind the counter, so I knocked and attracted her attention.'

He began to play a rapid twelve-bar tune, the strings muted under the pad of his right hand.

Robert remembered the young woman, dressed as a hippy, with a nose ring and a bindi dot on her forehead. She shook her head and tapped her wrist where a watch might have been, to indicate the shop was not yet open for business. Robert took his wallet from his pocket and waved it in the air, and the woman succumbed to the temptation of an early sale.

'She let us in and we had twenty minutes of welcome distraction. We left in a better frame of mind, with Hayley wearing this Stevie Nicks kind of flowing white witch outfit, as I called it. We had to rush back to Paddington or we would have missed the guys as planned at Maida Vale.'

Robert continued the series of staccato twelve-bar chords and started to sing, punk-like, bringing his hidden London intonations to the fore:

On our way to the gig, she wanted a costume
To light up the stage her very own nom de plume
She says 'it helps with the nerves, make me one of a kind'
Then she goes and buys a dress like Stevie Nicks.

Diaphanous cape, floatin' stage breeze
She got gossamer tresses, Rhiannon sleeves
Ethereal majesty, now she's got it all
'Cause she's bought a dress like Stevie Nicks.

Stevie, Stevie, nuffin' wrong with Stevie
But Hayley, Hayley, that's who I want her to be
But now she's bought a dress like Stevie Nicks.

Romantic gypsy, chaste witch-lookin'
All bustles and swirls when she gets it cookin'
The only thing missin': is a wand and rapid vibrata
Now she bought a dress like Stevie Nicks

Stevie, Stevie, got me very own Stevie
But Hayley, Hayley, that's who I want 'er to be
But now she's bought a dress like Stevie Nicks
'But she's gone and bought a dress like Stevie Nicks
Now she's bought a dress like Stevie Nicks.

'I love Stevie Nicks,' Nicky laughed.

Robert agreed. 'So do I. I would have preferred Hayley as herself but accepted it was her way of dealing with it all. As it turned out we were late and had to catch the next tube. Derry was wound up because we'd left him waiting so long on the platform. He growled and grunted, but I suppose relieved we'd made it okay. Then he told Hayley she looked super, which helped to lighten her mood.'

Robert began the opening bars of 'Here Comes the Sun', singing the first few lines, almost at a whisper. He paused to take another drink and habitually tweak the guitar's strings, then returned to the tune but no longer sang the lyrics. He continued to recall that day, how Hayley relaxed a little when they joined Derry and Pete on the platform. Derry stood with his guitar in its case while Pete was doing drum rolls in the air with the sticks he had bought especially for the day. Their excited banter somehow eased our tension.

Nicky was trying to paint a visual image of this woman who still held so much power over Robert.

'Did Hayley look like Stevie Nicks?' she asked.

Robert shook his head. 'She was fine featured like Stevie Nicks, I suppose, but her hair was darker, more honey blonde if you like. I used to think she looked more, you know, Welsh.'

'What does a Welsh woman look like?' Nicky said, without any mischievous intent.

Samantha appreciated Robert's courage in telling this story that she knew would end painfully. She hoped her sister hadn't pushed too far in her naivety.

Despite Samantha's concerns, Robert only smiled.

'Mum and Dad liked this sixties singer, Mary Hopkin, and I used to think Hayley looked like the face on one of her album covers.'

'She won the Eurovision Song Contest,' Dennis recalled.

'She did at that,' Robert nodded as he strummed a few chords and picked up on the story. 'We took our time walking from the station along Abercorn Place with plenty of distractions around there: Lord's Cricket Ground, Regents Park, London Zoo. We started feeling good, walking down that leafy road, three hopeful-to-be-discovered people with musical instruments, we felt we didn't look out of place so close to those iconic recording studios.'

'On Abbey Road, one wouldn't have looked out of place being dressed like Stevie Nicks,' Dennis sang, and Robert couldn't help but laugh.

'Then we got to Abbey Road and that famous zebra crossing, and of course we had to walk across it in single file, just like in the famous photo. Derry even stopped to remove his shoes for effect but then, before we knew it, we were standing there, looking up the driveway. Suddenly it all seemed very serious, staring at those nine stone steps, and that formal entrance. We weren't smiling any more, until Pete suggested we could always go to the zoo instead. I remember we all laughed at that, which calmed our wobbles a little bit.

'We stood for a while, reading some of the graffiti messages scrawled over the white wall out the front, until Derry checked his watch for the millionth time, and announced it was ten to eleven, and we had to go in.'

Robert paused and looked about him, so engrossed in that other world for a moment that he'd forgotten where they were. He registered the cold breeze on his neck and realised he urgently needed to pee.

'Just going for a biological break,' he said as he stood. He rested the guitar, strings in, on the chair and stretched his back. He turned up the collar of his shirt, rammed his hands in his pockets and trod, heavily, away into the darkness.

Samantha watched him as he went, guessing, assessing.

'All this talk of rock stars and Abbey Road Studios,' Dennis sighed, 'I need a drink. What'll it be, everyone? Speak now or get it yourselves.' He stood and headed for the Patrol for another bottle of red.

'We're okay Dennis, thanks,' Samantha said, 'still have half a bottle here.'

'Hey darling,' Nicky called, 'grab our jackets from the trailer will you? And a sweatshirt for Robert in case he hasn't got one – oh, and my beanie and gloves, please.'

'Yes, same for me,' Samantha said.

'Should have kept my trap shut,' Dennis murmured, just loud enough for all to hear.

· · · · ·

Robert stood in the dark night, and glanced over his shoulder towards the bright campfire. He watched his new friends milling around – Matthew tending the fire, Dennis walking back from the annex with his arms full of clothing, Samantha and Nicky chatting – and was amazed how at ease he remained. He thought back to that street in Burnie, when Samantha had spoken to him, and again at the Wheatsheaf, when she had ignored his rudeness, and he whispered a quiet thanks to her for it.

He looked in the direction of the dead tree, now in total darkness, and envisaged the net that held his *beast*. His mind checked the seams, ensured there was no possible way for the spinning cartwheels to escape and he believed, forced himself to believe, what his mind was doing was not only possible but also actually happening. *Controlling the beast ... my destiny*.

'You okay out there, Robert?' Samantha's voice, floating across the distance between them, was soothing, welcoming.

'I'm fine, just about to go wash my hands.' He flicked on his penlight and picked his way down to the water's edge.

As he turned back towards the fire he paused, looked over his shoulder and whispered, '*Just stay where I've put you, fuckers*.' He then walked back, running his hands down his jeans, and prepared himself to resume his story.

Nearing the pain.

His audience sat, jackets on, drinks in hand, a captive audience eager for him to continue. He willed himself to be strong as he slipped the sweatshirt on, picked up his guitar and sat. 'Thanks,' he said, for both the sweatshirt and the Drambuie Matthew held out for him. He took a sip and ran his fingers down his beard.

'Ever been to Abbey Road?' he asked his fellow Londoners.

Matthew laughed, 'Yes, Dennis and I went up there once and took the customary photo just like you did, but the street side of the gate was as far as we got.'

Robert nodded. 'Walking up those steps was about the most daunting thing I had ever done up to that time.'

'What – surely not more than plucking up the courage to ask Hayley out?' Nicky posed.

'Quite right, the second most daunting thing I'd ever done! Abbey Road is a musician's mecca, the most famous recording studios ever, as far as I'm concerned, all hidden behind that unassuming white Georgian facade.'

'There was certainly something hallowed about the place,' Robert reflected. 'Of course, nothing but bricks and mortar, but you can't deny the power of an icon. Nine steps of stone and mortar put the fear of God into us, as we went up them, one by one, to the entrance. The rest is really nothing more than history, expectation and awe.'

'That's us all over, Robert,' Matthew said. 'We put hats on everything. Pop groups, religious leaders, the holy microphone of All-saintez.' He parodied with exaggerated piety the artefact from *Monty Python and the Holy Grail*.

Robert grinned, remembering playing truant from school with a couple of friends and sneaking in to see a special screening at the Odeon Chelsea. 'I remember naming myself Sir Robert the Not-Quite-So-Brave-As-Sir-Henry-Cooper after watching that movie,' he smirked.

'Our 'Enery!' Dennis remembered the knighted boxer from Lambeth, whose main claim to fame was to put a young Mohammed Ali to the canvas.

'Don't start these two,' Samantha sighed, pointing at Dennis and her husband. 'We're sure they know the film word for word.'

'Who wants to cross the bridge of—' Matthew began, but was cut short by his wife's abrupt, 'Not now, Matthew.'

'Bet you can't guess my favourite colour?' Dennis said with a grin.

Nicky rolled her eyes. 'Please, continue your tale, Robert.' She pointed a finger at her husband as if to say, *do not dare.*

Matthew thrust his leg high, lampooning a silly walk from his chair.

'Sorry,' he said without meaning it.

Robert looked at them, fooling around while he grappled with the story of why his life had turned to hell. He didn't care, because they were helping him get through it.

'Nine steps,' Samantha encouraged.

'We made it to the entrance without being eaten by anything, and walked up to the reception desk. This young, fresh-faced woman asked our names. My head was swimming and I wasn't sure whether to say Hayley and the Tramp, or Hayley and Robert Aitken, Pete and Derry, or Rod or Roderick, but then Derry took control and wrote the relevant details in a big registration book on the counter. The receptionist pointed to a red leather sofa and told us to take a seat.'

He recalled her voice, a singsong Scottish lilt saying, 'Mister Bray and your technician will be with you soon'.

Robert remembered the scene: him and Hayley, hugging their guitar cases on the sofa, as if lambs to the slaughter. Derry sat fidgeting with excitement and Pete rattled drum patterns on his knees.

'After what seemed an eternity, this bloke carrying a black attaché case came through the main doors, flicked rain off his shoulders as if it were dandruff, and headed straight to reception to write his details in the book.'

Robert recalled how the man drooled over the receptionist, and it was obvious she didn't care for his attentions, as her smile wilted the instant he'd slapped the pen on the book and turned away from her.

'Derry leaped up to greet him, so we followed suit. He introduced himself as Gerald Bray: tall and thin with a comb-over, and a posh accent that oozed condescension, which did nothing to help our nerves, least of all Hayley's.'

Robert recalled how Bray quickly lost interest in them, and turned back to the young receptionist, who maintained constant eye contact with him. Bray may have assumed her attentiveness was due to his charm, but Robert assumed she was simply trying to take away any opportunity for him to gape down her cleavage.

'He, Bray, was a real sleaze. I remember turning to Hayley and making a silly joke to make us feel better: "The Derry and Gerry Show," I said as we stood there together, feeling out of place. She snorted when she laughed, had to search in her bag for a tissue. Bray swanned back over and told us we had to wait because the sound technician had been held up, and he waved his finger towards the red seats we'd already left backside imprints in. Then, instead of joining us, he went back to torment the Scots girl.'

'Sounds like a right prat,' Matthew said.

Robert nodded. 'We sat there for a few more unbearable minutes while Bray ignored us, then a woman came hurrying through those art deco double doors.'

Another light flicked on in Robert's memory, and his eyes glazed as he pictured the scene: a young woman, grasping a clipboard, flicking pages back and forward. She blew an errant lock of hair from her eyes as she checked the list, then looked up at them and smiled. Bray cleared his throat to catch her attention, she turned to him and her smiled briefly faltered.

'The woman greeted him and waited for an introduction. Bray looked as if a response was beneath him, and so Derry stood and announced us as Hayley and Robert Aitken, Peter Hardcastle and Derry Derrick, from Hayley and the Tramp.

'She was pretty, had a friendly face and melodic voice. I recognised Norwegian tones beneath her excellent English. She introduced herself as Elsa, stepped forward and planted a kiss on Derry's cheek. "Paddy hopes you play well today," she said. Derry, the dark horse, had kept to himself that he would know our technician, cheeky sod.

'Paddy was Derry's older brother. He was in a punk band, Piggins Hit, but we wouldn't have known of a connection until then. When she spoke about Paddy, it was evident he and Elsa had something happening, and the way she said the band's name was brilliant because she said it exactly as it had been intended: *pig in shit*. I'd met Paddy once or twice through Derry. A nice quiet bloke, but loud angry music.

'Bray definitely had tickets on himself, but Elsa certainly didn't, despite the fact she was a technician in the world's most famous recording studio. She showed us into Studio One then went upstairs. We could just about see her through the smoky window of the darkened room. She mimed for us to put our headphones on so she could communicate with us directly, along with her effervescent expressions and repeated thumbs up. There were just the four of us in that enormous space, apart from a man in a suit, who sat in a corner, watching.

'We did a sound check and quick rehearsal, then Bray waltzed right past us, without a word or a glance, and went upstairs to the control room. We watched him through the window, sitting like a self-proclaimed holy man. He spun his chair forty-five degrees, closed his eyes and tilted his face to the ceiling. His hand flicked at the air, a gesture for Elsa to start things off.

'She counted down, gave another thumbs up and we started playing. I think we were on auto pilot.'

'Must've been a fekkin' awesome experience.' Dennis sighed.

'If we had the time or nerve we might have actually enjoyed it. I mean, here we were, four unknowns from Fulham, in the same room where the Beatles recorded some of their masterpieces.'

'Amazing,' Matthew whispered. 'Robert, you're giving me the shivers.'

Want shivers? You ain't heard nothin' yet. Robert stared into space, strumming his guitar.

'We played three songs as requested, and despite Hayley's dread she made it through. To be honest, I have no memory whatsoever of performing the songs. Derry? Well, Derry would play for Her Majesty if she asked and wouldn't bat an eyelid. I do remember Elsa's voice coming through the headphones, and it was as if she had broken the spell. I looked up to see her pointing towards the stairs.'

Robert recalled removing his headphones, sitting his guitar in its open case and walking up the stairs with the others. They walked through the door that Elsa held open, and into the darkened room with an enormous multi-channel mixing console that almost seemed to fill the space. The console's regimented rows of coloured signal dials, knobs and sliders appeared an impossibility to master, but Elsa sat, cupped the headphones back over her ears and made adjustments to dials on the console, with the speed and knowledge of the professional audio engineer she proved to be. She beckoned them to stand close while Bray kept his eyes down, as if totally uninterested.

'Elsa slid the headphones off and asked if we were happy, and we all nodded as if we were. She said it sounded great and we went along with her again. She looked at Bray and asked him if he wanted to take over but he just waved his hand dismissively, as if to say, it's all yours, I'll just sit here wallowing in my self-importance.

'Elsa flicked a switch and the songs played through the room's speaker system. She was right, we sounded far better than we could have imagined, but Bray's apparent lack of interest made us feel as if we'd failed. Elsa said later the basics were good, we just needed to relax our hands a little more and work on our microphone and breathing techniques, but nothing we couldn't overcome. Then she checked her watch, referred to her clipboard and told us the studio was booked for another artist.

'It was then Bray came to life, almost as if he'd been holding off the torment until the last moment. He proceeded to tell us that he loved our work and, on behalf of Donnington Records, would like to offer Hayley and the Tramp a contract.

'We couldn't believe our ears! We had just stood in Studio One at Abbey

Road, played our stuff and now a label wanted to sign us.'

Bray had spoken, honey seeping from him like a beekeeper's harvest when he said, 'Follow me, good lady, and you gentlemen, to another room so the engineer can prepare for her next appointment'. As if his allegiances had shifted, he had walked from the room without another word to Elsa, and beckoned them to follow.

'Bray ushered us into a small meeting room and slid a contract into the centre of the table. Then he left us alone, telling us not to sign until he had returned. Back in those days we didn't even think about showing it to a lawyer first, but I do remember Derry saying he wished his brother was there to give us moral support.

'Derry, Pete and I were eager to sign – in hindsight, blindly – but Hayley was trying to make sense of some of the terminology, and threw up arguments against putting pen to paper. She would read out passages, paragraphs, and say things like she didn't know what this word meant, or didn't like that, or that sounded like a trap. The rest of us were on too much of a high, and wouldn't listen.'

'You thought it was a trap?' Nicky asked.

'I thought, or hoped it was legitimate. I mean, surely they couldn't afford for it not to be, but Bray was so up himself he'd have put anyone off.'

'Apart from you, Pete and Derry,' Dennis said wryly.

'Fair point,' Robert agreed, recalling how confused they all became sitting around that table. They had even begun to query the legitimacy of the band itself. Should they have created an official agreement before they got to the point of signing a contract? It was all getting so complicated; much of their questions brought about by Hayley's negativity, which she didn't understand any more than she could have justified to them.

'Elsa came in and we told her how this whirlwind session had all come about, and how confused we were about whether or not to sign the contract, but Elsa said she was in no position to advise us. She, of course, knew George Martin, and when I asked if he had recommended us to

Donnington, because that would have made us feel confident it was all above board, she doubted that he would have had anything to do with it. Then she had to get back on with her work, and left us to it.

'Bray came back a good ten minutes later, sat and looked at us each in turn and, in his smarmy voice, asked if we were excited about the life-changing opportunity Donnington Records offered. In truth, I was completely out of my depth and Hayley, well, she simply couldn't stand Bray. Well, none of us could particularly, but she refused to even look at him. I know it was stupid, but we didn't want to let Bray think we were idiots, so we didn't ask him questions that might have made us appear so.'

'The payoff was, of course, you didn't get the answers you really needed', Matthew said.

Robert nodded. 'I turned to Derry, hoping for some kind of leadership and because Hayley was making me frustrated. I remember saying this was what we had all been working for, and asked her, demanded really, to tell us why she was being so negative. All she did was shrug and say she'd sign if we insisted.'

'Hayley was right, though. We didn't understand half the terminology – you know, how legal speak hardly contains punctuation?'

'Feel like you're going to faint because there's nowhere to take a breath?' Dennis suggested.

'That's right. Bray left the room again then came back with the suit who'd sat in the corner while we auditioned, and introduced him as the witness to our signatures. I've no recollection of his name; only Bray insisting this stranger had no affiliation with Donnington Records.

'We had gone too far to turn back, so we took turns to sign the document. Hayley's mood seemed to lift once she had taken the plunge, and I noticed the beginnings of a smile on her face.

'On the last page there was a space for Bray and the witness to add their details and, there it was, Hayley and the Tramp were going to make records, maybe even become famous.'

CHAPTER SIXTEEN

'I tell you what,' Robert smiled as if the burdens of that session had only just lifted from his shoulders, 'we left the studios and it was like we didn't touch one of those steps on the way out. Even Hayley was bubbling, I guess after finding a way past the stress of being in that studio, the difficulty of playing through her own conflicting attitudes, and of signing for and contending with Mr Treacle. We headed for the pub to sit over a few drinks before going home, although we couldn't wait to tell our parents, couldn't wait for the world to know.'

'So, you didn't get to see Sir George, then?' Dennis couldn't hide his disappointment.

Robert shook his head, 'A hell of an experience, nonetheless.'

'Derry was a good bloke after all!' Dennis said, almost an apology.

'Derry was the best ... I loved him like a brother.'

Samantha felt Robert's enthusiasm wane in a breath. She kept her voice bright and asked, 'Robert, how was Hayley afterwards?'

Buoyed by Samantha's consistent, quiet support, Robert said, 'Hayley seemed fine, and I had assumed she'd turned a corner. We were on a high, and that night's Cauliflower gig became a celebration of our success at clearing the first hurdle. There was a big crowd in, and the reaction to our announcement nearly took the bloody roof off.

'From Monday we started planning a list of possible material. Derry even drafted an agreement between us four, to make Hayley and the Tramp more official, at least in our minds.

'None of us could relax as there was only a month 'til we had to be back in the studio. We already had the three songs we did at the audition, which Bray said he wanted to be included. We had some other songs we thought we could make good enough and would fit, so over the next few days we refined some and culled others. In the end we settled on nine: five of Hayley's, two collaborations, one of mine, and one of Derry's.'

Robert recalled Hayley was doing everything she needed to, but the dark pendulum of her moods gradually returned. Still she refused to discuss it, and Robert had no choice but fill in the blanks for himself, to make assumptions about why she was being so negative, to apologise privately to the others on her behalf.

He had repeatedly asked her to explain, to give him something to understand, but all she would say was she didn't know, apart from experiencing waves of alienation where the entire concept of writing, recording and playing live venues felt wrong to her. But surely, he would think, that didn't make sense. Surely she had to know.

Hayley remained a part of the planning, part of rehearsals, but without her usual spark, without the chemistry that made the talented, charismatic singer from Hayley and the Tramp.

'And then Derry told me one day that he was feeling increasingly uncomfortable being around us, so much he had contemplated leaving the band. We could get another guitarist any time, he said, as if people of his calibre grew on trees. I told him that was rubbish, he was just as important as the rest of us, and we four were the band.' Robert scratched an imaginary itch on his scalp. 'More to the point, I reminded him his signature was on the contract, and we might have a big problem with Donnington if he were to leave.

'That day I confided in him that Hayley was having second thoughts about being a star. Perhaps she'd realised that playing a Friday gig and writing some songs was one thing, but the rest – the contracts, the pressure, the expectation – none of that seemed to hold appeal to her any more. I told him if I pressed her for answers, she'd start to cry or get in a huff and walk away.'

Robert's playing had begun to sound edgy, agitated; less an underlying soundtrack to the story he needed to tell, and more a guard against the enchained demons from his past – and *the beast* across the water. Samantha sensed his mood darken, sensed all was not well with the story's unfolding.

Robert stood and propped his guitar against the chair, grabbed his mug and drained the remnants of his Drambuie. He began to pace slowly back and forth, his beard scratching now appeared less habitual and more the manifestation of his anxiety.

Samantha had to say something.

'Robert? Robert!' she repeated, 'why not take a break?'

He ignored her and continued pacing by the fire. Matthew stood.

'Robert, come and sit down.'

'I don't want to fucking well sit down,' Robert yelled, then groaned, 'Oh Jesus, here it comes.'

He glanced across the water and flinched, as if the spinning cartwheels were slicing into him. As Matthew stepped back, Robert allowed the mug to slip from his grasp as he fell to his knees and doubled over. His breathing sounded shallow and ragged. Samantha slid to the ground next to him, wrapped her arms around his shoulders and whispered into his hair.

'Fix the net, Robert.'

'I can't.' His words were thin and choked. He was sobbing.

'Robert, mate,' Dennis began, but Samantha looked up, her glance telling him to be silent.

'Robert,' Samantha said, 'you have done this before and we can do it again. Come on, with me now.'

She moved in front of him, held his hands and continued to whisper encouragement. While his breathing slowed, his head continued to hang as he focused his attention on Samantha's voice. There they remained while Robert battled against the wrenching despair that had ruled his past two decades. *But now I'm not alone.*

Dennis and Matthew went to the annex, more to give Samantha space than for the want of anything. After several minutes they returned, sat back and quietly reflected on the good fortune of their own lives while they watched the dancing flames.

Nicky had remained in her seat, feeling pride for the sister she had thought she knew well, awed by Samantha's ability to counsel a mind in such apparent turmoil.

Robert raised his head and stared into Samantha's eyes.

'Thank you, Samantha,' he said, 'seems we've managed to get the bastards back where they belong.'

Despite his distress he was determined to persevere. The churning cartwheels had been tethered again, enough for him to continue.

Samantha checked her watch.

'Robert, it's nearly two-thirty. Why not get some sleep? I think we all agree you've earned it.'

Robert reached for the Drambuie and refilled the mug that wavered in his trembling hands, and a little spilled down his jeans.

'If it's all the same, I need to keep going,' he shrugged, 'Can't stop now ... I'm ... so close.' He scratched at his beard and turned to the others. 'Unless you've all had enough?'

In truth his audience was riveted, but didn't want to make it seem as if the harrowing account was an entertainment.

'Robert, mate,' Dennis said, 'we're all ears if you want to keep going. It'll take a while to finish my wine anyway.'

'I shouldn't have put you all through this.' Robert sounded fragile.

Nicky might have been shocked by Robert's battle with this other entity for control of his wellbeing, but her empathy for him had strengthened.

'Won't hear of it, Robert. We wanted you to talk with us, and that hasn't changed one bit.'

Robert sighed, took another sip of his drink and sat back down in the fold-up chair. Matthew handed him the guitar, his safety blanket.

Robert ran a finger along the fretboard before revisiting his tuning regime. He began to play a sombre chord pattern as he remembered sitting with Hayley in their small ground-floor flat in Fulham.

'One morning,' he began, 'when Hayley and I were having breakfast, I told her I wouldn't leave the table until she spelled out what was wrong. I reminded her we had a fortnight until our recording session and said I felt there was no life in our work. Her rehearsals just sounded as if she couldn't be bothered.'

Robert's account was laboured, as if he could not, or did not want to reach its culmination.

'She was quiet. I demanded she talk to me about it. Demanded we clear the air. I'd never known her to raise her voice … it just was alien to Hayley's personality, but now her voice reached a pitch I had never heard in all the time I had known her.'

Robert could hear her voice as plain as that day over twenty years earlier: '"You are just not trying to understand," Hayley shrieked at me, "I don't want to be a part of this any more." I'd never seen her act so angry.

'She told me she hated the contract, hated the pressure and loathed Bray. "Don't you see how he ogles at me, looks down on you?" she said, "We're going to be trapped and you're too blind, too stupid to see it."

'At last, she had spoken. But, it didn't make sense to me, I mean, that was surely nothing we couldn't overcome? After all, she had dealt with Charlie Roddick and he was far more … actually dangerous than Bray could ever be. No, I figured there was something more, something she simply didn't want to tell me. I decided then and there she'd had enough of me, but didn't know how to end it.

'Instead of being the rational, understanding partner I should have been, I used her vulnerability as a lever to release my own frustration. Instead of saying, "that's great, at least we're talking, now let's work it through," I began to rant right back at her.'

Robert cringed as the metaphorical door, the one with the strongest locks on it, splintered into pieces. He did not want to but knew he must. He peered inside and remembered, but shame prevented him from sharing what he had said: *What the fuck do you think you are doing, Hayley? Screwing up everyone else's dreams because you don't like some sleaze?*

Don't swear at me Robert, I have no control over this.

'Even as the words were flying from my mouth I couldn't believe I was saying them, but I couldn't stop ...'

Okay so it's my fault then is it, you irrational bitch? I'm not the one who changes their mind every second minute without caring who you shit on.

'The more I vented, the more I said things I just didn't mean and didn't even know where they came from. The more I yelled, the more I didn't care, or notice, what it was doing to her ...'

Have you thought of me, or Derry or Pete? No of course you haven't because this entire universe revolves around Hayley fucking Sutton.

'And then I didn't stop until I was out of breath ...'

Those around the fire saw Robert flinch, as if he had been struck.

You think you can waltz into my life and take over my heart and then do and say what you want at your whim and I'll keep following you like a pathetic puppy? Well think again, darling, because I'll have no more of your fucking manipulation. You can stick your life and our marriage where it fits.

'And then ... it was like the fog lifted ... she had backed away to the kitchen door and I was right there, in her face.' He focused on his finger, pushing into her cheek and smearing the tears that ran down her face. 'She had fear in her eyes ... I didn't understand what I was doing, but I hated myself all the same.'

Leave me alone Robert. I can't listen to any more of this.

After all this time, Robert could not believe how he had acted, as if he was nothing more than an uncontrollable brat screaming in a supermarket aisle. He stared, wide-eyed into the fire. He lowered his accusatory finger and sighed. 'She turned away and left the room without another word.'

Little wonder he had locked it so deeply away.

Robert heard her in the hallway, the rattle of her car keys, and the front door closing. His irrationality had passed as quickly as it had come and he had stood for a moment, overcome by self-loathing.

'I followed her, but by the time I opened the door her car was pulling away from the kerb, into the traffic.'

The last snippet of Hayley's convulsive gasping, the profile of her wretchedness had etched itself forever into Robert's memory, so deep that nothing in heaven, or on earth, would ever erase it.

'Instead of chasing after her, instead of begging her forgiveness, instead of saying, "it's okay, Hayley, I want us to go back to how we were," I just watched her leave.'

Robert's face had turned pale, despite the glow of the firelight. He dug his fingers into his knees, and he rocked in the chair.

'I just watched her leave.'

CHAPTER SEVENTEEN

Robert's audience was stunned to silence. He dragged his gaze from the glow of the fire, and his head hung as he spoke as if in a trance.

'Didn't know what to do, I paced the flat, room to room.'

He found himself out in their tiny garden. He sat against the fence, wishing he could turn the clock back.

'All of a sudden I didn't give a shit about the contract, Gerald fucking Bray, fame ... anything. I just wanted to hold Hayley, tell her we'd go back to the way it was ... just us two and the rest of the world.

'Don't know how long I was outside. The sun had gone, air had cooled. I went inside, made myself tea, sat staring at her empty chair ... let the tea go cold. The flat was quiet ... just the hum of the fridge. I didn't even register the sounds of the traffic outside.

'I grabbed my guitar, to fill the emptiness she'd left behind, started playing – not anything in particular, just random chords. The guitar annoyed me, so I put it down, thumbed through the contract copy. I began to hate every bloody word. Just words, just legal-speak ... Donnington weren't monsters, but I hated that contract all the same.'

Robert looked up, his eyes pleading. 'What could I do? We didn't have a phone and I wanted to be home when Hayley returned, but wanted to go and look for her. Wanted to tell her we would break the contract no matter what, go back to our lives.'

As Robert paused to wipe his eyes, it was as if Ned's Camp held its collective breath, too afraid to make a sound.

'Why did she want to break the contract?' Nicky's voice was a grating disparity to the crackle of the fire, and the natural ambiance of Ned's Camp.

'Shush,' Samantha whispered, annoyed with her sister.

Robert waved it away, as if he could not deal with, or answer Nicky at that moment.

'Then ...' he hesitated. '... a knock on the door. I saw an awkward kind of shadow through the frosted glass ... knew it wasn't Hayley.'

Robert stared into the fire with an expression of hopelessness. 'I let them in ... two policewomen ... sat me down ... told me ... an accident. Told me ... my Hayley was dead.'

There was a collective intake of breath.

'Oh God, no,' Nicky gasped.

Robert dropped his head in his hands, his body ached with sobs.

'Hayley died and it was my frustrated anger that killed her.'

Ned's Camp, the place of serene beauty, hung in reverential mourning.

Samantha kneeled by Robert's chair, rested her hand on his forearm.

'We're here with you now Robert. We will help you get through this.' She hoped her words didn't sound condescending.

Robert nodded, shook his head, shrugged.

Matthew unclipped the guitar strap, and Robert allowed him to take the instrument.

Robert lifted his head and wiped his nose on his sleeve.

'Those police, Jesus, don't know how they do it. The one who'd done the talking got in touch with Mum, and the other one made some tea, then they waited with me until my parents arrived. Then the policewomen went on to, probably, their next disaster. Wonderful people, shit job.'

He leaned back into his chair, patted Samantha's hand and said, 'I'll be okay now.'

He studied his trembling hands, following the creases in his palm.

'It is like the point to living left me that day, and there has seemed little point to much at all since.'

They sat, staring at the flames, and for a while nobody felt much like conversation. Matthew became aware of a rhythmic squeaking sound and, realising it came from his chair, forced himself to keep his leg still.

The fire consumed their attention, as if contemplation of one of nature's most natural purifiers, flame, might help cleanse the tragedy that was Robert's tale. Their minds were absorbed with the account, the sound of crackling flame and the occasional flutter of moths, both attracted to and destroyed by the light and heat of the fire.

CHAPTER EIGHTEEN

Robert was exhausted. *There*, he decided, *I can't face any more.*

And not before time, the other voice in his mind added. While *the beast* had been mute, it remained a silent threat, no more distant than the very borders of his newfound sanctuary.

Everyone stared: Nicky and Dennis at each other, Matthew at the campfire and, Samantha? Samantha searched Robert's eyes, which seemed to silently implore her forgiveness. Ned's Camp endured, quiet and, despite the horror tale, peaceful. A place of refuge, and hope of healing.

You have nothing to answer for. Samantha's answer was communicated through her own eyes.

Dennis broke the silence. 'Mate, what a weight to bear.'

Robert had talked enough, and he felt as if he could not volunteer another word. Samantha reached out towards him, her fingers searching the air, just short of his own. He didn't react, so she drew her hand back.

'You haven't shared this with anyone, for how long?'

Robert's mouth twitched but again he didn't respond. Silence was peace, and in that peace respite may be found.

Matthew sat back and cleared his throat, as if to prepare them for his suggestion that Robert should take a break.

'It's got to be three a.m., Robert looks shattered and I think we're all pretty worn out after that. I think we should turn in, don't you?'

Robert nodded and blinked away gritty tears.

'I'm sure you have more to tell us, Robert, if you still want to,' Samantha added, 'and we want you to share it. But Matthew's right, let's get some sleep. Are you going to be okay?'

As if on cue, drizzle descended on Ned's Camp, settling softly on their hair and shoulders. The fire started to hiss. Robert looked up into the darkness, feeling the cool gossamer mist settle on his face … soothing, cleansing, but not forgiving.

'Swag's in the wagon,' he said without inflection. He stood, took the guitar, his lifeline, from Matthew, held it protectively to his body, and headed for the car. He opened the hatch, the globe had expired long ago but he fumbled in the darkness, through the jumbled mess of clothing and boxes for something to dry the instrument. He found and opened the lid of the case, slid the guitar inside. He grabbed the canvas handles of the bag containing the swag, swung it over his shoulder, closed the hatch and turned back towards the fire.

'You are welcome to sleep in the annex if you like,' Samantha suggested.

'I'll be fine here.' He nodded to them all, turned and walked to the other side of the campfire to set up.

'Robert,' Dennis called to his back.

Robert paused and looked over his shoulder.

'Thanks.'

Robert didn't respond. Dennis' simple word was not an accusation or condemnation. He could have offered meaningless condolences or overt compassion. Instead, he thanked Robert for sharing his pain, a lone syllable of appreciation.

Despite all he had confessed, he still felt as if these people were his friends. *Still not even a day,* he thought. *They are like family to me … like the family I lost.*

Robert unrolled the one person tent he called his swag, pegged the corners and secured the flysheet. He unzipped the side access and slid inside. He closed his eyes, exhaled a long breath and thought of the song he could not bring himself to sing aloud. They could not hear him. Robert didn't want them to, just yet.

I want to hold you, tiny bird
Light in the palm of my hand
I can't see you, or hear your breathing
I just dream you're here.

So small, so fragile, so full of promise
For your story to unfold.

But I know you must do other things
You've another life to learn
Before we had the chance to meet
You'd already flown away.

From that day, the day she left, Robert had always said goodnight to Hayley. The ritual would include an apology. 'Goodnight, Hayley,' he would whisper, 'goodnight tiny bird. Your story will have to wait for another day.'

Goodnight my love, her voice returned, as clear as if she lay beside him, *we are glad you have told them, we are happy it is finally off your chest.*

Did Robert believe Hayley reached to him from the grave? Damned right he did. He rattled a sigh and rolled onto his side.

Drizzle turned to rain. He always found its thrum on the flysheet pacifying and it seldom failed to lull him to sleep. Just as he was about to succumb, he lifted his head and stared, searching past the synthetic shell and over the water towards the dead tree. He had realised *the beast* had not stirred, still held firm in its incorporeal prison.

'*Goodnight, fuckers,*' he whispered.

· · · · ·

The sisters were standing inside the annex brushing their teeth. 'Going to get a wet bum in a minute,' Nicky spoke softly, trying to sound light.

'We brought a special night-time canister this time, and glad we did, too,' Samantha picked up an orange bucket and handed it to her sister.

'Go on, we can empty it in the morning. Only liquids, mind: anything else and you'll not be my favourite sister. I'll make sure Matthew doesn't surprise you.'

'All the mod cons, sis. Thanks.'

Samantha left Nicky to it and went into her sleeping compartment.

'Don't go out just yet, Nic's having a waz.' Matthew nodded.

She sighed. 'Are you still going to sit up?'

'Yes, love, Dennis and I will take turns, just to keep an ear out for Robert. His story is rattling around in my brain and I don't think I could sleep just yet anyway. I hope he doesn't do anything daft.'

'Clear,' Nicky's voice whispered. 'Goodnight, you two.'

'Night Nic,' Matthew whispered back. 'Need a last widdle, Sam?'

'Yep, won't be long. I'm bursting.'

When his wife was settled in the main sleeping compartment that sat over the trailer, Matthew whispered through the partition, into the second sleeper.

'Catch you in an hour or so.'

'I'll see you in a while,' Dennis returned.

'No worries.'

Matthew made himself comfortable on one of the chairs that had been brought into the annex, out of the rain. He stared through the PVC window at the fire, which grimly held on against the elements. He pulled up the collar of his jacket to meet with his beanie, thrust his hands deep in his pockets and reflected on the night and the story Robert had shared with them. While he gazed out he saw the fire eventually succumb to the drenching rain, which also now obliterated any view of Robert's swag.

CHAPTER NINETEEN

The footballer was running his thumbnail along the teeth of a comb, which was a strange thing to be doing in the midst of a Premier League game. While Matthew was watching from the second tier of the home supporters' stand at Stamford Bridge, the player was, strangely, floating right in front of him, his mud-smeared Chelsea strip glowing in a single spotlight. He was singing 'My name's Frankie and I just scored again', as he utilised the comb's teeth to provide a backing to his song.

Matthew's dream faded and he opened his eyes to the morning, heard Robert unzip the flysheet and crawl from his swag.

'Shit, nice one Dennis,' he mumbled, realising he had been asleep and Dennis had not relieved him. He wiped his mouth and eyes. 'Shit.'

He watched Robert push his hands into the small of his back and arch his shoulders back and forth, then walk down to the lake to gaze out across the water.

Matthew stood and stretched away the night of sitting asleep in a director's chair. He filled the kettle and lit the stove, placed mugs in a line and prepared the expected beverages. He dipped into the open biscuit packet, moved to the PVC window and looked out at the early morning sky. He studied the biscuit first, to ensure nothing else had been there before, then took a bite and chewed quietly, as if his crunching might wake his companions. There were a few breaks in the clouds now that the rain had passed, and the ground was wet with fine droplets glistening on the grass and leaves. He looked towards the lake but could no longer see Robert. The kettle began to rattle on the stove, and Matthew turned and switched the gas dial to off.

'Bugger,' Matthew heard Dennis say from behind the sleeping partition. Nicky mumbled at being woken. He heard the sounds of clothing being donned then Dennis came out.

'Sorry, mate,' he said, 'body clock failed me. Awake all through?'

'Yup,' Matthew lied, stifling a yawn.

'Hmm, coffee on the go I see.'

'Won't be long.'

Dennis looked towards Robert's swag. 'How's the guest?'

'He was down at the water, must have wandered off somewhere.'

'I was no bloody help. Here, let me handle the drinks.'

'She'll be right.'

'Nature calls then, so catch you in a mo.' Dennis picked up the toilet roll and the fold-up spade and wandered outside, collecting the orange bucket as he went.

A while later Samantha emerged, rugged up in her beanie, puffer jacket and gloves.

'Brrrr,' she jiggled on the spot, 'have you seen Robert?'

'Yes, good morning, love,' Matthew said sarcastically as he stared through the window.

Samantha wrapped her arms around him and kissed his neck.

'Morning my dahlink,' she said theatrically. 'Have you seen Robert?'

He handed her a mug. 'Yes, out there somewhere.'

'Thanks, love.' Samantha looked out towards the swag. 'Terrible tale,' she mumbled, and blew at the surface of her coffee without taking a sip.

'Morning, Sam,' Dennis said when he returned. 'There you go, bucket empty and rinsed.'

'Thanks. Nicky not stirred yet?'

'You snored like a trooper,' Nicky's muffled voice answered through her sleeping bag. 'I'm not getting up yet, out of protest.'

Dennis smiled and shrugged. 'Wasn't me, I was awake all night, standing out there, watching over Robert.'

'Bloody liar,' Nicky said.

'Bloody liar,' agreed Matthew.

'You can't talk, Matt,' Samantha said. 'You were imitating a freight train when I got up for a pee.'

'There he is,' Matthew changed the subject. They could see Robert back down by the lake, staring across the water again.

'When the tea's brewed,' Samantha said, 'I'll wander down and let him know he's welcome to join us.'

. . . . .

Robert heard the soft padding of feet on sand behind him. He dropped his head for a moment, then turned.

'Hello Robert.'

'Good morning, Samantha.' He accepted the mug with a grateful nod, noticing she had one of her own. *So she is here to talk*. He turned back and looked across the water. *How can she, after all she heard last night?*

'Still safely locked up?' she asked hopefully.

Robert shrugged. 'No.'

Oh hell, Samantha thought. 'Are they troubling you, I mean how are you feeling in the light of day?'

'Yes,' he said, looking about him. 'But, no.'

'Sorry?'

Robert turned to face her. He seemed calmer.

'I can't detect them out there, and they're not in here, and that troubles me no end.'

Samantha looked out to the tree. 'Don't you go missing them, now.'

Robert shook his head. 'Not likely, it's just ... they're always around, you know, that bastard *beast* depression.'

'Yes, I understand, it was your way of dealing with it.'

'I like the *was*.'

She smiled. 'No harm in trying, is there? Come on, why don't you come on up to the annex? You are welcome, you know.'

'Thanks,' Robert looked over to the campsite where Dennis was tightening a guy rope. Dennis glanced back and gave Robert the thumbs up. 'Morning,' he called.

Robert mirrored the gesture. 'I laid so much shit on you all last night and, well, I didn't want to assume,' he sighed. 'Besides, I needed to check things out.'

'Perfectly understandable,' Samantha said. She touched his forearm. 'Come on up when you feel like it. We'll get breakfast organised at some stage but not before we're all ready, Okay?'

'There is more,' Robert said, and left it hanging.

I think we all knew Samantha thought.

'You can talk to us if and when you are ready, Robert,' she said. 'We're an easy bunch to get along with.'

She began to walk away, and then Robert said her name.

'Yes?'

'Thank you, for everything.'

'Oh Robert, I think you deserve it.'

· · · · ·

They ate breakfast under the annex in the cool morning. Matthew brought out a cask of port and five plastic tasting glasses, which made Nicky feel the need to justify the extravagance. 'Only when we go camping, Robert. We're not pisspots, you know.'

'What are we up to today?' Dennis threw the question out to no-one in particular.

Robert felt awkward; *surely they don't mean to include me?* He was due back at the Wheatsheaf. It was one of the few times of the year when he allowed himself to be expected to play, when Rusty promised extra dollars in his pocket.

'I'm, er, playing this afternoon,' he said.

Robert's story was by no means over and there was still plenty he could, and needed, to say, but he would not utter another word without a direct invitation from them.

He was surprised that he still lacked a feeling of urgency to flee to his own space. His mind wandered through the dark, dank rooms of the house he had been living these past few years, he imagined *the beast* back there, lurking in wait. He did not welcome the thought of returning to that place.

'I want to see Stanley,' Nicky distracted him. 'I've heard there are lovely craft shops there and we've yet to have a wander around Wynyard.'

'You mean knickknack shops?' Dennis groaned, 'I'd sooner stick pins in me fekkin' eyes.'

'Oh, grow a pair, Dennis. You and your almost-brother can sit in a coffee shop while Sam and I check out Wynyard, then we can head up to Stanley,' Nicky said.

'A great coffee shop in Wynyard,' Robert added, but only because Adelina had told him so.

'Then we head west and you guys could walk up the Nut while the girls get some more retail therapy,' Samantha added, suggesting that climbing the town's remnant volcanic plug should provide an hour's distraction.

'Robert, what time are you due to play?' she asked.

'Rusty's expecting me for lunch, so I need to be there to set up around eleven-thirty.' Robert had a powerful need to not be alone; on his own *the beast* may seek him out.

'Finishing when?' Dennis asked.

'Four?'

There was an inflection in his response, Samantha noticed, a hope or need to hear an invitation.

Don't let them slip out of your life, my love. Suddenly Hayley's voice was no longer a folly, no matter how insane it must be to think she could still be with him.

'I, er ...' Robert stammered, 'I might catch up for a cup of tea with you all when I've finished?'

'Bollocks, Robert,' Dennis laughed. 'Come back for another night. We'd love you to, if you can put up with us again.'

Thank you ... thank you. Robert felt his face flush. *Impossible,* he thought, but his nod sealed the agreement.

'Done then,' Matthew decided. 'How's this: you come with us into town this morning, we drop you off at the pub and leave you to your lunch recital, and then pop back around four? Come back with us to Ned's Camp and it'll save you traversing the mud from last night's rain in your wagon.'

Robert was both overwhelmed by, and nervous about, the idea that he would be trapped with no vehicle, no escape, should he change his mind. *It is not a trap, my love.*

His mouth acted before his head could decide otherwise. 'Sounds good.'

'Perfic,' Dennis said.

Matthew nodded with satisfaction. Robert turned to Nicky.

'Okay by me,' she said, genuinely pleased.

'All settled then,' Samantha said, 'we'll take the Hoopermobile, but on one condition: everyone is to have a good wash first. I don't want to be stuck in that small space with four smelly campers – five, including me.'

CHAPTER TWENTY

Robert's mind was a confusion of emotions as he stepped onto the gravel of the Wheatsheaf's driveway. He closed the door behind him and watched his newfound companions drive away, awkwardly performing a motion that was alien to his world, but familiar to theirs. He returned their farewell waves, and felt a powerful sense of loss.

He turned, and his shoes crunched with every cumbrous pace towards the entrance, while his left hand possessively grasped the handle of the guitar case. He pushed through the front door and was immediately met by the familiar musty scent of old beer, cooking fat, stale body odours and angst. A fleeting memory of Ned's Camp made his throat close momentarily.

He walked past the darkened front bar and over to the stage to begin setting up. His crouching form cast shadows in the light that filtered through the kitchen swing doors. As he opened the guitar case, he heard the kitchen doors squeak. The few front-bar fluorescent tubes that were still in working order flickered into life.

'*Ciao* Roberto, I thought I hear somebody.'

The song in her voice was a joy to him. He stood and wiped his hands on his shirt.

'Hello, Adelina.'

She walked over and touched the back of her hand to his cheek. Considering his recent emotional disintegration, she was surprised at how well he appeared.

'How you feeling?'

Robert watched her reaction as she searched his expression.

'Feeling fine, thanks. What's up?' He resisted the urge to wrap his arms around her.

'You look *differente,*' she said.

I feel different.

'Do I?' he said.

'Yer late.' Rusty called in his usual gruff monotone.

'*Vaffanculo,*' Adelina mumbled and Robert snickered. He'd heard her aim that expletive at Rusty before.

'Held up,' he called back, and then whispered, '*Vaffanculo.*' Adelina slapped a hand over her mouth to muffle her laughter.

'Italiano,' Rusty yelled from the kitchen, 'here, NOW!'

'Sorry love,' Robert mouthed, fearing they had spoken too loudly, and he had landed her in trouble.

As Adelina turned towards the kitchen she realised that Robert had never before, to her knowledge, called her 'love'. He noticed an extra spring in her stride as she walked away, seemingly happy to receive another scolding.

'I'll get you out of here,' Robert whispered to her back.

Thirty minutes later, as the bar clock's hands clicked over to noon, Robert began to play his set to nobody but Rusty, Betty and Adelina, but of course they were busy being chef, manager and solo wait-staff, prepared optimistically for people to come through the door. Normally Robert wouldn't care, and yet today it irritated him. All of a sudden he wanted to be heard, just like he needed to be heard at Ned's Camp – and was by that intimate, attentive audience.

He sat in his usual place with the empty chair beside him, Hayley's guitar and Hayley's hat, the same Wheatsheaf views and the same Wheatsheaf smells. The place had been his link to society for years, he understood. The essence of the Wheatsheaf proved an integral part of the life, and *the beast,* he had created. He liked Betty and tolerated Rusty, and the same half-dozen old regulars who would ask him to play the same old songs whenever he was there. They were also a part of the brooding essence that had become Rob the Pom's universe.

But Robert Aitken decided he no longer wanted it, none of it, any more.

He played on autopilot as he looked around the room. Rusty was wiping smears from the bar with the same filthy cloth he'd just used to mop up a spill on the floor. Robert lowered his gaze, down past his guitar to his own well-worn trousers and shoes. Even in the dull light, he conceded, he was just as tired and unsightly as the Wheatsheaf itself. *A Tramp in an entirely different context*. He pulled his feet under the chair, as if that would hide his sudden shame about his appearance.

Adelina walked from the kitchen carrying a tray of clean glasses. She was different, he knew, and he wondered why she lingered. Did she, too, have her own *beast* to contend with? Too immersed in his own imploding universe, he had never before given that any consideration.

Why is she here, in Tasmania? Is she, too, running from something terrible?

That simply was not possible, he decided. Adelina had too much life in her, too powerful to allow a *beast* to come knocking on her bright door, and then invite it in. *But you never really know, do you?* Regardless, he had vowed to help her escape. Given the chance, perhaps he could do something real and good for a change.

So what was the difference, what was happening to him? At the conclusion of the song, as he tuned his guitar, he wondered if this new recognition that there was perhaps more to life than what he had made for himself was because he had finally given himself permission to move on. His head was telling him so, *and she* was telling him so, and he was certain *the beast* would not like it one iota.

There, at the end of the dark tunnel of his emotional myopia, sat this prism of coloured light, and it pulsated invitingly. With each shard of milling, rolling, twisting, colourful positivity, the churning cartwheels of depression were being displaced.

No, they were not being displaced, he told himself, *they were being dispensed with*. The all controlling *beast* was losing hold.

Wonderful thing, the imagination, he thought.

Yes, a wonderful thing, my love, her voice spoke softly in his head.

'Hello,' he said aloud.

'Hello,' a voice replied, and he looked up to see a couple had just taken their place at a table, assuming he was addressing them. They were young, well dressed and fresh faced.

'They must be lost,' he mumbled mischievously. Then, 'Great day,' he added with the hint of a smile.

Rusty looked up and studied Robert. Surprised at the performer's unusually positive manner, and still managed to look irritated. He watched Adelina, already on her way to greet the customers with her usual bouncing stride, and he wondered if her friendly smile was in some way broader due to this strangely different Rob the Pom.

The publican could not help feeling disgruntled by Rob the Pom's unexpected cheer.

Robert began to sing Simply Red's 'Holding Back the Years', a tale of sadness and regret. It had been one of Hayley's favourites, and usually he could not have contemplated performing it, but the last two days had changed a lot of things.

Rusty Faulkner was distracted from Rob the Pom for a while, being pleasantly surprised to see that more than half his tables were now occupied, and how well Adelina was coping on her own despite the extra numbers. He was feeling satisfied, considering he paid the hard-working woman a pittance. He always gave Robert cash-in-hand at well below what would be expected for a quality musician, too. *Good management*, he thought, as he envisaged achieving that elusive profit.

Betty toiled in the kitchen while Rusty leaned on the bar. He was, for a moment, considering that he might just get someone to fix that sign, when, at three-thirty, the doors opened, dispelling his pleasant musings in an instant. Samantha, Matthew, Nicky and Dennis walked through the door and over to the table they had adopted the day before. *Think they own the place*, Rusty scowled. As if Rob the Pom's demeanour wasn't already positive enough, now he was almost beaming. Rusty felt inexplicably insecure. He scowled again.

'*Ciao*,' Adelina greeted them.

How dare she wave, Rusty seethed, but wave she did and almost sprinted over to their table.

'Flat whites by four,' Samantha said with a grin. 'Hello Adelina, do you have cake?'

Adelina shook her head almost imperceptibly.

'No cake,' she whispered. 'Miss Betty have a bad day and Mr Rusty not help. We have biscuits with *cioccolato* – is good.'

'Ah,' Dennis said mischievously, 'bikkies sound tops, four of them, *per bleedin' favah*,' he said in London-flavoured, mock Italian.

Adelina smiled, and despite having her pencil poised over a small pad, as usual committed their orders to memory. As she turned to attend to a request from another table, Dennis dragged an extra chair across the floor from the table behind him and pointed to Robert. *Yours if you want to come over*, he mimed. Robert nodded and carried on with his set.

The musician took a short break. He wandered over to his new friends and said a brief hello before heading into the kitchen to see the Faulkners. After a few minutes he returned to the stage and played for another half hour, then switched off the compact amplifier and packed up.

CHAPTER TWENTY-ONE

The Pearson-Hooper party settled their bill and left, waiting in the car park until Robert emerged, guitar case in hand. When Robert had loaded the guitar into the Patrol's luggage compartment, Dennis closed the door and moved around to the front passenger side while Robert slid into the vacant back seat, next to Samantha.

As Nicky reversed from the parking space Samantha noticed Adelina, looking sad and lonely, watching them through one of the dining-room windows. She smiled briefly before turning away into the shadows.

'Is Adelina okay?' she asked.

'She'll survive,' Robert said. 'She's a tough cookie and it'll take more than Rusty's crankiness to upset her.'

'Does she have any friends?' Samantha waved to Adelina as they drove from the car park and onto the highway.

Robert shrugged. 'I'm embarrassed to say I don't really know, but after I picked up my dollars from Rusty I told Adelina I'd take her out to dinner tomorrow. Perhaps I'll find out more about her then.'

'Nice one, Robert,' Dennis winked into the rear mirror.

'It's her birthday, I know Rusty won't acknowledge it, and if Betty does, it will be on the quiet without him knowing.' Robert responded sharply, for a moment irritated by Dennis' manner. He suppressed a need to escape, to order them to stop, to get out and watch them drive away.

Breathe in my usual air of solitude. Wait for the beast to catch up so we can carry on, business as usual.

He felt nausea fluttering in his gut, slight but there all the same, and he recognised the need to tread carefully. Robert Aitken had been offered the opportunity for a very different future, as long as he could resist inviting his dreaded past back into his life. A future, he counselled himself as he sat in the window seat next to Samantha, different from anything that would have been in his wildest imagination only two days before. He folded his arms protectively.

After all, Dennis just banters, and there's the memory of Hayley and the tiny bird he knows nothing of just yet, he thought. *Besides, Adelina's got to be at least fifteen years younger than me.*

He shrugged to himself and tried to sound bright. 'It's only dinner to celebrate her special occasion.' He was not yet ready to accept that he did feel something for Adelina.

They pulled onto the highway and travelled in silence for a while. A question had formed in Matthew's mind but he changed it before he spoke.

'Do we need any provisions?' Instead of *Why not invite Adelina along?*

'Already sorted,' Nicky said. 'Retail therapy doesn't just involve mooching around knickknack shops at a snail's pace. We allocated time to whip through the supermarket to provide for our hunter husbands,' she added with a hint of mischief. 'Bags are at hubby's feet up the front here.'

Dennis turned the radio on. The piano introduction to 'Heaven Can Wait' had begun. *Wrong song at the wrong time*, Dennis decided, and quickly flicked the radio off.

'IPod choice, someone?'

Samantha scrambled to grab her player and find something upbeat.

Robert knew what was happening, knew the song and, yes, he realised they were trying to protect him. He was surprised he didn't feel patronised. Rather, their concern warmed him. Samantha must have picked the first track in alphabetical order: Aha's upbeat drums in 'Take on Me' thumped all too loudly through the speakers.

Robert noticed Dennis and Nicky sharing a glance that said *you've got to be kidding.* Even Matthew looked around at Samantha and, unable to help himself, Robert laughed, demanding, 'No, leave it on.' He began to sing along loudly and, as the song reached the falsetto section they all joined in, the discordant noise drowned only by their combined laughter.

Before they knew it Nicky had turned off the highway and stopped at the closed gate to Ned's Camp.

· · · · ·

As usual, the first chore was to fill the kettle and get water on the boil. Robert followed the other four into the annex and joined in with the general conversation, a stark contrast to the afternoon before.

'Fish again?' he dared to suggest.

'Yup,' Matthew agreed. 'Let's finish our drinks and grab the gear.'

· · · · ·

The fishermen returned after a half hour, and Dennis lifted the lid to the cooler box to show off their catch.

'What the hell is that?' Nicky recoiled.

'Eel.' Dennis said.

Nicky screwed up her face at the two dead creatures. 'I know what they are, you ninny, but I'm not going to eat them. What happened to catching proper fish?'

'We struck out,' Matthew said, 'but Robert landed these and reckons they taste brilliant.'

'Not a chance.'

'Come on love,' Dennis said. 'Robert says he knows how to prepare and cook them. For what it's worth I'm game, not to mention the poor things have already died for us.'

'There you go, mentioning it again,' Matthew grinned.

Robert nodded. 'Give it a try, Nicky. It really will be a nice meal.'

'Had eel in a Japanese restaurant once,' Samantha said, 'and yes it was delicious! Tell you what, let the boys cook that, we'll prepare some rice and veggies, and if you don't like it we can fry up some bacon for you in a flash.'

'I'm not happy,' Nicky pouted, 'but okay, on your head Robert, and if I don't like it you'll have to sing for your supper.'

'Reckon I'll be doing that anyway,' he shrugged.

Matthew set the fire as Robert artfully removed the slimy skin from the first eel. Dennis' attempt on the other was not so smooth and in the end Robert took over, and from there the rest of the preparation proved simple. Robert knitted eel fillets onto metal skewers, then basted them with soy and honey from sachets that Matthew had liberated from a previous hotel meal. Once the rice and other vegetables were ready, he cooked the eel over the open fire.

Samantha poured gin into five plastic glasses and served them with the meal. 'Sorry no *sake*,' she said, recalling the last time she had eel. 'Gin's the best Ned's Camp can offer.'

· · · · ·

'Okay, okay,' Nicky decided after she had finished her meal. 'You were right, it was tasty. I can't believe I just ate eel!'

While Dennis and Robert gathered the dishes and took them down to the lake, and Matthew rummaged beneath the trees for firewood, Samantha and Nicky prepared another round of hot drinks in the annex.

'How do you feel about tonight?' Samantha asked as she took a packet of biscuits from the shopping bag.

'A bit apprehensive, if I'm honest,' Nicky said. 'I can't wait to hear the rest of his story, but it's almost like I don't want to, because it's so personal.'

Samantha agreed. 'We heard a real campsite horror story last night, but Robert's hinted that there's more, and I fear something else tipped the scales, and sent him spiralling.'

Nicky watched Robert, apparently at ease as he and Dennis returned from the lake.

'He doesn't seem like the same person who told us that terrible tale last night, does he?'

He doesn't look like the same person who has been driven to despair and self-loathing, Samantha thought. 'No, he doesn't,' she said.

Robert gave them a smile through the annex window as he walked past and on to his car to store his gear away.

'Purpose to his stride,' Samantha watched, 'he looks committed.'

'To what?'

'To relate and, in his mind, repent, is my guess.'

The late afternoon remained clear and mild as they settled around the fire. Robert played a bracket of sing-along songs, taking ownership in a way that suited his voice and style of playing. He left an appropriate space between songs to allow for conversation, but would pick up when the mood suited him, or if he received a request.

They realised that, as he began each new song, none were his own. A continuation of Robert Aitken the entertainer, and not Robert Aitken the storyteller. They had, however, learned to show restraint, or patience, because he needed to do this at a pace he governed. While Robert sang, and they joined in, he was aware with every performance there was a limit of endurance, for both performer and audience.

Late-afternoon sun had dipped below the western ridge when Robert decided to take a break, for both himself and them, and while his guitar remained on his lap, he chose not to play it for some time.

Relaxed conversations were broken by periods of silence, during which the five friends gazed into the campfire, or followed spontaneous sparks as new timbers were introduced: flashes like dancing fireflies.

· · · · ·

Robert decided he could delay no longer. He poured two fingers of Drambuie into his mug, and sat back while he worked out where to, finally, resume his story. He put the mug at his feet without taking a drink, and searched for keys to unlock a few more allegorical doors.

'I had told them, the police, what happened that morning, before the accident.' His abrupt beginning surprised them. 'It was all dragged to the surface again during the inquest, how Hayley and I argued about the contract, our musical future, even our marriage.' Despite it being an inquest and not a trial, Robert had already assumed guilt. 'I might have even *admitted* to being guilty of murder, for all I remember.'

Robert inhaled and held his breath, as if he had decided never again to release, but he did, in a long, slow sigh.

'The coroner revealed that Hayley ... had been pregnant.'

'Oh God no.' Nicky spoke what the others were thinking.

Matthew absently poked at the fire with a stick, causing it to burn brighter. The cathartic glow washed over the companions, and for some time they sat without speaking.

'And you didn't know?' Dennis asked after a while.

'... had no idea ... wondered if Hayley knew.'

The crackle of the fire, again, took over the ambiance of Ned's Camp. None felt it would be proper to speak for some time.

'So you see,' he eventually continued, addressing them in turn, 'I, Robert Aitken, never sentenced and never served, at last confess to the murder of not only my wife, but our child as well.'

'I think you have served a very long sentence,' Samantha dared after a moment's reflection. 'Twenty years is enough.'

Robert lowered his face to stare at the ground, while his fingers worked around a simple tune, almost a baroque-style lullaby, the soft accompaniment to the words he sang in his head the night before. When his tune ended, the campsite sounds reverted to that of nature, and of fire.

'So, something as important, no, devastating, as this was kept from you?'

Dennis sounded angry. 'Why the hell would they do that?'

Robert shrugged. 'I have no idea why they would. At least I could have prepared myself...'

He recalled the room at that time, the gasps and murmurs, people turning in their seats to stare at him in shock, or pity, or judgement. Hayley's parents seemed to accuse with their looks, while his own mother and father chose to hang their heads instead of turning to him, which spoke the same condemnation, in his mind.

'To find out there, in that room of officials, family and strangers, made me feel even more like a criminal than I already did.

'And then fucking Bray appeared. He said whatever he saw fit, and the bastard seemed to be relishing the attention, like he enjoyed pointing the finger at me. Said he could tell Hayley didn't want to sign the contract ... I had badgered her, put her under too much pressure. It was an inquest,' Robert pleaded, 'but it felt like I was on trial ... twelve good men and true.'

'Could Hayley's pregnancy have accounted for her change of focus?' Samantha watched his manner carefully. 'Hormones controlling mind?'

Robert sighed. 'It had been suggested.'

'Poor woman,' Nicky said. 'Her subconscious telling her to start preparing a nest.'

'Perhaps she couldn't explain because she was too busy arguing with herself?' Matthew posed.

Nicky shook her head. 'What a nightmare. Poor Hayley.'

'Yes, and poor Robert,' Matthew added.

The inquest had officially determined that Hayley's car, colliding with the bridge pier, was an accidental fatality and not suicide. Robert would face no charges either way. Despite the findings, despite the authority's lack of interest in him specifically, nothing would assuage his self-condemnation.

'I probably looked and acted guilty, especially to her parents. They refused to speak to me, turned their back when I needed them.'

Robert had felt his own parents had alienated him, too, and that hurt him more than anything. He picked up his mug and took a drink.

'I didn't attend the funeral.' Robert's voice sounded groggy, although not because of the alcohol.

'You what?' Samantha could not hide her astonishment.

Her voice brought him back, and he shrugged. 'I sat outside during the service. I mean, I was a mess anyway and I didn't feel I deserved to be a part of it. Derry did come out to sit with me, but I just couldn't be in the presence of the Suttons, knowing they held me to blame for the deaths of their daughter and, as they now knew, their grandchild.'

Dennis shook his head. 'Robert, you should have been there.'

'Would you have, with all those people judging you?' Robert looked at Dennis, and guessed he would have been made of sterner stuff.

'For heaven's sake, Robert,' Samantha hesitated, 'Hayley was your wife and you loved her.' *No wonder you never found closure.*

'Everyone moved on to Hayley's parents' place, but I went to the grave and stayed there until it was dark. A lady, the churchwarden, came out twice from the rectory with drinks and something for me to eat. I remember feeling she was the only one to show me any friendliness.

'She came over to me a third time and asked if I needed a lift anywhere, as she was about to lock the gates.' Robert remembered it was raining heavily by then, and his clothes were saturated. He said no because he'd make her car seats wet. The churchwarden then escorted him beneath her umbrella and saw him out onto the street. As Robert turned away he heard the clink of the chain as it was secured around the gates, and for the first time imagined his cell door being locked.

'I can see now my negativity must've been hell for other people to contend with.' *Refusing to listen to anyone, or even respond to a smile.* 'I just hid myself away in my head, and in that flat, only going out when I needed to buy food.'

'Didn't anyone visit, offer support?' Matthew asked.

'Sometimes I answered the door.' *More often not.* 'I did let Derry in one time. He told me it was too painful to continue with the remnants of Hayley and the Tramp. Told me Pete had started working with another band. At the time I didn't care.'

Dennis hesitated before he asked. 'Devil's advocate here, Robert. Any chance people might not have turned their backs on you after all? Any chance you may've simply rejected them, built a wall around yourself?'

'That's not how my head saw it. I felt everyone was against me and refused to consider anything else. I had created the world I now lived in, and that was that.'

'What did you do with your time?' Nicky asked.

Robert recalled reliving that morning's events over and over and over, until he became physically ill doing it, but just couldn't stop himself.

'I'd sit in the same chair and speak to the empty one on the other side of the table.' He would talk to Hayley, saying out loud what he could, or should have said that day. Robert had shed tears of loss, regret, frustration and overwhelming guilt, but he decided that detail needn't be told.

'I did nothing much else, except I started to write a story.'

'Did you?' Samantha was surprised. 'As a distraction?'

'It was about how we had met and became a couple. The good times, the difficulties and ... how it all would come to a horrible end.'

'Do you have it with you?' she asked.

'I left it at the flat. Probably buried under a thousand tons of landfill by now ... After some months I started to drag myself from the gloom. You see, I had this need to do something for Hayley's memory and, despite what he'd done at the inquest, I wrote to Bray, hoping he'd give me the opportunity to record the music she had written, to honour the contract we had signed, to honour Hayley.

'The bastard's response was a crucifixion. He didn't need to say what he did, about me. Could have just said that, because Hayley was no longer a part of the equation, the contract was null and void. But no, he took the opportunity to stick the boot in again. He wrote that, in Donnington's opinion, Hayley was the talent, and it was she who they had really wanted. I was just a ten-a-penny backing musician, just a part player.'

'Did the arsehole actually say that?' Dennis gritted through his teeth.

'It's what he implied. There was no, "sorry for your loss," or, "it is with deep regret," or anything remotely human like that. Just matter-of-factly, "you were not the one we wanted and the contract will not be rewritten, so fuck off".'

'What a prize prick,' Nicky snapped, with more venom than Dennis or Samantha had ever heard from her.

'I slithered back into the hole I had dug for myself.' *Useless, unwanted, outcast.* 'Few friends, no family to console me, tell me everything'd be okay, and any solace I might have found in recording our music had been denied me by Bray.'

Yes, of course they might not have condemned me. I can see that now. Perhaps they simply gave up trying.

It doesn't matter now. 'I lost my wife, my unborn child, my career, my family – and the plot.'

'So, what happened?' Nicky wished she'd held her tongue the moment the words had left her mouth.

Dancing flames reflected in Robert's eyes. 'I walked away ... the tatters of my life in London ... had already buried Hayley ... the trauma ... couldn't move on from the funeral ... felt so alienated.'

He scratched his beard, took a drink.

'At the flat, I read Bray's letter again, over and over. It was late when I went back to the graveyard, scaled the wall and stayed until the early hours of the next morning, just being close to Hayley and our child.

'By the time the sun had risen I'd made a decision to leave. Not just to get away from the flat, but from the city that held all those memories and the people that pointed the fingers. I went back home, threw some clothes, papers and things into my rucksack, slung Hayley's guitar on my back and the rucksack across my chest and picked up my guitar. As I walked through the door for the last time, I grabbed one of Hayley's stage hats and slipped it into an old box and put it in the rucksack. Everything else I left behind. Clothes, photographs, every useless, unnecessary fucking thing that was our life. I walked to the station, stepped onto the first train to anywhere, and never looked back.'

CHAPTER TWENTY-TWO

'Where did you end up?' Matthew asked.

'Falmouth.'

'Where's Falmouth?' Nicky asked. *Shut up idiot*, she thought, all too late.

'Cornwall, love,' Dennis answered.

'You see?' Robert went on. 'Remember the song I played to you last night, "Cottage by the Sea"?'

'Powerful imagery,' Samantha said.

'Well, I found one just outside a village near Falmouth, a cottage near the sea, and I thought I'd rediscover myself there. I thought I'd be able to mourn Hayley without anyone around to judge me. It wasn't exactly a romantic hideaway. I shared the place with more rodents than you could possibly imagine.'

The cottage was little more than an old cowshed that the farmer who owned it had begun to renovate, but had lost interest in. In reality the building was hardly liveable but the farmer gave Robert permission to stay as long as he needed – without his official knowledge or he might have found himself in trouble with the authorities.

'The windows were all broken or cracked, the doors were half rotten and hard to close.' He recalled the holes in the stonework. The cottage was dank and freezing in winter and there was no electricity.

'The way the wind whistled and moaned through the place, it was like a theremin symphony, and in bad weather the place was almost unbearable.'

Dennis laughed. 'You wrote a beautiful song about dreams and closeness, from a shithole?'

'I wrote about a dream we had, plans for the future. It had to come out, regardless of the actual setting.'

Nicky had to ask. 'Sorry Robert, what's a theremin?'

'A musical instrument.'

'Remember "Good Vibrations"?' Matthew suggested. 'The Beach Boys used it for those weird sounds. Jimmy Page from Led Zeppelin used a theremin on a few of their recordings too, such as "Whole Lotta Love".'

Samantha looked at her husband and shook her head. 'Jeez, is there anything you don't know?' She turned to Robert and asked, 'Robert, how did you get by?'

'I had a few quid in my bag, and there was a decent pub within walking distance so I'd sing there and get enough to feed myself. They were a nice bunch down there. Polite enough, but generally left me to be myself.'

'How long did you stay?' Dennis asked.

'Two years I think, maybe three, I can't really remember. Some locals were kind. One guy used to bring me wood for the burner whenever I needed, and I repaid him with guitar lessons. The farmer's wife, a lovely old dear called, er ... Mildred, that was it. She used to bring me hotpots and occasionally invited me to join them for a Sunday roast. I'd do a bit of labouring for them if they needed help. Now and then the farmer dropped by with a load of timber and stuff on the tractor and we'd spend the day fixing the place up a bit. First the roof, then the draughts. By the time I left it was still a hovel, but less damp and at least held in the heat when I had the fire going.

'Though I felt like it was the best place for me to be at the time, I did meet someone I didn't care for, who has stuck with me ever since.'

Samantha understood. 'It's been with you that long?'

'What are you talking about?' Matthew asked.

'*The beast*,' Robert said, as if that answered all their questions.

Nicky expected another story, like the ghoulish tales the boys would tell. 'I'm afraid to ask, Robert, but what the hell is *the beast*?'

Robert considered his response. 'What one deserves? Punishment? A life sentence.'

Nicky made no sense of the riddles. 'I still don't follow.'

Samantha could see Robert was struggling, and didn't want to name it, but she felt he needed to in order to move on. He had progressed so far in the past twenty-four hours, and she was mindful just how much this could be taking out of him.

'Robert?' she asked. 'May I?'

She took his shrug as an invitation.

'You may have heard,' Samantha began, 'about Sir Winston Churchill's *black dog*? A metaphor for his depression, the thing that lurked behind him, taking the light and hope out of his world. He openly discussed it and to him the black dog was a very real entity, controlling his moods, and perhaps even his decision-making. Robert's *beast* is just as powerful, dark and oppressive. It first revealed itself all those years ago, while he was living in that cottage.'

As if to justify his decades-long silence, Robert said, 'I always felt men weren't supposed to talk about that sort of thing,' – he began to play a slow blues progression – 'so I wrote this, one afternoon last year. Decided if I couldn't take the piss, then I was doomed.'

I've got a beast, makes my highs disappear
When he nibbles at my brain and he pisses in my ear
Been a permanent fixture since coming to stay
Twenty long years, morning night and day
I wish he would leave, but the beast, he just won't go away.

He's over my shoulder, impossible to ignore
He drags me through the mud when this body wants to soar
The beast he belittles, the beast he bemoans
I've come to understand he's a devil to disown.

I wish he would leave, but the beast, he just won't go away

'Try to remove him from out of your head
I've got a friend,' the bartender said
When I sat on her couch it was as clear as it could be
As I looked into her eyes I saw her beast smile back at me
She had her own beast, and I guess it just won't go away.

I saw it there ghostly, a noose around her neck
Her attitude was ragged; disposition was a wreck
No point in remaining, no help for me here
Got up from my chair, into the night I disappeared.

Now I'm walking the streets as alone as I can be
The beast is right here and his shadow follows me
I've been wondering if he's lonely and needs company
I guess he can stay but best stop nagging me.

I call him the beast and that's his disguise
Why should I care when he doesn't sympathise?
I wish he would leave, but the beast, he just won't go away.

'I don't think there's anything to be ashamed of,' Dennis said. 'Even famous people own up to theirs. Shit, truth time,' he cleared his throat, 'I had a visit from a *black dog* in my twenties and, while I can't pretend it was as vicious as yours, I have an inkling of what he's put you through.'

Despite his tough London exterior, Dennis would occasionally show the sensitive, caring side to his character, which was one of the traits that had attracted Nicky to him.

'I love you, you big lug,' she said to her husband.

'Aw, shucks!'

'Did you talk to someone about it, like in the song?' Matthew asked, but Robert shook his head.

Samantha looked at Robert, and with some satisfaction said, 'Well, it's a good thing you're doing it now.'

'So, that makes us the best experts you've known, then,' Dennis said with an exaggerated wink.

Robert sat back and looked at them in turn. 'Where the hell did you people come from? This is, frankly, unbelievable.' He stood and placed the guitar on his chair. 'I need to take a pee.' He turned and headed off into the dark surrounds of Ned's Camp.

Nicky waited until he was far enough away, before she whispered, 'We can't just say goodbye tomorrow and leave him to it.'

'You're right,' Samantha agreed.

Dennis glanced over to where Robert had walked into the darkness. 'So, what do we do then?'

'I don't know,' Nicky shrugged. 'We just can't waltz into his world, be here for him to spew out all this to, and then disappear again.'

'So, we adopt him? Harry might get jealous.'

'Not funny, Dennis,' Nicky said.

'It's true,' Samantha reasoned, 'he doesn't have much of a life here, and I can't see him moving on in his head unless he changes his environment.'

'We could at least try and open some doors for him,' Matthew said, 'like suggest he move to a larger town where there may be better opportunities. Or, perhaps,' he paused, 'even see if we can help reopen a few old doors?'

'I don't follow,' Samantha said.

'You know, back in London.'

'Oi, Wonder boy,' Dennis spread his arms, 'we live in bloody Tasmania now mate, not Fulham ...'

'Shush,' Samantha hissed.

He lowered his voice. 'Seriously Matt, we haven't seen the place for a few years, and more to the point, what if he would prefer to leave those doors shut? We've no idea how it might be received, by Robert or the people on the other side.'

Samantha pressed a finger to her lips. 'No, but we have a telephone and the three w's, don't we? And we have some names. It can't hurt to just make a few enquiries.'

'Does anyone remember the names he mentioned?' Nicky asked. 'One was Gerald Bray?'

'Who we gonna call?' Matthew sang.

'Not Gerry,' Dennis snorted.

'I tell you what,' Matthew said. 'When we get home I'll do some searching, see if I can locate Derry Derricks.'

'Derrick,' Nicky corrected him, 'without the 's'. If we're to find him, we need to be specific.'

'I don't think we tell Robert just yet,' Samantha said. 'Just in case it scares him away.' They nodded their agreement. 'At least find out if anyone remembers, or is interested, first.'

'Hey,' Nicky said. 'He's been gone for some time. Should someone go look for him?'

Dennis looked over to where Robert had walked off. 'Give him another few minutes then I'll give him a holler.'

'I'll put the kettle on and break the seal on a red,' Matthew said.

Robert had still not returned by the time they had resumed their places by the fire.

'Tea's up, Robert,' Dennis called, but there was no response. Another minute passed when Dennis stood and said, 'I'll go for a butcher's.'

'Wait,' Samantha began, 'I'll go, if it's all the same to you, because I think I know where he'll be. Pass me the head light and his drink.'

She slid the strap around her forehead and switched the light on, picked up two mugs and left the glow of the campfire. As expected, she found him sitting down at the water's edge, gazing towards the dead tree.

'Want some company, Robert? I've got your tea.'

'Thanks,' he said, and gestured to the sand next to him. Its dampness seemed not to matter to him.

Samantha sat and flicked her head light off. 'Are they safely locked away?' she asked.

'Gone AWOL again,' Robert said.

'Hmmm,' she gazed across the black surface, not quite knowing if she should say anything more.

'She's still with me though.'

Who?'

'Hayley is. Hayley is still with me,' Robert sighed, 'almost as if she came to fight them, and has sent the bastards packing.'

'You almost sound disappointed they're not around.'

'Not at all, but Hayley's voice is so real, so comforting. I almost believe she is really here.'

'Maybe she is.'

'Christ, of course she's not. She's dead, remember? I feel a complete idiot just talking about her as if she was. The weird thing is, you know, it's not like her voice says things I expect her to. It's like I can have this conversation with her, but not know what she's going to say. She says stuff I might not have considered; stuff I wouldn't say. So doc, does that make me a lunatic?'

Samantha allowed his spoken thoughts to settle for a moment. 'I don't think you are,' her head turned a fraction towards those sitting around the fire, 'nor do they.'

She waited for a moment. 'Why are you here, alone?'

Again, silence. 'Robert?'

'My mind is reeling. You four have shown me something I thought I would never feel or see again, and it scares me.'

'The company scares you?'

'No. All this, the campfire, the company, the laughter. Finally finding my voice to talk about the past. After all this time I feel a part of something, and it's all about to come to an end.'

'Nothing has to,' Samantha whispered. 'Robert, this is all down to you. Either Hayley has come back to drag you back into the light, or you have manifested her as a weapon to help you do it yourself. Either way it's one hell of a positive change.'

He turned to her. 'And you don't think to take some of the credit?'

'Nothing I, or we, have said or done would have meant a thing to you unless you were receptive.' She squeezed his forearm. 'You, Robert, are doing it all yourself.'

'No,' Robert demanded, 'don't you understand? I don't have the strength to do this alone. There is some connection to Hayley's voice and you. She seems to have been more, er, present while you've been around, and I fear when you go, return to your own life, she'll pull back, or even go with you.'

'Hasn't she been around talking to you before I came on the scene?'

'Well, yes, but not quite as much. Samantha, there still seems to be a link between you and her.'

Samantha felt uncomfortable that Robert thought she was somehow associated with Hayley, even if only in his mind.

'I don't think you should allow that to confuse things, Robert,' she said. 'You see, I don't hear her. Hayley doesn't speak to me. In whatever way she is with you, it is for you and it is not from me. Perhaps she's with you more because you are getting stronger.'

As if he hadn't heard Robert said, 'I don't want her to go. I don't want you to go either.'

She didn't follow his reasoning. If he had been thinking she and Hayley were really the same entity, she had to put a stop to it.

'I've only helped you re-find yourself. You have to deal with it the best way you can.'

Robert turned to her silhouette. 'Sam, don't misunderstand me, I'm not falling for you or anything and I don't think you are Hayley reborn.' He didn't say that Samantha reminded him of Hayley, her build, her mannerisms and ... something in her eyes. *It was there the first time we met.*

Samantha exhaled slowly. 'Robert, I can't quite explain this because it doesn't make sense. There is something about us, the five of us, and I'm sure we've all felt it. Our friendship seems to span more than the two days it has. We're all feeling sad that this weekend is coming to a close, but that doesn't mean our friendship has to. When we leave tomorrow to go back to our homes, that won't be goodbye if you don't want it to be. Now, come back to the fire, play some more music if you like and let's share a glass, relax for the rest of this night, and work out tomorrow how we can keep in touch.'

They wandered back to the campsite. Robert picked up the guitar, went through his ritualistic tuning, and strummed a few chords.

He looked up. 'I have to say something to you all, in case the opportunity doesn't present itself tomorrow. You have been great, er, company, not that I've kept much of it of late. Don't think I'm not aware what you have all done for me. I will never forget these two days.'

It was Nicky who spoke first, despite her having the deepest reservations about the strange, brooding man.

'You are a good person, Robert, caught in a kind of inescapable spiral for far too long. Go on,' she said before she started sobbing, 'play us something.'

Robert closed his eyes and started to sing.

· · · · ·

Dennis woke, surprised to discover it was past eight. He slipped into a pair of track pants and donned a pullover. Still, he thought he was the first to greet the day.

'Coffee.' Nicky's muffled voice demanded from within her sleeping bag.

'One too many last night?' Dennis asked mischievously.

'Double sugars and don't be cheeky,' she said.

'Pssst, you awake?'

'Yup,' Matthew whispered, 'Sam's still snoring.'

'Don't talk to me about snoring.' Samantha had heard through her nonperforming earplugs.

'Heart-starters coming up,' Dennis said as he unzipped the thin, coated nylon partition door to the annex. He looked towards Robert's swag and could see the flysheet was open. 'You up, Robert?'

'I am.' The voice came, not from the direction of his swag, but from around the side of the annex. Dennis turned and saw Robert returning from the lake, evidence of a morning dip in his wet and tied-back hair. Dressed in fresh clothes, he carried a bag containing his toiletries in one hand and a towel in the other.

'Tea?'

'Yes please, be with you in a minute,' Robert said as he walked on past, towards his car. Becoming overwhelmed by one of his usual waves of alienation, he needed to sit, encapsulated by his own sensory world. It could have invited *the beast* back, but he needed that security nonetheless. *Only for a moment*, he told himself.

To Robert's relief *the beast* had stayed away, and after barely two minutes, wrapped in the familiarity of his car, he felt better able to face the morning, and his new companions.

· · · · ·

After a substantial cooked breakfast, they began packing up, with Robert enjoying the challenge of finding where to store things away for the journey. Robert would need to know for the next time. Robert prayed there would be a next time.

He unpegged, rolled and stored his swag in its carry bag, and into the back of his wagon. He cleaned his teeth and then joined the others to help with any last chores, noticing the chairs were still in a circle around the fire's ashen stones.

'Bring those in?'

'Reckon we've time for one last ceremonial parting drink,' Matthew said, tapping his wrist, which did not have the usual watch strapped to it.

With hot brews in hand, they made themselves comfortable one last time around the fire, this time at least.

'Cheers, everyone,' Dennis raised his mug and took a noisy sip. 'So, how did you find your way to this fair isle?'

'D'you want the long or short version?'

'I'm sure we've got time if you have,' Samantha said, looking to her companions for their approval.

They agreed with nods or smiles, and settled back in their chairs.

For once Robert sat without his guitar as moral support, and when he decided he was okay with that, began.

'Once *the beast* came to visit, I couldn't stay anywhere for long. No matter how new, or fresh, it would always feel wrong, almost as if wherever I went became contaminated by me. I remember hitchhiking around southern England but have no idea where. I do recall finding my way across the channel to France, then I just kept going.'

'To where?' Nicky asked.

'I didn't care; I was just trying to escape. I scored some work at bars playing music and being dish pig. At one place, a café in a village south of Lyon, the owners, a brother and sister called Zoé and Thomas, felt sorry for me when they discovered I was dossing in the shed where they kept the bins. They gave me a room and I stayed with them for some time.

'I helped out in the café, doing kitchen work and cleaning up around the place, and would sing for their customers on a Friday night. Life became quite good for me. Actually, Zoé and I had a relationship.'

Robert noticed Samantha raise her brows.

'I was only dead from the neck up,' he said.

She understood Robert had attempted a joke, although nobody laughed.

'But *the beast* found me and dug his claws in ... I had an urge to move on that was impossible to ignore. And that was that I suppose.

'I kept in touch with them over the years, sent them the occasional letter, even a photo once. Really, they are the only people who know where I am – from my old life, that is. In fact, it was so difficult travelling with two guitars, I left mine for them to look after.'

'Wow, that's some trust!' Dennis said.

'I had belief in them.'

'Why yours?' Nicky asked.

'I couldn't possibly leave Hayley's behind, could I?'

'So you moved on where?' Matthew asked.

'Kept heading east through northern Italy, but not because I was actually going somewhere, if you know what I mean. Every time I felt like settling, every time I'd start to relax, I'd be moved on by my inability to shake off that unwanted companion.'

'So, Robert Aitken has been on the run from himself for twenty years?' Dennis suggested.

'There was a time *the beast* wasn't with me. I found myself in Turkey ...'

'Turkey?' more than one of them exclaimed.

'Istanbul. I was working in this dump of a fish restaurant with three guys who'd all served in the Gulf War. Two were British ex-special forces, one a Geordie and the other from Edinburgh. The third was a demobbed Australian sapper. They were bloody tough but bonkers all the same. To accompany anything on their menu, they served *raki*, but of course you could get any kind of drink you fancied, you just needed to know who to ask. I've never drunk so much in my life,' he chuckled.

'Then, one day they had this harebrained idea of taking their old beaten-up Land Cruiser across into Iran, and asked me if I fancied a drive.'

'Why?' Nicky gasped.

'I asked the same question. "To see how far we get," one of them said.'

'And you said no,' Nicky demanded, almost motherly.

He shrugged, 'I had nothing better to do, did I?'

'You feckin' lunatic,' Dennis laughed, more with reverence than insult. 'The entire region was a bleedin' melting pot and you decide to go for a bloody Sunday drive?'

Robert grinned. 'Yes, but what therapy! I was so shit scared for weeks, *the beast* was too gutless to show his face.'

'I'm guessing you didn't dip your toe in, then back out to the safety of the bar?' Samantha asked.

'No, we kept moving southeast, through Iran and out the other side into Pakistan and India.'

Matthew whistled. 'Bloody Norah! Carrying Hayley's guitar and all?'

Robert nodded.

'How the hell did you not get caught, get through Iran, their borders?' Nicky said, shaking her head.

Robert shrugged. 'Who dares wins, I gather. First thing they did was find an abandoned truck and switch the plates. Maybe it was their training, and seeming lack of fear. They were very good at evading detection, blending in with the scenery as it were.

'We met some good people, normal. You know, like taking a weekend drive through the country, stop to ask a farmer for directions and he gives you fresh milk for your tea? Well, rural Iran wasn't that different.'

'Apart from a distinct lack of hedgerows, Jersey cows and sixteenth-century pubs?' Matthew joked.

'And I gather the Iranian coppers are not particularly receptive to the infidel dropping by for a singalong?' Dennis suggested, and Robert grinned.

'Not everyone was nice though?' Nicky suggested.

'Of course not, but we met some good, if nervous, people who seemed comfortable with the genuine friendliness of these larrikins. We were given food and sometimes a bed in exchange for music, a bit of muscle around the place and, well, fresh faces I suppose. Ash McBride, the Scot who served in the SAS, could speak a bit of Pashto and Balochi. It was funny listening to his refined Edinburgh accent trying to converse with Iranian people in their own language.

'They love their music, the Iranians, and they really embraced my playing.

Any excuse seemed a good reason to get their own instruments out to join me. Nobody knew what the other was doing, but it was great all the same.'

Robert paused to look over the lake to the dead tree, remembering that strange time living on the edge, singing, laughing, while expecting the military, or *the beast*, to smash the door in at any moment.

'Anyway, we never stayed more than a night anywhere because it could have been dangerous for us, and anyone who took us in – and you were right, Dennis, the locals were nervous when the Shahrbani were out and itching to kick down another door.

'One time we were ushered into a cellar, when word got around that they were coming. Nothing happened, but I wasn't asked to play again that night, and we left pretty early the next morning.'

'What are Shahrbani?' Samantha asked.

'Military police,' Robert said, 'or just young thugs dressed up like them.'

'Did the guys have any means to protect you if something nasty happened?' Matthew asked.

'Oh yes. Look, before they joined the forces these were probably the nicest, most normal characters you could ever meet, only their training gave them another personality.' Robert would never experience it directly, their silent abilities, but he sensed their underlying strength in the way they carried themselves. 'Don't get me wrong, they weren't full of themselves or anything, but I couldn't help but feel safe around them. Not to mention a number of formidable weapons hidden on their person, and in the truck.'

'Bet you were glad to get out of the place?' Nicky asked.

Robert shrugged. 'I felt relieved at the time, to be finally leaving Iran's borders, but we found just as much unrest in other, not so newsworthy countries along the way.'

Dennis laughed. 'Now I'm not saying I doubt the truth behind your story, Robert, but it seems amazing that you and these guys were able to slide your way through all these countries without permission, or detection. How the hell did you not go and get yourself arrested as illegal aliens or spies, or just plain murdered?'

'Oh, I agree with you, Dennis,' Robert said. 'Looking back I have exactly the same thoughts. But we did, and I could never put myself through it again, because second time around I'd not likely be so fortunate.'

He scratched at his beard. 'We found ourselves in Thailand, and that place was no picnic at the time either. Finally, we moved on to Singapore and hung around for a while. While we were there Nick Barker, the sapper, learned his dad was ill and he decided to fly back to Western Australia. I suppose he wanted some company, and because the Brits had chosen to stay in Singapore, he asked if I wanted to, as he said, pop over with him. He paid my airfare. I had to get my facts straight before I was granted a visa.'

'The Consulate?' Dennis asked.

'Yes, they were polite and helpful, but wanted to be convinced about me. It took a few weeks but they eventually said yes.

'We arrived in Perth in January of, I think, ninety-eight. A stinking hot and windy day, if my foggy memory serves. We were about to get into a taxi to his parents' place in Armadale when he made a call to his sister to let them know he wasn't far away, but she told him they were all at the hospital and Nick's dad had just died. I couldn't stand the thought of being a gooseberry at a wake so told Nick I'd leave him to it. We shared the taxi to the hospital, and that's where I said my goodbyes to him, and headed off to who knew where.'

'What a sad way to part,' Nicky said, and Robert closed his eyes, as if to say a momentary prayer to Nick and his departed father.

'I'm guessing the transition from Perth to here was more of the same?' Dennis suggested.

Robert nodded. 'Those more recent memories are a little clearer to me. I spent some time in Perth before hitching across the Nullarbor, and spent a year or two in South Australia. I busked in the Adelaide mall, played in a pub on some seedy street, and was dish pig and entertainment in a hotel in some small town in the Flinders Ranges.

'I moved on to Broken Hill for a month, headed south to Mildura, and kept on going until one day I stood on a pier in Melbourne, looking at this big red and white ship bound for Tasmania.'

'So, how did you get the other guitar here?' Nicky asked.

'I had been living here for a while, then one day, on the spur of the moment, I wrote to Zoé, and she sent the guitar to me, at the Wheatsheaf.'

'Great people,' Dennis said.

Robert's eyes glazed for a moment. 'Yes, they are. Zoé enclosed a letter, telling me she was married with a child.'

'How did you feel about that?' Samantha asked, sounding a little too clinical for her liking.

Robert shrugged. 'Very happy for her.' When he noticed Samantha's surprise he added, 'Okay, just a little sad.'

Samantha opened her hands. 'And here you are.'

'And here you are, too,' Robert said, 'and I know next to nothing about you all. I've waffled on for hours on end and I know nothing about you sisters, and only have an inkling about Dennis and Matthew here. But I've been the gasbag and we've probably run out of time.'

Robert did not want this to end but knew it had to. He wanted to drop a hint about seeing them again, but found there was no need.

'Fancy doing this again some time?' Samantha asked.

'I would really like that,' Robert said, 'But I have a feeling I won't be up here for much longer.'

'Where are you going?' Nicky asked, imagining Robert stowing away on a ship bound for anywhere.

'I can't tell when or where, Nicky. But you people have helped break the spell, and the thought of going back to my place, or even the Wheatsheaf, is daunting.'

'I'm not surprised,' Nicky said as she conjured up sights and smells of the dingy pub.

'I suppose you don't have a phone?' Samantha asked.

'Never had the need.'

'Have to do something about that,' Matthew said.

Robert peered at the cracked glass of his watch. 'It's eleven-thirty. I suppose I should leave you good people to it.'

'Robert,' Samantha began, 'this has been an amazing experience.' They all nodded in agreement. 'It's strange how you feel like family, and I for one don't want to lose you.'

Robert wanted to hug them all, and so he did. He said his goodbyes more than he needed to, slid into the driver's seat, closed the door and, as he switched the ignition, Matthew called, 'Hey, wait!' He grabbed a business card from the glove box of their vehicle and handed it to him. 'Find a phone and, please, let us know where you are. If you ever make your way down south ...'

'Or Longford,' Dennis added.

'Please let us know.'

'Just call us anyway,' Nicky said, her eyes welling with tears.

Samantha reached out and touched Robert's forearm as it rested on the open window frame. 'We'll come back as soon as we can Robert, and will look for you at the Wheatsheaf.'

Robert wiped his eyes, not tears of anxiety or sadness, just tears of longing. 'I'll call. I promise I will.'

He swung the car around and carefully negotiated his way over the flat rock and on down the rough track.

'Well, that's about it,' Dennis said as the sound of Robert's motor became distant. 'We've got things to discuss.'

CHAPTER TWENTY-THREE

Robert and Adelina arrived at the Wharf Hotel and ordered drinks at the bar before making their way to a window table in the dining room.

Something about his manner made Adelina curious.

'Roberto, you okay?' she asked after they had settled.

Robert opened his weathered jacket and took a small posy from the inside pocket and presented it to her.

'Happy birthday, Adelina. These are for you.'

He handed her the posy of late season wild blooms, picked from his garden and held together with twine.

'Flowers, for me?' The flowers looked the worse for wear after being hidden away, but she was nonetheless delighted with his gift.

'Yes, flowers for you.' He watched as she turned the posy in her hand, and then held it up to her nose.

He hesitated, feeling awkward. 'I suppose you know I don't make many friends, but you have been a support to me since we met. Whether you know it or not, I think of you as a friend. So on that note, happy birthday.'

She was perplexed by the positivity in his manner; it was almost as if a stranger sat before her. She took the purse from her backpack, more to distract herself, and checked her cash.

'*Scusa*,' he said, shaking his head. 'This is your day, and I will be paying.'

'No, no no no,' she said with a frown.

'*Sì, sì, sì, sì*,' he smiled, then finished with a poor imitation of Rusty's gruff voice. 'My shout, Italiano.'

Adelina laughed and absently flicked her hair from her face. She picked up the menu and started to thumb through.

'Okay Mister Rusty, I order something really cheap.'

'Oh no you won't.' Robert playfully snatched the menu from her hand as the waiter approached the table, and ordered for them both despite her protestations. He was determined to spend more than he could afford, if it ensured she felt appreciated for a while.

'You like Samanta, and the others?' she said, knowing he had left with them the day before.

'Yes, I like *Samanta*,' he answered, studying her expression. 'They have all been very good to me, like you are good to me.' He raised his glass. 'Cheers to you, welcome to the new me.'

'You need haircut,' she returned with a frown, and he laughed.

'Adelina, where do you come from?'

'You know, Italia. Why you ask?'

He ran his hand down his beard. 'I don't know anything about you. I was just wondering where, in Italy?'

She hesitated, and then shrugged. 'Ah, just a small town. You not know of it.'

He didn't press her. 'Do you have brothers or sisters?'

'Pietro my brother who is older, Concettina, little sister; we call Cocco.'

'Cocco, that means cook?'

'No, it is, eh, name for loved one. Why you ask?'

'Do you keep in contact with them?'

She smiled, feeling bashful because of his attention. 'I write Cocco and mama letters.'

'And, they write back?'

'No, I not give them address. Mister Rusty not like.'

'Well, Meester Rusty ees prick.'

She laughed at his poor Italian-English inflections. 'You funny man sometimes, Roberto.'

Robert hesitated. He wanted to ask her something more personal, but wasn't sure if his reluctance was because of a decades-old need to keep his distance, or simply because he did not want to hear the answer.

'Do you, um, have a boyfriend back in, where was it in Italy?' Adelina's smile wavered. 'Oh I'm sorry, I shouldn't have asked.'

Adelina turned and looked through the window, across the road to the boats swaying gently at their berth; her eyes appeared cold as marble. Robert felt awkward, felt *the beast* stir, felt the need to make his retreat, but he could not.

I must not do that, ever again. 'Forget I asked, Adelina.' He reached over and touched her fingers, but she did not respond.

Despite the discomfort, Robert refused to flee from there, or himself.

'I try to forget about *him*,' she whispered finally. She turned back to Robert, and could see that, he too, had withdrawn. She knew nothing of the weekend, nothing of his life story or the weight he carried, but began to place together the pieces of an enigmatic puzzle. She decided he had a need to talk, and so she relented.

'Salvestro Nicolai, my husband. He handsome man, like in the movies, but when we marry he show other side, jealous and mean. He beat me when say I look at other men. I have fear and hurting until one day I leave Salve and go back to mama. He come to our home and make threats to hurt me, hurt my family. I leave Italia, go far away so he cannot find me, and hope he leave my family alone. I also not tell mama address in case he find me.'

Robert sat in disbelief that Adelina, so full of energy and positivity, could be running from a beast. *So, she has her own after all, but this one made from flesh, bone and blood.* He reached for her hand again and this time she did not withdraw.

'I am so sorry,' he whispered.

'You not ask again? I not want to speak of it.'

'I promise not to ask again, but if you ever want to talk ...' He left the offer hanging, held his glass towards her. She raised her own and they touched lightly.

'Cheers, Adelina, let's put this behind us tonight.'

Adelina's smile returned and she nodded. Still, Robert wished he had not delved into her life. *It might be what she needs, my love*, the beautiful voice in his head spoke, and Robert tried not to let his reaction at her returning show on his face.

· · · · ·

While Robert and Adelina were sharing a meal and a deeper understanding of each other, Matthew and Samantha, Dennis and Nicky sat at their respective dining tables on a conference phone call. They discussed the past few days, which were dominated by the tragic tale of Rob the Pom.

'You could bleedin' well write a book about this stuff,' Dennis said.

'Or a musical,' Nicky sighed.

'A story needs a resolution, and musicals sort of demand a happy ending, don't they?' Dennis said.

'So what are we going to do about it?' Matthew asked.

'Find the solution,' Samantha said, 'so Nic can write her musical.'

Dennis leaned forward and drew invisible circles on the tabletop. 'I wager Derry is the key. I'm going to give Gabe a call and sound him out.'

'How is Gabe going?' Matthew asked, 'haven't spoken to him in years.'

'Going well, just like his daft brother,' Nicky laughed, poking Dennis in the ribs.

'I guess we can all do our own net surfing and pool our findings,' Samantha suggested. 'Sis, on the way home from Ned's, Matt and I talked about maybe coming up to your place for the weekend, in a couple of weeks, if it's okay. We can chat about Robert and help out with the renos while we're there.'

'Sounds great, Sam,' Dennis said, 'looking forward to it already.'

· · · · ·

'You pus-filled sewer rat,' Dennis roared down the telephone.

'Well, butter my arse and call me a cracker, if it isn't Denuair Tubthumper,' Gabe Hooper responded in his best attempt at a middle-class voice. 'What's afoot, brother? How are the Antipodes?'

'All good here bro, not that you give a toss.'

'Hello Gabe,' Nicky said, 'I'm well, thanks for asking.'

''Allo gawjus,' Gabriel said, the finishing-school accent suddenly giving way to his natural working-class drawl.

'Still a member?' Dennis asked Gabe.

'What, a country member?'

'Spurs, you muppet. The biggest thing I miss about England is walking through the turnstiles at White Hart Lane.'

'Sure am still a member, Den, the four of us are, and bloody 'ell it puts a dent in our pockets, but none of us would change anythin'.'

'Well, that's a turn up for the books,' Dennis said. 'I knew your boys took after their football nut dad, but yer missus never used to show much interest, as far as I remember.'

'Some of the older lads still ask after you, by the by.'

'That's nice. Say 'allo to those who remember, will you?'

'Sure will. Get to see any games on teev?' Gabe asked.

'See three or four a week on pay TV. Not like being there, though.'

'How 'bout you Nicky, follow the game?'

'Not really Gabby. I like Didier Drogba but Dennis gives me grief when I say anything about him, because he plays for the bad guys.'

'Ah, Monsieur Fall-down-a-lot, and we all hate him because he's not playing for us. So, chaps, what's been happenin'? How's the gallery goin'?'

'Should be up and running early next year,' Nicky said.

Gabe chuckled, 'A bloody 'Ooper running an art gallery. Still can't get my head around it.'

'Yes, well, you can just shut your cake hole. I'm sick of hearing Pearson here giving me grief about it, so you can leave it out.'

'Matt bloody Pearson,' Gabe said. 'How's that big girl's blouse goin'?'

'He's fine, Gabe, but we actually have something to discuss with you.'

'Not anuvver bleedin' bank robbery?'

Dennis laughed, 'Not quite, but no chance of a jail sentence attached to this one. We were hoping you could do some leg work for us.'

Gabe hesitated. 'Go on.'

'Remember Piggins Hit?'

'The band? Sure I rememba but would sooner not, Den. I'm a lot younger than you don't forget, and punk'd well and truly gone by the time I cared about music.'

'Bear with me, bro. Do you know anything about them?'

'Coincidentally I do. It seems like they got back together.'

'They haven't!' Dennis said.

'They bloody well 'ave.'

'I've come over all a-tingly,' Nicky said.

'I saw them on a poster at the pub a few weeks back.'

'Oh my God,' Nicky said, 'this is the universe helping out!'

'How much do you love me?' Dennis asked his brother.

'You're a prick, so not a lot.'

'Fancy going to watch your favourite band?'

'Not really.'

'Gabby?' Nicky said.

'Gabe or Gabriel, Nicky. You know how much I hate Gabby, and if you're scroungin' for something then don't call me bloody Gabby.'

'Gabe, honey,' she cooed.

'That's better, down boy! Now, something about a night on the town with my fave sister-in-law?'

'Sorry to disappoint you but I won't be there,' Nicky laughed.

'So, you'll go?' Dennis said.

'S'pose I'll have to now, despite just being jilted by yer missus.'

'I guess you won't remember one of the band called Paddy Derrick?'

'Nope.'

Nicky was on her laptop as they chatted. 'Seems he calls himself Pat Derrick these days, he's part of the reformation. He'll be there, according to this interview.'

'Wow, I didn't expect them to still be working,' Dennis said. 'Gabe, this means a lot to us, but it's a real long story. Please, go and see the band, find some excuse to talk with Pat, even pretend you're a big fan?'

'Bloody Norah! You don't want much, do you?'

'You never know,' Dennis said, 'you might actually enjoy it. This is what we want you to do.' Dennis gave him a few names and a brief outline. 'We'll give you another call in a week, to see if anything has come to light.'

· · · · ·

Robert and Adelina pulled into the Wheatsheaf car park. Despite it being only nine-thirty, the place sat in darkness. 'Need the light on to find your key?' he asked.

'Mister Rusty not allow me a key. Miss Betty say she come to door and let me in.'

Robert applied the handbrake and switched the ignition off. 'Adelina, when are you going to move on?'

'I not know,' she shrugged. 'I have not much money to go. Here I have warm bed and food.'

'Love, you work hard, you're paid a pittance and could do much better elsewhere.' *There, that word again: love.*

'What is pittance?'

'Like a slave,' he said. 'You are very good, and loyal to them but they don't give you your dues.'

'*Che?*' Adelina said, 'you speak funny words. What is dooss? Miss Betty, she nice to me.'

'Yes and Rusty is a bastard to you. Adelina, if they were good to you they would pay you better, and Rusty wouldn't treat you the way he does.'

'I have nowhere to go,' she sulked.

He thought for a moment, trying to get his thoughts into words. 'Soon, I am going to leave,' he said. 'Perhaps, we go somewhere together.'

'No, Roberto, I cannot leave Miss Betty and Mister Rusty. They have nobody to help them and Mister Rusty shout at Miss Betty.'

'Rusty shouts at everyone, Adelina. Anyway it's not your concern. I'll help you get away. We could even leave tomorrow.'

'No.' Adelina's eyes widened. 'If you leave, then Mister Rusty have no more singer.'

'When he's feeling generous, Mister frigging Rusty pays me fifty dollars' cash for three hours' work, Adelina, and how much does he pay you?' He realised he was almost shouting, and felt an unsettling flashback to a small flat in Fulham. Robert lowered his voice and continued almost at a whisper. 'If he cared he would do something about making the place more attractive, and learn how to treat his employees better.'

Adelina looked at her hands grasping the handles of her backpack, and crushing the flowers she still held. 'No go,' she began broodily. 'I will have nobody and be sad.'

'Come with me then.' Robert rested his hand on hers, not quite believing what he asked. Not just a lift, he had said the words, *come with me*.

He found her loyalty both remarkable and infuriating, but then, until the past few days, he had been as settled as *the beast* permitted.

A security light flooded the car park and they both turned towards its brightness. Robert squinted through the smeared glass.

'Miss Betty wait for me,' Adelina hurriedly said. 'She want to go to sleep.' She turned to Robert and thanked him for the flowers, kissed his cheek and said, 'I will go in, to bed now. Roberto. Please, do not leave.'

She shut the car door quietly, and he watched her as the front door opened and closed behind her.

Robert drove towards his home, his mind filtering events of the past few days. The nearer he came, the slower he progressed as his dread increased, and he recognised the shadowy churning of spinning cartwheels return. He pulled over, across the road from his home and switched the engine off. As he sat in the cold night staring at the house, the familiar black dread of hopelessness enveloped him.

For a while he could not bring himself to drive up and over the broken kerbing to the patch of rutted road base in front of the house that he used as a parking space. His hands gripped the steering wheel and he shivered, despite the beads of sweat on his forehead.

Twenty minutes later, he opened the front door and reached for the light switch. The usual damp, musty smells of the dwelling greeted him. He looked around and saw that nothing was his, not a chair, keepsake or framed picture. Even the cups, plates and pans he used for everyday living came with the house he had been given leave to stay in. He did not even have his guitar to fill the void of his loneliness, and he regretted his decision to leave it in the Wheatsheaf's strongroom for safekeeping while he took Adelina to dinner. His entire life was still no more than would fit in the old rucksack that sat behind the bedroom door, but without that, his guitars and Hayley's hat, he had nothing.

'I'm off to bed,' he said to no-one, 'and you can stay here,' he said to *the beast*. He cleaned his teeth and trudged off to the bedroom, and as he lay there he tried the techniques, the mantras Samantha had taught him, and was energised when he had some success.

While his spirits lifted, his determination remained. 'Goodnight, Hayley,' he said aloud. 'Goodnight, tiny bird.'

Goodnight my love; the soft sound of her voice, as real to him as his own, made his body tingle, and *the beast* retreated to the outermost reaches of his senses.

His dreams were always either wildly entertaining or deeply frightening. This night, the first was a confusion of Hayley, Samantha, Rusty and his entire life in Tasmania – and *the beast*.

The dream fused into a busy London street with hundreds of people going about their day. Robert wore nothing but a white vest, far too small for his body, the kind he would have been dressed in as a child. No matter how he tried, he could not stretch the material down to cover his privates. He felt so small, so exposed, and so vulnerable. Nobody seemed to notice, but Robert did, Robert cared.

Then, he was watching Adelina, huddled and homeless, cold, wet and crying in a corner of a stinking alley. He looked down and called her name. She raised her bruised and battered face and looked through him, didn't acknowledge his outstretched hand. Uttered two words, *help me*.

The dream changed. There was a sound of something moving, just outside his window. The noise suggested a creature, large and pacing, back and forth. Each outward breath was a deep rumble, like the coarse breath of a lion. His dream-self pulled the curtains back and pressed his nose against the pane, straining to see in the dark. A form grew through the blackness. It was darker than the night, oppressive and felt altogether evil. The Robert in his dream closed the curtains, lay back in his bed and pulled the covers up around his ears, the way he would have as a child, to protect himself from ghosts and other unknown terrors when the lights had been turned off.

Robert slipped into a deeper sleep, and did not stir until morning.

PART THREE

REALISATION

CHAPTER TWENTY-FOUR

When Robert woke, he realised the bedcovers were held up around his neck and ears, where his dream-self had tucked them. He looked up at the bedroom window, with the morning casting a faint glow around the closed curtains, and knew there would no longer be any stalking creature outside. He threw the covers off, sat and hung his legs over the side of the bed, and felt the cold of the linoleum floor bite into the soles of his bare feet.

He stripped the bed, and threw the sheets into the basket for his kind landlady to wash. He showered, brushed his teeth and packed his toiletries. Glancing into the mirror he ran his fingers through his hair. *Adelina is right, I need a haircut*. He emptied the bedside drawers of his clothing, folded each item and packed them all into his rucksack. One last look in every room, searching, or hoping there was something else he could call his own, but of course he knew there would not be. *The beast* was, for now, safely locked away, thanks to Hayley and Samantha – so far away he struggled to believe it. *If only I could leave the bastard behind, forever.*

Perhaps you can, my love, she said as Robert began to write to the owners of the house, thanking them for their help, and for washing his, their, sheets and pillowcases one last time. He put the note in an envelope, along with as much money as he dare part with, and placed it next to the house keys in a drawer. His unofficial landlord and lady were among an ever-growing list of people throughout his life who had showed him kindness and compassion, for little or no return.

They lived directly across the road from him and he could just as easily have knocked on their door and told them in person. No, Robert decided he could not face them, and hoped the letter would be thanks enough.

He made a cup of tea and went outside to walk in the garden one last time. He rested on the old tree stump that had become his place of contemplation. The year before, he had discovered some rusty woodworking tools in the half-collapsed stone shed, once overgrown with weeds and saplings, and used them to fashion the flat base of a stool. Sitting out there, in the middle of the small mossy lawn, gave him some comfort during his hours of reflection, or sleeplessness.

When time weighed heavily on Robert, he turned to gardening to fill the void, and had renovated the rambling yard into an open, colourful surrounding for his carved tree-stump chair. The once-proud garden, which had struggled to survive beneath ever-encroaching waves of gorse, blackberry and creeper, had been given a second chance to proliferate, by his care and attention.

He had even resurrected the dilapidated stone shed, and repaired the trusses under the old roofing irons. Not a quality home-handyman job by any stretch of the imagination, but it served its purpose by helping to hold the walls together, and kept the shed dry.

If nothing else, Robert would miss the haven he had created.

He knew it was time to rid himself of *the beast* and embrace life again, his new friends had shown him it was possible. He finished his tea and took the cup inside, where he washed it and put it away. He lifted his rucksack over his shoulder and stepped outside, pulling the door quietly until he heard the familiar click. Then he got into his car and drove away without a backward glance.

· · · · ·

It was eight o'clock when Robert pulled into the Wheatsheaf car park. The first thing he did was to clean out the rubbish from between the seats and in the back of the car, stacking anything of use against the wall and placing the rest in the pub's waste skip. He expected Betty would be in the kitchen, unless she was cleaning, because Betty was almost always in the kitchen, even when there were no meals to cook. The small, grimy television on her desk in the corner was her entertainment centre, and this is where Robert found her, watching morning television.

'Hello, love.' She reached for the remote and turned the volume down. 'What are you doing here?' She looked up at him standing in the doorway, his rucksack at his feet.

He knew there was no point dancing around the truth.

'Good morning, Betty. Things have happened and I've decided to move on. I've come to get my stuff, if that's okay.'

He watched her smile fade momentarily. 'Oh dear,' was all she said.

'Is Rusty about?'

'He's, um, still in bed. Rob, has something bad happened?'

'Something good, I hope. I can't keep living the way I have been and I need a fresh start, different surroundings.'

'Rusty will go spare,' she said, 'but you have to do what's best for you. Can I make you some tea?'

Robert had always liked the ever-suffering, ever-forgiving Betty.

He smiled at her. 'I'm going to miss you, Betty Faulkner.'

'Tea?' Betty's smile had returned, back where it was ordained to be.

'Oh sorry, no thank you.'

A noise behind him, and he noticed Betty's eyes widen.

'Who you talking to, woman? Oh, what the hell is Rob the Pom doing here? Piss your bed or something?'

Robert turned. While Rusty looked comical in his wrinkled flannelette pyjamas with his untethered hair reaching in all directions, the aggravation was still there. Rusty was still Rusty, even first thing in the morning. *No wonder Betty lives in the kitchen.*

'Hello, Rusty,' Robert began, not quite as freely as he had with Betty. 'I've decided to leave, so I've come to collect my stuff from your strongroom.'

Rusty's jaw dropped as he considered the repercussions.

'Why?' He could find no other words.

'No reason but time I was moving on, Rusty, I've been here quite a bit longer than I had planned.'

'What am I going to do without a muso?' He was starting to find his voice, and his irritation was rising.

'Find another, we're not that rare.'

'No, but the locals come to hear you.' His volume was on the rise.

'What, all six of them?'

Rusty roared, 'You're doing this on purpose, aren't you?'

'I beg yours?'

'Rusty, please don't,' Betty implored.

'Bloody pom. I gave you a start and somewhere to play and you just up and fuck off when you feel like it. What about loyalty, you prick?'

'Rusty, please,' Betty repeated.

'Shut up, woman.' Rusty redirected his anger towards his wife.

Robert spoke evenly, attempting to diffuse Rusty's ire, 'Rusty, this has nothing to do with you or the Wheatsheaf. This is to do with me, my health and my future.'

Rusty seethed, as so many words formed in his mind but failed to materialise. His eyes glowed with the rage that was inside him.

'I didn't come here for a fight,' Robert said, still surprised at how he was able to keep his composure, although he detected the slightest of flutters in his gut. *Have to be careful.* 'I just need to collect my stuff, and I'll be off.'

'Well, there's the small matter of storage fees for the past three years,' Rusty snapped.

'Sorry? A storage fee was never mentioned.'

'Don't get nuthin' for nuthin',' Rusty gloated. 'How much you got there in your wallet?'

'That's none of your business Rusty,' Betty said, wagging the television's remote control at him.

Rusty glared at his wife for a moment, before turning back to Robert. 'Show me your wallet.'

Robert had an instant vision of Rusty damaging the guitars. He reached for his wallet and opened it, to reveal a single fifty-dollar note.

'That it?'

'That's all I have. What you pay me is all I earn.' He now considered the cost of Adelina's birthday dinner to have been money even better spent.

Rusty snatched the note, folded it and slipped it into the pocket of his pyjama top. 'It'll 'ave to do then. Now get your gear and piss off.'

Betty stood, gaping at her husband. 'Charles Frank Faulkner, you have stooped even lower than I thought possible. I am disgusted at you.'

Robert had never heard Rusty's real name before, and he guessed it was Betty's way of displaying extreme displeasure.

'I don't give a shit what you think, Beatrice fat fucking Faulkner.' He turned back to Robert, his face crimson. 'Well, what're you 'angin' round for? I said get your stuff, I want you off my property.'

Robert resisted the urge to punch him on the nose. Instead he took a composing breath.

'Where's Adelina? I want to say goodbye.'

'She ain't here bucko, so you're shit-outa luck,' Rusty smiled as he opened a drawer, took out a key and tossed it to his wife. 'Help him get his stuff. You've got five minutes before I change my mind and decide to keep those guitars, and don't forget what's yours an' what's not or I'll come after you.' Rusty spun on his heel and stomped off, sounds of his bare heels thumping on the floorboards resonated down the hallway.

'I am so sorry, love,' Betty said as a distant door slammed. They listened as Rusty roared a string of expletives. 'Come on Robert, the quicker we get your things the sooner you can be on your way.'

Robert followed her from the kitchen, across the parquetry dance floor and through the far doorway, down the hall and to the strongroom. She unlocked the heavy steel door, pulled it open and followed him inside.

Robert brought the first guitar out and stood waiting for Betty to emerge with the other, but he saw that she carried his compact amplifier instead.

'Sorry Betty, I won't be taking that or anything else,' he said, 'It will have to be just the two guitars I came with. You can keep the other stuff for your next musician.'

Betty looked at him and smiled. She put the amplifier down. 'I'll just leave this here a moment while you get the other guitar.' Of course, she knew the car Robert drove did not belong to him, because it was owned and registered under her name. She had guessed he was about to hand the keys back.

Betty had warmed to, or felt sorry for, Robert the moment they had met, and without Rusty's knowledge had helped him out by purchasing the wagon for him to use. It had been a secret between them at the time, although Robert had assumed her husband would have found out at some stage before then.

'Robert, love,' Betty whispered, 'the car is a gift from me.' She held a finger to her lips and grinned. 'Just don't tell nasty old Rusty. So you can still take this amplifier here, and the rest of your gear as well.'

'I couldn't, possibly ...'

'Oh you can and you will, my dear, because if you leave the car and half your stuff he's sure to ask questions, and discover what we've conspired. Poor old Beatrice here will find herself in a world of strife.' She was still whispering. 'Come on, you'd best show signs of leaving or he'll start to holler again.' They headed for the exit and walked across the gravel driveway to his car. She placed the amplifier at his feet and said, 'You pack this and the guitars and I'll go and get the microphone and stand ...' she giggled like a schoolgirl, 'and the other stuff.'

While Rusty was often insufferably rude to Betty, she knew she could get away with many things that he was just too pompous to believe she would dare. This was one of the things Betty considered to be just payback for his constant ill treatment of her.

She returned with the stand and microphone, and watched as Robert packed them away. Lastly she handed him the bag he kept the cables in. As he threw the bag into the back and pulled the hatch down, she said, 'You'll find the car's transfer papers in there too. I've signed on the dotted line but you'll need to fill the rest out when you get a permanent address. Oh, there is also your fifty dollars back, plus another fifty for good measure.' She read his expression. 'No you will not refuse, Robert. Rusty'll never know what's missing from the till, and it will serve him right for not paying you better these past few years.'

Robert felt like arguing, but Rusty had taken the last of his cash, apart from a plastic zip lock bag containing three ten-dollar notes, which he usually kept hidden beneath the passenger seat's matting – emergency petrol money that he had transferred to his sock.

'Thank you, Betty,' he said, and knew he could never repay her.

He grasped her hands. 'Are you going to be okay?'

'Oh, of course I will be dear. While he can be a pig, he is still all mouth and no trousers with me. No matter how much he rants and raves, he's never ever raised a hand.' She looked at him, trying to read his thoughts. 'Where are you going to go?'

'At this minute, I have no idea,' Robert said. 'Any idea where Adelina might have gone?'

'After you dropped her off last night Rusty gave her another telling off.'

'Jesus, for what this time?'

'Who knows what sends him over the top? Perhaps she made too much noise coming in? I don't know. He had her in tears and when I came back from the shops this morning she wasn't in her room.'

'It was her birthday, for God's sake! You don't think she's walked out, do you?'

'I don't think so, dear. It looks like most of her clothes are still here. I hope she's not gone, she is a lovely girl and so good at her job.'

Then why not treat her better? 'I've chosen a bad time, then.'

'No time is a good time.' She patted his hand.

'Last warning!' Rusty hollered from the front entrance, still dressed in his pyjamas.

'I think you'd best be on your way, Robert. I'm really going to miss you and your music.'

'Can't say I'll miss the gaffer,' Robert smiled, 'but I'll miss you, too.' He gave her a brief hug before sliding into the driver's seat.

'I suppose you still don't have a phone?' she asked, and he shook his head. 'Adelina's number is written on the envelope with your dollars, back there in the bag,' Betty smiled, 'just in case you feel like calling her some time.'

'Will you say goodbye to her for me?'

'Of course I will. I tried to call her when I went back to collect the cables, but her phone was out of range, or switched off.'

'Oh, okay.' Robert didn't try to hide his disappointment. He started the car's engine and revved it a few times to let Rusty know he was making a move. Betty was watching him, trying to grasp the sudden change, from the depths of despair to an unexpected hint of positivity.

'Thanks for everything. Goodbye, Betty.'

'Goodbye, love,' she said. 'You know if you came back it would be water under the bridge with Rusty.'

'I'll keep that in mind. Thank you, Beatrice Faulkner.'

Robert said a last goodbye and, avoiding Rusty's glare, drove slowly out to the road, hoping that chance would bring Adelina back at that moment. He considered hanging around for her to appear, if for nothing more than a heartfelt farewell. She might be down the road hitchhiking, being picked up by a do-gooder ... or pervert. She could be walking around Wynyard, on the river or beach or off climbing a hill somewhere. How could he ever guess which? Still, he turned towards the town centre and drove around for a while without success. He crawled past the hotel where they had dined, before taking the scenic coast route out of town, past the basalt outcrop named Doctors Rocks, and east along the highway.

He did not look back, and was certain he would never see Beatrice, Rusty or the Wheatsheaf again.

Robert hoped he would one day rediscover Adelina.

CHAPTER TWENTY-FIVE

Determined to focus on their renovation project, Dennis and Nicky poured their energies into the gallery, and for them the days flew past. On the other hand, Samantha and Matthew were so preoccupied with Robert Aitken's story, their time seemed to drag. Despite each couples' differing circumstances, the next Saturday morning arrived to all at exactly the same time and, at six a.m. as planned, Samantha called her sister.

'Morning guys, are we all ready?'

'Morning, sis,' Nicky said, 'sure are – this is so exciting, I'm trembling.'

'Matt?' Dennis asked.

'Alrigh' mate, yerself?'

'Couldn't be better. Here goes then.'

Dennis dialled Gabe's number, pressed the conference call button and sat back, praying for the ringing to cease.

''Allo?' Gabe sounded rushed.

'Thought you'd never answer,' Dennis said. 'Not a good time?'

'Nah, just doing the dishes and dryin' my hands. How's Denmania?'

'Good, Gabe, but we're all gathered waiting for some positive news.'

'Wotcher Matt, Sam, oh and Nicky dahlin'.'

Dennis got to the point; 'So, what have you got for us bruvv?'

'Drew a dud, sorry,' Gabe said. 'We arrived at the Rose and Crown on Wednesday night to learn Piggins Hit had cancelled their gig, due to ... unforeseen circumstances.'

Silence relayed the disappointment around the room.

'Oh, okay, well, thanks for putting yourself out and giving it a go.' Dennis sounded as flat as they all felt.

'Thanks Gabe,' Matthew said, 'sorry we wasted your evening.'

'Well, it wasn't a total waste,' Gabe said, 'because what I just said was bullshite.' He laughed, 'Chaps, have I got some serious news about Piggins bleedin' Hit. They were bloody brilliant and we couldn't believe how much fun we had. I mean, not a pimple-faced anarchistic prat among them. Came across as a bunch of fun-filled blokes, despite recedin' hairlines and middle age spreads. I tell you we had a fekkin' ball – what's more I ended up buying one of their CDs!'

'You are a complete prick, Gabriel Hooper,' Dennis laughed.

'So, closet punk lover,' Matthew said, 'did you get to meet them?'

'Oh I did, Matty. Paddy Derrick does call himself Pat these days, a nice bloke he is – well, they all were. We must've chatted for half an hour over a pint. Pat remembered Hayley and the Tramp, and the accident, of course. Said he remembered Aitken going off the rails and vanishin'. Said Hayley's death and then Robert's disappearance hit Derry hard.'

'Pat said he'd speak with Derry?' Samantha hoped.

'Well, he did, and so did I as a matter of fact.'

Dennis shivered. 'You're shittin' us again. When? How?'

'I gave Pat me number then got a call from Derry yesterday, excited 'cause for all these years he'd thought Robert had gone away and topped 'imself. He can't believe Robert's alive and well on the other side of the bloody world.'

'I think "well" is stretching it, Gabe,' Samantha said, 'but Robert Aitken is certainly alive and kicking.'

'Now, I'm in two minds,' Gabe started, 'this has been so excitin' for me and I never was even aware of this Robert Aitken or Derry Derrick, and I don't know much at all, but I'm not sure I want to do the next bit.'

'What's that, bro?'

'I've, er, got Derry's number for you.'

'Holy fekkin' shite, Gabe, you are a bleedin' marvel!' Dennis laughed.

'Did I ever tell you I loved you?'

'Don't come over all gay with me, bro, I've only got you a bunch o' fekkin' numbers.'

'So why the hesitation?'

There was silence, and then, 'Seriously, this is too tantalising a tale, I don't want to be left out, after all this.'

'I'll make sure Dennis keeps you in the loop,' Nicky promised.

'Now Nic, you can tell me you love me,' Gabe said, mischievously.

'You old smoothie,' she laughed.

'Hey, focus, Don Juan,' Matthew said. 'Anything we need to know about Derry? How much does he know about us?'

'I assume Pat has filled him in on everything I told him, and we had a brief chat about the who's and where's,' Gabe said. 'He lives in ultra-posh Montpelier Square, here in London with his missus. They're both directors of an entertainment agency and other related stuff, and have done rather well for themselves.

'I never took much notice of Derry before this, apart from hearin' about him as a session muso, but his missus Elsa is quite the TV celebrity, so some of her fame has rubbed off on him. She manages some well-known acts, hosts a lifestyle TV series over 'ere, and rubs shoulders with the very rich and very famous.'

'Did you say Elsa?' Samantha asked.

'Yes, she's got a cute Scandinavian accent, I think she's from Denmark, or the like. Ain't bad on the eye, either.'

'No, that is amazing ...' Nicky said, '*Town 2 Country*. It's on TV and Elsa is one of the presenters. It's such a coincidence. Robert told us Paddy Derrick went out with a girl called Elsa, from Abbey Road Studios.'

'One and the same,' Gabe said.

'Someone's got something wrong then,' Dennis said.

'Hang on,' Matthew began, 'Robert did say something about Paddy and Elsa not quite being the perfect couple. Maybe things just didn't work out and she found more in common with Derry than Pat?'

'Well, it must have been amicable,' Gabe said. 'Pat spoke rather fondly of them both.'

'Anything else you found out we should know about, Sherlock bleedin' Holmes?' Dennis laughed.

'That's about it, in an eggshell.' Gabe would always intentionally misquote the idiom.

'You've been brilliant, Gabe,' Nicky said. 'Okay, I love you.'

'About time, now, 'ow do I whisk you away without my nasty big bruvver finding out!'

'See you, bro,' Dennis laughed, 'we'll get back to you with anything we discover, and yes, we promise.'

They all said their goodbyes and ended the call.

Dennis stared at his notepad and took a deep breath. 'There's no time like the present, I 'spose.' He punched into the phone the numbers he had scribbled on the page, and activated the conference option. They sat in wait for the call to be connected.

Click: 'Hello, how can I help you?' The accented voice was soft and confident, while politely detached.

'Hello, my name is Dennis Hooper,' Dennis said in his most refined way, 'am I speaking with Elsa?'

'Oh my word,' the voice said, 'Pat has told us you know where Robert is, and Derry is very excited! Derry,' her muffled voice could still be understood, 'it is the people calling about your old friend Robert!'

There was a pause, a click, and then another voice said, 'Derry Derrick, hello? We have you on speaker.'

'Pleased to meet you,' Dennis said. 'We are on conference call: my wife, Nicky and her sister Samantha ...'

'Hello,' Nicky and Samantha said.

'... And Matthew, Samantha's husband – he's the one who recognised Robert from his singing.'

'Hello Matthew,' Elsa said, 'what a keen ear you must have.'

'Hi Elsa, Derry,' Matthew said, smiling proudly. 'It's wonderful to find you and, I must say, easier than we expected. We are all so excited.'

'Yes,' Samantha agreed, 'we expected needles and haystacks.'

'Before we move on,' Elsa said, 'this is a private telephone number and we assume you will treat it as such.'

'Absolutely,' Dennis said. 'I'll stress that to my brother.'

There was a hint of mischief in Derry's voice when he said, 'Oh, your brother has been made completely aware.'

'Now that has been clarified,' Elsa said, 'we cannot wait to hear what it is you have to tell us.'

'I love your show,' Nicky blurted.

'Oh please,' Dennis shook his head.

'That is kind of you to say,' Elsa said, a smile in her voice.

'Now you're finished,' Dennis looked to Nicky, who mimed locking her lips and throwing the key over her shoulder.

'It all started last year,' Matthew began …

· · · · ·

They told the story, each continually interrupting the other, adding a point here or there. Elsa showed an interest, although she had only known Robert through their brief session at the studio, but Derry became emotional, and said, 'I should have done more, should have insisted he talk to me, not allow him to push me away.'

When the account had reached the present time, Elsa asked, 'So, where exactly do you all live?'

'Dennis and I live near Launceston, in Tasmania's north,' Nicky said.

'And Matthew and I are from New Norfolk, close to Hobart in the south of the island.'

'And where did you say you found Robert again?'

'Tasmania's North West,' Matthew began, 'Samantha and I were on holiday when we dropped into this pub, on the highway near a coastal town called Wynyard, where he happened to be playing.'

'You know,' Derry began, 'we were in Australia three years ago, and travelled all over. If only we had stopped in that pub we might have happened upon Robert while he was performing.'

'No point in thinking about that, Derry,' Samantha said, 'Robert might not have been there and, more to the point, you probably wouldn't have gone into such a ramshackle place, even if you'd been passing. Or you might have met him, but at a time when he wasn't capable of coping with it. I think we just turned up when he was emotionally ready to share his story.'

'So,' Derry started, 'how can we get to talk to Robert? Do you have his phone number?'

'He doesn't own a phone,' Dennis said.

'Wow,' Derry said. 'What about catching him at the pub?'

'The owner is a bit, er, feral,' Dennis warned them, 'one of the world's least agreeable people who's more likely to tell you to get stuffed than put Robert on the line.'

'If he happened to be there,' Matthew added.

'And there's something else,' Samantha said, for the first time revealing just enough of Robert's *beast*. 'We can't be sure if he actually wants to be rediscovered just yet. You see, he's had a pretty bad time of it all these twenty-odd years.'

'But he was willing to tell you all about his past and, with respect,' Derry tried to hide his confusion, 'you were virtual strangers.'

'Please,' Samantha said, 'this is difficult. Yes, he told us, but really it was like a confession, as if we were the priest behind the curtain, all listening and non-judgemental.'

'I think you are doing the right thing, Samantha,' Elsa agreed. 'You people have made contact with Robert's past world, to find out if the doors will reopen if he wants them to.'

'That's right,' Samantha said. 'Despite only having just met Robert, we care about him after the story he's shared with us. Really, I think it was about the most humbling, exciting and sad account I've ever heard.'

'That is different,' Elsa understood. 'We are excited at the prospect of seeing Robert again or, if nothing else, just glad to know he's still alive. You have our permission to give him our number, so he has control, but we ask for you to keep us informed.'

'Robert has a friend,' Samantha said, 'someone who works at the pub. I'll call her and see if she can corner Robert next time he goes to the Wheatsheaf.'

'Thank you all,' Derry said. 'I don't suppose you took a photo of Robert, by chance?'

'I took a nice photograph of him at the pub,' Nicky said, 'and videoed him when he was singing at night around our campfire. Just a snippet on my smart phone, so not very long, or the best quality.'

They heard a falter in Derry's natural confidence: 'Would you email them to us, please?'

'I'd be happy to,' Nicky said and took down Derry's details.

'If that is all,' Elsa said, 'we will say thank you for making this effort to contact us, and goodbye for now.' The call ended.

'Wow,' Nicky said, 'Elsa Soland, TV star, has a connection with this tramp we found in a random pub!'

'Okay,' Samantha said, 'I have to get a hold of Adelina and tee up a time to speak with Robert. Guys, I'll call her and get back to you as soon as I have an answer.'

Samantha ended the conference call while Matthew made a fresh coffee for them both. She dialled Adelina's number.

'Hello?'

'Hi, Adelina, Samantha calling.'

'Roberto, he has gone!' Adelina blurted.

'What? No!' Samantha cried as Matthew brought the drinks to the table. 'Why ... where did he go?'

'He come and tell Miss Betty he wish to leave, he take his things. Mister Rusty shout at Roberto and he go.'

'We have a problem.' Samantha looked at Matthew and switched the speaker on. 'Robert's gone,' she whispered. 'Adelina, when did this happen?'

'Tuesday morning he go.'

'Did you get to speak with him?' Matthew asked.

'No,' Adelina said. 'Mister Rusty shout at me and I go out for run. Roberto come and go while I still on the beach.'

'Shit,' Matthew whispered.

'I am sorry.' Adelina heard him.

'Oh Adelina, it wasn't your fault. Do you know where he went?' Samantha asked again.

'Miss Betty say she not know. I have to go back to work before Mister Rusty shout at me again.' Adelina ended the call.

'Working, this hour of the morning? We've got to help her get away from that place,' Matthew said.

'One rescue at a time, love. Let's focus on Robert first.' She dialled her sister's number.

Dennis picked up. 'What have you got?'

Samantha relayed Adelina's news.

'Rusty is such an arsehole.' Dennis seethed. 'I feel like driving up there and punching his fuckin' lights out.'

'No you won't,' Nicky warned.

'Well, if he doesn't, I might.' Matthew sided with his friend.

'This is not Rusty Faulkner's fault, guys,' Samantha reasoned with them. 'Robert went there with the intention of collecting his stuff and leaving. Rusty's reaction didn't affect his decision to go.'

Dennis had quietened. 'When did this happen? Did she say?'

'Tuesday morning,' Samantha said. 'Adelina's really upset.'

'I wonder if their birthday dinner didn't go well, and that helped with

Robert's decision,' Matthew suggested.

The conversation lulled, until Nicky told them her news: 'We were going to tell you something else, about Adelina this time, but this has put the tin hat on it, as Dennis would say.'

'Might as well say it anyway, Nic,' her sister sighed.

'The Tannery in Longford is looking for wait-staff,' Nicky said, 'we told them about Adelina, they're keen to meet her and will pay award rates. They only need one person, to do a whole range of tasks. I think Adelina would cope perfectly.'

'That's fantastic,' Samantha said. 'What about accommodation? And remember she has no wheels.'

'Don't know the finer details as yet,' Dennis said, 'but we've finished the gatehouse renovation so there's a place for her there for the short term, if she wants the job and needs a bed.'

'Also it's only a ten-minute drive, so either me or Den can be taxi service,' Nicky added.

'Why didn't you say earlier?' Samantha asked, 'I could have told her.'

'There was a message from the Tannery when we ended our conference call just a few minutes ago,' Dennis said.

'I don't want to call her again just at the moment,' Samantha said. 'I'll send her a text, tell her about the Tannery job.'

'So, what do we do now?' Nicky asked.

'Not much we can do, sis, but keep in touch with Adelina and hope Robert makes contact with her.'

CHAPTER TWENTY-SIX

A week passed by with no word from, or about, Robert. They all felt a growing concern for his wellbeing, as surely he would have made contact if he could have? Samantha even dared a call to the Wheatsheaf, hoping to catch Adelina, but it was Rusty who answered. He refused to put Adelina on the line, gave Samantha an earful of abuse, and blamed them all for Robert's departure. It was an accusation she found impossible to argue against.

It proved frustrating for Derry too, being tantalisingly close to rediscovering this spectre from his past. He and Elsa had no option but to be content with a single photograph, and to watch the snippet of Robert Aitken performing by the campfire, over and over.

· · · · ·

As Samantha emerged from a Friday-morning client meeting in Hobart, she felt her mobile phone buzz.

'Good morning, Sam Pearson speaking.'

'Hello Samanta,' the voice sounded bright.

'Oh, hello Adelina! Lovely to hear from you! Did you get the text message I sent you?'

'I not hear from Roberto.' Adelina made herself clear from the onset. 'Yes I get message but worry for Roberto.'

'I see, yes, I understand. How are you going? You sound better than the last time we spoke.'

'I am okay. I not work for Mister Rusty or Miss Betty no more.'

Samantha hesitated. 'Oh my gosh, what happened?'

'Mister Rusty, he shout at me and Miss Betty shout at Mister Rusty and I go to my room, put head under pillow and cry. I still hear them shouting with people in Wheatsheaf and I decide I will do no more. So I pack my things and tell them I leaving. Now Mister Rusty scream at me, Miss Betty yell at him and it all start again. Miss Betty not take *shit* no more.' Adelina spat the expletive with venom.

'Adelina, how terrible,' Samantha said, although she was relieved that Adelina had made the move. 'Where are you now?'

'No, it is good Samanta. I more happy now.'

Again, 'Where are you?'

'Backpacker place in Burnie.'

'Do you have work?'

'No work,' she sighed.

'Do you have money?'

'Miss Betty come look for me and find me on road. She take me to Burnie and pay two nights' sleep, then give me some money. Miss Betty she lovely and don't deserve *him*.'

'Adelina, can I call you back?' Samantha had to find out if the Tannery position was still vacant before she raised Adelina's hopes.

'Yes, sorry I call you at work.'

'No, you can call me any time. I will ring you back soon so keep your phone handy. Bye for now.'

Samantha dialled. 'Dennis?'

'Hello Sam, any news?'

'No, but Adelina walked out on the Wheatsheaf.'

'Good on 'er, I hope the place caves in on that arrogant prat.'

'What are you up to today?'

'Painting. It's all coming to fruition Sam, not long now.'

'I was wondering if you fancied a drive? I could call and see if she wants you to pick her up – if the Tannery job is still open, that is?'

'Give me five minutes while I check.' Dennis ended the call.

· · · · ·

Samantha saw the call was from Dennis.

'What have you got?'

'Nicky says the Tannery hasn't made a decision yet.'

'Okay. I'll call her and see if she's interested. Speak soon. Hey, are you in a position to put your brush down for a few hours and collect her?'

'Already washin' up.'

'You are a gem, Dennis.'

Samantha phoned Adelina and told her about the Tannery job and the Hoopers' offer of accommodation. Adelina was delighted. Samantha wrote the Burnie hostel address down and called Dennis.

'Adelina would love to come down for an interview,' she said.

'Nicky's excited and had a widdle cry,' Dennis said in a childlike voice after he had written down the directions and Adelina's phone number, just in case. 'I'll head off shortly; should be in Burnie in around ninety minutes. Call you then.' He hung up.

· · · · ·

Dennis found Adelina sitting on the pavement outside the hostel, engaged with the mobile phone in her hand. She looked up and waved, then changed the message she was writing to Samantha, to say that Dennis had just arrived. She stood and brushed herself down, threw her gear onto the back seat and slid into the passenger seat next to Dennis. She leaned over and gave him a peck on the cheek.

As they drove along the highway, passing the docks at Burnie, Adelina asked about Robert. What had happened over recent days to give him such a change of outlook on his life?

'He has an amazing past,' Dennis said. 'Some of it's been very traumatic for him.'

'What is ... traumatic?'

'Distressing, upsetting. Robert lost someone very dear to him and has carried the blame all these years.'

'A lady?'

'Yes, his wife. I can't go into details, as he must tell you himself if he wants to. We've been trying to reconnect him with people from his past in England, people who cared about him back then.'

Adelina turned and stared through the passenger window at a distant cruise ship on its way to dock at Burnie. Dennis heard her sigh.

'You like Robert, don't you?' he asked.

'*Sì*. He scruffy, but seems a gentle man.'

'How long have you known him?'

'I come to Tasmania since nine months. Mister Rusty and Wheatsheaf is first job.'

'Wow, you are loyal aren't you?'

Adelina shrugged. 'Miss Betty need good person to help.'

Like Robert needs a good person to help. 'Do you have any idea how old Robert is?' Dennis asked.

'He is *cinquanta,* eh, he fifty years?'

Dennis laughed, 'I don't think he's that old, love. Behind all that hair and hardship, he's probably not much older than me, I reckon late thirties, early forties. And you, if I may be so bold?'

'Bolde?'

'One should not ask a woman's age without having good reason to.'

'Ah.' She smiled. '*Ventinove*. Twenty nine.'

Dennis raised his brows. 'Well, honestly Adelina, I would have put you at much younger.'

She slapped his arm playfully and giggled. '*Casanova!*'

'Anyway, it's not my business.'

'Is okay, Denni.' She turned back towards the window and followed the passing coastline.

'So,' she said after a few minutes of silence, 'how we find Roberto?'

'I don't know how we can, love. He will either find us or he won't.'

They travelled in silence for a while until Dennis spoke: 'Adelina?'

'*Sì?*'

'What brings you to Tasmania?'

'It long story. Not happy story.'

The restaurant and Robert's question sat freshly in her mind, and she wished she had reacted better at the time. She said no more and Dennis assumed she did not want to talk about it, so he left the subject alone.

· · · · ·

It was mid-afternoon when Dennis pulled into the driveway and drove slowly past the gatehouse to the main dwelling. Harry poked his head through the pickets of the back garden gate and barked excitedly.

'*Cane!*' Adelina squealed. She had opened the door before Dennis had switched off the ignition. She ran to the gate, dropped to her knees, pushed her arms between the bars and wrapped her hands around Harry's face.

Lucky he doesn't bite, Dennis thought. Nicky appeared at the gallery doorway, dressed in paint-stained overalls, her hair roughly tied back from her face. Dennis thought his wife was a fine looking woman, and he was a lucky man. He noticed these things at the strangest of times.

Nicky beamed with anticipation. 'Hello Adelina, I see you've met Harry.'

'*Bellissimo*,' she pouted, and ruffled Harry's neck more.

Adelina was given a guided tour of the home, gallery and lastly the gatehouse, which would be her home for a while. She had accepted their offer of accommodation, irrespective of whether or not she succeeded in getting the job at the Tannery.

The gatehouse's slick contemporary interior might have been a jarring contrast to its classic eighteenth-century stone exterior, if it were not for the use of occasional period features to link the styles. Adelina loved the décor of her quarters and repeatedly promised to compensate their kindness in any way she could, and the Hoopers had little doubt she would do far more than they would expect of her.

After Adelina had a shower and change of clothes they all drove to the Tannery to meet the owners, who were so impressed by Adelina's presentation and quick responses to questions and tasks that they offered her employment for five days a week, to start as soon as she could. Adelina was overjoyed when they told her the official award rates, far exceeding her pay at the Wheatsheaf.

'I so happy,' Adelina said on the way home, 'you people good to me!'

'We're glad,' Dennis said. 'You've spent far too much time working in that madhouse.'

'*Che cosa*, eh, sorry?'

Before Dennis had the chance to clarify, Adelina's phone rang, and they all held their collective breath.

'Hello? Ah Miss Betty ... yes, I okay ... yes, I have place to stay. You hear from Roberto? Oh, you let me know, okay? Thank you Miss Betty. *Ciao*.'

She avoided saying she had met up with the Hoopers, who had found her another place of employment.

They sat around the dining room table while Nicky dialled her sister's number.

'Hello Nic. What have you got?'

'Hi sis, thought we'd let you know Adelina is sitting with us and we're on speaker.'

'Hello Adelina!' Samantha exclaimed.

'Samanta, I get new job today. You come soon?'

'Wonderful news, Adelina. We may come up next weekend. Any update on Robert's whereabouts?'

'Nothing,' Dennis said.

'Okay. Sorry, I have to go. Speak soon. Adelina, glad you are safe and well.' The call ended.

· · · · ·

Early Saturday morning Samantha woke from a dream, so real yet disturbing, it made her shiver. She squinted at the bedside clock, saw it was five-forty and, accepting her sleep-in had ended, slid quietly from the bed, slipped her gown around her shoulders and walked to the kitchen. She made herself a mug of tea and sat in twilight for an hour, mulling the dream over.

Matthew found her curled up on the sofa in their sunroom, cradling an empty mug. She stared out onto the garden, as low sunlight filtered through the windows and washed onto her hair and face.

'Okay love?' he called from the kitchen as he flicked the kettle on.

Samantha nodded. 'Fancy going for a drive today?'

'To the Hoopers?'

'No, a bit further than that. Grab your tea and sit with me. I have to tell you about my dream.'

'Do you remember at Ned's Camp?' she began when he had made himself comfortable, 'the dead tree on the other side of the lagoon?'

'Robert spent a bit of time looking in that direction.'

'The tree was a tool to help him focus against his depression, *the beast* as he calls it, remember?' Matthew nodded. 'Well, I helped him tether it to that tree.'

'Fascinating, Dr Sigmund, and how did you manage that?' Matthew may have reacted flippantly, but he respected his wife's abilities.

'I had him conjure an impregnable net, wrap *the beast* up tightly and hang it from the tree.'

'Jesus! If the RSPCA found out ...'

'Don't be a dick, Matthew! Seriously, it seemed to work, and after a couple of relapses, he said he was more able to control his moods.'

'My missus is a bloody marvel! You reckon he wouldn't have got through all that story without tethering *the beast*?'

'I don't think so, but listen to the dream I had. We were at Ned's Camp, the four of us, and Adelina. We could hear this calling, a sort of half-human, half-animal wail ... a horrible, pitiful sound. I looked across the water and there was this ... thing, wrapped up in a dark net, secured to the tree. Although the creature's shape was gloomy ... blurry, you know, as if our eyes were unfocused cameras, I knew it was Robert. He and *the beast* had become physically one and the same, and he was struggling to break free of the tangled mess. He, it, was crying for our help – a really wretched sight.

'We wanted to get across the water to him, but rain started pouring down and the river quickly swelled, forcing more water into the lake than it could deal with. The lake suddenly acted more like dangerous rapids, or surf, smashing on a cliff face at every bend. Our peaceful campsite was swamped, and it was impossible to get across to the tree. All we could do was stand and shout encouragement for him to break free of *the beast*, and the net, and the tree.

'It was horrible, Matthew. The pleading in his eyes, the desperation in his voice.'

Matthew put his mug down on the tiled floor. 'You think Robert's gone back to Ned's Camp, don't you? You think he's there, struggling with *the beast*, on his own?'

Samantha nodded. 'I don't just think, I'm damn well sure of it.'

'And we have no hope of helping unless we find him, because he can't find us. This dangerous river in your dream is to you the distance between you and him.'

'Spot on, hubby.'

'Going to phone the Hoopers?'

Samantha shook her head. 'I don't want to raise their hopes before we find him, and they might think we're nuts making such a journey based on nothing more than a dream.'

'Oh, they already think we're nuts, sweetie,' Matthew mocked her. 'But hey, listen, it's a helluva drive there and back in a day. What say we take the two-man tent and food enough for three? If it was only a dream after all, then we'll have a romantic night under the stars as compensation.'

'Agreed, and no time like the present.' Samantha stood, stretched away the hour of sitting on her feet, walked to the kitchen and rinsed her mug. 'I'm off for a shower.'

Matthew checked his watch. 'I'll pack the motor. We could be there by early afternoon if we get a wriggle on,' he shouted, already halfway down the hallway.

· · · · ·

They were on the road by nine-thirty, stopping only twice: firstly, to fill the tank and grab a couple of coffees to go, and secondly as a consequence of those coffees to go. They reached the old farm gate a little after two, Samantha got out to unlock the padlock, but saw that the rusting chain had broken and was coiled in the wet grass beside the post. She wondered if someone had forced the gate open, or the old chain had simply perished at that time. Her belly squirmed with anticipation as she climbed back in.

'Best replace that,' she said, 'in case Bushy thinks it was us and complains.'

'I think we've got a length of chain in the load bay that should do the trick,' he said as they traversed slowly along the boggy track. 'Thinner than the old one but no doubt stronger. I'll check it out on the way home.'

'Look,' Matthew said when they had rounded another bend, 'There's a car in a ditch up ahead.'

The car sat half off the track and half in the ditch. They stopped next to it and got out.

'It sure is Robert's,' Samantha looked around, 'God, I hope he's okay.'

A quick inspection revealed no obvious damage, and it appeared the car had simply slid off the track and become bogged. Robert was not inside, but his gear, including the guitars, was still in the back. That evidence caused them further concern.

They drove up and over the granite crest, and the welcoming vista of Ned's Camp lay below them. They saw the unlit fire, a swag and, sitting halfway down the bank by the lagoon, staring away towards the tree, they could see Robert.

Matthew stayed with the car while Samantha walked down to the water's edge. Robert looked up at her, and then returned his gaze to the tree. His eyes were cold, desolate.

'I prayed you'd come.'

Samantha sat. 'Fancy a bit of company?'

'I've decided being a loner is no fun any more.'

Still, he attempts humour. 'Matthew's with me, and he's about to make some lunch. You hungry?'

Robert stared at the tree. A single, subtle nod told her he had heard the question, but he chose not to respond.

'We also brought a tent ... in case you'd like some company tonight.'

Again, Robert nodded. The corners of his mouth twisted into the slightest of smiles. He sighed. Samantha turned towards Matthew, who knew what to do.

'We've all been worried about you, my friend.'

'Had to make the change. Things didn't go as smoothly as I expected. Then the bastards came back.'

They sat quietly for a moment, until Samantha said, 'I had a dream last night, well, the early hours of this morning, actually.' A shiver passed through her at the memory.

'You heard my call, then?'

'All very woo-woo, isn't it, Robert?'

Robert shrugged. 'I needed you, end of my tether and all that. I focused on you, spoke to you. Asked you to come and find me and, here you are. Helluva coincidence, wouldn't you say? Or woo-woo, as you call it.'

Samantha hugged herself. 'It was such an awful dream. I just knew you'd be ... we couldn't get here fast enough. Thankfully, Matthew believed in my intuition.'

'Read into it what you will, but,' he looked at her and she could see his angst begin to ease, 'I'm really glad you're here.'

They turned to the sound of footfalls padding down the sandy slope.

'Hi mate.' Matthew said.

Robert's simple nod did not relay his relief that they had come.

'You look like shit,' Matthew said.

Robert smiled. *Channelling Dennis.* 'I've been better, and want to be again, just can't do it on my own ... not just yet.'

'Important stuff first, rolls are made so come on up when you're ready.'

'Be there in a while.' Samantha watched Matthew turn and walk back to the camp. She adored her husband, no more than at that moment.

'Now Robert,' she began with conviction, 'let's you and me sort out this fucker together.'

He turned to her. It was the first time he had heard her utter such an expletive, and it made him smile, a proper grin.

Smiling made Robert feel good, as if a ray of sunlight piercing through his gloom.

They remained there for a while, and Matthew decided to take their lunches and drinks down to them, before leaving them alone again.

By the time they came up to the campsite, the fire was putting out welcome heat to contrast the brisk afternoon air. The Pearson's tent was set up, the portable camping stove ready and waiting on its stand, and three chairs were positioned around a card table where three plastic glasses stood, poised to be filled.

Robert sat, put his plate on the table and leaned back. He exhaled slowly.

'Red?' Matthew asked.

'Ordinarily no, but perhaps today is turning into a special one. Want to play some songs with me?'

'Sure, happy to sing along.'

'I mean play the guitar. I know you can.'

'What, on ...?' Matthew hesitated.

'Hayley's guitar. You've put up with all my crap and, well, I'm sure she would prefer that someone played it. You know, Samantha, she hasn't spoken to me for days, in fact not since the morning I left my digs. It's all been that bastard *beast*.'

'I'm ... not with you,' Matthew glanced at his wife, unsure if he should assume the comment was meant for him.

'It's complicated, love,' Samantha smiled at Matthew. 'One of these days, Robert might feel like telling us all about it.'

'One of these days,' Robert agreed. 'But for now, let's get the guitars.'

While they were away, Samantha checked her mobile, guessed there would not be a signal, but chanced a message anyway.

· · · · ·

Nicky heard the familiar buzz of her phone, and reached into her handbag to access the text message.

'It's from Sam,' she called. 'Oh my God, listen to this ... FOUND ROBERT SAFE AND WELL CAN'T TALK NOW SPEAK TOMORROW. I LOVE YOU ALL! Oh, I think I'm going to cry,' she said, while tears already made their way down her cheeks.

Dennis looked over to Adelina. 'Not you, too!' he laughed, as he chewed back his own feelings of relief.

· · · · ·

During their drive to Ned's Camp, Matthew and Samantha had agreed that, if they indeed found Robert there, they would avoid further talk about the past, or whatever plans he, or they, may have for his future. They simply wanted to offer him company, which amounted to food, drink, distraction and music. All the while Robert played his guitar, she knew *the beast* was in some way controlled.

The couple had also decided not to tell Robert they had tracked down Derry, until everyone was gathered in the same place. That is, if Robert accepted the invitation to go to Longford with them. Him choosing not to was an option they refused to consider.

Samantha watched as the two men walked back to the campsite, carrying a guitar case each. She was relieved that Robert had said he wanted to play. It was possible he left the guitars in the car to protect them from the elements, but she could not be sure of the reason, and she preferred not to consider the alternative.

· · · · ·

Robert and Matthew were jamming an earthy blues tune when Robert's strings faded to silence. He pressed the heel of his hands into his eyes and said, 'I've a cracker of a headache, and I'm really tired. If it's okay with you, can we leave it there so I can go and put my head down?'

'No problems,' Matthew said. He lifted the guitar strap over his head and slid the revered instrument into its case by his chair. 'Thanks for allowing me to play, it's been great. Come on, we can put them in the back of our truck for the night.'

When they returned, Robert hugged Samantha and grasped Matthew's hand. 'My thanks to you two, yet again. Goodnight.'

Without another word he trudged towards the shadows beyond his swag and the reach of the firelight, to relieve himself.

'Sleep well, Robert,' Samantha called. 'See you in the morning.'

Through the gloom they saw him raise a hand in acknowledgement, before he was engulfed by darkness.

Samantha and Matthew sat for a while by the fire before retiring to their tent. They nervously anticipated the invitation they would put to Robert in the morning, and both rehearsed in their heads how it might best be delivered. Would he accept and go with them? That remained to be seen in the cool light of Sunday morning.

· · · · ·

Matthew woke to a dawn chorus of birdsong, slid from his sleeping bag and wandered down to the lake in his T-shirt and underwear to fill the kettle. He expected to find Robert there, gazing over at the tree, but there was no sign of the man anywhere along the bank. On the way back to light the gas under the kettle he passed close to the swag. 'Tea, Robert?' he asked, but heard no response.

'Tea for me, darling,' Samantha cooed through the lightweight tent. 'Morning, Robert,' she added.

'I guess he's, um, at nature's latrine, Sam.'

Matthew and Samantha were well into their first drink when Robert showed, with a towel and his toiletries bag in hand. 'Hello,' Samantha said, 'we wondered where you had disappeared to.'

'Part of the new me, Sam, a dip and a morning walk so brisk *the beast* can't keep up.' He bent and flicked a leech from his exposed ankle before it started its own breakfast.

'Can't do anybody any harm,' she said with a smile. 'Take a seat while Matthew gets you your tea. We've something to ask you.'

Robert hung the towel over the director's chair arm, sat and brushed sand from his feet before slipping his socks and shoes on. He took the mug from Matthew, looked at them both and said 'Well, out with it, before I start to get nervous.'

Samantha leaned forward on her elbows. 'We'd like you to come back with us today.'

Robert's gaze flickered between his companions. 'And ... that's to where?'

'Longford,' Matthew said, 'Dennis and Nicky's home.'

Beyond hope. 'Is there work for me? I need to be doing something, to keep *him* over there.' Robert gestured towards the tree.

'We all want to discuss something with you, something important.' Samantha said. 'Dennis and Nicky are a part of it and, well, we all just want to see you again.'

'That's some carrot you're dangling.' The corners of Robert's mouth creased into the faintest of smiles, while the hairs on his neck bristled.

You have no idea how big, Samantha thought, while Robert closed his eyes in apparent contemplation.

'Well, what do you think?' It was as if she snapped him from a trance.

'Car's in a ditch,' he said, as if it would be a factor in the equation.

'Did you bend something putting it there?' Matthew asked.

'It was more of a slide, so I don't think so.'

'Okay then,' Samantha sat back, satisfied, 'let's get ablutions out of the way and pack up.'

'Breakfast first,' Matthew said. 'Men can't go and fight a battle on an empty stomach.'

'Oh all right, if we must,' Samantha grinned.

'Nobody said anything about a battle,' Robert mumbled, loud enough for them to hear.

A simple breakfast of toast was shared, before they took down the tent and swag, cleaned up and left Ned's Camp. Despite his recent harrowing experience, Robert was still sad to leave the place, while Samantha and Matthew made their own private pacts to return as soon as they were able.

As they journeyed along Ridgley Highway, Robert was relieved there was no need to pass by the Wheatsheaf again. That was a chapter in his life he considered read and closed, never to be reopened.

· · · · ·

'Morning Nicky,' Samantha sang down her mobile as they passed along Bass Highway through Burnie.

'Hello sis. Oh God, what's been happening? I haven't slept a wink, you know this is so exciting!'

'We're on our way to yours, if that's still okay?'

'Of course it is. Where did you find Robert?'

'I dreamed he was at Ned's Camp, and that's where he was. We had to pull his car out of a ditch.'

'Oh my God, is he okay?'

Samantha reassured her he was.

Nicky hesitated while she tried to process the vision. 'You could always do stuff like that.'

'What, extracting vehicles from ditches?' They all laughed.

'When will you get here?'

'I guess we're still over an hour away.'

'How much does he know?'

Samantha checked the side mirror to see Robert's car, holding its position several car lengths behind. 'We've not said anything about Derry, or Adelina for that matter. How is she, by the way?'

'Settled in nicely. She wants to extend her visa so I'll take her into Launceston next week and help her get the process under way.'

'That all sounds lovely. We've lots to talk about. See you soon.'

· · · · ·

Harry sat up in his bed and growled when he heard tyres on gravel.

'They're here!' Nicky called, and looked around the open-plan kitchen-dining room to ensure everything was *just so*.

'Okay love,' Dennis said as he walked up from the cellar. 'You get 'em Harry,' he called, and the schnauzer leaped from his bed and raced from the kitchen and up the hallway, barking with expectation.

Nicky turned to Adelina. 'So Adelina, are you excited?'

'*Sì*, ah, yes, Miss Nicky,' she returned as she sat her folded apron on the breakfast bar.

'*Sì*, is fine Adelina, but please just call me Nicky – please?'

A knock, then Matthew's animated voice called, 'Hello, barmy dog.'

Harry barked, and then scrabbled the length of the timber-floored hallway into the kitchen, leaped onto his bed and attacked his rope toy.

'In the kitchen,' Nicky called as calmly as she could, when she heard the muffled voices down the hallway.

'Hi sis,' Samantha walked around the corner and hugged her sister, 'I'd like to introduce our old friend, Robert Aitken,' Samantha winked, 'Come on Robert, don't be shy – he's been missing in action, you know.'

Robert appeared nervously through the doorway, holding his guitar to his chest as if he feared another inquest.

'Hello Nicky,' he said softly, and then he saw Adelina. His awkward smile broadened. 'Oh hell, Adelina! I didn't expect to see you! How on earth did you get here?'

'Ciao Roberto, is good to see you safe.' Adelina moved to him and kissed his cheek.

'Likewise, mate, but you ain't getting no kiss from me!' Dennis walked into the kitchen, weaved around the dining table and grasped Robert's hand in his. 'Welcome to our home for stray waifs. It's a pleasure to see you again, old chap. You really have caused us some worry, you know.'

Robert nodded as he moved aside to allow Matthew to bring in the second guitar and Robert's rucksack. 'It is good to see you all, again,' he said genuinely.

'Put the stuff here if you like,' Matthew indicated as he placed Hayley's guitar case in a corner, and leaned the rucksack against the wall.

Harry leaped from his bed and trotted over to inspect the new items and their smells. Dennis noticed Robert looking nervously at the dog. 'Don't worry, Harry won't damage anything.'

'Hungry?' Nicky asked.

'Starvin',' Dennis said, 'whatever it is smells fantastic.'

'Not you, garbage guts,' she returned. 'You're always hungry. Adelina and I have made some lunch for you all. Anyone need to wash their hands, laundry is through there.'

When they heard Robert was on his way, Nicky and Adelina had gone to the Sunday market and returned with ingredients for a wholesome Italian-style lunch of bruschetta with garlic and tomatoes, and an antipasto platter of pepperoni, mushrooms, artichokes, cheese and olives. Robert couldn't remember the last time he had eaten such food.

While Robert remained silent, he appeared more at ease as the murmur of conversation grew around him, like an enveloping, comfortable shawl. Mostly focusing on the gallery and Adelina's departure from the Wheatsheaf, their conversation avoided questions concerning Robert and his situation, for the time being.

When lunch was over, Dennis opened a bottle of Moscato, followed by coffee from the Hoopers' new machine, purchased for but not yet housed in the gallery kitchen.

Samantha felt her belly bubble with nervous anticipation. She knew someone had to broach the subject, and understood it was best coming from her.

'Robert, we have something to tell you. Please, promise you won't be mad at us for meddling – because we have been, but only because we care, and I mean we all, really, care.'

Robert sat back in his chair, a vision of himself getting into his car and driving away vanished as soon as it had appeared.

'I won't know what I should be mad at until I know what you're on about,' he said with a hint of uncertainty. 'No promises, but I'll give it my best shot.'

'Dennis rang his brother Gabriel, in the UK. Gabe went to see a band you would have heard of: Piggins Hit.'

'Pig ...' Robert paused, 'they, they can't still be together after all these years, surely?'

'Well that's the funny thing,' Dennis said, 'they recently reformed. Gabe met a guy called Pat Derrick, who remembered you.'

Robert pushed his chair back, feeling his breath catch. 'Paddy?'

Samantha continued; 'Calls himself Pat these days, Robert. Anyway, he was really excited to learn that we had found you. So much he called his brother to tell him the news.'

'Noooo,' Robert sighed with dismay as memories flooded his senses like a movie on fast forward. He was becoming overwhelmed. 'This cannot ... how could you do this to me?'

Adelina had only been told a few snippets of information, so that she would not be totally ignorant of his past. She reached for his hand.

'Roberto, please,' she whispered.

Robert pulled his hand away.

'Mate,' Dennis said, 'Derry was over the moon. He was so overwhelmed to know you are okay, he evidently broke down and cried.'

'It was good news to his wife as well,' Matthew joined in. 'She knew you, too, evidently.'

'Derry's wife?' Robert sniffed and looked dazed. 'Derry wasn't married ...' His mind attempted to make sense of it all, still saw Derry as the young man he knew.

'Elsa, the Abbey Road producer,' Samantha said.

'Bullshit. Elsa was Paddy's girl.' *Why are they lying to me?* Robert was trying to find a reason not to believe any of it.

'Well, believe it or not, she married Derry,' Samantha continued. 'Pat, and especially Derry and Elsa, want so much to talk to you.'

Robert reached for the edge of the table to counter a wave of vertigo. 'Can't be true. After all these years ... why would they remember me? After what happened ... why would they care?'

'You have no idea how much Derry misses you still, Robert,' Samantha said. 'Remember when you told us, around the campfire, how you loved Derry like a brother? Well, he told us that when you disappeared it was like *he* had *lost* a brother.'

'So there you go,' Matthew continued, 'you are both like brothers to the other, which means he has every right to still care.'

Samantha added, 'And this is right after he lost Hayley, who was like the sister he never had. Elsa knows how much you mean to her husband, and because of that it means something to her, too.'

Nicky wanted to soften the mood. 'Elsa is a celebrity. I've watched her on television.'

'I don't ...' Robert hesitated, failing to find the words. 'Too much,' he mumbled then, 'I need some air.' His chair screeched on the tiles as he got up and staggered into the laundry. They heard the outside door clunk behind him, saw him walking out in the garden with Harry at his heel. They watched him sit on a garden chair and lean forward with his fingers scratching at his scalp.

Adelina made to follow him outside.

'Wait,' Samantha said.

'This has to have been a helluva shock,' Dennis said. 'Maybe we should have broken it to him over a few days.'

'We have been matter-of-fact, Dennis,' Samantha said. 'He has to process whatever we say, and however we say it, the best way he can. I think he's doing it the only way he knows how, and that is on his own.'

'Apart from Harry,' Nicky said, as they watched Robert run his fingers through Harry's short coat, then sit back in the chair and wipe his eyes on his sleeve.

'Samanta?' Adelina said, and Samantha shrugged, aware it wasn't her place to tell anyone what to do, because nobody really knew how to deal with the unfolding situation.

Adelina walked through the laundry to the back door, closed it quietly behind her and walked, hesitantly, to where Robert sat. The others watched as she spoke to him, and he looked up at her. He shook his head, and returned his gaze to his hands, as they rubbed at the material covering his knees. She sat next to him and watched Harry dance around with a stick in his mouth. Harry dropped the stick by her feet, and she threw it for him.

She turned to Robert. 'I not understand why these people can make you so unhappy.'

He spoke slowly, as if in a trance. 'People from the past ... a lifetime ago.'

'Were they bad people?'

'No, not bad, just a part of the world that took my wife away from me.'

'But it not their fault, no?'

'Nobody's fault but mine.'

'They were your friends and miss you.' It was not a question.

'I realise that, love.' *There was that word again, so easily spoken.*

She rested her hand on his. 'You punish yourself, and you punish them also?' He looked up at her, a sudden flare of anger in his eyes made her snatch her hand away. '*Mi scusa*, I am sorry, Roberto.'

Robert stared into her eyes, and his irritation melted. He reached for her hand and wrapped his fingers in hers. 'No, it's me who should be sorry,' he said. 'You're right.'

He turned to watch Harry playacting with the stick, strutting around as if it was the most important thing in his life. At that moment it was, including the people who loved him, fed him, and all those other things that make a dog feel an integral part of a pack.

Since the day of the argument with Hayley, and the devastation that followed, Robert Aitken had denied himself the essence of those most human of necessities: love, safety, community. He closed his ears to the world for a moment. Still no Hayley, the voice that had come to him in times of dire need, the tamer of his *beast*.

Or was that, really in the end, just me?

Robert looked around the garden. A modest lawn was surrounded by callistemon, banksia and grevillea growing over a carpet of fresh rich mulch that bordered the old stone wall surrounds. He watched honeyeaters, bees and myriad other flying insects darting among their foliage, feeding, existing. It reminded him of the garden he resurrected in Waratah, a task that proved a pastime of necessity, and therapy.

Robert realised that when the Pearson-Hoopers stepped into his life, they offered a new world to him, and now they had helped open a door to the old one. Adelina? He'd never found the need to let her in, no matter how much he may have liked her.

He stood, still holding Adelina's hand and inviting her to stand with him. He turned and took her other hand.

'I can be such an arsehole,' he said and drew her to him, pressed his face into her neck and breathed her in. They remained together, swaying slightly in their comfort until he looked up and, seeing their audience on the other side of the window, smiled.

'Feel like a couple of movie stars? Look over your shoulder.'

Adelina turned to the window and laughed through her tears.

'Best go back and face the music,' he kept firm hold of her hand as they made their way inside.

· · · · ·

'Roberto will sing for us!' Adelina announced loudly as they returned to the kitchen.

'What?' Robert said.

She looked at him. 'You say you play music?'

Robert realised what it was Adelina had misunderstood. 'Yes, you are right Adelina, I'm going to play some music. But first we must talk about this stuff, if that's okay?'

He noticed six wine glasses had been filled and, at that stage, untouched. He picked the closest and took a sip before turning to the others.

'Before you ask, I'm not angry with any of you. I'm confused and, frankly, scared out of my wits more than anything else.' He took a deep, rattled breath, let it out slowly and resumed the same seat. 'This, really is too much.' *To handle – or to hope for.*

He studied their faces, read the same compassion on them all. 'So, what happens? You have been in touch with these people, you say they're happy to know I'm alive ... what is supposed to happen next?'

Dennis pushed a notepad forward.

'What's this?'

'Derry's phone number.'

Robert stared at the numbers as if they were as priceless as an ancient artefact – or as evil as Satan's own memoirs, he couldn't decide which. Nicky pushed the telephone towards him.

'No. Really?' Robert's belly churned, but it wasn't *the beast's* doing.

'Yes, really,' Nicky said.

'I ... I can't,' he mumbled. They all sat around the table, staring at the telephone. 'I can't,' he repeated.

Dennis took the phone and said, 'Anyone mind if I give them a call?'

'Sounds like a plan,' Samantha said. 'Robert?'

Those nine steps to Abbey Road? Finding courage to finally speak with Hayley? They all seemed to pale in comparison. Robert was dumbstruck, terrified at the thought of speaking to Derry after all these years. He managed the slightest of nods.

Dennis picked up the pad, dialled the number.

'What time is it there?' Nicky whispered.

'Around six in the morning,' Matthew counted on his fingers, 'I think.'

Dennis felt his own belly churn. 'Hello, Elsa? ... Yes, it is Dennis Hooper speaking. How're you going? Hope it's not too early... That's good... is Derry there as well? ... Brilliant.' He put his hand over the mouthpiece. 'They put me on speakerphone ... Derry! Can you hear me okay? ... Great.'

Robert's face paled as he sat on his trembling hands, a barely controlled adrenaline surge.

'Yes, Robert is with us now. What? Oh yes we agree, he has led us on a merry dance but he's here now, safe and well. I'm excited and I reckon Robert is too, though he's feeling a bit bashful,' he looked at Robert and winked, 'but it's time to put the old boy on. Speak later, ta-ta for now.'

Robert took the phone, staring at it first before slowly bringing it to his ear. He hesitated.

'Derry?' was all he could manage before he cried, 'Derry I can't believe ... I am so sorry, so sorry.' Tears ran down Robert's cheeks and through his unkempt beard.

'Come on,' Samantha whispered, 'let's go outside and leave him to it.'

Adelina shrugged Samantha's hand away. 'I stay with Roberto,' she whispered. Samantha nodded and stood, squeezed Adelina's shoulder and headed for the garden.

Dennis left the open bottle on the table and grabbed another on his way out. They sat around the outside setting in the cool afternoon air and watched Harry show off with his stick.

Adelina sat quietly and listened to half the conversation, understanding little, but was no less engaged.

'Yes,' Robert said, his nerves subsiding, 'I heard you married Elsa... How long? ... God, have I been gone that long? ... It's these meddling people, I was enjoying myself being fucked up with the world and they came and dragged me back into it ... Yes,' he said as he rested his hand on Adelina's, 'so many changes in such a short space of time ... Yes, I understand, Derry. It's so great to hear your voice again too.'

Robert did not want to let go. 'I'm sorry, Derry ... yes I'd love to speak with you again ... and you too Elsa... Listen, it's been hell for years and, really, I don't know how I've survived ... it's a surprise why these people bothered ... Derry,' he hesitated, 'please don't turn your back on me like I did to you ... Yes, it has been an amazing call. You two have no idea ... until next time, goodbye. Derry, please... Okay,' he afforded himself a small laugh, 'speak to you later ... Goodbye, for now.'

He placed the telephone softly on the table then turned to Adelina and wrapped his arms around her.

. . . . .

'Oh Jesus!' Dennis diverted his attention to Harry and his antics. 'Get a room, you two.'

'They've got one if they both want it,' Nicky laughed, and wept at the same time.

CHAPTER TWENTY-SEVEN

During the afternoon, the Hoopers received an email from Derry outlining a proposition for Robert. They were excited, but feared that it would be emotional overload for him, so agreed not to tell him for at least another day, to allow his nerves to settle.

'Let's see how tomorrow pans out,' Dennis suggested quietly to Nicky, Samantha and Matthew. They agreed to call Derry on Monday and let him explain to Robert in person.

An hour later they sat over a drink at the Tannery, outside in the garden, rugged up against a cool breeze.

Robert's nerves had calmed down while he and Adelina sat on a bench facing the South Esk River, and the magnificent backdrop of the Great Western Tiers. Deep in thought, Robert contemplated how so much of his life had changed in such a short time: *all down to these strange, wonderful, caring people.*

Only a day earlier he had been battling with *the beast*, alone at Ned's Camp. Now he was in a town new to him, surrounded by strangely familiar people who believed he had some worth, although he had deemed himself worthless long ago. As if that was not enough, they had created a wedge in a door he had closed many years ago, where tendrils of his past were now finding their way through. It felt good. It felt wholesome. But he was almost afraid to blink, in case he reopened his eyes and discovered it all to be nothing more than a cruel fantasy.

The joy of hearing Derry's voice, somewhat older but still recognisable as his young friend, was overwhelming. He felt like pinching himself, so many emotions he assumed had been dead in him. He struggled to comprehend the scope of this second chance he was being offered.

He thought about Hayley's presence, how she spoke to him, guided him, helped him. A voice that could be a torment, and a wonder all the same. *If I change my life, will she be allowed to rest in peace, and so, leave me forever?*

Robert breathed in the air, studied his hands. He turned to his friends at the table behind, 'Do you think your local pub might take on a resident muso, in part exchange for lodgings?'

'There's two bedrooms in our gatehouse,' Nicky suggested, 'You're welcome to stay there for a while, if Adelina doesn't mind.'

Adelina turned to them and shrugged, 'It is not mine to decide, but I am happy.

'I've no money to pay,' Robert said. 'It's not possible.'

'Okay, here's a deal,' Dennis began, 'it's unlikely we'll get any paying guests until the mess from the renovations has been carted away, the landscaping's finished and the gallery is open, so you staying at the gatehouse for a couple of months to help you find your feet won't affect us. You may well get a gig at the hotel and could do some work around here to help pay your way. We're not talking rent, just a bit here and there.' He looked to his wife for support and she nodded.

'That's too generous,' Robert said.

'That's why we'll never die rich, and wouldn't have it any other way,' Dennis smiled. 'And of course you'll have to play at our grand opening, if you're still around.'

'That I can promise to do.'

· · · · ·

Samantha and Matthew were glad they had decided to stay over and share one more evening, hopefully to reflect on Robert's life-changing telephone call and Adelina's escape from the Wheatsheaf. The atmosphere was the most relaxed it had been since they met Robert, and they felt that the pleasure of sharing a few more hours would be worth the inconvenience of having to make an early start in the morning to get back to work. Adelina, especially, was delighted to be able to spend a few more hours with Samantha.

After returning from the Tannery, the men were standing around the barbecue, cooking the meal they all had a hand in preparing, while the women sat in the sunroom and talked. They were all enjoying the serene and welcoming surroundings. The excitement of the gallery renovations had, almost totally, been overshadowed by the powerful events of the past few weeks, but Nicky did not feel inclined to chat about their domestic matters now.

Later, after they had eaten, they relaxed around the outside dining table, comfortable with their new friendships. Samantha had maintained her quiet study of Robert, aware that he had not brought his guitar outside; in fact, it had not left its case since he arrived. She studied his face and decided it was okay, that he simply did not require what she had referred to as his safety blanket, at that time.

Robert finished his meal, picked up his glass and wandered around the garden. 'I bet lots of work goes into keeping this so presentable,' he turned and said to them. 'Who's got the green fingers?'

'Neither of us at the moment,' Nicky said, 'The gardens were in a shocking state when we moved in, so we focused on bringing this private garden up to scratch and got a landscaping team in. We'll get them to tackle the other beds and borders once the builders have finished.'

Robert had an idea. 'Well, maybe there's something I can help you with while I'm here,' he said, and told them about his passion for gardening.

· · · · ·

Eventually a chill evening drew everyone inside to the lounge, where they sat talking for a while. Adelina told them of her last hours at the Wheatsheaf, they had a laugh at Rusty's expense, and reflected on the life Betty had to contend with.

Robert, conversely, avoided speaking about his final moments with Rusty and Betty, or his lonely struggle at Ned's Camp, nor did he feel like discussing the amazing telephone call with Derry. There was far too much for him to comprehend. He preferred to sit at peace and let others do most of the talking.

Robert held his glass of Drambuie under his nose, breathing in the herbal and honey aroma as if it were incense; breathing in, too, whatever that other uplifting essence was, of having friends around him.

The beast was nowhere to be seen, heard or felt, but then nor was the essence of Hayley. It was as if Robert could not have one without the other. He almost longed for the dark negativity of his unwanted companion, if it meant he could hear the angelic voice of his wife again.

Throughout the evening his guitar sat locked away in its case, and none were disappointed or offended that it remained there.

Because of their planned early-morning departure, the Pearsons retired to the guest suite at ten. Adelina said goodnight half an hour later, quietly excited about her important first shift at the Tannery. Robert sat with the Hoopers for a while, delaying solitude for as long as he dared. Eventually, though, he said goodnight, and Dennis helped him with his gear, across the driveway to the gatehouse.

They entered quietly so as not to disturb Adelina.

'I'll leave you to it then.' Dennis spoke quietly. He put the guitar and amplifier in a corner, grasped Robert's hand, wished him a good night and closed the door behind him.

Robert stood in the room, his rucksack over one shoulder and guitar case in the other hand. He looked at the large bed, covered by a pristine white spread with embossed patterns, the generous pillows propped against an ornate oak bedhead. On the corner of the bed, a large towel had been folded perfectly, with a small wrapped chocolate in its centre. He looked down at his tired clothing and felt, suddenly filthy. *I am, truly, a tramp.*

He laid his guitar next to the other, opened his rucksack and dragged everything out onto the floor, searching for something appropriate to wear. He swore under his breath as he stood and looked around, feeling it would be impossible for him to soil the Hooper's spotless linen. It was then he noticed a robe and pyjamas draped over the back of an ornate timber-framed armchair in the corner of the room. He picked the top up, held it to his nose and breathed in its aroma, the lingering after-hint of laundered perfume. His eyes welled with tears of anxiety, chagrin and relief.

He took a long hot shower, put on the pyjamas and slid under the covers.

· · · · ·

Samantha and Matthew departed the next morning while it was still dark, without waking anyone but Harry. Samantha left a note addressed to her sister in the kitchen, reminding her of when they would be home after work, and ready to be witness to Derry and Elsa's plan.

Robert opened his eyes at the sound of tyres on gravel. Backlit by the headlights, the bedroom curtains brightened momentarily. He had not been asleep. Throughout the night the smell of fresh paint instead of dampness and mildew reminded his senses that he was no longer in his old, borrowed bed in that tired house. He considered a headache from the fumes was small price to pay for the security he felt, awake or in dreams, being constantly reminded of where he lay.

In the next room, on the other side of the plaster and wainscotted wall, Adelina would be asleep, he thought, and that comforted him more than anything else. Robert constantly repeated his mantra, created by him and Samantha, to keep *the beast* away from his metaphorical door, and knew there would be no more sleep for him. That mattered little as he lay there in the dark, counting his follies and fortunes, and longing for the coming of a new day.

At six-thirty Robert knocked on the Hoopers' laundry door. Although he saw Dennis and Adelina in the kitchen as he walked past the sunroom windows, he still waited for an invitation.

'Come in,' Nicky said, but opened the door for him instead. 'Good morning Robert! Go on through', she said as she loaded clothes into the washing machine.

'Hello, Nicky,' he returned, sidling past her and into the kitchen.

'Sleep well?' Adelina asked as she stood with a tea towel in hand. Feeling awkward, Robert nodded.

Dennis stood at the sink, washing dishes from the previous evening's barbecue before handing them to Adelina.

'Great timing, Robert mate. First job in earning your keep is to take Harry for his morning walk, if you fancy some fresh air? We've given Adelina directions so I suggest you take him together if you like, but not before a heart-starter.' He indicated where the mugs were kept so Robert could help himself to coffee.

Once Robert and Adelina had left with Harry, Nicky and Dennis donned their overalls and continued with the last of the painting. Some time after eleven they heard noises at the door and turned, expecting Adelina and Robert, but were surprised to see the Samantha and Matthew, wearing overalls and grins.

'Got a couple of spare brushes?' Samantha asked.

'What the hell are you two doing back here?' Dennis laughed.

'Checked the diary,' Samantha said, 'We had no planned appointments today so I emailed the office to say we weren't going to be in until tomorrow.'

'I thought you had urgent things to attend to.' Nicky said.

'We made an executive decision that the staff will just have to cope without us for a while – and it's about time we gave them more responsibility, rather than us feeling as if we have to hold their hands all the time. So, we nipped home, grabbed some clobber and headed back, *voila*, just like magic.'

'How reckless of us,' Matthew boasted.

'Reckless indeed,' Dennis smiled. 'Clean brushes over there. Don't you go and balls anything up now, cause I'll be watching you,' he sang.

. . . . .

The friends spent an hour painting the last of the gallery's multi-pane window frames, mostly working to the accompaniment of music played on their portable CD player.

'Dennis reckons he's going to write a song for launch day,' Nicky spoke over the music, 'and we'll ask Robert to perform it.'

'Why not the three of them?' Samantha suggested. 'Work on a few others and play for an hour?'

'We'd be in that if Robert's keen,' Matthew said.

They heard Adelina before they saw her, chatting with Harry as she came down the new connecting hallway between house and gallery. Delighted to see the Pearsons back, she announced it was almost time for her to leave for work, and said Robert was already preparing lunch, and would drive her to work when he was done. She turned and, with Harry in tow, went back to finish getting ready.

'Looks like Matt isn't Harry's fave human any more,' Nicky said.

'Easy come, easy go,' Matthew agreed.

The four stood at a window and watched Robert's car exit the driveway towards the Tannery.

By twelve-thirty they had cleaned up and made their way back to the kitchen. First through the doorway, Nicky was startled to see a stranger at the sink. She held her breath, until the man turned around.

'Good God, Robert. You gave me a start!' she laughed.

Gone were the long locks of peppered hair and thick, unkempt beard. 'A gift from Adelina,' he said.

'Wow,' Samantha sighed, 'what a handsome man you were under all that facial fuzz!'

'And you can cut that out, missus,' Matthew joked. 'I see your Italian friend is getting her claws into you already!'

'I don't mind at all, in fact I like the new me. Cold around the ears on the way back, mind you.'

· · · · ·

That evening, while they sat around the dining table sharing animated discussions or enjoying comfortable silence, Robert's hands continually toyed with a coaster. Dennis turned towards the clock and announced, 'I reckon it's time.' Robert swallowed back an urge to flee as Dennis picked up the phone and dialled the number, this time activating the telephone's conference speaker as soon as the call tone sounded.

'Hello?'

'Hi, Elsa,' Dennis said, 'Robert's here with Nicky, Samantha and Matthew, and Robert's friend Adelina is also with us.'

'Hello all.'

'Hello,' Robert said, his voice questioning, 'Derry?'

'I'm here, Robert. We'd like to tell you a story, if you're up for it?'

Robert felt the hairs on his neck bristle. *Please don't speak of Hayley's death.* 'What you have been doing over the years?' he hoped.

'That's right. Well, Elsa and I have been married now for twelve years. We've been pretty good, or lucky, at business, both individually and together. Elsa not only set up her own recording studio but she expanded into act management as well. Me? You always joked about how I seemed to know everybody, and I guess I made it my job to find any excuse to befriend people. Some of them knew other people and, well, a benefit of being gregarious.'

'Bands?' Robert asked.

'Not as such. I suppose after ...' he hesitated, 'you know, I decided I could never be in a band again, but still wanted to play. A few acts I knew asked me along to recording sessions and the word spread that I was a pretty handy player, and I started to get regular session work. Once I was stand-in guitarist for Whitebeam Fox on their UK tour, but I guess you wouldn't have heard of them over there, Robert?'

'Sorry I haven't. Did you finally learn how to read music?'

'No, all still by ear. I went with the flow, rather than by dots on a page.'

'We never seemed to know what you were going to do next ...' Robert hesitated, hoping Derry would understand his offhand compliment.

'Added to the excitement, didn't it! Eventually I met up with Elsa again through her studio. Hey, do you remember Gerald Bray?'

'That arsehole?' Dennis interrupted.

'Absolutely,' Derry agreed. 'The way he treated Robert at the inquest was disgusting. Evidently he even bragged about it. Maybe he resented you because he fancied Hayley.'

Robert laughed bitterly. 'She thought he was a sleaze.'

'He was,' Elsa agreed.

'Well, what he did to you got back to Donnington Records,' Derry said, 'and he was given an unceremonious boot out of the place. Word came to me that, from their perspective, the contract could have been honoured at the time, just you ... Pete and me, I guess.'

'Prat got his comeuppance then,' Dennis said.

'I suppose, after all these years, that contract would be useless now?' Robert posed.

'Without doubt,' Elsa said. 'I hope it gives you some small satisfaction to know that, as far as we've heard, Bray never found another job in the industry. I am sure Derry would had made noise if Bray had tried.'

'Not really, but I'm glad you told me. Wish I'd been there to see it happen. I might have helped him down those studio steps for the last time.'

'Me too,' said Derry, 'Just an obnoxious individual who big-noted himself at any opportunity. Anyway, back to the story. Things didn't work out between Elsa and Pat – they had parted company years before I started seeing her; there was no going behind Pat's back about it – just in case you wondered. Elsa and Pat get on famously now they're in-laws.'

'Derry and I were working together more and more and our relationship slowly grew,' Elsa said. 'We became close, and I saw Derry would fit in well with our team, so I invited him to become a director of the studio and my management business.

'Our ideas and personalities really clicked. With Derry there I could branch into other areas that interested me, we devised a television talent show called *Forget Dreams, Here's Your Reality.* And back in ninety-eight it was first aired, with me as one of three judges, more to keep our costs down than a desire to be in front of the camera.'

'The pilot's ratings were pleasing,' Derry continued, 'so we refined the format and the first season hovered around mid-ratings on a Tuesday night, which was better than anyone could have hoped. Elsa was a total natural and a bit of a darling of the show's fans.'

'Okay, but I haven't seen it.' Robert sounded apologetic.

Dennis laughed. 'Guys, our Robert probably hasn't watched much telly in recent years,' (Robert agreed with a shake of his head) 'but later we'll find the show and record it, so Robert can see Elsa.'

'Sounds a good idea. Anyway,' Derry continued, 'we scored a second season, then a third, and then Elsa stepped back a little. Not hosting so many shows gave her more time to devise another lifestyle program called *Town 2 Country.* *Forget Dreams, Here's Your Reality* and *Town 2 Country* both hold their own against ... well, you won't know them, but let's just say bigger-budget rivals. I guess the mix of personality and pace is just perfect. Now, this is where we want to put an opportunity to you.'

Robert stared at the telephone, took a deep breath and said, 'Keep going, I'm listening.'

'We think you would be brilliant on *Forget Dreams*,' Elsa said. 'They will ask you questions about why you are there, and it would make an amazing story for people who love a happy ending.'

'No,' Robert was not comfortable with where this was going. 'Hayley was the one with all the talent.'

'With respect, it wasn't just down to Hayley,' Derry said, carefully. 'You had, and I guess still have, an amazing voice, with so much character. You could write music. You could knock 'em dead.'

'Knock who dead?' Robert asked.

'A sell-out live audience and perhaps millions more on television. What an opportunity to gather up the old threads.'

Robert sat back, speechless. He looked at the smiles on Dennis, Nicky and Matthew's faces. Turning to Samantha he held her gaze longest, hoping she would tell him this was all a joke. Nobody did. He felt the blood drain from his cheeks as another wave of nausea enveloped him.

'What do you think, Robert?' Derry asked.

Silence.

'Hello, Robert?'

'What do I think?' Robert chewed on the bile in his mouth. 'For starters I can't afford to go back to London, I've not played in front of more than twenty people for years, and even then they're too busy stuffing food in their mouths to be bothered with what I'm doing, and thirdly ... thirdly ... I can't do that shit.'

He slid his chair back, strode from the kitchen and down the hallway. The front door slammed behind him with clanging reverberation.

They sat around the table in silence, all looking at each other.

'Shit,' Derry's voice sounded thin on the line.

· · · · ·

Aware of the rhythmic crunching of shoes on gravel as he walked across the driveway towards his car, Robert reached into his pocket for his keys. His mind churned, a confusion of abject fear and anger. Fear of his own inadequacies and hatred for *those who keep fucking meddling*.

Hello Robert, thanks for inviting me back.

He stopped and looked around. Clear as day, a voice of honeyed pretentiousness that made him feel like retching. Why had he not realised before that the demeaning, condescending tone of *the beast* was the voice of Gerald Bray? *Bray the beast* had goaded him with his words, tormented Robert's memories and realities, held power over him for years.

However, with that spark of recognition it was as if *the beast's* hold slipped fractionally. *With recognition comes hope of control from within.* He turned and looked back to the house to see Adelina standing by the door, arms folded across her chest, her face expressionless. He could sense, even taste, her disappointment in him. *Not her ... not another one?*

What are you doing? His thoughts echoed over the deep, guttural laughter of *the beast.* Not Hayley but his own conscience. *Fuck off out of my head, Bray, you bastard. Hayley,* he called out in his mind, *come back and help me.*

She's not coming, Robert. Let it be just me and you, the talentless, unhinged murderer.

Robert clenched his hands into fists and pressed them into his temples. 'I've done it again, haven't I?'

Adelina wasn't sure if he spoke to himself or her, so kept her silence.

He looked over to her. 'I turned my back again, didn't I? Adelina?'

She responded, and while her voice was calm it still stung him.

'They try to help you, Roberto. They offer you something better than life you have, help you find something you lost, and this how you treat them?' She tilted her head back and held a determined stance. 'If you drive away, I not come looking for you.' She turned and moved back inside, closing the door quietly behind her.

In the act of putting up a barrier between them, it was as if the door, the house and the new life he had been offered started to fade into the distance, speeding away from him. He felt himself panic. *The beast,* the voice of Gerald Bray, laughed louder and he felt the creeping terror of loneliness wrap its grimy arms around him. The familiar churning nausea of spinning cartwheels threatened to overwhelm him and he gripped his belly protectively.

'No,' he groaned. 'I don't want you here.'

He clenched his jaw and staggered back towards the house. *The only hope for me is here.* As he reached for the door handle, his ears rang, hums and high pitches built in his head to intolerable levels. Vertigo took hold, his sight dimmed; he pitched forward and thudded to the ground.

Adelina had not moved far away, and had been watching through the side windows by the front door. She was with him almost before he hit the threshold. '*Aiuto*! Help!' she cried, and within moments footsteps echoed up the hallway, and Samantha and Matthew were standing with her.

'What happened?' Matthew asked, turning Robert onto his back to see blood seeping from his nose, and a split over his eye.

'Roberto *faint*,' Adelina cried. 'He not well.'

'Robert? Robert!' Samantha's tone invaded the numbness of Robert's torpor. He had a brief dream of *that* day, on the bridge.

'Roberto*, per favore*?' Adelina said as she held her fingers to his cheek.

Robert mumbled groggily, 'What ... happened?'

'Looks like you met our new slate tiles, old boy.' Dennis stood at the door. 'They're not very forgiving, are they?'

Matthew helped Robert prop himself against the wall. He hooked his elbows around his knees and sat, hunched and stunned. *That's never happened before.* He was shattered but energised as well, an inexplicable contradiction, but he now knew who, or what *the beast* was. He exhaled slowly and sighed, 'Derry not still on the phone?'

'No mate, told them we'd call back another time,' Dennis said.

'Is it too late now?'

'We can try if you want.'

'Help me up, Matthew. I really need to do this.'

Robert sat at the table in a cold sweat, pressing a wet flannel to his eye.

'Tea for you, love?' Nicky said.

He nodded, feeling his gut, feeling the cartwheels subside. *Fuck you beast, you're not going to control me, ever again.*

'Ready?' Dennis asked, and Robert nodded again. Dennis dialled the number and pressed the conference button.

'Hello?'

'We're back,' Dennis said.

Elsa apologised. 'Robert, we're sorry to put such stupid, unrealistic expectations on you. We did not think it through.'

'My fault,' Robert said. 'You offered me something inconceivable, and I panicked. Because of, well because of who I have become, and that panic came out as aggression. It's me who should be apologising, and I am.' His head and heart felt numb, while the dark cartwheels fluttered, ever so slightly, in his belly. *Losing their grip.*

'We're sorry anyway,' Derry said. 'We were bloody idiots.'

Robert tried to reason with himself, and them. 'Really, it's something I simply could not afford to do. All I have is a few dollars Betty gave me before I walked out on the Wheatsheaf.'

'Chaps,' Dennis spoke to Derry and Elsa, 'Betty is the long suffering wife of the bonehead who runs the pub Robert played at.'

'Ah, the feral?' Elsa repeated an earlier description of Rusty.

'Yes, but Miss Betty is lovely,' Adelina said.

Another in the long list of angels. Robert thought. 'When I told her I was leaving, she gave me an extra fifty, which is generous considering they probably don't have much themselves. Another thing,' he added, 'my visa may well have run out.'

'Problem solved,' Dennis said, 'you might just get deported back to the UK.' Dennis' usual offbeat humour helped lighten the mood.

'Elsa and I are quite prepared to sponsor your trip, and your stay,' Derry said, 'so that wouldn't be an issue, and it need not cost you a penny.'

'That's generous …' Robert hesitated. 'But consider my perspective. I've spent years shunning society, and you might all say senselessly, but it's what I did, and I just can't envisage walking onto a professional stage.'

'Perhaps so,' Elsa agreed. 'Hence, our offer to sponsor you does not hinge on you coming on the show. We are happy to bring you back, simply so we can see you again, in person.'

Robert took a drink of his tea and sat the mug on a coaster. He looked at his hand and noticed it was shaking, through the fall, nerves or both, and realised his subconscious seemed to be processing the concept. He rested his hands together on the table edge, and Samantha reached over and touched them. He couldn't believe he was about to say what he did, his fears told him not to, but his future considered otherwise.

'Okay,' he blurted, 'now I'm not saying yes or no, but hell I'm willing to talk about it. Shit, shit.' He wrapped his hands around his cheeks and shook his head.

'Oh, I think I'm going to cry,' Nicky giggled.

'Me too,' agreed Samantha.

'Wow, great,' Derry said, '—no, not that you girls are going to cry.'

'We'll leave it up to you, Robert,' Elsa said. 'This has to be your decision alone. Our offer is there, on the table. We will sponsor your return to England, whether a holiday or permanent will be for you to decide, and whether you appear on the show or not. If you decide to take up the offer, you must speak to us and say so.'

'And if I decide no,' Robert said, 'what happens to … to us?'

'You are back in our lives now, Robert,' Derry said, 'whether you want it or not. If we never get to meet you face to face again it'll be a terrible shame, but we are your family – and God, it's so good to know you're still with us.'

'Robert,' Elsa said, 'talking of family, did your parents ever know where you were? Would you like us to try and locate them?'

Robert hesitated. Resentment lingered from what he perceived as a lack of support from them after Hayley's death, but he delved further back into his memories, to a childhood of love and safety, and especially remembered nights of singing harmonies with his dad.

'I did send them a letter, years ago, from Turkey, but didn't give a return address. I decided it was okay just for them to know I was alive.'

'Well, you let us know your decision,' Elsa said, 'okay?'

'Okay. But how long can I think about it?'

As Adelina balled a tissue and wiped a smear of blood from Robert's eye, Samantha touched his shoulder. 'Robert, the longer you take, the easier it will be to say no.'

'Fair enough. Derry, Elsa, can I call you same time tomorrow?'

Derry laughed. 'You can call us whenever you are ready, and whenever you feel like it.'

They all said their goodbyes, ended the call, then the six of them stared at one another.

'How are you feeling?' Samantha tried to read Robert's expressions.

'Confused. Terrified. It's a big ask, you know. Oh, also a little depressed, if I'm honest.'

'Be honest,' Dennis said, 'It won't hurt you or anyone else. But you are among friends now, and that should make a world of difference.'

Robert needed time to consider the situation, and had put himself under further pressure by not giving himself much of it. Samantha suggested he tell Derry and Elsa he needed another week but he refused. 'You were right, Sam, if I don't know tomorrow I won't know in a week. So I'll sleep on it, and have my decision in the morning.' He rubbed at where his beard used to be. 'I think I'll head off now, if that's okay with you all? My brain hurts, so does my face, and I need a shower. Oh, thanks for the pyjamas, by the way.'

Robert stood, caressed Adelina's neck for a moment, then turned away from the table.

He avoided saying he just needed to be by himself. Perhaps he would play his guitar? Perhaps he would try and summon Hayley. Perhaps he would look for *Bray the beast*, just so he could test its weakness and his resolve.

Perhaps he would close his eyes and thank the Lord, or the universe, for bringing these wonderful people into his life.

Robert said his farewells and left through the laundry door. They listened for the side gate to scrape shut before Dennis whispered, 'Don't fancy being in his shoes at this moment.'

'I don't think I'd ever have wanted to be in Robert's shoes,' Matthew added with a shake of his head.

'No, good point.'

'I take him something to eat later,' Adelina said.

A change of focus was needed.

'How was your day, Adelina?' Samantha asked.

'Good,' the Italian said with a smile. 'They nice people, the place smell clean and the food is good. At Tannery, nobody shout at me.'

'I don't think anyone shouts at anyone at the Tannery,' Dennis smiled.

'So,' Nicky hesitated, 'I wonder what Robert will say in the morning ...'

· · · · ·

Their alarm sounded, and Matthew and Samantha knew they could not put off their return to the agency any longer. Samantha tapped on her sister's bedroom door.

'Yes?'

'It's me, Nic.'

'I'm awake,' Nicky said. 'What time is it?'

Samantha pushed the door open and tiptoed in.

'Five thirty. We're off, have to make sure the staff know what they're doing,' she whispered, and sat on the side of the bed.

'Okay, drive safely.'

'Let us know what happens, eh?'

'Of course we will, the moment anything does.'

'Wonder what Robert's decision will be?'

'Why don't you go and ask him?' Dennis mumbled grumpily through his pillow.

'Sorry for waking you.'

'Oh it's all right, I had to be awake to answer,' Dennis drawled. 'Draw the curtains will you?'

'You're a dag.' There was no more need to whisper but Samantha did. 'Still dark out though.'

Dennis didn't respond.

'Where's Matthew?' Nicky asked.

'Making coffees to go.'

'Tell him he's a right royal prick,' Dennis groaned as he stretched.

'Feck off, Hooper,' Matthew said from the door, coffees in their travel mugs in his hands.

Samantha reached over and kissed Nicky's cheek. 'As soon as you know,' she said again.

Nicky nodded. 'Have I got dog breath?'

'Yup,' Samantha smiled. 'Speak later. Close the door?'

'Don't bother,' Dennis said. 'Harry will want to go out soon anyway.'

· · · · ·

Cold rain beat down as the Pearsons threw their bags into the back of the Mitsubishi. They buckled up and Matthew reversed out of the parking space. Headlights washed over the gatehouse window as the vehicle turned up the driveway, but there was no sign of activity.

'No point waking them,' Samantha said as Matthew pulled out into the wet street.

They'd travelled only a short distance when he braked suddenly.

'What the...?' Samantha called out. She looked at Matthew as he studied something through the rear-vision mirror. She turned to see the silhouette of a person running towards them. 'Someone's coming.'

Matthew lowered the driver's window.

'Wanted to catch you,' Robert stuttered through clenched teeth, 'before you left.'

Matthew looked him up and down. 'You're not wearing shoes.'

'No time.'

'And you're in pyjama bottoms,' Matthew added.

'Get in, you silly man,' Samantha ordered.

The back door clicked shut and they turned to look at him.

'You're drenched,' Samantha said.

Robert shrugged. 'I wanted you to know, be the first to know,' he hesitated as if he still wasn't sure, 'I'm going back to see Derry, and, you know, whatever else they have in store for me.'

He grasped their outstretched hands, leaned forward and kissed Samantha's cheek.

'This is all because of you, Sam, and you, Matthew. If not for you two and your wonderful, meddling family, I would still be rotting away in my self-made hell.'

He cut across Samantha's response: 'No wait, Samantha, you two have to understand how much you mean to me, what you have done. Now, this isn't goodbye yet, and I hope not ever. You see, I've so much to sort out before I can go. I ... you had to be the first to know.'

Passing headlights illuminated the tears that ran down Samantha's face. The car passed and the light faded.

'This is wonderful news, Robert,' she said while she fumbled in her bag for a tissue.

'We're bloody proud of you, Robert,' Matthew said, as he bit back his own emotions.

'None of it is going to be easy, you know,' Robert said. 'Frankly, I'm shitting bricks just thinking about heading back to England, let alone the television show stuff but, you see, I know it's the only way to truly put the past behind me.'

Samantha blew her nose again. 'Oh, Robert,' was all she could say.

Matthew gripped Robert's hand. 'Remember we're only a couple of hours away. Anything you need, just ask. If we can help, we will.'

'Come and stay with us before you go,' Samantha snuffled. 'Promise me you will.'

'That I will do,' Robert said. He kissed her cheek again. 'You'd better be off. This is just *ciao*, for now.'

Robert allowed his fingers to slide from theirs. Only then did Samantha notice the note in her palm.

'What's this?' she asked as she unfolded the paper. She read the title, saw some chord symbols scrawled above the words. 'You've written a song called 'No Ordinary Day'?' She glanced through the verses, and as her eyes again welled with tears, folded the paper quickly and lowered it to her lap.

'It's for you, Sam. Kind of like a thank you.' Robert looked away, feeling suddenly bashful. 'I wrote it last night. Maybe I can sing it to you, sometime soon, or definitely before I go.'

He opened the door, got out quickly and patted the car roof. Samantha and Matthew watched Robert Aitken trot back to the gatehouse in the pouring rain, his arms wrapped tightly around his chest.

Robert Aitken turned, waved, and was gone.

PART FOUR

REDEMPTION

FORGET DREAMS, HERE'S YOUR REALITY

A tiny desk-mounted LED flashes rhythmically in front of Jon Haversham. The *Forget Dreams, Here's Your Reality* team leader and official 'bad boy' has quietly enjoyed, but publicly suffered most of the eleven contestants who have already auditioned today. He does, however, look forward to the last act on his list. The LED ceases its flashing and he counts in his head; three, two, one, and Haversham's smile vanishes before the camera light indicates that the ad break is over. He has reverted to his unimpressed public persona by the time the contestant walks onto the stage, guitar in hand.

'Hello, who do we have here, then?' Jon Haversham asks his trademark question in a well-rehearsed attempt-to-sound-interested-though-mind-numbingly-bored style. As usual, members of the audience ape his delivery.

The contestant sidles up to the microphone. 'Robert,' he croaks, clears his throat and tries again, 'Robert Aitken.'

'And Robert, Robert Aitken, what do you do?'

'I'm, um, I'm the Tramp.'

'Enigmatic. Does one care to elaborate?'

'I used to be known as the Tramp, many years ago.'

'... And that's because?'

'I played in a band in the eighties called Hayley and the Tramp.'

'Hmmm, Hayley and the Tramp? Doesn't ring a bell I'm afraid. No hits I gather?'

Robert lowers his eyes. 'No hits.'

'What's with the second guitar?'

'It's Hayley's.'

'I guess the hat too?' Melanie Wicks, the darling of the show, probes. Robert nods with a nervous smile.

'And Hayley's running late, we presume?' Words Haversham immediately regrets saying, because he knows.

Melanie Wicks, who is also aware, glares at her co-host. 'Jon!' she whispers, almost angrily.

How dare you! You know where she is, you bastard. 'No, she's right here.' Robert presses a hand to his chest.

Melancholy sighs emanate from the audience. Haversham sighs too, although his is from the impatience demanded by his on-air personality.

'So, what have you got for us today Robert, Robert Aitken?'

Despite having previously met the personable Haversham at Derry and Elsa's home, Robert struggles with the host's public derision. He takes a breath and says, 'My life in a song.'

'Is that the title or the subject?' Haversham drawls.

Robert stares at him. *Don't you understand how hard this is, and you're just making it worse?*

'The song is called "Real Life Passion Play" and, yes, it's about me.'

'Can we gather, then, that this is your own composition?'

'Yes.'

'Take it away, Robert Aitken, AKA the Tramp.'

A backing track begins, one they recently recorded at London Notes, Derry and Elsa's recording studio, but Robert only stares at the floor by his feet, suddenly so terrified he can hardly move, hardly make his fingers work. *Come on, play it, damn you.* He hears mumbles emanating from beyond the reach of the stage lights, imagines contemptuous sniggers. He lifts his gaze to see Jon Haversham staring blankly, impatiently tapping his pen on the desk, a regular staccato as if Morse code: dot dot dot, dash dash dash, dot dot dot. *Save our souls? Save our ship? Save my song? Save me, Hayley.*

The backing track stops as suddenly as it had begun, revealing the audience's impatient murmur.

Although Haversham retains his outward persona, he is inwardly urging Robert on, hoping he can break the shackles of fear, sing up a storm, and gain them more publicity and ratings. No, he doesn't want this, he truly wants Robert to perform well, because Robert is a dear friend of his dear friends and bosses, Derry Derrick and Elsa Soland.

He wonders if they will tell him later that he was too abrasive, the direct reason for Robert's anxiety overflowing?

An imaginary hand has gripped Robert's throat so tightly he can hardly breathe. He glances to the wings to see Derry and Elsa urge him on, sees Adelina's hands clasped in front of her face and her eyes are tightly shut, as if she prays.

Robert's senses have numbed; he feels as if he might swoon.

He turns to look past the four judges, out to the vague shapes of members of the audience. A distant EXIT sign glows on the far wall. He sees a glint of hair, a black shoe, a red stocking, illuminated by the aisle lights. He imagines those silhouettes fidget in expectation. But, too indistinct for him to recognise, four of them sit together, people from his past, vastly changed from the last time they saw him at the inquest so many years ago, when he already looked at the world through the bars of his mind's prison.

His parents and Hayley's parents sit, their hands linked in a daisy chain of happiness, relief, pride and reopened grief. Even Pete Hardcastle sits in the row behind to watch his rediscovered friend. Robert is not aware they have come tonight. No, Robert is too focused on his own terror.

Then her voice: *Come my love, we are with you. Play for me. Play for us.*

'Hayley has come back to me,' he whispers. *Truly.*

The muscles in his fingers relax as he responds to her presence, and his head begins to clear. He takes a breath, turns towards the wings and nods, a signal for the sound engineer to restart the backing track. As he follows the introduction on his guitar, the shackles of dread disintegrate and the invisible fingers that had gripped his throat fall away.

His confidence builds and, with that so does the presence that audiences of old connected with. He looks again to his left, to see – surely they all can – Hayley beside him, standing ghostly by her guitar. She looks at him with silent, beautifully graceful encouragement.

He turns back to the judges and begins to sing in a strong, clear voice:

The secrets that we keep, dreams we conjure in our sleep
Emerging from our past lead to feelings that could last
Games that people play we leave for another day
The things we wish to last become echoes of our past.

My book of secrets, all its prospects – bitter, challenging or complex
I keep revisiting the chapter that tells of happier times and laughter
The smile we give the most, the love we have the need to boast
Those echoes of our past, those memories …

I don't know why I did it; can't say why I did it
It was my life, I turned away from my real life Passion Play.

Faith of soldiers to their leaders. As infirm would to their healers
An excuse to carry on when it seemed there wasn't one
Fools who suffer sages, I find I'm either, in those pages
It keeps me reading to the end – the secret forced me to defend.

My secret had a reason, and I knew it was deceiving
I missed the comforts of a home
I didn't own this secret, but the secret had captured me
I see it written in the tome.

And it would not set me free.

Anyway, it is such a mystery, all those options that were blind to me
While I was led astray by my own naivety
Now the walls have broken down, thanks to you I have come home
All those things no longer secrets, but you're still asking.

I don't know why I did it; can't say why I did it
It was my life, I turned away from my real life Passion Play
I don't know why, can't say why
It was my life. But now's another day.

I'll still remember, I'll still remember. I'll still remember you
I've really closed that book today – but I'll still remember
I'll still remember you.

Robert feels *Bray the beast's* tenuous presence jolt and evaporate like smoke on a breeze, and is convinced he, *it*, cannot possibly, ever return.

He looks over towards Hayley, standing by her guitar. She smiles. She whispers something that he will forever keep, a different kind of secret, and with a blown kiss she fades. As she vanishes, his gaze settles on Derry, Elsa and Adelina watching him with pride, admiration and love.

He then hears a sound rushing into his senses, like a sudden hailstorm crashing on a tin roof; applause, whistles and roars from the audience.

His song complete, tears stream down Robert's cheeks, and those who are there to witness his return cry with him.

The cameras continue to roll, capturing all forever, all but the beautiful face of Hayley Louise Aitken.

I would like to acknowledge the heart warming support I received
from so many friends, who helped get this project over the line
by pre-ordering the novel, CD and other merchandise:

Special thanks to:

Pat & Radonna Cannon
Gary Day & Linda South
Birgitta Magnusson-Reid
Kay & Michael Waldmann.

Also to:

Yvonne & Jeff Dale, Dave & Judith Harvey,
Ian Jones, Gina Merry, Judi & Tony Swain,
Mike & Val Talbot, Nigel & Jo Walsh.

Richard Cannon, Mandy Foot, Terry Gostlow,
Patricia & Manohar Hullan, Greg Leong, Maree Luxford, Barbara Owens,
Anna Radford, Bruce Sexton, Michaela Waldmann, Graham Walsh.

Keith Arnold, Geoff Dobson, Stephen Scott.

Brendan Clough, Pedro Cubiles, Surinder Hullan, Josh Owens,
Domonic, Gabriel and Izaiah Swain, Blake Waldmann, Julia Wheaton.

Thanks for believing in me.